(17) £1

'Enjoy a snappy style and wise-cracking dialogue that'll keep you on your toes – just what you'd expect from the authors of *The Nanny Diaries*' *Glamour*

'A convincing picture of the rollercoaster of teenage love, peppered with references to 1980s Americana . . . Crackling dialogue and Kate's pragmatic, self-deprecating voice make this an incisive read for anyone who remembers the agony of their own first love' *Financial Times*

'An essential read for the beach this summer' *Elle*

'From the bestselling writers of *The Nanny Diaries*, this novel is another surefire hit. Hilarious and heartbreaking in equal measure, it expertly explores how you sometimes have to go back before you can move forward. Vividly capturing the feeling of being a love-struck teenager, it's a must-have read for the sunlounger' *Woman*

'An accessible, enjoyable story about growing up and the trials of true love. Anyone who grew up in the '80s will instantly connect with the evocative description of the sights and sounds of the period . . . Perfect for enjoying on a sunny beach with the sand between your toes' *Arena*

DEDICATION

A Novel

EMMA McLAUGHLIN

and

NICOLA KRAUS

POCKET
BOOKS

LONDON • SYDNEY • NEW YORK • TORONTO

First published in the USA by Atria Books, 2007
A division of Simon & Schuster Inc
First published in Great Britain by Simon & Schuster UK Ltd, 2007
This edition first published by Pocket Books, 2008
An imprint of Simon & Schuster UK Ltd
A CBS COMPANY

1 3 5 7 9 10 8 6 4 2

Simon & Schuster UK Ltd
Africa House
64–78 Kingsway
London WC2B 6AH

www.simonsays.co.uk

Simon & Schuster Australia
Sydney

A CIP catalogue record for this book is available from the British Library

ISBN 978-1-84739-124-7

Printed and bound in Great Britain by
CPI Cox & Wyman Ltd, Reading, Berkshire

For Joel
&
David
with deep love and gratitude

DEDICATION

1

December 22, 2005

"He's here."

"Laura?" I ask into the phone, disoriented, voice sandy with sleep.

"Kate."

"Yeah," I murmur, my head sinking, pushing the receiver deeper into the pillow.

"He's here," she repeats. "In Croton."

Her words register and my eyes fly open. I sit up.

"Awake now?" she asks.

"Yes." I look over to my bedside table, tilting up straighter to see over the stack of books. The glowing numbers on the clock read 4:43 A.M. "How—"

"Mick's been throwing up—some kind of stomach flu slash candy cane binge with the baby-sitter. I look out the bathroom window and his mother's house is lit up like Disney World, called the sheriff's office and they confirmed it. He's here. He's *here,* Kate."

I fling off the duvet. "I'm coming." Dropping the cordless into its metallic stand, I swing both feet to the smooth wood floor of my bedroom.

He's here—there. Jake Sharpe. Of course it's not three P.M. on a Saturday. Of course you reappear in the middle of the night like some nocturnal blood-leech.

Adrenaline surges.

I grab yoga pants from the chair, pull them up under my nightslip, and tug the little black cardigan from the doorknob. Throwing open the closet doors, I stand on tiptoe, fingernails catching the edge of my suitcase handle just enough to avalanche it off the shelf, business trip toiletries raining on my head and rolling across the hardwood. I scramble to retrieve the miniature bottles, an anxiety-dream sweat dampening the silk of my slip. Only I'm awake. And Laura's flare finally hovers in the night sky over the snowy hills of our hometown.

Indignation fuels the whipping open of drawers, fistfuls of underwear, T-shirts, and pajamas filling the case, my mind moving ahead to the important items—skinny jeans, date sweater, dangly earrings—the heels that knock me up to five-nine. The two zipper toggles collide and I shove my brass travel lock through the holes.

Rolling down the hall I push my feet into my sneakers, yank my trench from its hook, open the front door to the cricket quiet of my suburban street, and reach into my pocket for the keys—shit, my purse. I whirl in the dark apartment, spotting it hiding on the kitchen table among the boxes of unwritten Christmas cards, rolls of wrapping paper, and my laptop. No. I don't need my laptop. Just bring the binder to read on the plane. Then I might start the report. Then I might need my laptop.

Just bring the laptop. I try to unclip it from the docking station, but my fingers fumble. I flick the light switch on, startled by the jarring brightness. But, oh, this is good, yes, okay, good, light helps. Okay, reality check. I take in my reflection in the kitchen window, face creased from sleep, eyes puffed from deprivation of same, brown hair tangled from passing out in forgotten ponytail holder.

This is insane.

I flick the light back off, swing the front door shut, stalk back to the bedroom, flop on top of the bed, and pull the still-warm duvet over me like a taco. Letting the keys drop from my grip, I will the adrenaline away, will back the peaceful dead-to-the-world repose I was beneath just moments ago.

Sleep, Kate. Go back . . . to sleep. You've been working nonstop—the conference, the meetings, the forty-two-hour round-trip to Argentina. This bed was all you could think of. Aren't you comfortable? And relaxed? Living your life? Sleeping in your bed? Isn't it nice to be an adult . . . who can get into her own bed . . . in her own apartment . . . and go to sleep . . . on her own timing. My pulse deepens. And not be reduced to some stupid . . . knee-jerk . . . adolescent . . . obsessive . . . lunatic behavior . . . just because Jake's finally shown up—finally shown up—

I sit up. Breathless.

And within minutes find myself flying along Route 26, counting off the exits to the Charleston airport.

• • •

I pull the suitcase from the backseat and lock the Prius with a double beep, glancing up once again at the LONG-TERM PARKING sign. I ignore the implications. This is a swing through, that's all. An eight-hundred-mile swing through.

The sky still black behind me, I pass between the sliding glass doors into a brick-walled trough of canned air and canned music. The lone ticket agent, wearing three-step eyes and impressively pronounced lipstick for predawn, smiles in greeting. "Checking in?" she asks. I blink at the crimson foil poinsettia pinned to her uniform. "Checking in?" she repeats.

"Yes?" I answer uncertainly.

She looks at me inquisitively as I look at her inquisitively. "Are you sure?"

"Yes. Yes. I'm going to Croton Falls, Vermont. Burlington is closest, but I'll take whatever you have." I drop my purse on the counter and rest my messenger bag heavy with my laptop between my ankles.

"Can I see your I.D.?"

I flip open my wallet and slide the plastic over.

She looks down at the card with a frown. "Solutions for Sustainability?"

"Sorry." I trade her my office badge for my license.

"And ticket?"

"Actually I don't have one, but I need to get on the first flight. What do you have?"

She taps the keyboard, and I watch her stare intently at the obscured screen, all the possible routes back to him. "Well, let's see, there *is* one seat left on the commuter to Atlanta, then a two-hour layover, which would get you into LaGuardia by three and then another layover . . ."

"Is that really the earliest I can get there?" I lift my wheelie onto the metal scale.

She tears the outdated baggage tag from the handle. "Two days before Christmas—yes."

"Right. Great. Thank you."

"If the weather cooperates you should be in Burlington by six P.M." Almost twelve hours from now. Rock on.

I take my ticket, with its two layovers and one leg in cargo, and make my way to the gate, wishing for a Starbucks, but settling for a man selling the bare basics from a brown Formica cart.

Slinging my messenger bag into the overhead bin I take my seat in row thirteen with a bruised banana and large black coffee. I nestle against the plastic wallpaper and let my hair down from its makeshift topknot, my lids drooping shut, blocking out the sensation of everyone settling in around me.

"Ladies and gentlemen, the captain has informed us we may be hitting some turbulence, so we will be turning the seat belt sign back on. Please make sure that they are fastened." I reflexively open my eyes to double-check that I'm still buckled in beneath my neglected binder on Argentina's revised pollution regulations. My gaze locks with the headline of my seatmate's *US Weekly*. "First photos ever! Jake Sharpe and Eden Millay spotted ring shopping in St. Bart's. Is it WEDDING BELLS?" We hit an air pocket and the plane drops, my stomach lurching.

"Ladies and gentlemen, we're now beginning our descent." Twisting the opening of my bag toward me with my foot to keep it level, I pray those aren't prescient words.

I peer out the window for some visual landmark to orient me—a landing strip, the distant lights of Burlington, but the blackness seems thick and impermeable. Then the clouds clear the full moon, the snow-covered fields suddenly gleaming as if lit by a flashbulb. I rub my eyes as the wheels touch down.

A chapped-cheeked luggage handler emerges through the plastic flaps from the tarmac, pulling the laden metal cart behind him, trailing tread marks of sleet on the tile. He deposits its contents before us, and immediately there's a flurry of grabbing hands, the snapping of handles extending, as my fellow passengers take what's theirs and go. I stare for a moment in disbelief at the empty steel trolly. Shit. "Sir?" I make a beeline to where the man is checking off arriving flights on a clipboard. "Is that all the bags?"

"Sorry, ma'am, there're baggage delays coming out of New York. If yours isn't there, check with Velma at the desk. She can help you fill out a report."

I drop my head. "Thank you."

As Velma and I fill out the forms she repeatedly promises with a big smile that they will bring my little rolling bag to my door *the minute* it arrives in Burlington, *the minute*. Only, she concludes brusquely, as she taps the layers of forms neatly back together on the countertop, it's Christmas and she can't make any promises. I nod, heaving my bags back onto my shoulder, the realization sinking in that I'm going to be trying to make someone regret his entire existence in yoga pants. I walk to the sliding glass doors and—ohfuckohfuckohfuck—run through the snowdrifts in my sneakers to the few waiting taxis, their mufflers steaming. I slam the door shut behind me with a rusty squeak. "Hi, I'm going to Croton Falls, please."

"Croton!" the driver coughs, resting the cigarette on his lip to shift the car into drive. "My cousin's in Fayville—with the Christmas traffic, that could be an hour, easy."

"I know." I let my bags slide off my shoulder onto the torn vinyl seat. "I'll pay your return fare." I re-count the fold of twenties from the LaGuardia ATM. "Please?"

"Suit yourself." He grumbles our destination to his dispatcher on the CB duct taped to the dashboard.

"And, sir?" I flap the clammy Lycra hems away from my bare ankles. "Would you mind rolling up the window?"

7

He flicks the glowing butt onto the road as he reaches for the circular end of the handle. "Didn't think it was gonna be snowing?"

I huddle against the maroon vinyl, tucking my legs up under me in an effort to warm the damp fabric. "I didn't think it was going to be December."

2

SIXTH GRADE

Mom's right hand grips the gearshift, her knuckles pulsing above Grandma's cameo ring. She turtles her head forward to peer through the windshield at the clouds rolling across the lightening sky. "Looks like it might rain."

"Brolly's in the trunk," Dad says from the backseat, his Etonian temperament out of patience with our dawdling.

I stare past her mutton sleeves at the empty lot, beyond the rows of extra-long parking spaces for the buses en route with my new classmates, to the beige brick two-story complex that is Croton Elementary, Middle, and High. A maple leaf flutters onto the windshield, its stem catching in the wipers, momentarily blocking the view of the middle school entrance before blowing on. "It's just *huge*," I repeat for the billionth time since she took me on a tour of the carpeted hallways linking room after empty-desked room of a whole new life.

Turning from the hulking structure, she really looks

at me for the first time since the alarm clocks set us running in circles, and I feel the fear break in my eyes. Her face mommabirds. "You're going to love it here, Katie, I promise."

I shrug, my body tight with the potential waiting yards away.

"Yes. You're all going to love it. It's heaven, it's nirvana, it's the single greatest public school in the world. I regret not taking the job here already. Now, Claire, *Principal* Claire." Dad pulls himself forward with our headrests, the tip of his blue tweed blazer coming into view out of the corner of my eye as he squeezes her shoulder, deflating her blouse like a soufflé. "It's an hour's drive to Fayville. My interview's at eight. You *have* to get out of the car. See there, your first charges are arriving."

A yellow bus emerges through the break in the dense green hedges, making a wide turn into the parking lot, and we watch it weave through its painted maze to the high school.

"Tomorrow I'm taking the bus and getting up at a normal hour, right?" I ask again, hating that I couldn't have done this First Day thing on my own, knowing that if I was on a bus right now, I'd have seen their faces, maybe already be talking to someone.

The door accordions open and a stream of much older boys tumble off, staggering groggy and dazed. I slump out of view, my nose level with the glove compartment. "That must be a sports team." Mom reaches to the floor mat for her purse. "I don't have to worry about that. No early practices in the lower school."

"They don't have peewee football or something?" Dad smiles. "Something really violent for the little Visigoths to exhaust themselves with?"

She flips the visor down and takes a swift glance in the mirror, widening her lips to check her teeth. "Ready?" She flips it back up.

"Ready," I confirm, heart galloping.

Exchanging a kiss, they both open their doors to the thick humidity of summer's end, making me feel like I should be drifting on a floaty in Megan's pond. I shake out my new chin-length bob one last time, praying it's right—that they do chin-length bobs here—and slip my arm under my backpack strap as Mom sets her patent-leather pumps on the asphalt.

⚸

"Indian hop! *Indian hop!*" the gym teacher hollers into the chlorinated air. He jumps from one slimy floor tile to the other at the middle school pool's edge, arm and opposite knee raised to the fluorescents. I stare up at him, still immobile from the shock of being plunged in icy water when an unseasonably early freak snow is covering most of the pool building's windows.

"You." He bends down, his red face leaning in.

"Katie," I offer eagerly, hoping he's about to acknowledge I'm turning blue and should get out and into a warm towel immediately.

"Katie! Let's see you MOVE!" He extends his hairy arm over the shallow end like a 700 Club guy, blessing the other sixth graders who are chopping through the water with varying success, depending on where they are in their growth spurts. I smile weakly. "Come *ON!* No one's leaving this gym class until every single one of you has crossed this pool at least eight times, and I'm not giving late passes! Now HOP!"

"I'd like to strip him naked, stick him in a block of ice, and see him hop."

I turn to the wry voice coming from my left, where a girl in a purple O.P. swimsuit is gingerly holding her blond French braids above the water.

"This *can't* be legal," I agree.

"This *can't* be liquid," she matches me. "Laura Heller."

"Katie Hollis." Exactly the same height, we wave pruned fingers over the splashing swell.

"You just moved here, right?" she asks, trying to knot the long braids on top of her head.

"Yup." The drumbeat of longing for the familiarity of Burlington. "In July actually."

"I DON'T SEE YOU HOPPING!"

"Well, welcome to Croton Falls." With a grimace, Laura carefully lets her goosebumped elbows drop beneath the surface. "We also have a thirteen-lane bowling alley and a Pizza Hut—*with* salad bar." Suddenly we're blinded as two boys slap the water hard in our direction, drenching us both.

"Nice nipples," they heh–heh.

"You're so lame!" she shouts, slamming them back.

"Laura!" the gym teacher barks. *"Less talking, more hopping!"*

12

Eyes narrowed to slits, Laura surrenders her golden plaits to the sloshing current and raises her fist in the air.

I throw mine up in solidarity. "Okay, on two!"

❦

"Gimme." Moving a stack of magazines aside, Laura takes the snack tray and sets it down on the glass coffee table of the Heller den. Popping an orange curlicue into her mouth, she flops to the chocolate-colored shag and, slipping onto her back, points her bare toe against the TV's worn power button. I lower myself beside her to sit Indian style, unsure whether or not to sprawl. "So you've *never* watched *Santa Barbara?*" she asks again, waving for the bag, which I hand off as tacky strains of violin fill the room.

"My best friend, Megan, in Burlington, has MTV. So we pretty much only watch that—" I stop speaking as the phone rings atop a nearby stereo speaker.

Laura reaches over me to answer it, licking off her cheese-tipped fingers, the corners of her mouth tinged orange. "Hello?"

Taking advantage of the moment to look around unobserved, I finger the purple mane of a plastic pony in an abandoned corral on the board-game-crammed bookcase behind me. Suddenly Laura slams the receiver with a hard *thwack* startling me into knocking over the rainbow row of horses. I right them, watching as she pulls a cushion into her lap, squeezes it, and stares off at the television, not seeming to see the screen. The commercial for Mount Airy Lodge blares, the couple toasting each other in the wineglass bubble bath.

"So," I begin, unsure what just happened, nodding as if we're mid-conversation. "Um . . . so Megan, in Burlington, her aunt watches soaps all day . . ." I trail off as Laura twists to me. "What?" I ask, my new-girl antennae snapping to attention.

"You talk about Burlington like you're still there."

"I do?" My eyes drop to my tumbler, watching the tiny bubbles rise and pop.

"It must be hard to be stuck here in the middle of nowhere," she says testily.

"Burlington's not so great," I rush, aiming to sound like I believe it. "I love to skate, and they just closed the rink down. And my new room here is, like, twice the size of my old one—you should come over," I finish, lifting my Coke to take a long nervous gulp.

A barrel-bellied Lab moseys in and sniffs the snack tray, its white eyebrows lifting. "Shoo, Cooper." Disappointed, he hangs his head and lopes out.

The phone rings again, "Want me to get that?" I offer. But she just hugs the pillow to her chest as a man on the TV wearing a turtleneck under his suit screams about lowlowlow prices. The ringing stops. "Laura? Is something wrong?"

She looks at me for a long minute, her finger absently twirling a loose fringe thread. "Jeanine Matheson and I were best friends until she just stopped talking to me at the end of last year."

"Why?" I put my glass down on the paper-towel-lined tray. "Why'd she just stop talking to you?"

"I don't know," she says quietly, taking an Oreo from its package and slowly twisting the top off, separating it smoothly from the white filling. "Her parents got divorced last year. Are your parents still married?"

"Yes," I say, realizing I've never been asked the question, darkly wondering what I would do if, like Jeanine, the answer suddenly changed.

"Mine, too. Anyway, it was really bad and when she found out she was going to be at camp with Kristi she got totally obsessed with being popular and was, like trying to devise some master plan to break into that clique."

"But you're popular."

"Not like Kristi Lehman and those girls." She licks the creamy middle, looking down at the tracks her tongue leaves. "The boys all like them. No big whup. The whole thing's stupid."

"I'm sorry. That must have really—"

She finally meets my eyes. "It did. It really did." She sinks her chin into the brown cushion, denting its piped border in a deep triangle. "So were you at the top at your old school?"

"What?" I ask, cheeks reddening.

"I don't know," she slopes her head to the side and lowers her lids at me. "Michelle Walker said you look like Justine Bateman."

"Oh my God, thanks. But my school was *so* small. People hate—sorry, hat*ed,* past tense, people and loved people every other day, but it was like one or two were popular, not a whole football team. Here's a lot more complicated."

"Unlike Santa Barbara," she says wistfully, tracing the outline of her lips with the tip of her braid. "I'm moving there as soon as I graduate. I was totally born in the wrong climate. You in?"

"We'll get a convertible." I lift my head at the commercial where two smooth legs scissor from the backseat.

"Pink." She pops a whole cookie in her mouth. "After this we can watch *Dynasty*. My grandma tapes it for me." It rings again and she freezes. I freeze. "It's her," Laura's voice drops. "Them."

"What, they just call and hang up?" I drop mine, too, as I instantly feel like they're standing over us.

"I think Kristi makes her do it as a test. They scream stuff."

"You're kidding."

She shakes her head, looking so scared that I can't take it anymore. I reach up and grab the receiver. "Hello?"

"Laura's a bitch!" I hear giggles. Mean ones.

"I'm sorry." The wrongness of it raises me to my knees and summons Mom's most principal-like tone. "Laura can't come to the phone right now. She's busy thinking about how little of a crap she could give. Have a pleasant evening." I hang up.

Laura stares at me, a huge smile spreading across her face as I realize I'm about to pass out. *"Crap,* I like that."

"Shit was overhitting it."

"I do agree." She twists apart another cookie.

"Thanks." I drop back to the base of the couch, sprawling happily beside her.

Laura can't stop grinning. "Hey, want to be my partner on that Social Studies project?" She hands me my own lap pillow. "I think we have to say who we're working with by Friday."

"Sure," I mellow my answer, despite the cartwheels I feel at finding out that not only might I have found someone to move to California with, but she still wants to be friends with me on October 22, when the Renaissance binders are due.

❧

"Whad'ya mean, you don't like anybody? Everybody likes somebody," *the* Kristi Lehman states as if I've just challenged the Swatch. "Everybody." She pulls her headband off, shakes out her dark blond hair, and slides it back and then forward, creating a perfect crest.

"It's true. That's how it works," Laura confirms from where she slumps on the other side of me against the gymnasium bleachers; Laura and I have a pact to get out of whatever sport is being inflicted on us immediately. Not a huge feat when it comes to dodgeball.

"Didn't you like somebody at your old school?" Jeanine leans around Kristi. Laura rolls her eyes. "What? I can't talk to her?"

"Like I care." Laura re-smooths her new bangs, which were supposed to make her look more glamorous, but so far all they seem to do is annoy her.

"So?" Kristi persists, her heart-shaped face pinching in exasperation.

"Yeah, of course." I aim for a carefree shrug. "I just, you know, haven't met that many of the boys here yet, so . . . who do you like?"

"Benjy Conchlin," JenniferOne volunteers from where she's pulling at her stacked rubber bracelets. "And Jeanine likes Jason Mosley."

"His brother just moved to New York. To be a *dancer,*" Kristi whispers, holding her splayed manicure at the corner of her mouth.

"He's having a really hard time with it," Jeanine confirms. "I wrote him a note. He wrote back. We've been writing," she says as if they've been sharing a toothbrush.

JenniferOne continues, "So, JenniferTwo likes Todd Rawley, Michelle Walker likes Craig Shapiro . . ." She goes down the whole line of girls chatting along the bleachers as balls thud loudly off the walls and occasionally off the stomachs and groins of the boys trying to hold out on the court.

I check the caged-in clock over the scoreboard to see if I'll be able to get out of here before coming up with a name, buy myself some time over Thanksgiving break to do proper research.

"So who?" Jeanine leans in and I can smell the tacos from lunch. "Come on, whisper."

I scan the contenders—the survivors hurling rubber balls at each other with the focus of gladiators, and the downed and wounded nursing their egos.

"Come on, kiss it! You know you want to kiss my butt!" The butt in question is shaken tauntingly.

"Yeah! Kiss his butt! Butt kisser!"

"You do have to like someone," Laura urges. *Really?,* I think, continuing to survey my options.

"Someone," one of the Jennifers echoes.

"Michael J. Fox?"

"IN SCHOOL!" they chorus.

"If he's been on the cover of *Tiger Beat,* he doesn't count," Kristi scolds, her headband slipping out of place, requiring a repeat of the ritual.

"Okay, okay."

She pushes her fingers into her hair, lifting it inches above the band as a new thought occurs to her. "You're not a lesi, are you? I hear there's a lot of that in Burlington."

And now, according to my parents, I am supposed to lecture her on being a horrible person. Next year. It's a rain check. Her and me. Big lecture on being a horrible person. I'll bring slides.

"Well?"

My eyes land on a scrawny kid with floppy brown hair absentmindedly hugging a ball to his chest. He bobs his head and appears to be . . . whistling.

"That guy." I nod toward him. "The one with the, uh . . ." I squint. "Palm trees on his Jams."

"Jake Sharpe?" Who?

"Yeah, okay, uh, Jake Sharpe. I like him."

Laura pats my arm approvingly.

"No one's ever liked *him* before." Jeanine sneers.

"That's GAME!" The teacher throws his meaty hands toward the locker rooms. Jake Sharpe, apparently in his own whistling world, doesn't hear him.

"Well,"—I stand and dust gym grime off my shorts with the rest of the girls—"that's who I like."

3

December 22, 2005

Antsy, I lean forward in the cab, peering up through the frosted glass as we pull into my parents' snow-covered driveway, the headlights illuminating the colonial's façade. I knew they painted the shingles yellow last year, but part of me is still shocked at the change, as though time should have stopped out of deference to my absence.

"So, that'll be fifty-three bucks." He turns off the meter and flips down the visor, a pack of Camels dropping into his hands.

As I reach across the seat to where my messenger bag has tipped and lodged on the floor behind the driver, I catch sight of a Prudential realty sign sticking out of the snow. I squint in the near darkness to make out a rectangular SOLD placard lodged in the top of the drift. Excuse me?

"Miss? Fifty-three bucks."

"Right . . ." I rummage in my wallet while replaying the last months of phone calls to pinpoint where I might have missed that the house was for sale. "Thanks." I pass him my remaining cash and reach for the handle, look-ing out to the black branches of the towering Chinese maple they planted the day I graduated Croton Middle. That someone *else's* grandchildren will apparently be swinging on.

"Miss? You don't want change?"

"Sorry? No, keep it. Merry Christmas."

"Hey, you, too."

I release the door handle, a lash of icy wind blowing against me as I swing my legs outside, the snow envelop-ing my feet, the fabric immediately soaking through, short-circuiting my shock. "Hah! Hah! Hah!" I bleat as I run for the house, flashing to myself racing brazenly out to collect the mail barefoot at an age when being impervious to the winter was a sign of social cool.

I pause by the trellises to dig manically in the dim spillover from the neighbor's Christmas lights—"Hah! Hah! Hah!"—where the zinnia bed should be. I feel around, snow spiking pins into my bare hands, until I find a rock whose surface is artificially smooth. I pull it out, extracting the key from its hollow plastic center. Thanking God they never got around to improving their security system, I bolt up the porch steps and let myself into the entryway.

Slamming the door behind me, I rest my bag down and kick off the wet sneakers, crouching to squeeze warmth into my bare toes. Flipping on the overhead, I automatically turn the thermostat dial up to a reckless sixty-five degrees, disbelieving that, despite being yet another decade from their postwar childhoods, they still regard heat and electricity as special treats. The furnace clanks to life one floor below, joining the steady tock of the wall clock and I hug my arms to my chest, trying to land here, trying to anchor, trying to get a grip on the fact that our house is sold. I reach under my slip to peel my wet yoga pants off and hang them on the hat rack beside the faded Venetian mask I made at art camp. I touch its glittered triangle nose and look down at the red sparkles on my fingertip, affected to see my presence still tucked among Dad's collection of Red Sox caps. But beneath the rack, visible on the cream paint, is only the dark outline of where the hall mirror should hang. I look to the stairs, where more rectangular smudges mark the places of the seed catalog illustrations I helped Dad hang when we first moved in.

My stomach sinking, I pass the door to the dining room, coming to an abrupt halt when I see Granny Kay's walnut table gone, the oriental rug rolled along the wall, and the floor littered with boxes of bubble-wrapped pictures. I twist up the dimmer, letting the pewter chandelier cast a glare on the bare walls. Through the door I can see into the living room, its pine bookcases stripped clean of their prodigious shelf-sagging contents, its rug also rolled up, its furniture gone. I flick the switch off.

I step back into the front hall, pausing at the boot bench, which is now laden with every piece of displaced bric-a-brac—dusty kachina dolls standing side by side with Brahmin elephants and the base slivers of every Christmas tree trunk we ever had, each one scrawled with the year of its service in Dad's permanent marker.

And it strikes me that this is what it will be like when they die. I'll get a call, scramble onto a plane unexpectedly, dressed inappropriately, to process the artifacts of their interrupted existence. All of this, from the useful—can openers—to the vital—pill bottles—to the frivolous—ugly wooden fruit from Guatemala—will lose its context, most of it transformed into rubbish at the moment they stop living—and I suddenly want them home with a childlike urgency.

Braced, I step into the den, but find it thankfully unchanged. Swapping my damp trench for the age-softened afghan, I nestle into the overstuffed green couch, retreating from the agglomeration. The clock chimes for seven o'clock. The refrigerator hums faintly from the kitchen. Unable to snap out of the morbid frenzy I've worked myself into, I reach for the phone to call Laura.

"Ulo?"

"Mick?" I ask, winding the cord around my finger, unsure which of her twins has answered. "Keith? Is that you?"

"Ulo?" the three-year-old voice says again. "I'm Keith. Mick is frosting."

"This is your Godmother Kate—"

"Fairy Godmother!"

"Hi, Keith. Is your brother better?"

"He barfed. It was Christmas color. But it didn't smell like Christmas."

Smiling, I tuck the afghan around my bare feet. "I heard. Is Mommy there—"

"Kate?" Laura takes the phone.

I pull out my ponytail. "Word is you're frosting."

"We're making holiday blobs." Her voice drops to a conspiratorial timbre. "You're here?"

"Tah-dah. I took the first flight." I slide the black elastic onto my wrist. "Did you know they sold the house?" I rise up onto my knees.

"They sold the house?"

"Uh-huh. My parents sold the house," I say slowly so I can hear it, too.

"You're *kidding.*" Her incredulity soothing as always. "I didn't even know it was on the market. Where are they moving to?"

"I have no idea! There're boxes everywhere. It's so creepy. So—"

"Completely irrelevant at this moment. Did you really fly all the way here so we can discuss real estate and shirk the long-distance fees? Turn on your TV, my friend. It's the second coming."

I reach for the remote, its batteries still held in place with masking tape. "What channel?"

"Every channel. Start with E!."

I flip to a woman in a pink wool coat standing on our Main Street under a banner that proclaims WELCOME HOME JAKE!

I taste bile. "You must be fucking kidding me."

"You didn't see it?" she asks.

"We didn't come through town—the cab took the back roads."

"Well, they've erected a statue of him made out of

Spam, covered Main Street in one long red carpet that runs all the way to his bedroom, the mayor has declared this National Jake Sharpe day, and twelve vestal virgins will be blowing him at tonight's Christmas pageant. This town—has gone—insane . . . Kate? You there?"

I shake my head, incredulous.

"Kate?"

My jaw agape, I click through the news channels, all of which show some pastel-coated blonde trying to blink against the snow while locals bounce up and down with HI, MOM! signs in the background as if outside the *Today* show.

"Multiplatinum recording megastar Jake Sharpe has just announced—"

"In—of all places—his hometown—"

"His engagement to international recording super-star, Eden Millay—"

"MTV sat down with Jake six months ago—"

"E! will be bringing you live coverage as the story unfolds—"

"Some cynics have noted the announcement of this relationship dovetails conveniently with the pending release of her first film and his greatest hits album—"

"Here at CNN we are all very happy for him and wish the couple a very Merry Christmas indeed—"

"Some say this is just the tip of the love iceberg—" comes through the receiver in stereo.

I shut it off. "Fuck."

"Do you think it was a *love* iceberg that sank the *Titanic?*" I hear the tin clang of a baking sheet hitting the floor and the twins "uh-oh"-ing in chorus. "Gotta go. Stay strong, The Moment has arrived."

Furrowing my eyebrows, I click the screen back to life, the town center just a few hundred yards outside the picture window falling under siege as I fire through the channels . . .

"Jake Sharpe—"

"Jake Sharpe—"

"Jake Sharpe—"

"Hello?" Mom calls out, her voice tinged with apprehension. *"Kate?"*

"Yes, hey! I'm in here!" I call.

"No." She wings into the doorway, ankle-length down coat still on, her pale cheeks flushed. "Dammit. I knew it. Who told you? I wasn't going to tell you. Laura. Laura told you—"

Ready since I boarded the first plane, I stand, clasping the blanket around my shoulders. "Mom, you could've put every resident of Croton under a gag order and I'd still be at the gym in Charleston right now getting a blow-by-blow from Anderson Cooper."

"You're kidding." She comes around the corner and stares at the screen as I click through the channels to demonstrate. "The world's gone mad." She takes the remote from me and presses OFF.

Indignity flickers like a lit filament through my jaw. "And what about you two?" I point accusingly through the door to the entryway's stripped walls. "Why haven't you told me anything about this?"

"We didn't want to do it over the phone. Good Lord,

it's broiling in here." She rips the snaps of her coat apart. "We thought we'd wait until we saw you at the beach."

"Okay. That's one strategy. Where are you moving *to?*" I peer at her as she looks down to unzip the lining layer.

"Oh, Kate, the agent said it was going to take months and then we got an offer the first weekend and it's all happened very fast." She shakes off the gray down and drops it on the couch. "Your father's left his post at the library—"

"He's *what?*"

"He's done. He needs a change of scenery." She lifts her shoulders, her characteristic move to summon positivity. "So I just do a little bit of packing every weekend; it helps me adjust to the idea."

"Of *what?*" I cock my head, unable to imagine them anywhere but here doing anything else but what they do. Did.

"Sarasota. We're going to move to the condo for a year and then see what we feel like doing next. Dad needs a break from the snow." She gives me a wan smile. "And I'm adjusting."

"Adjusting?" I ask, low panic a rumbling submarine beneath the surface of my mission.

"I'm retiring at the end of next semester."

". . . Retiring."

"So!" she cheers. "We're going to sit on the beach and figure it out."

I spin to the doorway as I hear Dad stomp off his

snow boots in the front hall. "The Cashmans' collie's been digging up our zinnia bed again."

"Simon, in here!" Mom calls. "With your daughter."

"Katie?" He rounds the corner, hazel eyes lighting up. "Oh my God, Katie." I let him wrap me in a hug while I inhale his scent of ink-stained cuffs and newsprint. I stifle my questions, knowing any direct inquiry will only be met with infuriatingly enigmatic redirects. He pulls back, holding my elbows. "Well, let me look at you." Given the news, I study him in turn, the attuned expression, the meticulous shave.

"Yes." Mom puts her hands on our huddle and pushes us toward the door with renewed purpose. "She can drive and you can look at her the whole way back to the airport."

"Mom."

"Don't 'Mom' me. You are getting on the next flight to anywhere and we will see you as planned in Sarasota on Friday for our vacation."

"No." I throw the blanket off my shoulders. *"This* is The Moment. This is it."

"He's not worth it." She tugs at her cashmere scarf. "It's a hundred degrees in here. Simon, open a window."

"I know he's not worth it," I reprise as I pull off her knit hat, her gray bob rising in the static, and hand it to her. "I know that."

"In that flew-four-hundred-miles-in-your-nightie sort of way," Dad snorts, lifting the sighing mullioned panes.

"*This* is my Alamo. I've waited *thirteen years* to have the home-turf advantage."

"What's the news on Kyrgyzstan?" Dad rolls up the sleeves of his burgundy cardigan and reaches for the remote. "NPR said thirty people were killed in the capital today."

"You have not been *waiting* for anything," Mom picks up the thread. "You have a very happy, successful—"

"Yes," I concur as the chant of *JakeSharpeJakeSharpeJakeSharpe* resumes in the background. "The point is that The Moment has arrived."

"Nothing? Maybe BBC America," Dad mutters, peering over his wire rims.

"At last count forty-two bodies line the square."

"That's better—"

"SIMON, WOULD YOU TURN THAT OFF!" Principal Hollis surfaces.

Dad clicks it, dropping the remote on the ottoman, and we both watch as he pats the pockets of his corduroys for his wallet. "Right, then. I'm going to go get a tree. When I get back I expect you two to have come to some sort of consensus on the plan of action here." Smiling, he lightly squeezes Mom's nose between his knuckles as he passes to the front hall.

Mom swiftly crosses to me. "You can't do this," her voice an urgent hush.

"Uh, three flights and two layovers says I can."

"Don't be glib." She takes my arm. "You can't do this now, not now."

"What, should I just tell him to come back at a better time? When it's convenient for you?"

"This is your family, Kathryn. You're putting your family at risk."

Her audacity renders me speechless.

"Kathryn."

"I'm putting this family at risk?" I manage as I tug free before yelling past her, "Dad, we don't need a tree!" He returns to the doorway. "And we most definitely do not need a consensus." I keep her shocked face out of my visual periphery. "This is going to take twenty minutes. Tops. I just need to swing by there and make him regret his entire existence. I'll be back in time for dinner, catch the first flight back to Charleston in the morning, and we'll all be drinking Mai Tais in Florida by Friday." Dad retreats to the hall. "Where I will be giving you a PowerPoint presentation on why retiring and selling the house with no game plan makes you both—"

"His entire existence?" Shirking my indictment, Dad interrupts as he steps in with a hanger and picks her coat off the couch. "In twenty minutes?"

"And that still leaves me nineteen for a stroll home," I reflexively surrender to his pressingly lighter current. "Have you *seen* Jake Sharpe's existence?"

"I'm sure MSNBC will be doing a two-hour feature of it at nine." Mom stalks over to the window, sticks her head out, inhales deeply, then leans back in, closing it. "Followed by five minutes on Kyrgyzstan," she mutters as she swivels the lock.

"I'm going upstairs to change." I move toward the stairs, reaching down to pick up my messenger bag and purse from the floor.

"Why not run over like that, looking as deranged as this idea," she hollers after me.

"Thanks," I call back flatly as I raise the bags. "I appreciate the support. I'll be sure to return it as you sketch out the next thirty years of your lives with a seashell."

I stand, waiting for them to round the corner, defend themselves, make their argument, go there. But instead I hear the set click back on, the volume rapidly swelling as reports of the coup's toll continue to mount.

4

SEVENTH GRADE

I lift the brittle ends of my hair to my nose, nauseated by the sweet stench of Salon Selectives I've sprayed, squirted and squeezed over the last two hours of alternated crimping and curling with Michelle Walker's mother's beauty supplies. "My hair is broom straw," I mutter to Laura as she listlessly raises and lowers the trays of the professional expanding makeup box at this slumberless slumber party.

"God, what time is it even?" she asks, dropping a tube of liquid eyeliner onto the gold-flecked Formica counter of the basement bathroom Mrs. Walker has rigged as her salon. "It's so bright in here it could be lunchtime." She squints against the glare from the baseball-shaped bulbs framing the mirror, as if this were a Hollywood dressing room and Mrs. Walker doesn't primp wedged between a dented Maytag and a badly burnt ironing board.

JenniferTwo wipes off yet another shade and I reflexively lick my own lips at the sight of the prickly irritation spreading around her mouth. "Two forty."

"Two forty A.M.?" Laura asks as a wave of exhaustion breaks over the pizza, caramel corn, Coke, and Carvel birthday cake making a gushy mess in my stomach.

"Yup," she nods, two curlers flapping against her face.

"The movie *must* be done by now." I flick the OFF buttons on the heating devices that have been keeping those of us not wanting to watch the third seventies-era horror video in a row or examine Mr. Walker's *Penthouse* stash *again,* entertained.

All of a sudden Stephanie Brauer pushes the door open, bouncing in her long T-shirt, knees pressed together. "Movemovemove, I've gotta pee!" The sound of a chain saw revving slips in behind her before she pulls the door shut and dodges between us to the saloon-style shutters at the far end of the room.

"Is the movie almost done?" Laura asks, wilting. She rubs her Cleopatra eyes.

"Oops." I point to the black football player streaks. "Bad move, Bubba."

She wearily raises her index fingers and takes in their smudged tips. "Crap."

"Ooh, gross," Stephanie groans. "Michelle's dad's, like, underwear is hanging up in here. Gross," she repeats over the flushing toilet.

"He moved out and left his underwear?" Laura asks as Stephanie pushes back through the sprung shutters. "That's so weird. Don't you guys think it's so weird?"

While Stephanie retreats to the mirror, Laura holds open one of the doors so the three of us can cram into the toilet alcove. Sure enough, on a white plastic rack over the sink hang five pairs of Hanes boxers, dried stiff.

"C'mon, guys." JenniferTwo backs out and starts clacking the lipsticks into their plastic slots. "We better put this stuff where we found it or she'll spaz."

"Did Michelle know?" Stephanie asks, and JenniferTwo, self-appointed guardian of Michelle, pauses, her hand full of warped hotsticks halfway-shoved in their case. "How?" Stephanie stares intently at Jen's bent head. "What was the sign?"

"Separate beds?" Laura asks, leaning in. "Separate rooms?"

Ignoring her, JenniferTwo resumes packing the colored foam rods. But Stephanie steps intently over to her. "Did they fight?" The pink band of fabric slips out of her hair. "Did they? Just tell me, Jenny."

"All the time."

Sucking in her cheeks, Stephanie nods to herself as she retrieves the band from the floor, wrapping it twice around her wrist. The only sound is the burble of the refilling tank. JenniferTwo clears her throat, "You guys better not tell Michelle I said anything." She stands up and bores her eyes into each of ours as she goes to open the door. For the first time all night, the sound of bell-bottom-wearing teens mid-slaughter does not bounce off the veneered walls and into our hair-sprayed refuge. Instead, in its place, come the hushed tones of tense negotiation. Stumbling over each other to get out, we follow JenniferTwo across the mess of sleeping bags littering the orange carpet. She steps over the snoring

Dunkman twins to where the birthday party is in some kind of standoff in front of the sliding door to the yard. Fully dressed in their identical acid-washed perfection, Kristi and her friends have their backs to the glass.

"So are you staying?" Kristi asks matter-of-factly as she swipes on a coat of iridescent lipgloss and passes it to her friends. Jeanine opens her mouth, but is at a terrified loss. She looks from Kristi to Michelle.

"Spaz," one of Kristi's minions gets haughty. "We're just meeting the boys at the falls to have a smoke, it's not like we're having an orgy."

Kristi cracks up.

"Seriously, guys, you have to be back really soon," Michelle pleads. "If my mom wakes up—"

"Yeah, sure." Kristi tugs the door open, letting in the chilly fall night. "Make sure Jeanine has her Pampers on when you tuck her in."

"Don't get an ulcer." Her other minion slides it shut, sealing us in.

As we watch the It Girls disappear outside the arc of the floodlight there is a moment filled only by the snoring behind us. Michelle turns, wild eyed. "I'm so screwed! I'm so totally screwed! It's my goddamn birth-day! And now I'm *screwed!*"

"You're the one who had to invite Kristi," Laura mutters.

"Thanks!" Michelle spits at her. "Thanks a lot, wench!" She pushes between us, trying to run through the mess of sleeping bags toward the bathroom, but she trips over a Dunkman and we all watch as she flails in slow motion, limbs like a runaway marionette, before hitting the carpet with a slamming thud. Frozen, we stand with our hands over our mouths—is she dead? Dana Dunkman makes a kind of gargle half-snore before rolling over, still out cold. Dazed, Michelle sits up. Laura clamps her hand tightly on her mouth, but her shoulders start to shake as she fights it. I instantly start to giggle. Laura grabs her stomach and drops into a crouch she's laughing so hard. "Sorry. I know . . . it's . . . not . . . funny. It's not."

JenniferTwo runs to Michelle, helping her up as she clutches her nose, her eyes still wide in surprise. "Ohmygod, she's bleeding," JenniferTwo announces. "I bet she has a concussion."

"Ice," I manage to get out.

"Get her ice." Laura wipes her palm across her eyes and stands up.

"You'll wake my mom if you go up there!" Michelle wails in alarm as a patrol breaks out for the stairs. Someone grabs a pair of ruffled pink socks to stuff against the blood trickling from her left nostril.

"Let's get her into the bathroom." JenniferOne helps to lift her up and the group half-carries half-drops Michelle to the other side of the basement.

"Laura," Jeanine's voice comes from behind us.

We spin around to see her still facing the black glass, her eyes fixed on the illuminated wedge of leaf-strewn grass. "Let's go," she says.

"Duh. We can't," I remind her.

Jeanine turns, her face hard. "I wasn't talking to you.

I was talking to Laura. Wipe that stuff off and let's go meet up with them."

I look over to Laura, psyched to see her tell Jeanine to screw herself. But she doesn't. Jeanine tugs off her pajama pants, pulls up her jeans, and pushes her feet into her loafers. "Rick Swartz is going to be there. He's friends with Jason after soccer camp this summer." She pulls off her top, her worn training bra, probably her sister's hand-me-down still on underneath, and, embarrassed, quickly shoves her head through the neck of her sweater. "So come on."

"Why don't you just stay, Jeanine?" The uncertainty in her voice makes my chest tight. "You know your mom'll kill you."

"I have to." Jeanine pulls a Kissing Cooler from her pocket and swipes it on, rubbing her lips together.

"No you don't. That's only four girls out there. There are, like, thirteen still here."

"Thirteen who'll be playing makeup for the rest of seventh grade." Jeanine's eyes narrow.

"So, why do you have to do everything Kristi says?" Laura finally asks what she's wanted to for so long. "She's not even funny or . . . I mean, she sat here all night making bored faces in the corner. She's just . . . I don't know. So her mom's a manager at the mall and she gets to wear designer clothes—"

"She's fun. A lot of fun. And I don't want to sit around with a bunch of babies who don't even talk to boys on the phone playing nurse to Michelle Walker all night. So are you coming or not?"

Laura looks at the floor. "Not," she says softly.

Jeanine's face turns the ember color of her hair. "I hope you two will be really happy together. Be sure not to invite me to the wedding."

"Fuck you," I say, surprising myself.

"Fuck you both." She seals the sliding door soundlessly behind her.

Laura holds my stare, her expression stunned. "Wait," she says. And I ready myself for the moment I have known was coming since the day Laura told me about Jeanine: when Jeanine would realize she'd made the biggest mistake of her life throwing over the best best friend a girl could hope for and she'd want Laura back. The moment Laura would go. Because they have history. They have lower school. They have learning to read and all sorts of things I will never—"Who am I?"

And she face plants onto the nearest sleeping bag.

✿

"Stop," Laura mouths sternly, tipping me past the point of being able to contain my laughter.

Overtaken, I slam the receiver back down. "Oh, God, I'm gonna pee." I roll on the raspberry carpet in the doorway of Laura's parents' bedroom, where I've stretched their phone cord to its limit.

"Katie!" she moans from the opposite end of the hall, where she's stretched her brother's phone to *its* limit so that we can see each other for the First Call.

"I'm ... I'm sorry." I gasp for air. "I don't know what's so funny."

Laura sits cross-legged in her prairie dress as she broods. "Okay, maybe this isn't a good idea, you being able to see me. Maybe you should go inside the door."

"Maybe I shouldn't be on the line at all. I mean, why am I on?"

"So you can tell me what I sounded like. And what he sounded like. Like a witness."

"Witness," I sigh. "Let's call Harrison Ford." I break into another fit of giggles.

"You're such a dork; I don't know why I recruited you for this job."

I take a deep breath and sit up. "Okay. Okay, I can do this. You can do this. Today we call the boys. Go." I wave at her, putting the receiver back to my ear. "Dial."

Laura exhales slowly, pointing sternly at me before dialing Rick Swartz's number. As the line rings my heart speeds.

"Hello? Who's on the phone?" suddenly Mrs. Heller's confused voice breaks in.

"HANG UP!" Laura drops the phone, shouting down the stairs. "OH MY GOD! MOM! HANG UP!" We both bolt from our posts to meet at the railing, frozen in terror.

"This is Martha Heller. Who's this? No, I did not call you. Well, then *you* hang up . . . good-bye."

"I . . . I . . ." Laura becomes zombielike. *"My mother* called Rick Swartz. Jeanine's going to—the entire seventh grade's going to . . . *My mother* called Rick Swartz!"

"Laura, listen." I swivel her face to me. "Just call him

back and say, um, that your mom's been really sick and she's just, like, got a really high fever and has been, um, calling random numbers and being, like, delirious." I nod hopefully.

"Really?"

"Yes."

"But how would I know that she'd called him unless I was on the line?" Her blue eyes grip me with desperation.

I chew my lip. "Say you just came into her room and she was murmuring about calling Rick Swartz like she murmurs about the other stuff she's doing while she's sick. Come on, Lor, we're losing valuable time here. Just call."

"MOM! DO NOT PICK UP THE PHONE!"

Mrs. Heller appears at the bottom of the stairs. One hand in a yellow rubber glove, she uses the other to re-clip her hair away from her face. "Are you paying the bills around here now?"

Laura hangs off the banister. "Mom, *please,* I'm begging, just give us five minutes? *Please.*"

"Are we calling boys?" She rests her gloved hands on the hips of her stirrup pants.

"Mom," Laura moans.

"Laura," she moans right back. "All right, but start your homework, please."

"Okay!" I chime as we each resume our posts. The second she's out of earshot, Laura dials. I press my palm into the door frame as it rings.

"Hello?" he answers.

Laura freezes. I scissor-kick my legs at her to snap her back.

"Rick?"

"Yeah?"

"Hi. This is Laura Heller." Her small hands clench the receiver so tightly her knuckles turn white.

"Yeah?"

"Yeah, so I just called 'cause my mom has this major fever. She's really sick and I don't know, we think it could be malaria because she's just totally sweaty and out of it and . . ." I kick my legs again. "Anyway she's been doing all sorts of weird stuff because she's, like, delirious. We have to watch her all the time and my brother was supposed to be watching her but he had band practice so she was alone and she, I think she picked up the phone and called you and acted crazy. Because of the malaria. I only know because I just walked into the room and she was mumbling something about your name and I thought, you know, God, I better call you and let you know that she's just being weird like that because she was sick and dialing random numbers and so . . . so that's why I called."

"Okay."

Out of material, Laura shrugs at me in desperation. Reminding her to play cool, I toss my hand in exaggerated nonchalance.

"So, uh, what are you up to?" She drops into a slouch.

"Wait, who is this?"

"Laura. Laura Heller."

"Your mom didn't call me."

"Oh!" She turns nuclear red. "Oh, okay, then . . . uh, bye."

"Bye."

Laura carefully puts the phone down before slumping to the floor. "Crap. Crapcrapcrapcrap."

I hang up and run the length of the banister to her, kneeling to pat her head. "Maybe he won't tell anyone."

She looks up at me through her hair, her face beating. "Anyone, like who? Like Jason and the other jocks? Who'll tell Kristi so she and her clique can act it out at the next assembly?" She rubs her cheeks with her hands and groans. I am momentarily speechless at this very real possibility.

"Just deny it," I decide.

"What?"

"Deny it. If anyone asks you about calling Rick and saying your mom has malaria just say you don't know what they're talking about. Like, they're the crazy one for asking you."

"I can't say *Rick Swartz* made it up." She exhales. "Okay, your turn."

"What, are you nuts?"

"Katie, I did it, you have to do it."

"Yeah, and that went so well."

"Shut up. Get the phone book in the pantry and let's look up Jake Sharpe."

"No." I'll just keep carrying the fact that I'm supposed to like him because I said so in gym class around along with my library card, my Red Cross babysitting certification, and my house key.

"We made a vow!" Laura sits up on her knees. "A birthday vow!"

"*You* made a wish when you blew out *your* candles! It's not the same thing. Laura, let's just finish Science. My dad's going to be picking me up soon." I stand.

"Uch."

"What! Volcanoes are cool. Come on." I reach a hand down to seesaw her to her feet. "I'll help you. You'll learn to love the volcano from the inside out."

"Fine, but next time you're calling Jake Sharpe. First."

✳

I put my sandwich back down on its Baggie and tap Laura's untouched yogurt, my voice lifting over the din of the packed cafeteria. "No good?"

She points to the silver wires on her teeth. "This no good." She slumps forward, pushing her old folks' home lunch away. "I can't believe I had to get these the same week as . . . as—"

"Move it, Malaria." Benjy Conchlin bumps Laura's chair as he slides through to his table, his red curls poking out above the size tab of his Sox cap.

"As that."

Just then JenniferThree plunks her tray down, the ohmygod look on her face silencing the entire table.

"Something the matter?" Laura asks, refusing to play into her dramatics.

Jennifer pauses another beat, until she's sure she has our undivided attention. "Jeanine. Got a big red stain. On her white pants. In shop."

We collectively gasp.

"That *has* to blow you calling Rick Swartz out of the water."

We all nod in agreement, and, gloom lifted, Laura returns to tackling the Yoplait. I offer her a slice of apple. "Suck on it."

"Squish it against the roof of your mouth with your tongue," Michelle, the longest brace wearer at the table, instructs.

"There she is." Jennifer gestures to the double doors of the cafeteria and we all turn to see if she is still alive— if getting a period stain in a room full of boys, does not, in fact, kill you.

Jeanine is wearing her gym shorts—ah, good move. But still, most every head turns. Despite her being a colossal bitch, I feel genuinely awful for her. Our eyes meet and I offer a sympathetic smile. She nods. Good for her, she'll just walk through the maze of round tables and sit with the weirdo clique that took her in when Kristi's group was done with her, and—she isn't walking. She flips her newly blackened hair over her shoulder and looks around.

"What's she doing?" Laura whispers.

We all shrug in response, riveted.

She walks directly to the nearest table and leans down, displaying a stain-free butt to all, as she talks to—the whole lunchroom watches—to Jake Sharpe. He scans the tables and then she points. Points right at me.

And then . . . they all turn, the whole cafeteria turns. The whole room looks at me and then back to Jake Sharpe, who stands to get a better look. At me.

"Ohmygod."

"Ohmygod," Laura echoes.

"She's telling the boy you like that you like him," JenniferThree Howard Cosells the moment as we all stare at each other, agog. Then the bell rings, signaling the end of lunch and my life. Motion resumes. But Jake and his friends stay put. To wait. Because they're right by the exit. People continue to blatantly stare as they shuffle toward the racks of dirty trays.

"We'll go together." Laura stands, tossing her bag into the nearby trash.

"No," I hear myself say, "I have to just—I'm just going to . . ." And then I'm moving, speed walking, pimply faces a blur. I grip my lunch bag and books to my chest and focus on the glowing exit sign over the doors, moving along the waves of stares and whispers. But then I hear, "Hey, Hollis!" and automatically turn in the direction of Randy Bryson's voice and, in the slowest of slow motion, Jake's angular face locks on mine, hair falling in his green eyes as he cocks his head, like Laura's Lab when he's watching a deer out the back window. And then it's loud and fast again as I step into the crowded hallway, continuing on to . . . where? I look at the doors to the parking lot. Pouring April rain splatters the cement. I could just walk and keep walking. Instead I find myself carried by the tide up the stairs to Social Studies.

"That's her."

"She likes Jake Sharpe."

"Katie likes Jake Sharpe, wants to marry him and have his babies."

I find myself at my seat and slide my shaking legs under the attached desk. Mrs. Sandman comes in and the overheads flicker on.

"Katie wants to lick Jake Sharpe's wiener," someone whispers in the row behind me. I see the rest of my life at this school playing out as if I'm Rocky Dennis while Jeanine gets to stroll in here every day with maxi pads stuck to her face and no one even notices—"Lick it, lick it—"

"Mrs. Sandman?"

"Yes, Katie?" She places her coffee mug down and peers through her glasses at her lesson plan.

"I'd like to make an announcement." I would? A picture of Krystle Carrington appearing in my head, I feel myself step onto the seat of my orange plastic chair and then onto the desk as if about to correct a rumor campaign whirling around the grand ball. Then I'm tossing my hair back over my imaginary beaded shoulder pads. "Yes, so, um, I believe you have all heard that I like Jake Sharpe. I just wanted to put an end to the rumors. Yes, I, Katie Hollis, like Jake Sharpe. So, there you go. Now we can all get back to our lives." Okay. I step down, one Bass loafer at a time.

Ms. Sandman blinks at me. The class blinks at me. I pull at my rugby shirt and retake my seat, noting I have not dropped dead, and not yet sure if this is a good thing.

❦

"No. Way," Laura's voice lowers.

"What?" I ask, pulling the Gruyère off my sandwich and rolling it tightly before biting off an end, enjoying that people have finally stopped staring at me like at any moment I might hop on the furniture and announce I like *them*.

"Your Jake Sharpe is sitting with Jason and those other jocks." Laura darts her head at the cafeteria table of top guns a few feet away.

I fold the rest of my cheese roll into my mouth. "Not mine. We've never even said hi."

"He was yours enough to stand on a desk and claim him."

"That's *not* how it was supposed to go in my head. And that was days ago and I'd appreciate if we could all drop it. Besides, don't forget whose scandal of the week I knocked off the charts, Ms. Malaria."

She shrugs, working her way through an apple with slightly more expertise. "I just thought you'd be interested to know that since your big announcement he's been supremely promoted. Your dramatics were apparently an escalator to popular."

"So that's why it feels like I'm being stood on."

We munch as the lunchtime screams and giggles around us bounce off the mint-green walls, *ascending,* our new vocab word, to a deafening level. Having avoided looking even in his general direction for the past four days, I let my eyes wander casually back to the rowdiest table. Sure enough, spastic, whistles-to-himself-in-the-halls Jake Sharpe sips out of a silver Capri Sun between Benjy Conchlin and Todd Rawley.

Laura squints while carefully sucking apple skin from her braces. "Doesn't it look like he got a haircut?"

I glance over one more time, using my paper bag as cover. "I guess, yes, he seems, more . . . more something." More in color. Like if River Phoenix had a younger brother. "I don't know! It's not like I study him or anything. I've just been trying to live him down."

Jeanine stops in front of our table, pushing open her milk container, her spiked hair looking extra porcupiny today. The girls around us fall silent, looking from her to me. I take a breath and try Mom's suggestion. "Hey, Jeanine, why don't you join us?" I smile with as much real kindness as I possibly can, watching with satisfaction as her face clouds in confusion. "Jen, why don't you and Michelle move over a seat so Jeanine can sit down?"

"I don't . . . need a seat," she says weakly, and it is awesome to see her so uncertain of herself. "Hey, Katie, don't you like Jake Sharpe anymore?" She pointedly flicks crumbs off her Anthrax sweatshirt, and I fight a smirk at how flat her preplanned one-liner falls after my Gandhi setup. "Or are you holding out for Laura?"

"Uch, screw off, Jeanine," Laura says in a tone so indifferent it actually makes Jeanine just shrink away with a two-fingered salute and an "Okay, whatever. Later."

I look around the table at everyone waiting anyway for an answer to Jeanine's question. "Of course I still like Jake Sharpe, okay?"

Laura clamps her hand on my shoulder, lightly pressing down. "In case you get the urge to reassure the entire cafeteria."

Breaking a smile, I lift my bread slices and slap her cheeks.

"Gross!" She pulls back giggling. "Oh, so gross, now I'm coated in mayonnaise!"

"*Seventeen* says it's supposed to be the best moisturizer," JenniferTwo informs as she stands back up with her brown plastic tray.

I hand Laura a napkin. "God, what's the big deal? Everyone likes someone, right?"

Laura thoughtfully wipes Hellmann's off her cheeks. "But no one ever stood on a desk."

5

December 22, 2005

Turning the porcelain knob, feeling the resistance as
the white door drives against the faded pink pile carpet-
ing, I'm immediately struck by the chilly, vaguely stale
air and the smell of mildewing paper and hidden dust.
I push it all the way open to see in the stark moonlight that, other than a few concessions to accommodat-
ing overnight guests, my old room continues surreally as
I left it in high school.

I step in and drop my bags on the bed beside the towels Mom always leaves waiting atop the comforter under
brochures for the local pumpkin picking farms and
maple sugar refineries, an unironic commentary on my
refusal to leave this house once safely ensconced. I move
the brochures aside, revealing the monogram, EHK, and
remember the fight we had over those towels—"They're
hanging in *your* bathroom, Kathryn, *whose* towels would
they be?" But Michelle Walker's had her initials on them
and I was determined to have a set. Twelve mowed lawns
later and they were mine.

Smiling at my tenacity, I reach out to turn on the

bedside lamp, illuminating the Katie Museum in all its cluttered glory. Stunned as always by the sheer volume of visual information, I drop onto the quilt to take in the layers and layers *and layers* of memorabilia I meticulously assembled, added to, and detracted from all through high school, as if Johnny Depp might suddenly arrive at any moment and need to get the complete picture of my marriageability solely from these four walls. I marvel that I slept soundly amidst this dense collage of objects proclaiming my allegiance to shows now long off the air, a presidential nominee retired, legislation that will not be enacted in my lifetime, and a rockstar who died of AIDS; as well as pigs, James Dean postcards, angel figurines, and an impressive assortment of bobble head dolls. Bobble head dolls. Sweet Jesus. And now I will finally dump all of it into as many lawn bags as it takes to strip the place bare.

I cross to the bookcase, running my fingers over the dusty volumes—J. D. Salinger and *Tender Is the Night* pushed out in front of the Jackie Collins I didn't want found. On a lower shelf sit all the CDs I didn't take to college—Morrissey and the *Pretty Woman* soundtrack bookending my yellow boom box. I press PLAY and a disc starts to whirl. Music pounds from the speakers and I fumble to lower the volume, smiling as soon as the driving, electronic melody registers.

"Ready to duck. Ready to dive," I hum along with Bono, remembering Laura's own words of encouragement as we packed The Bag and formed The Plan.

The Plan.

Wondering if Laura, in all her infinite wisdom, could

have foreseen my lost luggage, I drop to my knees and lift the dust ruffle. And there it still sits, waiting for me, the black DKNY duffel we stuffed nine years ago with everything I would ever need to Make Him Regret His Entire Existence. I heave it up onto the bed and pull down the zipper, reaching in to pull out . . . a spaghetti-strapped silk minidress, and then another . . . and another . . . each patterned with . . . butterflies. And then one . . . two . . . three . . . *four* fistfuls of Victoria's Secret. I reach to the bottom of the bag and take out first one and then two pairs of strappy patent leather sandals. With RuPaul platforms.

Platforms.

I lift the bag up and tip it to the side as I reach in for the last item, praying for perfectly cut jeans, low-V cashmere, and a fitted shearling coat; but instead find one very overstuffed makeup kit, which I unzip to discover concealer that has gone—whew! *Off.* Annnnnnnnd—this should come in handy—several palettes of MAC silvers and aquas. And glitter.

I look down at my options, and then out the darkened ice-latticed window, my lips pressed taut, church-giggle tears springing to my eyes. Hitting STOP on the CD, I go back to the top of the stairs and crouch down. "Mom?" I call tentatively.

From the kitchen I can hear the sink running over the Queen of the Night's aria. "Mom?" I call again, reluctant, but desperate.

"You rang?" She appears at the bottom step, an apron protecting her gray cowl-neck sweater, carrot in hand.

Chagrined, I stick the tip of my tongue into the corner of my mouth. "I'm sorry I was an asshole."

"What did the asshole say?" Dad calls from the kitchen.

"I'm sorry!" I shout.

"Tell her she can stay for dinner," he says as the sink shuts off.

She just looks up at me, waiting, and I drop my head against the spindly banister rails. "Okay, so my suitcase is MIA. I've just unhooked the rip cord, and all that's flying out are strappy sandals. Actually strappy everything." Because that bag was packed back when the objective was to be a naked disco-ball.

"Uh-huh . . ." She bites her carrot, unappeased by my humor.

"So . . ." I lift my eyebrows hopefully.

"So this might take more than twenty minutes," she confirms.

"So," annoyance cracks back through. "I might need to borrow the car and see if Laura'll meet me at the mall."

"You? Leave the house?" she says in exaggerated disbelief. "You're not just going to hide behind drawn drapes, make Laura come to you?"

"Okay, I have a very logical, informed strategy for navigating this town—"

"Your Belle of Amherst routine?" She waves the carrot in a circle.

"I can go to the mall."

Her brow furrows. "Two days before Christmas. It'll be mobbed."

"So?"

"So, on further thought, I think this may be an appropriate time to continue your logical, informed strategy."

"Mom?"

"Yes?" she replies evenly.

"I am asking to borrow the car and drive to the mall."

"And I'm saying in the twenty-four months since you last graced us at the holiday season, driving to the mall has grown into a much bigger endeavor than you think it is."

I take a breath, trying a new tack aimed at the core of her concern. "Okay, Mom, I'll be superfast and back in time to have dinner with you guys. And we're spending the whole week together in Sarasota. You'll be sick of me by New Year's."

"No, that's fine." Her mouth tenses, despite my effort.

I knock my head against the banister rails. Thank you, Jake Sharpe, I am now actually crouched on my parents' stairs negotiating, *negotiating,* to borrow the car. "I wasn't even supposed to be here," I moan, rocking back on my heels.

"Well, it's a *pleasure* to be your obligation," she says with sarcastic cheeriness.

"Mom," I sigh, but unable to deny it. "Mom," I say again, grasping for some sentiment I can offer to mollify, to connect. But, as always, I'm stymied in a way I never am in Sarasota or Charleston, only here, where the

specter of Jake thins the air between us. And now the prospect of this fresh revisitation is sucking us to a new altitude altogether. I rest my head against my out-stretched arm. "Mom"—I reach for her—"can you drive me to the mall?"

"Say that again." She cocks the carrot by her ear, her eyes drifting closed.

I peer down, smushing my face between the rails. "Can you drive me to the mall? *Please?*"

She smiles, her expression soft as she opens her eyes. "Aah. For a moment . . . I was forty-six."

6

EIGHTH GRADE

"Every man's got his patience and here's where mine ends." I shake my hips from side to side as we speed in a circle around the gym at the September Skate Social. Dancing one wheel in front of the other, I spin about and glide confidently backward until I lock with Laura's wide eyes. Seeing the bead of sweat on the tip of her up-sloped nose, I spin around Tom Finkle attempting to robot dance and take her hand. Her damp fingers clutch mine as her blond curls jerk back and forth with her geisha steps.

"You're so good at this," she says in tense puffs, clutching my arm with her other hand for additional support.

"First time I've ever *not* hated being in here!" I arc my arm on the beat at the gym walls dotted with a few half-hearted construction paper leaves and pilgrim hats courtesy of the PTA.

"Help me off so we can talk without being run over?"

Nodding, I guide her through the whirring wall of jeans and mock turtlenecks to the unfolded bleachers. "Easy." I help her down.

"Look," JenniferOne nudges her front wheels into my lower back. I follow her pointed finger jutting over my shoulder to where Stephanie Brauer has glided in wearing yet another brand-new Limited sweater. "It's insane."

"I wish my dad bought me new shit every time he missed a weekend," Michelle says from behind us as she unlaces her skate and taps it against the bleacher, a tiny grain of gravel tumbling out.

"Shiiiiiiiiiiiiiiiiiiiiit!"

"Tip forward to brake: Brake!" I cry as Maggie comes barreling into us. Laura and I grab her waist as she ragdolls over our shoulders into JenniferOne's lap.

"This is *bullshit*," she gripes as we flip her around to sit between us. "The only person who doesn't look totally retarded out there is you," she accuses me.

"I used to take lessons with my dad when I was little, on ice."

"Why can't we just have dances, like a normal school?" Laura unclips her rhinestone earrings, her lobes indented with red rectangles.

"Middle school graduation dance in May," Jennifer-One says as she peels off her nail polish. "It's gonna be awesome."

"And the best is everyone goes with dates. It's a couple-thing," JenniferTwo says like she's supposed to be at a couple-thing right now and her parents just dropped her off at the wrong gym.

As though the DJ overheard her, the electronic drum-beat of "Lady in Red" comes on and half the lights flicker off. I lean into Laura and make fluttery eyes. She returns with kissy fish lips.

"Girls' choice," the DJ's voice breaks into the song. Everyone looks around the emptying wood floor, charged with held breath.

"You should ask someone." Laura nudges my shoulder.

"No way," I murmur, watching the It Girls glide carelessly over to their chosen, bracelet-laden arms out-stretched. My stomach drops.

"Holy crap. That's Kristi Lehman asking your Jake Sharpe," Maggie murmurs as a hand takes his sweatshirt sleeve.

"Not mine," I say automatically. But I don't look away. We're all watching. As a girl, The Girl, just goes right up and grabs him.

"Sure his parents didn't pay you to move their son up the food chain?" JenniferOne quips.

They round toward our end of the bleachers, slipping in and out of pockets of light and shadow. Jake, ever so slightly moving his lips along with the song, Kristi pop-ping a bubble and sucking it back in, her white-blond hair sprayed into a banana clip. As they move past us my eyes are caught by his free hand, thin fingers slightly curved, moving in time with the synthesizer.

"Are you so jealous?" Michelle Walker sticks her head between us, her Impulse body spray clogging my throat.

"You must be. Kristi can be pretty slutty." Jeanine leans over from where she sits with the head-banger clique as Kristi releases Jake to his It friends. "I'd be jealous."

I try to tap my wheels like I could give a crap, meanwhile allowing myself in the half-darkness to study this boy who has gone from nobody in stupid Jams to top tier in under a year, which is fine—I mean, whatever. But now to become a couple-thing right in front of me. . . .

The lights flicker back to full wattage as the opening bars of "Lean on Me" drown out the last beats of the slow song. As if hearing a whistle blow, the boys blast out of the moving circle, skating where they please, owning the floor, snapping bra straps as they fly past. What would it be like to be so . . . not-caring?

At the reggae bridge Kristi awkwardly tries to move her hips in a way she must think looks Jamaican and just as the boys are about to laugh Jake loops around her and smiles. She grabs the hem of his shirt and trails him to the drinks table.

Yes. It would be amazing to have a boy beside me. Everyone watching as I'm transformed from a desk-scaler into someone enviable, fabulous, free. It would be . . .

"Well," Jeanine scowls, her split-end inspection completed. "Are you?"

I nod. I am.

Laura tiptoes in her ankle-socks, pivoting side to side under the buzzing lights of the Lord & Taylor dressing room. I automatically do the same, pulling the almost extra foot of bodice satin behind me, struggling to fist it all tightly together where the zipper drapes away from my spine. "You don't think it looks just like the new wallpaper in my dining room?" she asks, lifting her boobs up in the snug corset.

"Uh, no." I clench the tent with my elbows while I hook the flat fan bow over her butt. "It's really pretty." I drop my heels and step back to lean against the Formica wall. "Who are we going with that we have to be so tall?"

"Katie?" Dad beckons from where he's trapped on the threshold and I hoist up the voluminous folds to follow his voice. "There you are." He steps back into the racks of evening suits crowding the dressing room entrance, holding an armful of V-neck sweaters, corduroys dangling off his elbows and a peach dress swinging from his hooked finger. "I found *this*. Any good?"

"I'll give it a whirl."

"Great." He looks me up and down. "Because I know you're fond of large and shapeless, but I think you may be rather taking it to extremes with that one."

"I know, Daddy. It's headed for the reject pile."

"Your mother's rifling the sales racks in the men's department. We're going to play Lions Romans Christians with these jumpers. Holler if you need a third and fourth opinion."

I point at my head, my sign for him to smooth his hair, which has duck fluffed in the mall static. Carrying the peach candidate, I find Laura flopped on the carpeted pedestal in a pitiful flowery pouf.

"Who do you think I should ask?"

"Michael J. Fox?"

"In school," she completes our routine as I turn sideways, wondering what I'd look like with cleavage.

"You gonna ask Jake?"

"Uh, *no.*"

"Don't get defensive." She lifts her palms. "And your mom's busty—they're coming."

I crouch on the floor in front of her. "I can't ask Jake. It took forever for all that to die down. Besides, he's always hanging out with the Kristi girls. Are you asking Rick?"

Her nose wrinkles.

"So, there you go." I stand back up.

"What do you think of Craig?"

"Craig, your-lab-partner-Craig?"

"Yeah." She pulls the scrunchie out of her fading perm, shaking the limp waves to her shoulders as she slips the burgundy velvet onto her wrist. "I think you guys would look cute together. He's tall and blond. You're tall and brunette."

"Aw." I pat the top of her head and, momentarily forgotten, the bodice drops to my waist. My hands fly to my bare chest. "Yeah, both of us and our grandbabies could get in here."

She stands, taking the peach one off its hook, and turns me toward my stall. "Try this. I think it'll be really pretty on you. Plus it has straps. Which maybe is a good idea."

"So, you're admitting I have no boobs."

"I'm saying your boobs would be extra flattered by straps." She smiles sweetly before shutting my door. "So, what about Craig?" she calls.

I think about him as I kick off the heavy satin and unhook the hanger straps of the Gunny Sax. "He's cute, I guess."

"*And* nice. *And* smart."

I step into the scratchy crinoline. "I just never really thought about him that way."

"What way? The Jake Sharpe way?"

I swivel my head around the door. "Yes."

She narrows her eyes at me. "Katie, we can't let everyone get boyfriends but us just because of Rick Swartz and Jake Sharpe. We have to move on." She looks down to double wrap the scrunchie around her wrist. "I'm asking Randy Bryson."

"Really?"

"Yes. I think his eyes will look good with these flowers." She lifts her skirt and relays it gracefully around her legs. "So get that dress zippered and let's move on already."

❦

I concentrate every ounce of my energy on the one hair that refuses to lie flat with the others sprayed and twisted in the peach satin bow clip. I'm about to rip the flyaway right out of my head when the door to the bathroom opens and loud music pours in, followed by Kristi Lehman.

She pushes into a stall door, tugging layers of white lace in behind her. "You're here with Craig, right?" she calls out.

"Yup!" I stop with my hand on the girls' room door, not sure if she's finished talking to me, not wanting to slight the Queen.

"He's nice. He used to live down the street."

"Yeah, yes. He's very nice," I say, though he is not very anything else as far as I can tell. He checked the *yes* box on a note during Social Studies and here I am with a boy who has, other than smiling shyly, said nothing but, "Please pass the rolls," since 7 P.M.

The stall swings open and she steps out, adjusting her strapless dress over her infamously large breasts. "Yeah, I'm here with Jake. Oh, crap, you like him, right?" So I'm told. "You don't hate me, do you?" Answer irrelevant, she turns to the mirror to reapply her lipstick. "We're going out now. You know, officially."

I take this like all ten of her Lee press-ons have just lodged in my rib cage. "That's great! No, I—that's great."

She pauses for a moment in the mirror, the ridged silver tube poised above her lips, studying me in the reflection. "You're sweet."

"You guys look really good together," I hear myself add. "Well, have fun!"

I shove back into wailing guitar and walk straight to the drinking fountain. Leaning over, I press my hand against my chest to keep any of the pervs from staring down my dress and pretend like I'm getting a drink, but instead just watch the water circle into the drain. So Jake Sharpe has gone all the way to the top. Without so much as a word to me.

I release the metal button and straighten, broadening my shoulders so that the whole of the cutout back is exposed, and step around the huddle of blazer-clad teachers to look for Craig among the boys whipping each other into a frenzy with their liberated ties. The staff quarters in *Dirty Dancing,* this is not.

Immediately giving up, I find Laura and the other girls who've also given up, dancing by themselves in a circle by the picked-over buffet. Laura tugs me to her and cups my ear.

"Jake Sharpe told Randy your dress looks hot." She pulls back to study my face, holding down both my arms as if I might fly away.

"Seriously?" I scream through the music. She nods emphatically.

"But I just heard he's going out with Kristi."

Laura shrugs, her drop puffed sleeves lifting and lowering. I look over the tan line on her bared shoulder to see Kristi return to her gaggle, all of them in flounces of shiny lacy white. As Benjy careens into Kristi, she tugs the tie from his hand and flicks him, cleverly pulling her girlfriends into the frenzy. Then Jake comes up behind her and wraps his arms around her waist, lifting her up, her legs bent. She flails, waving the tie like a gymnastic ribbon as her giggling friends join the boys in their roughhousing.

"Dance!" Laura commands me back.

I shake off any momentary urge to be locking eyes with him, a tie whipped between us like a bullfight cape. My dress is hot. I am . . . hot. I AM HOT! Giddy, I throw my head around with utter abandon, walking like an Egyptian. A *hot* Egyptian.

Laura and I descend the hill into town surrounded by the lulling buzz of sunshine-fueled cicadas. Given our summer of serial sleepovers, we're bleary eyed as our laceless Keds scuff the pavement in unconscious unison. Our gas-station sunglasses doing little to cut the glare, we both squint in the flat noon brightness.

I replay the last few minutes of *Sixteen Candles* in my mind's eye, my chest rising as I imagine what it must be like to sit atop a glass table while the Hot Guy of Your Dreams leans over to give you a birthday kiss. "Think high school'll be like that?"

"Like what? Shit!" Laura's hand goes flying to her purse. "Thought I forgot the video. Sorry, keep going."

"Like, the hot guy you like finds out, and then just

shows up, and wants to kiss you," I mull as we cut across the school's playing field.

She lifts her ponytail and pats her hand across the back of her damp neck. "I'll say a prayer every night if you will."

"Deal." I reach my pinky out and she swipes it with hers.

A humid breeze lifts across the vast green. "Oh my God, don't look up," Laura suddenly whispers into her pocket tee. I ever-so-slightly follow her not-gaze through the waves of heat rising from the dusty turf to a figure riding a bike slowly while another trots alongside him, bat in hand.

"Who?" I ask, tight mouthed, even though they're halfway across the field.

"Jake," Laura whispers back.

"Is Kristi with him?" I ask, nauseated.

She shakes her head. "Only if she's had a sex-change. I think it's that new kid, Sam—the one who moved in across from Michelle—in that lame Green Bay jersey he's always wearing." We continue our controlled stroll. I pretend to scratch my shoulder and see the bike cut diagonally across the grass.

"Anything in my teeth?" Laura slightly parts her lips, not breaking the pace.

"No. Me?"

"You're good."

Taking Laura's cue, I keep my eyes trained on the turf. Then the front wheel of a red bike comes into my vision, just beneath the horizon of my bangs. It does a lazy circle around us as I watch Jake's open high-tops, the tanned muscles of his calves. And then another circle. Long shadows covering our bare legs. Think of something to say—anything . . .

We walk; Jake bikes around us in fountain-size circles and Sam, trailing behind, tosses his bat up in the air and catches it, with an *oomf.* Okay, I will concentrate very, very hard on getting her to say something. Say something cool. Something really cool. *Sayitsayit-sayit—*

Then the shadow pulls back off my feet. The *oomf*-ing gets quieter.

Turning around, I catch a glimpse of boxers sticking out of basketball shorts as he bikes away, Sam jogging along, bat held behind his neck like Frankenstein shoulders.

Laura tugs my sleeve before suddenly breaking into a run, her purse flapping. I take off after her, flying across the field. "Why are we running?" I huff.

She flaps to a stop once we get under the cover of the bleachers and grips her knees, laughing, her ponytail flopped over her face. "I don't know. Why didn't you say anything?" She rights herself and reaches into her shirt to adjust her bra.

"Why didn't *you?* That was so weird."

We move back into the sunshine, walking the last few blocks in thoughtful silence. As we cross Adams Street and climb the steps, Laura makes her summation, "And in September they're going to hunt us down and confess their undying love." She slides the video box out of her purse. "I'm so sure."

"He didn't confess his undying love. He bought her a birthday cake," I correct.

"Same difference." She pulls open the door, a blast of arctic air hitting our damp faces as the attached sleigh bells jingle our arrival.

7

December 22, 2005

"Only for you," Mom shakes her head as we inch the Honda down Main Street, television vans abutting us on every side.

"Only for him," I retort as a pack of ski parkas with cameras aloft appears suddenly in the headlights.

She brakes sharply, her right arm automatically extending, pinning me against my seat. "This better *not* be for him."

I smile at the reflex as she returns her hand to the wheel. "I told you, I'm here for me." I gesture to the fogged windows. *"They* are not."

"You mean not yet."

I sink down, tucking my nose under her borrowed scarf.

She takes a left out of traffic onto the relative quiet of Adams Street. "What happened to Rent-a-Flick?" I ask as we pass the shingled two-story building with a Curves sign in the front window.

"The Blockbuster out by the mall," she says with dismay. "But Trudy's done a great job with the Curves. I've been going three times a week."

"Mommm." I give her a mittened thumbs-up. "Very impressive."

"The secret is earplugs. I can't stand that racket they play so I just stuff my ears and then nod and smile at everyone. It's quite pleasant, actually. Now I know why your father always seems so relaxed."

At his mention I turn my gaze from the hypnotic flow of taillights to her patrician profile. "How's he doing with all this?"

"He's fine," she answers lightly.

"What about you?"

"I'm fine."

"Really?"

"Well . . ." She brushes her hair from her eyes. "Tired, of course, with the move and the holiday and whatnot, but I'm fine."

"Really?" I ask again, trying to discern if she's lying just to me or herself as well.

"Yes."

"Your husband suddenly forces you into early re-tirement from a job you love and you're just fine?"

"*Yes.* I'm fine and you're just running a little errand." I stiffen. "So." She lifts her shoulders. "Now he wants to write a book in the sunshine and fish. And that's what we're going to do. It was just—really taking a toll on him, it seems. And we have to respect that."

Feeling the muscles around my eyes twist, I dig in my

purse for my drops, squeezing the liquid in and blinking as it splashes onto my cheek. "No, of course. He's still on the Zoloft, right?"

She nods to herself, reassuring me as she traverses us through the recently plowed streets, slowing to a halt at each stop sign as she navigates the back way. "It's not like he didn't try at the library. Honestly, the people in this community. They hire you to effect change and then make it impossible."

"Unless you want to put in a Curves."

"Yes, then we welcome you with open flabby arms. You're still having the problem with your eyes?"

"Only when I'm tired." And stressed. I wipe the condensation off the window and peer through the wet streaks left by the wool as we emerge out of the valley into a sprawl of lights. "Wow. It's so built up. It's all so—"

"Oversized, gaudy, trumpeting the end of civilization as we know it."

"I was going to say 'much.' "

We haltingly circle the football-stadium–size parking lot a few times, a salt-crusted sea of cars stretching out before us over every inch of asphalt. I bite the inside of my lip and look around pointlessly for a spot.

"Screw it." She pulls onto the snow-covered meridian abutting the lot and takes the key out of the ignition. I crane my head, calculating the hundreds of yards of frozen vehicular tundra to get to an entrance. But she's already heaved her purse onto her shoulder. She gets out, slamming the door closed, and I jog against the wind to reach her and take her arm. She squeezes my mitten with her elbow and we duck our heads down for the trek.

"She said they'd be in the food court!" I shout back as we round the corner into the bustling atrium lined with queues of hungry, holiday-addled families. "There!" I point to where I spot them sharing a burger at the far-end table. As we make our way over I watch Laura laughing at something with her boys and have that momentary pang of awe and jealousy—will I be at the boys' wedding still thinking, "Oh my God, Laura *made* them"? Or worse, still be the spinster aunt with three hundred godchildren because everyone took pity on me? I raise my hand and wave; she beams.

"Fairy K, my dog threw up! I'm eating a cheeseburger with fries!" Mick stands on his chair to announce these two updates with equal emphasis over the blaring bossa nova of the carousel. Laura laughs again, putting down her yogurt as he hurls his forty pounds into my arms. "You're wet." He puts his small hand to my cheek and pulls it away to examine. I return his feet to the vinyl.

"Claire wanted us to get some exercise." I wipe the sheen of sleet off with a McDonald's napkin as Mom tears open her coat. Then I lift Keith up in turn, ruffling his bangs with my chin.

He kicks his miniature blue moon boots out for me to examine. "Yours are brown."

"Pretty stylin'." Grinning at my borrowed Lands' End ensemble, Laura stands to engulf us both.

"Mommy! You're crushing me!" Keith wriggles down our legs.

"Kate Hollis standing in the Croton mall—and without a fake nose." She laughs in my ear. "Look at you, being all brave."

"Look at you," I murmur as I pull back, my hands going to her rounded belly, and again, the pang. "You look beautiful."

"Please, minus the braces, I'm having a second puberty. Actually, make that a third. Do you know what it's like to be buying Clearasil at thirty?" She leads Keith back to his seat and licks a napkin to wipe the ring of ketchup from his mouth.

"You're radiant, Laura," Mom insists, helping her consolidate the fast food detritus. "Pregnancy suits you."

"Well, drink me up 'cause this is my final round." She hands me the tray of wrinkled wrappers, which I carry across the floor and dump in the trash, stopping short as a posse of toddlers runs past. I pull back, narrowly avoiding felling a laughing mother in hot pursuit. She steadies herself, giving me a once-over.

"Katie?" I'll be taking that fake nose now, please. She stops, blowing her bangs up and allowing the kids to race another lap. "Katie Hollis?"

I blink for a moment at the thick red hair and glowing skin. "Jeanine?"

"Oh my God, Katie!" To my utter surprise, she lunges, wrapping me in a hug, her poncho emitting a musky trace of incense. "That is *so* bizarre." She releases me, smiling with her whole face. "How *are* you?"

"I'm good, thank you," I laugh, her enthusiasm contagious. "How are you?"

"This is so crazy." She scoops up one of the lapping boys to the hip of her leggings. "Anne and I were *just* talking about you in the car on the way over!"

"And is this your son?" I rub the pink cheek of the child squirming in her arms, deflecting us from my auxiliary celebrity status.

"Timmy," she smiles tenderly as she ruffles his hair. "Yeah, I'm meeting Craig here to do the family gifts. Our last year." She looks up at me. "We're getting d-i-v-o-r-c-e-d. I'm shedding Shapiro."

"Oh, God, I am really sorry to hear that," I say, sad our class is already joining the ranks of the didn't-make-its.

"Thank you," she reaches out and touches my shoulder. "But it's for the best for all of us." She shifts Timmy to her other hip, her flexing thigh muscles visible through the spandex.

I admire her serenity. "You look fantastic."

"There you are," Laura calls, swaying over with Mick balanced on her boots. "Hey you!" she greets Jeanine as she lifts Mick to the floor, sending him darting back to the table. They exchange a truncated half-hug over Timmy and Laura's pending Number Three.

"Are you doing the poses at home?" Jeanine places her palm solidly on Laura's belly. Not tentatively, the way I do it.

"I try! I do." Laura mugs embarrassment. "When the boys nap." She turns to me. "Jeanine teaches prenatal yoga."

"I'm so impressed," I marvel.

She bounces Timmy back up to her waist, turning intently to me. "You *have* to take a class with me. I teach a whole roster at Yoga H'om up there." She points to the escalators. "Just past the Sunglass Hut. You have to come. You'll thank me, seriously."

"That would be great." I nod.

"So your folks' house sold?"

"Yeah, it did," practical stranger who knew before I did. "They're pulling up stakes and heading south."

"Yeah, Anne and I toured it when it was on the market. We're looking for a three bedroom. It's a beautiful space, really good positioning. But the energy." She waves her free hand, her face darkening. "Completely congested. And your old room, wow—the whole place needs to be smudged."

I look down to see ketchup smeared on my thumb. Laura pulls a napkin from her pocket and puts it into my hands. "We've really gotta boogie." She shrugs apologetically.

Jeanine nods knowingly. "You're here to see him, huh?"

"Him?" I crumple the red-streaked paper, trying to signal to Mom with my pinky at my hip to bring the car around.

"Jake."

"Yup." I exhale.

"Babe." She puts a palm on my trapezius, pushing Mom's coat open to give me a brisk three-stroke swipe. *"Let it go.* God! Yoga would be so good for you! Your whole aura is *starving for it.* You have got to take that on when you get home—where do you live?"

"Charleston."

"Wow, he *really* did a number on you."

"No, no." I look to Laura, my smile faltering. "I just hate living in the cold."

"Cold is a state of mind, babe." She stares squarely, making no motion to let us leave, signaling she is just beginning her list of what my aura is starving for.

I lean over and give her a quick kiss. "Great to see you, Jeanine."

"I teach tomorrow. Get the schedule from Laura. Yoga saved my life."

"Definitely!" I wave good-bye. Glancing back I see them wend their way to a blond guy waiting at a table with two overstuffed Target bags and my gaze pinballs from the burgeoning beer paunch to the sun-damaged forehead to the utility belt to the duck boots to the *Us Weekly* with Jake on the cover he's flipping through. I tuck my head down and take Laura's elbow, darting us out of Craig's visual range. *"That* is why I will only meet you behind closed doors. Everyone here is talking about the pathetic girl who got ditched by the rockstar— which I'm only known as in a forty-mile radius of that Pretzel Time." I point up at the hot-pink sign as we pass.

"Okay, everyone here is talking about their *Christmas lists,* for starters. And I hate to burst your reclusive bubble, but we are a far-flung group. Right now Jason Mosely is probably thinking about how pathetic you are as he tends to his hydroponic lettuce in Olympia. JenniferTwo is taking pity on you all the way from Philadelphia, and I'm sure when she wakes up tomorrow Maggie will spell out 'Katie is lame' with breadcrumbs for the pigeons in Trafalgar Square. Get a grip."

Chastened, I nod. "Hydroponic lettuce?"

"Check out his Friendster page."

"Okay, grip gotten. And who's Anne, her guru?"

"Uh, no." We wait as a security golf cart passes, its orange lights flashing. "Her girlfriend, soon to be partner."

"Shut the fuck up."

Laura grins. "And sometimes we get stoned. Now you're completely up to speed."

"Laura!"

"Not while I'm *pregnant.*" She cracks up. "You try having twin boys. It's a miracle Sam and I aren't crushing Valium into juice boxes." The cart clears and we cross to Mom and Keith playing patty-cake. "Okay! Let's do this thing. I want to get the boys in bed by nine."

"Yes, I love you—and I appreciate being included," Mom acknowledges. "But you're right, I can only take about forty-five minutes of this—" she circles her arms at the crazed pre-Christmas masses surrounding us. "Before I expire. Why don't I take the boys to the carousel while you two do your thing." Keith and Mick look rapturously at the garland-strewn apparatus spinning beneath the domed night sky. "All right, gentlemen, I'll take a hand from each of you, *per favore.*"

She stands and the boys grab her hands, giving in to the magnetic pull of the plaster horses. For a second I feel the sensation of her fingers enclosing mine at that age, the assurance. "Forty-two minutes," she mouths, deftly steering them into the crowd.

"*. . . had a very shiny nose . . .*" My cranium reverberating with cheer, Laura and I let ourselves be carried along by the shoulder-to-shoulder madness. Bypassing the chain stores optimistically featuring cotton "resort wear" in their windows, we somehow manage to jostle ourselves to the women's department of Lord & Taylor.

"Does this come with a free bikini wax?" I point at the mannequins sporting waistlines all of an inch above the crotch.

"Try finding a pair that covers your ass when you're pregnant. It's feast or famine. Either your tailbone's sticking out or you're in an army tent. How 'bout these?" She lifts washable suede toward me.

"Uh, no." I flip the hanger around to show her where they lace up. "I'd rather not go as a VJ."

"Didn't you get the memo? We're all supposed to look fourteen now."

"Kristi Lehman would be so bummed." I flip through midriff-baring sweaters. "She didn't even look fourteen when she was."

"She's running the mini-mart out in Fayville now."

"Shut up!" I spin around and give her a shove. "Shut up! How do I not know this?"

"What?" Laura smiles, savoring my reaction. "We never go out that way. Sam had to install some equipment in Clarkson and stopped to get gas. He said, and I quote, she looks . . . tired."

"Tired!" I shake my head.

"Tired!" She throws her arms up, her purse sliding up to her shoulder. "Merry Christmas!"

"God, right back at you." We stare blissfully at each other. "Crap, what time is it?" Laura asks, checking the clock on her cell and immediately pivots me forward.

"Twenty-eight minutes, move."

Damp with sweat, I grab anything that looks remotely spectacular-grown-up-and-over-you. Laura throws her own selections on the pile, which is soon higher than my sight line. I follow blindly as she leads us, snaking around circular racks of velveteen and faux fur, to the hallway of dressing rooms. She stops abruptly and I tip forward, the pile slipping. She catches it in her arms as we take in the long line of miserable women balancing their heavy coats with their potential purchases and pulling at their turtlenecks.

"This is ridiculous."

"I say drop to your skivvies or we're going to be here all night."

I do, taking more and more off beneath each item until I'm down to my underwear and mom's knee-high argyle socks. Laura, sitting on the makeshift cushion of her down coat, pulls her hair back with her scarf to better keep up with rehanging the heap of discards as she gives me her vote. "Uh. . . . no." "No." "Nope." "Do you miss working with Sonny?" "Definitely not." "Out of the question unless a revival of *Carousel* comes to town." And she finally collapses in giggles, managing to snort out, "You . . . look . . . like . . . Charo!"

I slump down in front of her and drop my head into my hands. "I've done this all wrong."

Laura dries her eyes, "No! No you haven't. But, Kate, come on, why do you care *so much* what you're wearing?" She takes a wistful breath. "You've had great boyfriends. I mean, you date fabulous men—"

I snort.

"You have big sex." She pushes the remaining outfits off of her.

"Sometimes," I concede, unzipping myself from the velour bustier. "You have a husband," I volley back.

"A very very tuckered husband. You've got this great career doing important altruistic things. You fly to Buenos Aires at a moment's notice."

"I was on a plane, in a hotel, in a factory, and then back on a plane. I could've been in Cleveland."

"With framed pictures of Eva Peron behind every cash register?"

"No, probably not. That part was cool," I concede. "I had to keep reminding myself they were portraits of the actual woman and not Madonna."

"See? You've had an adventure." She pulls out a pack

of gum and pops a piece from its foil pocket. "And the farthest I ever got is visiting you in Charleston."

"Okay, you're not eighty—'the farthest I ever got'— and you have a *family!*"

She crosses her arms over her belly. "You still have your body."

"Which I work at for the express purpose of some day having what you've already achieved, which is a man who'll pledge to love me when I'm senile and two— three great kids! Laura, if I told you, in three hours, you could have a face-off with Rick Swartz, what would you do?"

Her eyes glaze over. "Take out a second mortgage . . . get Chanel to whip something up for me to drape this and minimize that. Get every square inch, new square inches included, highlighted, waxed, buffed and polished so I'd look so fucking great that all of mankind would be stopped in their fucking tracks and little Rick Swartz would have no choice but to regret his entire fucking existence."

"Right, and all he did was tell the seventh grade you made a phone call." I hand her the angora shrug.

Her face refocuses with renewed resolve. "Okay, let's just try to find you a decent pair of jeans and then get you some makeup. Here." She reaches into the bottom of the pile and tugs out an array of denim. I stand back up. "So, what are you going to say to the little shit anyway?"

"What would you say to Rick Swartz?" I push the

first aborted pair off with my socked feet and she hands me another.

"I told you I think he's in prison now, delightfully enough."

"Merry Christmas to you."

"That was last year's present. Ah, Croton High, the gift that keeps on giving. But should I deign to visit him and address that whole chlamydia—"

"Malaria," I correct her, swiping another pair.

"Right, malaria. Oh my god, chlamydia, can you imagine? Anyway, I would purse my perfectly lined lips and ever so slightly push out my currently humongous cleavage and tell him the whole thing was *so not cool.*"

"Yes." I turn to show her where the majority of my butt-crack is exposed. "Basically along those lines. There will most definitely be a not-very-subtle theme of So Not Cool."

"You don't have an exact plan? Really? We didn't pack some notes or bullet points in that bag?"

"I don't want to talk about that bag and it's been forever since I've given this any serious thought. Thank God. I mean, there was Plan A." I tug the denim from her arms and she gives, letting me fall back a step. "We'd hear he'd been spotted singing for quarters on the sidewalk in L.A. beside his empty guitar case."

"Sadly, no go."

"Plan B, One-Hit-Wonder. He'd fade into total pathetic obscurity, only resurfacing to appear gray and bloated on *Where Are They Now?*"

"Plan C," Laura continues as she stretches up to stand with one hand on the mirror and the other supporting her back. "Straight-up O.D. You'd arrive at the funeral in a stunning, yet tasteful, black sheath, your Nobel prize on a grosgrain ribbon around your neck, and his mother would take your hand, look into your eyes, and tell you—"

I zipper up the final pair. "You know, dear, although he had such success, he never knew a minute's true happiness after he left." And I would squeeze the old crone's hand and say, "I'm sorry for your loss." And, "Was he really found naked in his own feces sucking his thumb?"

"Oh, I did love Plan C." Laura studies the fit in the mirror over my shoulder.

"Yeah, well, last we left Plan Negative Z involved locking eyes with him across the aisle at your wedding. Late that night we'd meet at the gazebo, I'd be in a sexy little nothing—apparently with butterflies on it."

Laura grimaces. "I still, *still,* don't know why Sam thought he'd come back for that."

"Because those boys always want to believe the best about Jake." I sigh.

"Well, believe me, that well's run dry. Anyway, cut to mad passionate almost."

"Cut to him regretting his entire existence," I pick up her cue. "I get on with my fabulous life. There. That was the plan."

"And *those* are the jeans. What about on top?"

"It's not here; there must be something at home that'll work."

"Great. Come on, we've got six minutes for makeup. You run to the Lancôme counter and I'll pay for these. Break!"

We both step in opposite directions before I spin back, "Lor—"

She turns, her blue eyes scanning me. All I can manage is a goofy smile as my own are suddenly moist. "I know," her voice softens. "You, too."

"You guys have your own rage, I totally defer to that."

Her expression darkens. "You know how his label just got bought out by Bertlesbrink?" I nod. "Well, they've hit us with a cease and desist. They threatened, quote, *aggressive* legal action if we don't drop it. We got the letter Monday. So Merry fucking Christmas."

"Jesus. What are you going to do?"

She shakes her head as she cradles her tummy. "Sam says we can't afford to keep pouring money into this."

"And you?" My eyes go to the small tremor beneath her hand.

"I sat there in that fucking basement," she says, her face taut with anger, "right alongside you, while my husband wrote the melody for the longest-running number-one of the 'nineties. So I can't let it go, I can't—the second we cease it's like saying what he did is okay." Closing her eyes, she takes a steadying breath. "I can't get this upset." My heart going out to her, I squeeze her arm and her eyes open. "So if you can make Rockstar Fuckhead's evening even a little less fabulous it will be a total success as far as I'm concerned. Okay?" I nod. "But not looking like that."

"Right." I run my hand through my hair. "I love you."

She smiles shyly, her cheeks flushing as her Scandinavian side gets embarrassed by the declaration. "Shucks, okay, I have too many hormones to do this now. Go!"

"Okay!"

"I mean it." She waves me away. "You're kicking his ass for all of us. I don't want you doing it with puffy eyes."

8

NINTH GRADE

"Sam, you're *so* retarded," JenniferTwo declares wearily as Sam slides our minivan's rear door shut, catching his Charger jacket in the hinge.

My eyes fly to the back of the driver's seat, but her offense did not make it to Dad's good ear, which is angled toward the dashboard. Thank God NPR is more fascinating than a bunch of fourteen-year-olds. That we are listening to a droning debate about Nicaragua, and not my new Guns N' Roses tape, was a requirement hotly negotiated in exchange for his chauffeuring our group date. Final compromise: misery, but only on the front speakers.

"Are we going to make the two forty-five?" I ask over the whir of Sam dragging the heavy door open and shut again, the "ajar" bell dinging steadily.

"Out and over, Sam. *Out* and over," Dad twists back to instruct.

"Katie, I told you." JenniferTwo reapplies her Clinique Black Honey gloss in the backseat, the first coat already making her lips flake off in dark red chunks.

The fact that she shared a lifeguard chair with Kristi this summer has doubled her wenchiness, as if she has to quick use her new status in case it fades like her tan did. Not that Laura and I aren't using it, too. It *did* make this date happen. But at least *we* don't have attitudes. "If we don't make *Indiana Jones,* we'll hit the three o'clock *Pet Sematary.* Don't be retarded." This time she's loud enough for Dad to catch my eye in the rearview, his nostrils flaring to convey that he does not in any way approve of the teenage misappropriation of the term. I nod right back to convey that, of course, this is unacceptable, but it's just something people say so can he please just keep driving and continue with his silent protest, silently.

"Any more stops for you charming young folk?" he asks as the door clicks closed.

"Jake's, Fifty-three Bluebell." Sam slumps back with Benjy and me, absentmindedly wiping the greasy black streak on his jacket, clueless to Dad's sarcasm. Laura glances back from the passenger seat, panic passing between us on an invisible current over the cup holder. *I'm going to be sitting in a car with Jake Sharpe?* I ask her with my eyes. *Yes!* she replies with her eyebrows. *Oh my God!* I shout with my forehead.

"He said he'd be waiting—" Sam suddenly yelps as Benjy grabs his blond head and a noogie love match erupts. "At the! . . . End of the! . . . Driveway!"

"There. That's him, Mr. Hollis," JenniferTwo resumes orchestration of this date. Her status, her coordination, her Black Honey lipgloss on our lips. Flaking off them. My stomach knots as I see Jake in his leather jacket kicking wet leaves into a pile on the curb. He doesn't *look* heartbroken. Maybe Kristi dumping him for Jason has made not just me, but also Jake, a stronger person. Maybe he feels like everybody else does about the whole thing, that Kristi and Jason at long last going out is like a fulfilled destiny for the entire freshman class. That, somehow, now that these two have paired off, the universe might actually be able to focus on the rest of us for a change.

Sam, utilizing his newfound expertise, slides the door open and he and Benjy jump out to pull Jake inside "abduction style." Dad sighs as Jake tumbles onto the seat, his huge high-tops landing in my lap on a wave of damp chilled air.

"Sorry," Jake Sharpe speaks to me for the first time ever as he whips his feet off my lap and then crams against my side. Benjy and Sam pile in next to him, head to head, Jake's dark brown hair completing the Neapolitan.

"Aw, you reek!" Benjy tents his jacket over his nose.

"My dad's burning leaves." Jake flicks Benjy's forehead.

We crane to see the smoke from the field bordering the lawn, where a man leans on a rake beside a reddening blaze.

"That's not your dad." Benjy scowls.

"The guy who cuts our lawn or whatever."

Benjy flicks Jake. Sam flicks Jake. Jake flicks them both at the same time, his elbow narrowly missing the bridge of my nose and I don't even care.

"One of you boys is going to have to get in back, *now*. Everyone needs a seat belt." Dad's losing patience.

Havepatiencedadhavepatiencedadhavepatience.

The flicks turn to shoves.

"Sam?" JenniferTwo extends an invitation and to a round of mock girlish *"Saaaaaams"* he gets into the backseat, bright pink stains spreading over his freckled skin.

"So gay," JenniferTwo tosses under her breath to my snorting seatmates.

"Seat belts or we aren't going anywhere," Dad orders. A bead of sweat slides down my chest. *Oh my God, please. Please Dad, let's just run the risk, live on the wild side, chance it. So much better than ordering these guys around—traction, losing limbs, dying—all tiny prices to pay for being able to show up at school on Monday and not hear about you being a total—*

But everyone clicks their belts without attitude and I'm jolted by the reminder of their behind-the-scenes lives, with parents who insist on socks and bedtimes and finishing milk.

Dad pulls onto the highway and the boys talk about the *Appetite for Destruction* album, currently banished to the glove compartment—"Sorry, our cassette player's busted, *isn't it,* Dad?" Overcome, Sam finally whips his Walkman out of his jacket and plays it on 10, all of us leaning to hear the tinny echo dancing out the padded earphones atop the grumble of the Sandinistas. Straining to listen, Jake is at last still and his body solidly borders mine from heel to shoulder. Touching. The feeling of his shoulder, arm, thigh and calf. Just suddenly right here, next to me. Weird. Completely weird. As weird as touching the TV screen and feeling warm skin on Kirk Cameron's face would be.

"Take me down," the guys cry out together while Laura and I sit in frozen anticipation of what the afternoon holds. Vibrations move through my arm as Jake starts nodding his head to the beat and soon Jake and Sam are air-guitaring as Benjy drums the back of Laura's seat, his hands and feet working in synchronicity.

"I figure if I pick up another shift after school, I'll have enough saved for the drum kit by the end of next summer," Benjy says in rhythm, his head slamming back and forth.

"Our band's gonna rule," Sam declares, "Just like GNR."

Jake takes a deep breath and then blasts Axl's chorus into Sam's face.

Benjy and Sam join in, shouting the response. Dad turns up the volume on the dashboard.

"Anybody found a bassist yet?" Jake asks the car.

"Um," Laura swivels from the passenger seat, peering around the headrest. "Todd Rawley plays for Mrs. Beazley in choir sometimes?"

"Jake, you should check that out," Sam says. I see Laura blush from the taken suggestion as she swivels back, sinking into her coat. Having nothing to offer I just let myself be rocked by Jake's motion as I look down at the scuff mark left on my thigh and replay his first word to me, searching for some deeper, encoded message.

But it doesn't happen until we're in the theater, as we collectively squirm to our right to gain at least an armrest's distance from JenniferTwo kissing Sam like it's the next thing on her To-Do List—that I feel this thing take root in my stomach, this rubber band thing as Jake Sharpe comes back from the concession stand. A twinge tells me to turn around and, sure enough, he has just walked in the doors at the top of the dark aisle. The band tightens as his narrow silhouette approaches. Then, when he slides past I tuck my legs up on my chair and our eyes meet, stray kernels tumbling onto my lap—and it is taut between us. Loosening again as he plunks himself at the other end next to Benjy, who lunges for the tub of popcorn. I slide my hand to the center of my chest while staring up at the screen. This thing is different from living down Jake Sharpe, different from avoiding Jake Sharpe, even different from knowing Jake Sharpe thinks about what I look like. This new Jake Sharpe thing is happening inside me, all the way at the core.

People shriek, Laura dives her head into my shoulder, but I watch unflinching, my mind not connecting to the images—the old man grabbing his blood-spurting ankles, or even the gnarled spine of the dying girl. I am piano-bench straight, every inch of me realigning to this new state, this Jake Sharpe Compass I have just become.

• • •

"I'm going to kill my mother." Laura runs her hands down the back of her thighs, smoothing her oversize letter jacket under her as a barrier against the cold curb, and sits.

"What'd she say?" As cars pull in and out circling for rest, I stare across the dark lot to the food court carousel's twinkling lights, visible through the mall's atrium. Jake Sharpe leans against the brick wall of the Cineplex. About twenty feet behind me, to the left.

"She wasn't there. Just my sucky brother, who bit my head off because I'd woken him from his sucky nap."

"She'll be here soon." I pat her knee reassuringly. "Let's just hope JenniferTwo brings her sex slave back before she gets here."

"So disgusting." We squint into the tall trees lining the edge of the parking lot where JenniferTwo marched Sam off as soon as she saw that Laura's mom wasn't waiting. It's what we're all not talking about. With the exception of Benjy screaming, "Don't forget to swallow!" met with the screeching, "You wish, asshole!"

The chilly October night blows through us and I withdraw my hands into my sleeves, wishing I could be wearing the ski hat Mom made me tuck in my pocket.

"All that calling and picking out outfits for *this.*" Laura waves her hands around at our pathetic clusters. "Ugh." She stands and steps out into the lot, peering up to Route 14A. "I'm going inside to try her again."

"I'll keep guard," I volunteer.

"I'll guard for bloodthirsty toddlers back from the dead." Benjy extracts the straw he's been chewing for three hours and waves it like a scalpel, showering spittle on the concrete.

"I feel safer already." Laura backs out of mucus range.

"Actually, I have to take a whiz." He grabs the theater door as she drops it and follows her into the purple-carpeted lobby.

Jake drums the top of the garbage can. I focus very hard on the rippling outline of the mall carousel's horses because now it is just the two of us and the band is getting tighter, tighter until his high-tops are next to me. "Stupid."

My eyes fly up.

"The movie. Pretty stupid."

"Yeah." I nod, the wind blowing into the coat I can't zip up, must keep off my shoulders like I've just shrugged carelessly and couldn't be more comfortable this way even though I can see my breath. His toe nudges an empty can of Squirt soda off the curb. He rolls it lightly to my ankle and back again.

"All that from burying a cat. Seems kind of extreme," I offer.

"Yeah," he laughs. I'm riveted by the lolling hot pink letters under his red rubber sole, seeing if I can anticipate the direction it will go next. A test. "You see *Big?*" he asks. "That was pretty cool."

"I loved *Big!* Where he has to say good-bye to Elizabeth Perkins because he has to grow up and she has to let him. Oh, it was so good."

". . . Yeah." *Wrong! Wrong! What else happened?! What else?!*

"And the whole thing where he plays the giant keyboard, that was cool."

"Totally!" Yay! "It'd be awesome to get all that stuff without having to live with your parents or finish school or go to college or any of that. Just stick a ticket in a machine and bam! You're there. Wicked pad. Cool job doing cool stuff. Hot girl." The can slips out and his foot falls onto my toes, pain shooting up through my leg and I bite my lip.

The Heller station wagon honks, approaching through the maze of mall stop signs, and I wave. Then his feet are opposite mine, toe-to-toe, his hands dangling in my face. He flicks them in insistence and I realize what he wants. I push my numb fingers through my sleeves, our shivering skin meeting. He grips my wrists and then leans back, pulling me up. I arrive just beneath his face, looking into the break in his oxford at the tender hollow of his exposed neck.

"Thanks," I breathe as he releases me, no idea if I got out any actual sound.

"Katie, hon," Mrs. Heller rolls down her window to speak to me. "P & C was a zoo. Where's Laura?"

"She went to call you. I'll go get her."

I reach out to the leather covering Jake's arm. He looks down at my hand, his face surprised. "Sam." I withdraw my palm to gesture to the trees. He nods and I move toward the glass doors, the band stretching the length of the parking lot as he jogs to the edge of the pines.

At the sight of Jake's bike rounding the corner I rise to standing on the warped steps of the Whiteforest Settlement Historical House and quickly pull my hands from my coat pockets. I press my lips together, making sure my gloss hasn't evaporated in the November wind as Jake hops off at the edge of the gravel and walks his bike up to the front stoop. "I didn't even know this place was here." He looks over my shoulder, up the steps to the little gray clapboard house. "It's only like a ten-minute ride from my house, too. Weird." He smiles, effortless cool.

"I know, I didn't even know we had so many historic sites in Croton . . . which, I guess, was kinda the point of the assignment."

"I'm glad you called." You are? "I totally would've left this till the last minute."

"Yeah, now we've got three weeks to work on it. Not that I plan on working on it for the next three weeks," I backtrack. "I mean, Laura and Benjy are at the battlefield right now, so they're also getting a head start, yeah." I lean against the bottom of the old wood railing, willing the cold to numb my nervousness.

He pulls his hat off and stuffs it in his pocket before flattening his hair with the palm of his red hand. "My dad was so impressed I was coming here on a Sunday he just handed me twenty bucks for, like, nothing." He looks down at his handlebars. "So I'll just . . ." Jake walks the bike over to the rusted rack bordering the empty gravel parking area and kicks the stand. The metal drops between the stones.

"Yeah, should be fine." I try to keep my hands out of my pockets as the biting air whips around us. "I doubt the millions of other Whiteforest Settlement Historical House visitors will steal it."

"I don't know, I think we just beat the Whiteforest Settlement Historical House rush." He jogs up the steps as I laugh. I didn't expect him to be funny. "I bet there's a bitchin' souvenir shop." He opens the door and holds it for me to walk in behind him. As we stand, thawing in the humidified heat, I realize that the same classical music that was on Mom's car radio is playing from a black transistor on the windowsill.

"Hello!" An elderly woman in a lavender nubbly suit stands behind a wood table displaying a few stacks of brochures to lower the radio. "Hello there!" Our arrival seems to have brought a flush to her hollow cheeks behind the two circles of rouge. "A donation is suggested, but not required, and I will just put my book aside to give you a tour."

"That's okay," Jake and I speak at once. He continues. "We've been here before."

"Lots," I add.

"It's our favorite place, so we know our way around." Jake smiles winningly.

Placing her liver-spotted hands atop the brochures, she sinks back into her chair, her shoulders sagging in disappointment. "All right, if you know your way around . . ."

"Thanks, though," Jake says. "So, um . . ." I turn to him, raising my eyebrows encouragingly. "You always like to start with the, uh, upstairs, right?"

"Yes," I say. "I love the upstairs." I follow him to the narrow staircase and, my eye line level with the yellow stitching on his back pockets, we steadily climb, stooping as we clear the last step to a small room blocked off at waist level with Plexiglas. We stand for a few minutes while I pretend to look at the worn quilt, its surface mottled by the straw mattress poking up from beneath, breathing in the sweet smell of him.

"I was hoping for more," he says. I start laughing again. "No rides? Not even a tram or something?"

"She's going to hear us," I whisper.

"So? We're enjoying the Historical Settlement House," he whispers back.

I glance to the stairs. "We didn't even make a donation, I feel bad. She really wanted to give us a tour."

"Of what, though? This place is tiny." He smiles, the gray light from the small window filtering in from behind him, the faint sound of the wind blowing around us mixing with bits of symphony from downstairs. I force myself to stay perfectly still, not to wrap my arms around him. "Miss?" he calls out, his eyes still on mine. "If it's not too late, we actually would like a tour."

From below we hear, "Not too late at all, I'll be right up!"

Standing inches from him in each of those five rooms, as she prattles on about loom weaving and coal-warmed beds, her face alight, all I can think is, *this* is the beginning. All the drama and the humiliation will be Before. And today marks the beginning of After. I will become the girl who is dating Jake Sharpe.

I follow him to the door as he fishes the twenty his dad gave him from his ski jacket and drops it into the donation basket. "Thanks a lot." He waves at her as he opens the door for me. "It was a great tour."

"Oh, my goodness, thank you." She looks down at the crumpled bill, probably having just set some record.

"Yes, thanks! It was great!" I cheer. Be sure to invite you to the wedding!

We jog down the steps into the crisp dusk. Jake zips up his coat. "That was really . . ."

"Boring?" I smile.

"No!" He laughs. "The part about dipping candles was cool." He pulls the folded assignment sheet out of his pocket. "I think I'm going to use that as one of my three artifacts. So don't steal it. I'm calling dibs on the candle dipper. How 'bout you?"

"Yeah . . ."

He grins. "You weren't even listening in there!"

"What?" I laugh. "No! I was!" I straighten my face. "She's really happy now." I point over his shoulder at the window where our guide tidies the table with purpose, a smile on her ridged lips. "We did a good deed."

We both watch as she folds contentedly back into her

chair with her dime-store paperback. He looks at me over the collar of his ski jacket grazing his chin, and tucks his lips around the zipper tab. "Is your family big into church or something?"

"No." But they absolutely could be if you want. "Why, is yours?"

He cocks his head. "It's just . . . I don't hear people talk about good deeds so much."

"That's my parents, I guess." I shrug, trying to figure out how I can move us toward hot chocolate at the diner.

"But not you?"

I look up at the darkening indigo sky. "I guess I am. I mean, if it's easy to do something that'll make things better for somebody . . ."

He laughs, his green eyes warm on me, "Oh, I see, as long as it's easy."

"Was that tour easy?" I dart a daring finger into his chest.

"Like a history test." He grabs it.

"Next weekend we've definitely earned a cheesy movie."

And I don't know if he actually steps back or just leans, but all at once my finger is released and he's gone. He looks to his sneakers, his hair falling forward. I want to tuck it back—a second ago would have, but he sighs with frustration, digging his toe into the gravel. "Katie, I'm not going out with anyone."

"Sure! Of course!" I push myself. "No, I just meant—"

"After Kristi." His lips twist as he stares past me, they're chapped. The wind is building in fierceness, irritating the browned nettles along the fence. I pray for it to lift me right out of this, sweep me across the field and all the way to California.

"No, totally. This was just for school. I didn't mean . . ."

He steps away to reach for his bike, kicking the stand up. I race for some way to save this, some way to take it back, but he starts talking again, his voice low as he tugs out his hat and pulls it on. "I should get home. My mom wants me to help get the decorations and stuff down from the attic tonight."

"Yeah! Go ahead. My mom'll be here any sec, so . . ."

"Thanks for the tour." He looks at me before throwing his leg over the bike. "Seriously, Katie."

"Sure," I manage.

He looks like he's about to say something else, but doesn't. Instead, standing to grind the wheels across the gravel, he turns away and, launching into the pedals, takes off down the street.

My eyes sting, my everything stings as Jake Sharpe gets smaller. Our minivan comes into view three blocks down, lights on, slowing when it passes him. I don't move as Mom rolls toward me and stops the car.

She lowers her window, her face bright with barely contained curiosity. "So?"

It is my turn to stare at the gravel. I tuck my head into my chest and round the front to get in, the scent of her

Chloe enveloping me. I grit my teeth, trying not to fall apart, willing her to just take me home. Her hand gently brushes my hair as she goes to grip the headrest to back the car up. "Craig Shapiro called for you," she offers tentatively as she makes the K-turn. "He wants you to call him back."

9

December 22, 2005

"Manicotti's getting cold, and we're ravenous," Dad calls from the stairs as I'm hastily rifling my closet of yore—the Betsey Johnson bodysuits, the babydoll dresses, the military jackets.

"I'll be right down!" I say as I finally unearth Mom's college sweater. I shake out the black cashmere, pressing the wrinkled three-quarter-length sleeves against my chest, and try it on.

Dad knocks. "You okay?"

"Yup," I say as my head reemerges, needing to keep moving.

He pushes the door farther open, coming in to take a seat on my bed. Stepping over the heap of my airplane-aromatized outfit, I wait for him to say something. He doesn't.

"So, full-time sand, huh?" I feel him out, reaching for the Lord & Taylor bag.

"Round the clock." He nods. "That looks nice."

"Thanks. But you always stay on the deck under the umbrella. And you hate the mosquitoes."

He flexes his fingers. "Have you checked in with your office?"

I swipe my old Mason Pearson from the dresser top and tap it against my thigh to shake the dust free. "No, I'm waiting for them to file a missing persons—see if they really love me."

"I'm sure they really love you. I do. Most days."

"Thanks." I flip over to brush the flight knots out of my shower-damp hair. "Actually, I was on conference calls during both layovers and after working straight through Thanksgiving and this Buenos Aires thing, they should be able to deal if I take off for Christmas two days early."

"Fair enough."

"So what's the story, Dad? Why are you fleeing the state?"

He pulls a Kleenex from his pocket. "That's a funny question coming from you."

"Ha ha." I dump the makeup out on the bed, catching my side view in the mirror. "Crap—there's a hole." I lift my finger under the tiny puncture. No time for, and even less interest in, excavating Mom's underwear drawer for a camisole, I swipe a Sharpie from my desk, lift the sweater up an inch and draw an eraser-sized dot on my ribs. I flip the fabric down and—"Voila!"—no hole.

"You are a genius." He blows his nose.

"Thanks." I turn back to the mirror. "I just can't shimmy, which is fine, as there is no shimmying in my game plan. My game plan is devoid of shimmying—and details."

"Mine, too." His hearing aid begins to whistle and he reaches in with his pointer finger to adjust it.

I hunker in front of him, studying his face. "So, Dad, how are you feeling?"

"Knock on wood." He raps his knuckles on his scalp, then, realizing his hair has fluffed, smoothes his hand across it.

"How are you sleeping?" I touch the knee of his corduroy trousers.

"No worse than anyone my age." He starts patting down his pockets, his comfort reflex, and I instinctively stand and step back to give him room. "You walk down our street at three A.M. and you'll see everyone's got their telly on."

"Are you? Walking down the street at three A.M.?"

He slaps his palms against his thighs. "Come, your mother's waiting to eat."

"Hold on. Dad, are you still seeing Dr. Urdang?"

"Katie, unless you are renewing my insurance during this visit—"

"I just want to get a handle on why all the subterfuge."

"I'm boning up for a second career with Her Majesty's Secret Service."

"Dad—"

"Katie." He slips the tissue back in his pocket.

Infuriated by his childish obfuscation, I start ripping

the cardboard packaging off the new makeup. "Okay, can you please give me a real answer here?"

He stands. "Listen, bun, I have cartons of notes from the research center that I've been wanting to turn into a book for years." I nod to that oft-heard sentence. "And I was sitting in that god-awful fluorescent-lit library listening to the same five people have the same stupid budget fight they have every year, and I just snapped. What was I waiting for?" I don't know—your IRAs? "I feel fantastic. We've finally unloaded this albatross— I'm cooking again, I've been catching up on my reading. I'm off those bloody pills that made me feel like a zombie—"

"You're *what?*" I sputter.

He steps over the threshold. "Come on, Katie, my puttanesca sauce is at its best hot."

"Does Mom know?"

Pretending not to hear the question, he pulls the door shut. *Fuck.* I look at the alarm clock. I look at the makeup piled in a crashed pyramid on the quilt. I flip open the compacts, quickly applying the colors in the mirror backing the door.

"Kate?" Mom calls.

"Right down." I hold the mascara wand up to see my hand is shaking.

I jog into the kitchen as Mom turns to me, innocently proffering a bottle. "Care for some wine?"

"No, thank you," I say, staring at Dad, imploring him

106

to speak. But he looks down obstinately, continuing to ladle manicotti onto plates.

"Milk then?" Mom cants her head inquiringly as she reaches for the refrigerator door. I cannot take my eyes off of Dad's mouth, set in a grim line.

"Thanks, but I need to . . ."

Dad sighs.

"Get this over with. Now."

Lifting her shoulders, Mom chirps, "Car keys are on the side table."

"Thanks, but I've gotta walk," I say, kissing her cheek, my heart clenching as I round the island, not looking at him. "I still have to figure out what to say."

10

NINTH GRADE

Laura crosses her eyes in my direction from the alto section of the risers. I scrunch my nose, making a rabbit face in response. "We need to wake up! The concert is three weeks away and you don't want to embarrass yourselves." Mrs. Sergeant waves her man-hands at the baritones, and a sad trickle of "We Built This City" ekes out into the choir room for the millionth time.

Backed by Todd Rawley on bass, little Mrs. Beazley attacks the piano keys, her pink beads jumping against the flopping bow of her blouse. A row beneath Laura and me sits Jake, and I watch as his finger slides along his song sheet in time with the actual song. Not the Muzak-nerd version Mrs. Sergeant is aiming for.

"Sopranos, let me see those 'ooooo' faces, big and round! And! *Say you don't knooooow me ooooor recooooognize my face.*" Her mouth opens so wide I see the outline of her tonsils. "Now really enunciate here—*ea-ting. Up. The. Night.*" Sergeant stops us with a frustrated shake of her Play-Doh beauty parlor perm, but Mrs. Beazley joyfully continues.

As does Jake. Pitch perfect, his voice fills the air like light unearthed from beneath the soil of all our breathy singing. Everyone twists to watch. He's good. Really good. Buy it at the mall, listen to it in your car, good. And much, much better than molar-mouthed, oversinging with her feet planted, doing her best Valkyrie, Mrs. Sergeant. Red splotches appear on her jowls and everyone studies their music folders. Mrs. Beazley purses her lips, pushing back her pink glasses. Jake clears his throat and Laura takes the moment to make a huge "o" face. I snort.

"You think this is funny, Katie Hollis?" Mrs. Sergeant spins to me, seething.

I freeze. "No—"

"You think someone trying to steal the show from forty-eight of his classmates is worth laughing about?" Her shoulder pads lift above her earlobes.

"No, I—"

"You *what?* Or were you just trying to get his attention?"

I sit at the edge of my chair. "No, I just . . . remembered something . . . funny someone said at lunch."

"What?" She raps her music stand. "What was the funny thing someone said? You think it's worth being so rude about, you should let us all enjoy it."

"Nothing." I shrink. "I'm sorry."

"It takes years of work, hard work, school and practice, years of practice, before you can just sing wherever and whenever you like." She narrows her eyes. "I want you and Mr. Sharpe here to take your huge egos and put together a presentable duet with a descant of your own devising. The last section of the song, through 'Marconi plays the mamba,' to be performed for all of us, let's see . . . a week from this Friday seems fair. That should be something two freshmen can handle if they think they're prodigies." A sneer forms her last *s*. "And Katie?"

"Yes?"

"Enough flirting." A blast of heat explodes in my face. With a satisfied smile, Mrs. Sergeant nods and Mrs. Beazley begins again.

Benjy bounces a Hacky Sack from one hand to the other as he sits slouched against the locker next to Laura's. "It's 'cause Sergeant's not doin' it."

"Shut up," Laura and I chime. "Neither are you," she adds, to clarify her sexual status for anyone in earshot as she wriggles the *Daisy Miller* CliffsNotes out from a pile of textbooks wedged into her locker. He tugs at her bare calf and she collapses into his lap shrieking, "Ben–jy!"

"It's not like we can just use the sheet music," I say, starting to panic, "We have to devise a descant. I have no idea how to do that!"

Craig, slumped with me against the lockers across from them, doesn't even look up from the car magazine he's leafing through with his free hand. I pull mine from the other to ruffle his hair. "Hey, I need advice."

"What? You have to do a song." Craig flattens his bangs back the way he likes them.

"A duet," Laura corrects as Benjy's hand tries to push under her sweatshirt. Giggling, she grabs it through the fabric, holding it at bay below her under-wire. Craig drops his arm around me in an attempt to keep up, and I pull my legs in so I can curl against his sturdy frame. The tallest frame in the class. The frame that for the last four months I am proud to call my boyfriend's. The frame that's had a secret crush since the Middle School Graduation Dance when he was too shy to talk to me. The frame that thinks of me as KatieHollis, one word. A cute frame, a nice frame, an honest frame. The frame of someone who would never, ever, in a billion years, say they don't want to go out with anyone and then, less than a week later, start going out with Annika Kaiser.

"You have a good voice, Katie." Craig squeezes my shoulder as he flips another glossy page. "Just practice and do it. It won't be such a big deal, you'll see."

Exasperated, I give him his arm back and stand up. "Thanks."

"Katie, I'm sorry," Laura responds, swatting Benjy away and standing in turn.

"It's just . . ." I scan her eyes. Now that I've publicly clarified my lack of enthusiasm for this assignment, I suddenly find myself not wanting to go any further in front of Craig.

"I know," she says, squeezing my hand. "It'll be fine.

I'm sorry I got you into this mess. Just let him figure it out. Follow his lead."

The crocheted sack flies past our knees and Craig dives to avoid it. "Should I be jealous?" He hurls it back at Benjy.

"No!" we cry in unison.

❦

Three days later Jake Sharpe has not done anything— that I can follow, or otherwise. I walk over as Biology ends and inch in between his friends as they pack up their books. Closer than I've been to him in the five months since our "date," I try to ignore the lingering freckles from his spring break tan. "Jake?"

"Hey." He fidgets with his pen.

"Hey. So we should probably plan to practice or something." Sam and Todd turn and push their heads over his shoulder, sticking their tongues out like Gene Simmons.

"Cool. Whenever."

"I have fourth period free on Monday. Do you think it'll be enough time to prepare? If we wait till Monday? That's only five days."

Suddenly his eyes land on mine and he smiles like he just remembered the idea of me and likes it. "Yeah."

"So, fourth period, Monday. Think the music room'll be free? Maybe that's better. I think the gym is free. The gym is definitely free. What do you think?"

"What do you think?" Todd mimics, grinning stupidly.

"Whichever." He shrugs.

Yeah, I get it, you don't care. "Fine. The gym."

"Cool." He nods, slinging his backpack onto his shoulder. As they walk away a dime slips from a hole in the canvas where he has ball-pointed a lizard. I pick it up.

⁂

I get into the gym at the start of fourth period. I get a hand-cramp flipping that f'ing dime between my fingers. I get a sore butt from sitting on the hard wood and keeping my hair fluffed just right for three hours. I get detention for skipping fifth period in case I had the time wrong. I get annoyed on a whole new level.

⁂

"Jake." I tap him on the shoulder at the drinking fountain. "What happened?"

"Hey." He pulls back like I stung him.

I drop my offending hand. "Hey. So, what happened?"

"What?" He wipes the droplets from his chin. "Fourth period, Wednesday."

Sam strolls by and punches him in the arm.

"Monday. That was yesterday," I say as he reaches around me to punch Sam's departing back. "So, what do you want to do?" I crane my head for his attention, trying to keep from biting the inside of my mouth in annoyance.

"How about Wednesday, you know, fourth?"

Of course I can't fourth on Wednesday. "I can't fourth

on Wednesday." I switch my books to my other hip. "How about after school? The music room should be free."

"Cool."

❦

So not. So far from cool. So very far. Mrs. Beazley stops in some time after dark to pick up her forgotten fuchsia glasses and wakes me on the risers, my hands asleep from resting under my hair to keep it fluffed.

❦

"Hi, Jake?"

"Hey."

"This is Katie Hollis." I lean against my kitchen wall.

"Yeah, hey."

"Hey." I repeat.

Laura rolls her hand at me, helpfully prompting. I take her cue, "I'm calling because—so, what happened?"

"Right," he says like he knew I was going to call.

"Oh my god!" I mouth to Laura, throwing my palm out. "Yeah," I try to relax my voice so as to avoid further fulfilling any expectation of me as psycho. Laura makes a stern face and I turn my back to her, focusing instead on the stove clock. "Well, we only have two days left."

"I know. After school?" he volunteers.

Arms crossed, I stare at the braided rag rug, puckering my mouth to the left. "How about before, just to be safe. Is that too early for you?"

"No way. I'm there." I hear the twanging of a guitar being tuned in the background. "Sam, dude, hold on."

I pivot back to Laura, who is practicing her twirling with two spatulas. "Okay, Jake, so, seven A.M. tomorrow. Music Room. You sure?" She catches them to give me a thumbs-up.

"Definitely."

※

"Stood up! Again! Detention! No sleep all week! Three chapters behind on *House of Mirth!* And I have to get up in front of everyone tomorrow and Mrs. Asshole and try to wing a descant with Jake Sharpe, who may actually, now that the evidence is in, be clinically retarded. And I'd say that to my dad's face!" I grip my books to my chest as I stomp up the hill home with Laura.

"I'll pull a fire drill. Or Benjy can call in a bomb threat? I think he'd be up for it, I really do."

"No! This is now officially Jake Sharpe's to fix."

"Agreed." We nod at each other as we hoof through the last patches of snow giving way to full-blown spring.

"Except I'm the one who's going to sound like a beaten cat."

"That's so sad!" She stops her stride to ponder. "Such a sad picture, a cat that's being beaten, who would do that?"

"Laura!"

"Katie! Just, I don't know, march over there and tell him what a retard he is!"

My eyes widen as the reality of the idea passes between us. "What if I do?" I murmur.

"You'd be my hero and I'd bake a whole batch of devil's food cupcakes just for you."

"Step aside."

I tug one arm free from my backpack, raising the other shoulder against its load, because I need every ounce of cool right now and will not risk precious points for proper spinal alignment. I push the glowing doorbell again and glare at the Easter garland. I'm going to stay here all night, that's what. I'll just wait for him until he comes out in the morning and we'll practice this stupid freaking duet all the way to stupid freaking school—

"Hey." Jake slouches inside the doorway, holding a box of Kraft macaroni and cheese.

"Hey."

"So, come in." He waves me inside with the blue cardboard. Thrown by his expectant demeanor, I dumbly follow. I go to drop my bag in the front hall, like at Laura's, but am struck that a worn green JanSport would look very out of place on the gleaming hardwood. His socked feet sliding Tom Cruise–style, he's already retreating through the door on the other side of the living room like a sweatpant-clad white rabbit. I try to keep up, but I'm mesmerized by the wood paneling, Chinese pottery, and little smushed-face porcelain dogs on the mantel—the bar with rows of crystal decanters. The closest I've been to a house like this was the lobby of the Boston Ritz-Carlton, where we met my cousins for tea when I was nine.

I find him in the kitchen, which is wallpapered in a lilac pattern with matching fabric in the breakfast nook. But no pictures. No tchotchkes. No art or good grades stuck to the fridge. No Mickey Mouse ears resting on top of the cookbooks. Sitcom kitchens, trying to look like real family kitchens, have more stuff in them than this real family kitchen.

Jake is stirring in the cheese powder on the stovetop. I stand behind him, gripping my books. Finally satisfied, he turns around, slides the pot onto the counter of the island, and hops onto a lilac-cushioned stool.

"You going to put your books down?" he asks, taking a big, wooden-spoon mouthful. I rest them on the counter and slide off my backpack. He puts the spoon down. "Sorry. Want some?"

"Sure," I say automatically and he leans to grab two forks from a drawer, bouncing one over to me like a skipping stone. I catch it as he shoves the copper pot between us.

"Where're your parents?" I ask, taking a forkful of orange noodles.

"My dad's traveling for work. Somewhere west. Texas, or New Mexico this week, I think. Mom's asleep. Upstairs."

"She doesn't work?"

"No," he half-laughs, stabbing his fork around in the pot, his hair flopping down.

I nod awkwardly and try to figure out how I suddenly found myself in this intimate activity, made all the more intimate by the ringing silence of this house. Because in the two feet between us, mostly what I am doing right now is not throwing our forks across the room, grabbing his face, and kissing him. Right now I am the girl not kissing Jake Sharpe. I am the girl not kissing Jake Sharpe who will now clear her throat.

"So, Jake, I'm really pissed. I mean, I pretty much got roped into this stupid duet because you couldn't keep your mouth shut, and I've wasted, like, half the week waiting for you and you just completely blew me off."

I tilt my head and wait for an answer. He has stopped eating and stares intently at me.

"You're going out with Craig."

Wha—"I am."

"For how long?"

I can hear the blood in my ears. "I don't know. November sometime." I stare back. "You're going out with Annika," I return evenly.

"Yeah." He nods down into the pot. "I am."

"So . . ."

"So, I'm not that good at schedules."

"Okay . . ."

"But you're here."

"I am."

"So, let's practice."

"Okay."

He pushes back from the counter, the stool tipping as he jumps off to place the pot in the sink, running water into it as someone must have told him to. "Sam and I have been working on some band stuff with Todd. We played with the Jefferson Starship song, and I think we've rigged up a descant. Want a Klondike?" He holds open the freezer, steam billowing out over a few boxes of pops and at least five gallon bottles of vodka.

"Thanks, sure. Your parents having a party?"

"What?" He glances back at the stocked wire shelves. "No," he bristles.

"Oh, I just thought—"

"It's cool." He grabs two bars and swings the door shut. It makes a shushing sound as it seals.

"Um, I'm not really a singer," I say, needing to divert. "I mean, I like doing it in a big group, but I'm not really a soloist or anything." Understatement of the century.

"I know. That's cool. You've got your whole science thing. This way." No time to stop and absorb that he knows what my "thing" is, or call Laura, or take out an ad, once again I'm following. I catch sight of him disappearing into a doorway halfway down a long corridor running the length of the house. I find it leads to a flight of tan-carpeted steps.

"You coming?" He looks up at me standing on the threshold, his face illuminated by a low-watt bulb. "I have to practice in the basement." He pauses. "My mom gets headaches." His eyes implore me.

"I'm sorry," I say, finding myself replying in earnest, not to his words, but to the look on his face that asks me to understand.

⁂

Sergeant towers above the spindly black music stand, arms crossed over her polyester turtleneck dress as she waits for us to fail. Behind her, the entire chorus shifts in their seats along the risers, studying their nails, scrawling notes to each other. All except Laura, who stares straight into her lap, hands balled in shared horror. As Todd strums his bass and Mrs. Beazly pounds out the opening chords, nervousness is being redefined in my lower intestines. To my left, Jake, redefining relaxed, slips his hands out of his jeans pockets and lightly taps the top of the piano percussively as if this were a real performance and not just straight-out torture. Will falling into a coma get me out of this? Could I drop chorus right this second? Or should I just start dancing, as if that was the assignment, just take off doing *West Side Story* moves around the room. Really throw myself into it. Or start reciting something, like that *Beowulf* thing. Or just turn and walk out. I picture Sergeant chasing me through the parking lot, dragging me back through the halls by my hair—and suddenly Jake is singing. He nods his head in encouragement and I feel my lips moving, sound pushing out. I realize Jake has subdued the strength of his part so that mine can be heard. I breathe

more sound out, letting my shoulders drop like he re-
minded me when we practiced. The more I sing, the
more he sings, and suddenly we're halfway there. Feeling
prickles of relief, I notice then that the edges of Jake's
eyes and mouth are curled into a smile as he continues
guiding me, lifting me, helping me survive this with his
voice.

11

December 22, 2005

I let the storm door slap shut behind me as I jog down the snow-packed bricks into the bracing air. Flipping up the collar of my eleventh-grade peacoat, I note with chagrin how indistinguishable it is from a recent J. Crew purchase. Well, minus the holes in the pockets. My fingers slide through the ripped satin, my hands settling into their well-worn niches. My old motorcycle boots provide traction as I set a brisk pace. Willing myself to feel the distance gained from my parents' kitchen with every step, I look down at my breath puffing into the night air like locomotive steam.

With the full moon to illuminate my path, I tromp past sparkling lawns dotted with glowing snowmen and twigged reindeer frames. Shuffling down the hill, I turn behind the school and cut across the playing fields. As the rubber treads crunch snow beneath my feet I recall his bicycle making lazy circles in my periphery, its wheels streaked green from the morning's mowing. My mind careens through memories. Then memories of when those memories became anecdotes.

I follow the bank of the frozen creek to the tonier side of town, where the houses are spread out on multiple wooded acres delineated by the low stone walls the colonists used to carve up Croton. The moon disappears behind the clouds, but I find my way on instinct, history both local and personal guiding me. I try to quell my adrenaline, slow my heart, breathing in through my nose out through my mouth, as if this were only mile three in the predawn. I find a pace, clear my mind, trust that when I see him the words will just . . . be there. They will be there for me.

I round the bend onto Bluebell Lane, immediately sensing a density in the black. "Someone's coming!" and suddenly I'm blinded by a barrage of klieg lights flooding my vision.

"Who are you?" "Are you here to see Jake?" "Are you a friend?" "How do you know him?" "Are you a friend of the family?" "Did you go to high school together?" "Hey!" A finger is snapped in my face. *"What's he really like?" "What was he like in high school?"* The hysteria building, questions fly at me in an indistinguishable cacophony. *"Was he always so talented?" "Was he the most popular guy in school?" "Was he always so hot?"*

"Um. . . ." My utterance silences them. Every national news outlet hangs on my next words, microphones jockeying for position under my chin. *Saysomething. Say. Something.* "He . . . I . . . I'd just say . . ." But then their faces are harshly illuminated in turn and I follow their shifting gaze to the halogen headlights announcing a cavalcade of limos arriving behind me.

"EDEN!" And I'm forgotten. Absorbed like amoebas, the vehicles roll into their mass; they slap the metal frames loudly with their palms, exhorting her to "ROLL DOWN THE WINDOW!" Tempting, I'm sure. Taking advantage of the distraction, I turn and book it back into the darkness, taking a quick left onto the Ackermans' land and jogging into the woods—in this era of electric fencing—my face flushes at my recklessness and I slow my gait. Yes, my message is bound to lose impact if delivered with black smoke rising from my hair.

I hit the gully and start snaking back toward the Sharpes', to the north of their acreage, where the stone wall breaks and about a hundred yards of barbed wire delineate their kingdom. I feel my way, my fingers carefully running over the barbed metal, praying the additions to their mushrooming estate haven't included closing the hole. And then I feel it, the place where the top row was pressed up, the bottom scooped down, and the middle cut with a pair of pliers. I duck through and run, stumbling down the incline in awkward side steps, my adrenaline pushing me on, the only sound my huffing breath.

As I clear the copse I get my first sight, and I stop, stunned. Still standing in a good acre-size clearing, the addition of a third story makes it look even more like a layer cake on an oversize porcelain platter. Susan always did hate having trees anywhere near the house— they made her "nervous." Wonder how her "nerves" are standing up to a ground floor that looks like it's been chosen as the site of the Ascension. A force of white light gusts from each window, creating a spectral ring of artificial sunshine around the domicile. I hold my hand in front of my eyes. Momentarily riveted on the back lawn, I watch the heat from the lights melt the snow in the flower beds. Of course the Sharpes need not be confined by such petty considerations as actual time of day.

I tuck my head down and make the final dash to the house, the old basement dormer window catching my eye. I drop to my knees, my fingertips finding the groove I made in the wood, and tug. Amazingly it flips open, and I swing my legs through until my feet feel something firm beneath them. I shimmy my upper body down.

"Hello, Katie." I freeze. Crouching atop the washing machine I push my hair out of my eyes as nonchalantly as possible and look over to where Susan Sharpe is perusing a wine label while she fingers the velvet ribbon trim of her cashmere cardigan.

"Hello, Susan," I reply evenly, enjoying her flinch at the use of her Christian name. "How are you?" I ask politely, even though the faint web of broken capillaries across her cheeks and the bottle in her hand have already answered the question.

She levels her gaze at me, the frosty expression of contempt familiar. "The noise is a bit much upstairs. I can't for the life of me figure out why Jake would want to double the amount of hysteria around him." She replaces the bottle and extracts another while I jump down to the concrete floor and straighten my clothes. "Ah, this is the one, the Reserve." She pulls her glasses down from her gray blonde hair to scrutinize the label, the tortoiseshell frames concealing her watery eyes. "Well, I better get back upstairs." And she smiles that country club smile that somehow got enticed to the wilds of Vermont. "Do shut the window behind you when you go." She closes the crosshatched glass door and glides back upstairs in her Ferragamo pumps, flicking the lights off when she gets to the top.

"Thanks," I mutter, hearing the door shut. I look around in the stark light cascading through the dormer as I unbutton my jacket. Minus the transformation of half the room into a temperature-controlled wine cellar, it's fairly unchanged. There's that old green couch and the ghostlike band equipment silhouetted beneath sheets. I look back at the machine I just hopped off of—still the old Maytag. Warmth pounds my cheeks.

Okay, enough.

I put my hand on the railing, my foot pausing on the bottom step. It isn't the summer. I'm not tan. And I don't have a husband to buffer me. And I could go away. Scramble back through the window and wait another ten years. I take a breath—all adrenaline suddenly suctioning me back toward the tilted glass. But I can't. I can't have come all this way only to stand beneath him.

I climb the stairs and let myself into the long back hallway, which, Susan once proudly told me, in the eighteen hundreds, was designed for servants to scurry back and forth while causing minimal disturbance. I follow the sound of tumult laid over a thumping bass beat to the living room and cautiously peek my head around the door. While it's immediately obvious that she's combined the old dining room and living room and knocked out the ceiling to create a "great room" I've no idea what else she may have done, because the space is overrun with camera equipment, video equipment, backdrops, prop sets, racks and racks of clothes, two hair and makeup stations, and yards and yards of thick cables snaking over it all.

"Here, Larry." The teamster-size man next to me tosses a boom to his colleague, gouging the wood paneling. Merry Christmas, Susan.

Taking cover behind a rolling garment rack, I inch forward, following the sound of shouting, which has the tenor and urgency of an emergency room. "ANDY, MORE BLUSH!" "CAN WE DO SOMETHING ABOUT THE BLUSH?" "SWAP THE BLUSH!"

"Could someone toss me my Fiji?" a voice asks. "Thanks." It is at once both deep and somehow breathy. My eyes water and I look up at the ostentatious egg-and-dart molding that marks where the ceiling used to be. I blink until everything's in focus again. Deep breath. And I peer around the flat. John Norris, Eden Millay, and Jake Sharpe sit in a rugged, bear-claw-laden, L.L. Bean, MTV reimagining of what Jake Sharpe's childhood living room would look like. Jake Sharpe is maybe twenty feet from me. And he looks familiar. Not just the ghost of his seventeen-year-old features in a thirty-one-year-old face, but the recent-familiar—the lighting, the set, the mikes, the camera—this is the Jake Sharpe I recognize—from the videos playing overhead at the gym, the interviews I click on by accident at home, the magazine covers I catch sight of at the supermarket—this, this . . . packaged person—*this* is who I recognize.

Behind him, atop a ladder out of frame, someone is shaking detergent flakes over the fake window in the fake wall, creating a bucolic Christmas scene where, I'm sure, at any moment, some MTV intern trussed up as a moose will peer in.

"Rolling sound. Whenever you're ready, John." At the director's go, Jake lifts his arm and Eden nestles against him.

John nods, pulling his eyes up from his index cards to look into the camera. "We're sitting here with two of the most in-demand stars in the music business, Jake Sharpe and Eden Millay. Hi, guys."

"What up, John?" Jake nods.

"Happy holidays," Eden says, her voice surprisingly earthy for someone with such a narrow ribcage, her toffee-hued hair catching the fake moonlight.

"Now, Eden, first off, you just celebrated a significant birthday, the big four-o, and MTV was on location for the festivities at Red Rock." Jake takes her hand, the spotlight caroming off her multi-carat diamond.

"It was a blast," she squeezes his affectionately. "There's something really special about that place. The land has an energy that you just don't feel anywhere else."

"Great. Here's where we'll cut in with b-roll of that show." John takes a sip from a paper coffee cup. "Okay, so, Eden, you've just finished your world tour promoting your latest album, which features your take on twelve classic country-western songs. This is quite a departure for you," John politely broaches the subject of her commercially disastrous experiment.

Eden smiles with calm self-assurance as she pushes the waves framing her heart-shaped face from her sightline. "Yeah, I know, it was a risk, but that's the music I was raised on." Her fingers flit against the gold feather dangling from her lariat, the taut definition of her biceps appearing in the split of her blouse sleeve. Whatever. "Listen, I'm extremely grateful for all the opportunities the success my first two albums brought me, but I felt it was time to share something more honest."

John clears his throat. "And you did have record-breaking ticket sales all through Asia."

"I'm big in Japan." She laughs with undeniably winning self-deprecation.

"Cut," the director calls, and people scramble back into frame to check the lights.

A coil of cable is thrust into my shaking hand. "Hold this," the teamster barks.

John's voice drops to its non-TV timbre. "So, Jake, this is where we'll cut away to the montage of your Grammy speeches, your Earth Day performances, the Oscar for best song, all that stuff, and there'll be a voice-over giving all your stats, the forty million albums, yada yada."

"Great." Jake waves him on. Eden whispers something in his ear and he nods, smiling. You have a big dick, maybe?

"And roll sound!"

"Rolling."

"So, Jake." John shifts in his chair. "We're here in your hometown of Croton Falls, a very scenic region of Northern Vermont, whose influence you credit with the rustic imagery in so many of your songs. Much like Sting writes repeatedly about the life of the bygone English port town, you sing a lot about the lost New England industries."

"Well, I think in the age of global commerce, it's important to remind the younger generation that there were jobs here once, that America had thriving industries in textiles and manufacturing—jobs that have gotten sent overseas out of greed."

John asks the appropriate follow-up questions about how their viewers can help and get involved. Eden nods thoughtfully while Jake pontificates, trying his best to look earnest, and I have to move my gaze. I stare at a table of congealing sushi as John continues, "Now, you have a box set coming out in the new year. A decade of all your number-one songs, starting, of course, with your hit single 'Losing' off of your breakout album *Lake Stories. Rolling Stone* famously credited you with 'taking America's virginity.' "

Jake smiles, casting his green eyes down to his knees as he demurs.

Barf.

" 'Losing,' it bears repeating, was the number-one hit single of the nineties and you've reflected that by including not one, but *three* versions. There's the original, of course, a live acoustic performance, as well as the version you performed with Bono and Michael Stipe at Live 8."

"Yeah, we wanted to include the Muzak and pan flute remix, but there just wasn't room."

John laughs. "Now, I'd like to discuss the theme of infidelity, which you first introduced on the title track of *Lake Stories,* and is one you've revisited over and over." And over, and over.

"Yeah."

"Why the fascination?" Uh, yeah, Jake, why the fascination?

There is a barely perceptible pause. Eden laughs lightly. Jake speaks, "I just think in this age of globalization, we have so many options. It gets so much harder to commit to one place, one person, one profession. We're emotional chameleons, man."

"Hmmm." John nods. Eden nods. "Interesting." Interesting *bullshit.* "So," John continues. "There's one new song on this collection and it's titled . . ." John flips his index cards. "Let's see . . . um, okay, yes, here it is. 'Katie.'" "Wait, *what?!*

"Katie," Jake echoes, sending a tsunami of voltage through my system.

"So, we here at MTV haven't heard the song yet, but advance buzz is it's your most erotic song since 'Losing' and it's going to be huge. So, who's Katie?"

Jake pushes at his jeans again. "It's just a name." YEAH, MINE, ASSHOLE!

"Eden shouldn't be jealous?" John smirks, Eden laughs.

"Nah," Jake grazes his jawline with his knuckles.

"Really?"

"Katie's just a lyrical device."

The coil of cable slips through my hands, landing with a thud. The teamster swipes it off the floor in a huff. "What are you supposed to be doing?"

"I have no idea." Head down, I scramble backward, pushing through the crowded kitchen, still devoid of so much as a newspaper clipping about Jake.

"Excuse me," I sputter, reaching for the back door as my eyes meet with Susan's before she looks down to continue pouring her Reserve.

12

TENTH GRADE

I hear insistent scratching at the screen door. "Craig, I think your cat wants to be let back in." I elicit no response. "Craig?" I pivot my head from where it rests on his shoulder and realize Craig is out cold, his head flopped against the back of the den couch, his mouth open, white crusts at the corners as if he were in a coma.

I get up to open their door. What if Craig was in a coma? Playing through various scenarios, I press the metal handle and wonder how I'd feel . . . stunned? Bereft? Relieved? Would I be allowed to marry someone else? Or would his parents expect me to remain faithful to his prone, atrophying body?

Boxer brushes past my ankles and I reshut the screen just as the music swells and Mel Gibson and Michelle Pfeiffer give in to their sensual passion in the wine cellar. I look back at zonked-out Craig, then down at the dark spot his sweaty palm left on my jeans. Sigh.

A burst of gunfire from the speaker above the couch rattles him awake, his eyes opening and rolling back before focusing in on me. "Sorry." He sheepishly wipes the spit lolling from his mouth on his cuff. "Hey, come here."

I sit back down beside him on the leather sectional, but lean forward, propping my elbows on my knees. "It's fine."

He glances at the green numbers glowing from the VCR. "Your mom's going to be here soon." He reaches up and clasps his fingers, before dropping the weight of his arms around my waist and leaning in to kiss my forehead. I don't punch my way out of his clunky confinement. I don't move. "Are you still mad I picked the wrong movie?"

"No. Sorry, I just wanted something funny tonight, that's all."

"I heard they're gonna have a bunch of movies at the Lock-In next weekend—we'll only go to the funny ones, okay?" He lifts me onto his lap and I become deadweight at the idea of spending the tenth-grade Lock-In locked in this exact same position. "Think the teachers will be chaperoning everywhere or there'll be a room we can hide out in and . . ." He slides his hand into my jeans, darting it under the waistband of my underwear. I grab his wrist. *"What?"* He throws his hands up in irritation. "Why are you so mad all the time lately?"

I push myself off him to stand. "I'm not. It's just . . . I'm sure school's locking us in, or whatever, till ten with activities so that we'll . . ." I shift my weight from hip to hip between his long legs in the L corner of the couch, unable to see his face as I block the television glare. He must not be able to see mine, either. "You know, hang out, be social, not . . ."

"Hook up." He slumps back, his chest caving in. "So we're back to this. Look, Katie, if you don't want to do it, fine, but we should at least be able to—"

"I don't want to go out anymore."

His dark silhouette is suddenly perfectly still. The air leaves the room.

I said it to hurt him, to embarrass him for how blah this has become, to slap him back for how sick of him I am, how disappointed I feel that this is not what First Love is supposed to be about—constant zipper negotiation.

But I'm instantly sorry. A burst of shooting breaks out again, sending Craig digging into the cushion crevices for the remote. He leans around me to point it and, in the light of the TV, I see his stunned expression as he locates the STOP button. He blinks down at the remote, his eyes filling.

"Craig." I sit beside him and reach for his hand. He lifts it away from me. He sniffs. "Craig, I'm sorry. But we've been dating for over a year and I just don't feel like . . ."

He clears his throat. "You don't love me anymore." Hurt vibrates through me. I don't. I really don't.

"I do. But I think . . . you know, more like a friend." He inhales sharply. "I'm sorry." I grab his hands again, always warm and moist, now cold and dry. "I'm sorry, I'm not doing this very well—"

"Breaking up with me? You're doing it fine. I mean, you're good at everything, right? Your parents would be proud." He pulls away, crossing his arms, and it is unbearably quiet. The snow on the screen sends out a whitening glare, flattening everything in the room.

"I really thought you were going to be the first, Katie."

"I know." I nod, my eyes prickling. "But it's just not like at the beginning. I feel like an old married couple and I'm only fifteen." Tears break on my cheeks as the disappointment that had hardened beneath my annoyance finally surfaces, mixing with the terror of feeling like I might be screwing up my fate and ripping Craig's heart out in the process.

Standing, he clicks off the TV, tossing the remote across the smooth surface of the cushion. I wipe my nose on the edge of my sleeve as he walks to the door. "Are you going to tell everyone you dumped me?" he asks, his broad back to me.

"No!" I jump up and run over to him.

"Well, then, what?" He doesn't turn.

"Anything, Craig. I'll say whatever you want."

"Fine." His arms hang at his sides. "We'll tell people it was mutual."

"Okay. Sure." I nod.

"And you can go wait at the end of the driveway for your mother." He walks out of the room.

"Claire!" Dad urges Mom to join us in their bedroom, where my closet pilfering has unfortunately woken him from his Saturday predinner nap.

"You rang?" In the dresser mirror reflection I see her appear in the doorway, white plastic laundry basket balanced on her hip.

"Claire, would you please tell your daughter she cannot keep wearing my suit jackets?"

I turn from where I've been experimenting with various blazer/ wide-belt combinations. "Simon, would you please tell your wife to take me to the Salvation Army, as requested, so I can get something big enough?"

We have a face-off while they take in my fabulous outfit. Dad sits up to clean his glasses on his shirttail while Mom strains for a poker face. "You look ridiculous," she finally pronounces.

"Utterly," Dad adds, stretching to stand.

A cracker popping in my chest, I swipe the *Sassy* magazine I've been consulting from the dresser top and remind myself that she's the one in the smock-top. At least I'd know to belt it with some leggings. "As educators I would think you'd both appreciate the importance of fitting in with your peer group." There's some glaring. "Fine." Blowing out a breath that sends my bangs aflutter, I take off the blue tweed.

"No."

"Mom," I begin, but, now directly drawn into the debate by her black cashmere sweater I'd been using as a base layer, she shakes her head and sits on the coverlet, resting the basket on the pillow beside her.

"Our clothes are our clothes, Kathryn. Yours are yours. You have a whole closetful of your own clothing and, I believe, half of Laura's. Where did you even find that?"

"At the bottom of your sweaters. I need a base layer and all I have are turtlenecks. It's too hot for those." Through their open window the May breeze lifts the linen curtains. "This is perfect. It's really thin."

"It's really cashmere. Go up to the attic and get your summer clothes down."

"Don't have time." I check the clock radio on Dad's nightstand. "School's closing in, like, thirty minutes for the Lock-In and I still have to dry my hair."

"*Like* thirty minutes? Or thirty minutes?"

"Mom." I sit on the edge of the bedspread and face-plant into her hand. "Please. Please, I'm beg-ging you. I will be so careful. It fits me perfectly. I am *begging.*" I turn to look up at her, my cheek fitting her warm palm that smells faintly of fabric softener.

"It *is* nice to see you in something that doesn't make you look like Charlie Chaplin." Dad rehangs his jacket in the closet and pointedly closes it before stepping into the bathroom, calling through the shut door, "How late are your teachers expected to baby-sit tonight?"

"Ten. And I believe the term was *supervise,*" Mom shouts back. "So they don't run in the mean streets of Croton Falls. Start gangs."

"Hijack the video store. Burn the Seven-Eleven," I add.

"I bought that with my first paycheck." She nods at the sweater before pushing herself up and lifting the basket. "I guess it should get another moment in the sun."

I throw my arms around her. "Thank you!"

"But back in my closet first thing. And if we catch you shopping in there again we're really going to be furious. Permission first," she says into my hair.

"Gotcha." I release her to salute.

She lifts an eyebrow. "And I want my Laura Ashley blouse hanging back in my closet before you leave tonight."

"Absolutely!"

"And my suede skirt. We'll start with that."

I wait for her to leave and then sneak into the back of Dad's clothes to pull out his old university blazer, carefully tucking it behind me as I pass her unloading the hamper into the washing machine.

"That's a ballsy choice, black." Laura eyes my outfit as I jog toward her, up the high school's main steps. "No worries it'll fuel the rumors of tragedy?"

"There is no tragedy. That's the message." I slip Laura's dangly beaded earrings into my lobes, feeling their weight as they graze my shoulder.

"Necklace?" she asks. I reach in my pocket and pull out the string of turquoise beads, which match her aqua tube skirt. She drops them over her head, lifting her ponytail out and touching my sandal with hers. "Ready for an evening of good-old-fashioned, fun-filled entertainment?"

"With a side helping of incarceration?" I rejoinder as she pulls open the front door and we slide in among the other tenth-graders clustering around the foldout table, where the adults have set up camp. As we become aware of a not-so-subtle amount of whispering and finger-pointing in my general direction, we shimmy through the waiting crowd to Mrs. Beazley.

"Hello, girls. Now, here's your sheet of activities, a list of rules, a schedule of events, a map of approved areas, and, of course, your contract. Sign here." She flips our sherbet-colored handout packet to a sheet that outlines our promise to stay inside the Lock-In until 10 P.M. and abide by school codes.

"So then I should leave my pot with you?" Laura asks.

"Yes." Mrs. Beazley nods reflexively before her coral mouth puckers. "Oh, no. No, then you shouldn't come in. No, there is to be no drug use on school property. Are you using drugs, Laura?"

"I was only joking, Mrs. Beazley. We came for the . . ." Laura scans the mint-green sheet. "Marshmallow Eating Contest. Where's that?"

"Now let's see." She pulls up her glasses and studies the map. "The eating contests are in the cafeteria. That's down the hall, and then take a left—"

"Yes, we know. Thanks for your help. Come on, Katie, we don't want to miss it!" Laura grabs my arm and we scamper away.

"That one doesn't joke," I reprimand as we walk down the hall of classrooms, checking out the kids sitting on floors watching movies, playing games, and generally hanging out while supervised by pairs of bored-looking teachers gripping coffee mugs.

"This is weird," Laura says as we pass by the glass wall that looks out on the now-dark courtyard. "Feels like we should be getting ready for a choir concert or something."

I cross my arms. "So, what are we doing?"

She drops into a squat, laying the sherbet sheets on the floor for perusal. "I don't know. The marshmallow thing should be good for a laugh."

"Or a vomit." I tap my fingertips on the top of her head. "You go ahead. I'm going to check out what else is going on."

"The middle school pool's open for the Lock-In. Maggie and Michelle said they'd be down there."

"Okay, I'll head in that direction and work my way back."

She straightens up. "But, Katie, are you going to be okay on your own? You're not going to kill yourself, are you? Remember, he's not worth it." She crumples her face in soap opera sympathy.

"Yeah, thanks."

"I'll probably watch a movie." We give each other the thumbsup and split paths. I wander farther down the hall, glancing at the paper map.

"Katie—hi."

Ca-rap. I reluctantly double back to the door I just

passed, where Craig and his friends are setting up an air hockey game, supervised by Jeanine, Craig's rebound girlfriend, and her twerp sidekick, Leslie.

"Hey!" I say, sending bouncy cheerfulness out of every pore. "You guys having fun?" Jeanine averts her eyes to the white leather sleeves of her Hysteric et Vous collegiate jacket.

"So, how are you?" he asks, radiating concern for my well-being. His friends look from the side of their eyes as they fiddle with the table.

"I'm good, Craig! I'm really great!" And if I'd known I was going to be turned into the Anne Boleyn of Croton Falls I would have dumped you at high noon in the cafeteria.

"Well, it's good to see you." He withdraws his hand from his khaki pocket to shake mine, like I'm his dowager grandmother lying on her deathbed.

"You saw me eighth period, Craig." I restrain myself from wiping my palm after he drops it.

"Right. Well, I hope you can have fun tonight." He pats my shoulder.

"I am having fun. I hope you have fun. Hi, Jeanine! Leslie! Hope you guys are having fun, too!" I wave. Jeanine scowls.

"As long as you're not upset."

"Craig, I'm not upset," I mutter, getting upset.

"I know. I know." He steps closer and I'm hit with a wall of Drakkar Noir. Lucky Jeanine.

"Craig, I don't like you. I'm happy not to go out anymore, which is why I'm the one who brought it up. It's fine. Really. If you had a Bible I would swear on it."

"Of course, Katie." He puts his lugging arm on my shoulder.

"Craig!" Jeanine screeches.

"Chick fight." His friends punch the air and Leslie jumps to her feet, her green sweatshirt making her look like a Ninja Turtle about to blow.

"You guys, I'm fine! Jeanine, I'm fine! Seriously, if you guys want to go out that's totally cool with me. I swear. I'm being completely honest. I just offered to say it over a Bible."

"That's really big of you, Katie," Craig says solemnly because he is really, like, forty years old and already retired in there.

"Thanks, Craig. Jeanine. Leslie. Guys. Later." I twist my palm in a half-wave at my shoulder, pivot, and continue on my way down the carpeted hall of the middle school, but not fast enough to miss Jeanine's "I don't know, Craig, she seemed *really* jealous."

I sigh to my sandals and keep walking, following the relatively empty halls linking the two buildings toward the middle school pool. It's weird, actually, the lockers look shorter, as do the drinking fountains and bulletin boards.

I pass through the double doors that lead to the sports area and am greeted by the muffled sound of whoops along with the not-so-muffled stench of chlorine. I cross the hall and press my face against the mesh-wired windows to see what looks like summer camp free swim on a hundred-degree day.

"Katie." I look around the hallway—no one.

"Katie," his voice says again. I look to my right, up the staircase that leads to the darkened balcony and there he is, sitting on the landing in basketball shorts and water-spattered T-shirt, a striped wet towel over his head. My heart in my ears, I climb halfway up the flight of stairs until I'm standing on the same step his flip-flops rest on. "You were in there?" I ask, referring to the frothing pool.

"Yeah." Jake drops his head back, the towel slipping to his shoulders, his brown hair tousled in a million perfect directions. "It's pretty crazy. You going swimming?"

"Oh, yeah," I laugh before realizing from his blank expression that the joke didn't make it out of my head. "Because I don't have a bag." He just looks at me. "I don't have a swimsuit or anything. So, no, I'm not going in." Shut up! I lean back against the banister and study the grout grid of the wall tiles.

"So, you having fun?" I feel him still looking at me.

"*Yes!* I'm having fun! I'm fine! I couldn't be happier! God, I'm the one who broke up with him! I was just try-ing to be nice and let him save face and now I seem like some pathetic loser. It really pisses me off!"

"You and Craig broke up?"

"I'm sorry. I thought . . . Jeanine was telling everyone he dumped me. Didn't you hear?"

He shrugs, clasping the ends of the towel with both hands. "Nope. Just wondering if you were having a good time. But thanks for the update." He smoothes the ends of his shorts over his knees.

"Sure."

"You don't really hold anything back, do you?"

"I'm not sure how to take that."

"And if you were, I bet you'd tell me." He grins, his green eyes glittering as he slides his flip-flop across the stair next to my sandal, the tip of his toe touching mine. "What's your deal, Katie Hollis?"

My breath quickens. "I don't know . . . I guess I just think people should say what's on their minds."

He lies back on the landing, his face in shadow, his shirt riding up, revealing the ivory contours of his hip bone, the muscular indentation, the downy hairs running from his belly button into his shorts. Our toes touching. "So?"

"Yes?" I ask.

"What's on yours?"

"Like, what specifically?"

"Like you and me," he says into the darkness. I am rabbit-in-rifle-range frozen—the banister digging into my back—not moving a muscle—not wanting to startle him from this train of thought.

"Okay . . ." I say, willing him to guide me.

"There's always this thing about you."

"My good deeds?"

"Your good deeds." He grins up at the ceiling. "And this intensity thing, how you take class so seriously and take all those notes or, like, you made that announcement about raising money for stuff in South America."

"Central. Central America."

"It's weird. I don't know, sometimes it really pisses me off. Sometimes . . ." He sits back up, flipping the towel down between his knees.

"Sometimes . . ." I prompt.

"What are you doing tonight?" He looks up, his eyes on mine.

"This. What are you doing?"

"Sleeping over at Sam's."

"Yeah, Laura's coming over."

"We should all leave together or whatever."

I nod, willing to feel the pain of the metal railing digging into my spine if it means I can stay in this moment for the rest of my life.

"Now you're not saying anything. That means you don't have an opinion, I guess." He bats my bare calf with the damp towel.

"I have an opinion." I bend to grab the cool terry, my hair falling into my face, a thin wall between our lips. "Sounds like a plan."

Then he reaches for the banister and pulls himself forward and up so he's standing on my stair. "I mean, it sounds like you were having a totally fun night. I don't want to get in the way or anything." He looks down at me as my gaze flickers to the hollow of his throat. "We should do something together. See what happens."

"So we're not hanging out tonight?"

"We are. I meant like sometime, you know, go to a movie or something."

I keep my eyes from widening at the significance

here, letting the moment obliterate the lingering humiliation of making the same suggestion to him well over a year ago. "I can go to a movie."

"So, we'll go tomorrow." His finger weaves into my hair and lifts it gently over my ear, his skin grazing mine. So close. Right here. In a haze of chlorine.

He inches closer—the edge of his damp shorts touch above my knee and I am paralyzed with the terror of this moment, standing an inch from my face. Of doing it wrong, of scaring him off. He leans in. "Jake."

"Katie."

"Let's not. Let's wait."

He turns away. I blink at the wall—Oh God, rewind! *Please* give me another take. Instead, he lunges up to the landing.

"Jake," I say, desperate to get the moment back. But he reaches into one of the ficus plants lining the turn in the stairs and tugs at something, unhooking something blue from the branches. He comes back down to my step to inspect it while I try to act natural. Like, this is stotally natural, like me and Jake standing an inch apart in the near dark happens all the time.

"A Smurf."

"It is," I say confidently, trying to regain ground.

"It's got glasses. Which one is that? The poet one?"

"Um, the poet one carried something like a pen or a quill or something."

"Of course you know that."

"What do you mean, of course I know that? You asked. It's not like I sit around thinking about the Smurfs.

I mean, that's from when we were kids—that thing's gotta be, like, eight years old or something—"

"Brainy!"

"Excuse me?"

"The smart one was Brainy. He always took everything so seriously." He turns the figurine around and lifts my hand, enclosing it inside. "For you, Brainy."

"I'm the big nerd, thanks."

"Uh-huh. So, Brainy, what's the deal? We gonna meet up?" I let myself stare up at him, into him, let him be the one to wait.

"We are."

"Then, come on." He jogs loosely down the steps, the *thwack* of his flip-flops hitting the metal echoing. I follow as he continues under the stairs to the side door.

"Wait, first I have to—"

He turns. "I didn't bring a bag either."

"Okay, but first I have to talk to Laura."

"See?" he grins. I shake my head, not understanding, but brave enough to admit it. "The bag joke doesn't work. I don't have my stuff. I had to borrow a towel and swim in my shorts. I'm going to run back to my house and change, 'cause I'm rank."

"Oh! Okay." He reaches out and grabs my hand lightly to pull me forward, placing my fingers on the door. "But you have to let me back in, cool?"

"Sure." I tense as he steps out onto the asphalt, my stomach telling me not to lose sight of him. He gets to the streetlamp where the football turf begins and turns back to smile like a little boy, and only then do I allow a return smile that overruns my whole face.

.He takes off into the shadows, and I continue to beam into the night, relishing the darkness and the mild rain that begins to sliver into the ring of light where he was just standing.

I AM . . . WE ARE . . . THIS IS HAPPENING!!! Joy bounces through me like an electric photon—ohmygod—I have to tell Laura. Figuring, even if Jake sprints it, I have at least twenty minutes, I drop the door and take off running through the halls, past the pool, past stupid Craig and stupid Jeanine, down the long corridor of the high school.

"Laura? Laura? Laura?" I duck my head into each room. "Laura?"

"SHUT UP!" I'm shushed by the riveted pile of bodies lying beneath the screen where Batman is swooping onto the Joker.

"Sorry," I whisper, "Laura? Is Laura in here?"

"Katie?"

I reach down, grab her up, and haul her out to the hallway over a chorus of hostility.

"What the hell? Are you trying to make me new friends?"

I throw my hand over her mouth. "No time. Ran into Jake Sharpe by the pool. We touched toes and he gave me a Smurf. He thinks I'm intense and say what I think and wanted to know what I think about him and me. Him and me, can you believe it?" She nods no. "I know.

I can't believe it. Wait, it gets *so much* better. He gave me a Smurf, wait—I told you that—anyway, he went to kiss me and I was all, 'What's the hurry?' And we're going to a movie tomorrow and I think going to be Going Out. So, here's the thing, he wants us to hang out tonight with Sam Richardson, so please say that it's okay." I release her mouth.

"Sam Richardson?"

"Laura, I am asking this one thing. Just this one. Just put up with Sam for tonight. You don't have to touch him. Just get him talking about the Packers, put up with him, and I will owe you forever. Any jewelry, any clothes, my parents' clothes, I'll do your Science homework, and your laundry." I lift the turquoise necklace. "You can have this forever. Anything, just say yes, please?"

She narrows her eyes. "Sam Richardson?"

"Laura, please?"

"I'm taking the necklace."

"Awesome! I love you!"

"Where are you going?" she calls after me as I race back toward the middle school.

"Jake had to run home. Got to hold the pool door for him to get back inside. I'll find you!" I stop at the end of the corridor and turn back grinning. *"We'll find you!"*

She throws up her middle finger as encouragement.

I lay by the door, my eyes long adjusted to the dim red glow of the exit sign, the nearby pool having grown still. Gripping the Smurf, I look out into the now pouring rain as it puddles in the field. I feel Laura softly touch my shoulder.

"Katie, it's over. They're closing up. My mom's going to freak. I'm sorry, we have to go." I shake my head. "I'm sorry," she says again. "Really."

I pull my bare knees into my chest and cry.

13

December 23, 2005

So, the strap of that Tahari dress broke the first time I wore it . . . I've gone through three cars since high school . . . my DVD player only ejects with the aid of a letter opener . . . and yet—the double-sided tape I used to attach Keanu Reeves's face to the ceiling over my bed in 1991 is still going strong. Fantastic. We should get NASA in here to conduct a full study.

I puff up my cheeks and blow out a stream of hostile air into the freezing cold of my bedroom. God, *what* is wrong with my parents? How is it not snowing in here? I watch a cloud of condensation form and hover over my, I'm sure, blue lips. "So, Keanu, any exes you'd like to cop to?" His surfer scowl remains unchanged. "Anyone? No?"

I roll over. Again. Getting tangled in my mother's flannel nightgown. I flail my legs, tugging the fabric clear of my irate limbs. I arc my head back, staring up at the frosty debating trophies on the shelf above my headboard. So I thought I'd just . . . what, exactly? Grow Jake Sharpe a conscience by the sushi table? Reach back into his childhood and peel his mom off the floor? Make his dad remember his seventh birthday so he could develop attachments like normal people, with a sense of mutual responsibility and outer-directedness and empathy—

Something hits my window.

A hailstone?

Again.

I turn my head.

Again.

A little hollow *thwack*.

I sit up—mentally struggling, in the absence of any visual cues that it is 2005, to remain thirty. Sliding out of bed I move to the dark glass pulled by a tiny blue-and-white blur, feeling as if the universe has slammed on the brakes and is trying to reverse into a good parking spot, time truncating, compressing, a roiling like seasickness as I find myself going to the window in the middle of the night because Jake Sharpe . . .

. . . has pinged a plastic Smurf against it.

I look down, momentarily expecting chin-length hair and that black-and-white plaid jacket, instead seeing the bizarre stylist's take on Vermont/après-ski getup, complete with dead beaver on head.

"Oh no. No, no, no, no, no, no, no." My head shaking in righteous indignation, I storm downstairs, throwing a coat over Mom's nightgown and shoving my feet in whatever boots are there. I hurl the front door open. "I'm a LYRICAL DEVICE???!!! A *LYRICAL DE-VICE???!!!*"

I pause, letting my ire sink in through his asinine

hat and thick skull to the impenetrable blob of self-aggrandizement that is his brain.

Lights go on in bedroom windows of neighboring houses. A dog barks.

"I'd prefer you weren't one for the entire neighborhood, Elizabeth Kathryn." Mom's head protrudes from her bedroom window, as, ashen, she takes in the spectacle.

"Hey there, Mrs. Hollis. How are you?"

"I don't know how you live with yourself." She lets her window crash shut.

For once in agreement about Jake, I motion for him to come closer, hissing, *"A lyrical device?!"*

"You'd prefer I tell John Norris that Katie is actually Elizabeth Kathryn Hollis, a thirty-year-old who lives in Charleston, North Carolina, and works as a sustainable development consultant? And if they want a chat, she's currently visiting her parents at thirty-four Maple Lane?"

Disbelief. My head tilts. "You know what I do?"

"I keep tabs." He shrugs, smiling.

"You keep tabs?" I lean in.

"I Google."

"Wait! This is *not* how this goes."

"Oh? How does it go?"

I fix him in a dead stare. "You. Are an asshole. A cosmic-size, grade A, redefines-it-for-a-generation, asshole."

His smile fades, his expression crumpling. "I deserve that, I guess."

"You guess?! You *guess?!* The last thing you said to me was 'See you tomorrow!' "

His mouth twists to the side, his shoulders and moss-hued irises lifting. "Yeah."

"That was thirteen years ago!!"

"Okay, I don't remember exactly what I said—"

"Odd, you remember every other fucking detail like you have it tattooed on your ass."

"Maybe I do. Wanna see?"

And I fucking smile. Dammit.

Regaining my composure, I look past him, my eyes landing on his old ten-speed propped against the maple. "You *biked* over here?"

"As soon as my mother said she'd spotted you crouched on our washing machine."

"They didn't pen you in like the Tour de France?"

He shakes his big stupid hat. "I snuck out the back way. I had to get out of that house." His eyes smile as he takes me in. "God, you look beautiful."

"Don't." I lift a warning finger.

He slips his hand in his jeans pocket, his shoulder hunching. "Look, I'm sorry."

"You are?" I lunge on his words. "For what?"

"For calling you a lyrical device."

"Oh, oh, great." I mime opening a *Book of Kells*-size ledger, flipping back through *masses* of pages until I scroll down the columns to . . . "Calling me a lyrical device . . . check. Great, well, that's taken care of." I slam the "book" shut. "That just leaves lying to my face, disappearing in the middle of the night, harvesting my adolescence into a multimillion-dollar empire, um, apparently now using my name—"

"I know what happened."

"Yeah, you know what happened. Casey Kasem knows what happened. Ryan Seacrest knows what happened. People singing karaoke in Japan right now . . . know what happened. 'I slid into her, my eyes on the towering golden Gods.' Like that's some deep metaphor. If they only knew how untalented you really are."

His cell rings. "You Shook Me All Night Long." I roll my eyes.

"Yeah?" His gaze fixed on me, he braces the tiny phone to his red ear. "The back road . . . I took my bike . . . No, no one saw me—chill." His attention is suddenly absorbed by the fur trim coming loose from his boot. "Yeah, no, I'll be right back . . . No, don't send a car, I'm not riding around fucking Croton Falls in a limo . . . Well, tell Rai Uno to keep their pants on." He flips the phone shut, slides it in his back pocket, and returns his attention to me. "I'm sorry."

I lunge again. "You are? For what?"

"They need me. But you're here." He points behind me at the Colonial igloo.

"No. No, I'm not. We're leaving tomorrow. Right after you announce that song is now called 'Tallulah' and it's about your dental hygienist. Or I swear to God, Jake."

He starts to walk backward, shuffling a reverse trail in the snow. "Don't leave. I'll come find you tomorrow." He picks up his bicycle, throwing his leg over. "I want to hear more about how untalented I am!"

"That hat makes you look like a jackass," I hiss down my drive.

He swerves to a stop beneath the streetlamp. "So then if I just take the hat off I'm—"

"A jackass *au natural.*"

"I've missed you." And he grins that lopsided grin of his, the one that, thank God, gets me less since he had the chip fixed . . . and speeds into the darkness. Forgotten coat open, I stand watching the lamp lights bounce off his wheel reflectors, blurring into a contiguous circle until he is gone.

14

ELEVENTH GRADE

"And it's *you* who is the love God . . . and it's *you* who makes me—"

"Excuse me," Finkle interrupts my backup vocals. He gestures his cheese-dusted fingers at the Tupperware bowl on the table behind me, clumps of white powder flecking the patch of Michelle Walker's living room carpet between us. Swigging my beer, I dance away from the side table of dwindling doodles, pretzels, and puffs and, in the low light of the piano lamp, Finkle angles his back from me and the other juniors so he and the Smartfood can have some privacy.

"OhmyGodthereyouare!" Laura slurs through a glassy smile. She weaves in from the kitchen and slides her hand into mine, her glimmering eyes trained on my face, her elation pulling me into her orbit. As the Soup Dragons moan from the speakers she leans her forehead until it's brushing mine, the quartz crystal on the leather cord around her neck tapping my chest. "Ilovethissong!" Without dropping my hand she begins to dance, her hips, her arms in fluid motion, and through my own

"That's the word," I say with disdain.

He shuffles the sheet music on the floor. "Why"— he clears his throat—"Why have you been such a bitch to me all year?"

My forehead furrows in disbelief. "You can't be serious."

He sits back on his heels, tapping the stack together on his thighs. "I am."

"Uh, the Lock-In?" I remind him, sarcasm raising my eyebrows.

He looks down to the floor as the tank continues to burble, rubbing his knuckles absentmindedly along his jaw. "That was . . . yeah, that was bad."

"Yeah." I turn and start rifling the plaid couch . . . useless in the blue shadows. Switch on the light? Or not. Is he like a stain only visible under infrared? Would the fluorescent overhead make him disappear?

"My mom, uh . . ." He pauses as I dig my hands behind the cushions, feeling a concession stand's worth of old popcorn. "When I got home her car was kind of rammed into the elm next to the garage."

"Oh my God." I twist to him, wiping the dusty salt from my palm.

"Yeah, the front was crumpled like a beer can."

"Oh my God, I didn't know. I'm so sorry, Jake. Is she okay?"

"She was passed out in the front hall, so yeah." He laughs dryly. "She was fine."

"Wow, I'm really sorry," I say, meaning it. "You could've told me, you know, I wish you had."

"I am." His eyes return to me and he smiles that half-smile. "You're the person I'm telling." I am? "Nice dress."

I run my hands down the front of the Betsey Johnson I found at Filene's Basement—the rayon embodiment of over twenty hours spent watching the Haberman twins. "Thanks." Nonchalantly. "Got it in Boston."

"Cool. Whatcha lookin' for?" He shoves the ream of music in his knapsack, his hair still damp to his forehead from playing.

"Your friend, Sam, seems to have divested Laura of her undergarments."

"Divested." He smiles to himself, slipping his guitar pick into the outside pocket. "That's a new one." I drop to the floor and push my arm under the couch, feeling the rayon lift up my thigh. Feeling him watch. "Having fun?" he asks.

I withdraw half a broken poker chip. "Oh, yeah, I haven't let loose like this since the Easter egg hunt."

He laughs. Really laughs. And the thing I always thought was a rubber band pulsates into a hormonal electrical twist, primed my whole life to charge at only this sound. "You guys were good," I offer, probing under the La-Z-Boy. Really good. JenniferTwo screaming, "Take me, Jake," good. "I especially liked the new song, the acoustic one."

"Really?" He smiles. "Thanks, but I don't know . . ." We seesaw as I stand back up and he lowers onto his heels to reach into his backpack and extract a dry T-shirt. He whips off the Dinosaur Jr. one he played in, tossing it to the carpet. "We're working with a new amp, we fucked up the bridge on the third song, and Benjy's drumming was kinda all over the place, but—"

OHMYGODWHERE'DYOUGETTHATBODY-WHOAREYOU?

"Yeah," I half-squeak to what I don't know haven't heard don't care, the stab of lust leaving me feeling like my car just did a one-eighty on black ice. I step back, the base of the stairs grazing my ankle.

He pushes his head through the T-shirt, shaking out his hair. "Okay."

Okay.

The breeze blows past me. I look at him, silent.

"Well, see ya around." He picks up his guitar case and slides his backpack over his shoulder. But, instead of heading out the open door, he comes toward the stairs and as I watch him get closer I steel myself for him to pass out of my night, out of my weekend, out of my May. But he comes straight forward, slowing as he gets to me, bag over shoulder, guitar in hand, arriving, pulling in, the thrum of his engine perceptible to my skin.

He stops. His face mere inches, his hips, not even seconds, from mine.

"Hey," he says again, simply, on the way to the stairs, on his way out.

"Hey."

He doesn't move. He's just there. Inches. Seconds.

I reach out my fingertips and slip them under the hem of his shirt, finding his taut stomach. He shivers, his eyes fluttering closed and then opening to find me. I hold his gaze as I delicately rake my thumbs outward across the line of his jeans, feeling the pulse in the flesh beneath. A moan. Better than the laugh. Much better.

I step in, releasing his hips to run my fingers up into his hair, my thumbs along his cheekbones, and then we merge, his tongue on mine, tasting of beer and Parliaments and Jake. And the case falls, the backpack drops. We have never done this. Your skin, your hair, your touch, is new is new is new—we have always done this—always your skin your hair your touch.

"That song," he says into my mouth, his hands pulling at the pearl buttons, poppoppop, his fingers finding my breasts.

"Yes?" I half-gasp.

"It's called 'Katie.' "

The never.

And the always.

And the never.

☙

I slouch against my bed's dust ruffle in front of the floor fan, the pink carpet pressing into my bare thighs as I trace the symmetrical dime-size bruises on my hip-bones. My finger slides from the edge of my black eyelet bikini to circle the marks left by seven straight days of Jake's grinding. Desire and confusion combust as I lay my hands over my stomach, leaning my head back onto the bedspread and focusing on the whir of the fan. The phone rings and I lunge for it.

"Hello?" I clutch the receiver.

"Hey. Oh my God, how hot is it for the beginning

of June?" Laura asks. "I keep sweating off my eye shadow. Ew."

"Hi," I sigh, disappointment pouring through the receiver.

"He didn't call."

I shake my head at the fan, my hair whipping across my face.

"Katie?"

"Nope." I pick at a blush yarn.

"It's a party," she tries to cajole me, "I'm sure he couldn't call everyone he wants to come—"

"He called you!"

"He called *Sam,*" she corrects me.

I rip out a carpet loop, a chunk of adhesive clumped at its roots. "But he probably said, 'Tell Laura she's invited.'"

"He probably held the phone to his ass and farted."

"Which Sam understood to mean—"

"We're all invited. Fart invite's all inclusive."

"Laura." I extend my legs. "I'm serious."

"Katie!" she yelps in frustration. "You guys have been fooling around all week!"

I look down at my Hester Prynne bruises. "Thank you."

"You don't talk at all?" she asks, disbelieving.

I shake the settled crystals of my ice tea. "There's a lot of heys."

"I think you're his girlfriend," she says definitively.

"Fantastic. Could you also think I have a fourteen hundred PSAT?"

"Don't *you* think you're his girlfriend?"

"I don't know!" I hear parental footsteps stop outside my door and lower my voice to a hush. "I think he's writing songs about me, he's grabbing me the minute the bell rings, and now he's throwing a party at his lake house and I'm finding out about it from everyone who did *not* dry hump me all week!"

"This is ridiculous, it's already four. Sam's picking me up in five minutes; we're coming by to get you."

"No!" I flail, accidentally knocking over the fan, its plastic frame grinding into the carpet as it vibrates away from me.

"Why?" Laura moans.

I yank the plug from the wall by the wire. "What if I get there and he's sitting with his real girlfriend?"

"And who would that be?" she asks flatly.

"I don't know." I right the machine, smoothing the deep pile beneath to stabilize it before setting it down. "Someone we don't know about."

"Okay," she humors me. "So you get there and Jake is sitting with some girl his parents have been keeping caged in their barn since birth. Then what?"

"Then what if he sees me, rolls his eyes, and is, like, 'What are *you* doing here?'"

"Whip out the bruises."

I wipe my hands down my damp ribs. "Or worse, what if he doesn't acknowledge me at all?"

"Still voting for the bruises."

"But there must be some sort of ground rules and if I just show up when I haven't been invited—"

"No one has been invited. There are no engraved invitations. He mumbled something to a few people—"

"Kathryn." Mom picks up the line.

"Off in a minute."

"If you're going to sit around all day, how about mowing the lawn?" she offers.

"Mom!"

"Just a suggestion." *Click.*

"I love how she says that," I marvel, "Like, how about taking a spa?"

"Please just come? Come on, decide. I have to quick wash my face before Sam gets here. I'm all sweaty again."

"Okay, my decision is . . ." My chest pounds.

"Katie, you come to this party with the rest of the eleventh grade. You toss your hair, you swish your black bikini, and screw him."

I'm so shaky as Sam drives us down the dirt road that I just try to focus on my skin sticking and resticking to the vinyl seat to calm myself. When we get to where the cars are parked, all half-leaning into a ditch, Laura reaches back and squeezes my knee.

"Wow, he's got the place rockin'." Sam pulls over and silences the engine, the buzz of cicadas rising and falling over the sounds of splashing and laughter. I unfold from the car, the long grass scratching at my ankles as I pull my ponytail holder out and attempt a toss. I catch up and walk behind them in the chalky dirt, towel around my neck, stomach in my sneakers. Sam, picking up the faint tune drifting over the trees and humming it, takes Laura's hand and we all shift our path to the shady side of the road.

Where the line of oaks end we round the last parked car and see a small cabin sitting atop a yard that slopes to the water. Head tucked, I dart my eyes over my sunglasses to the faces surrounding a keg being kept cool in the shade of a willow, its branches trailing into the water. No Jake. I scan the clusters dotting the grass, the porch, the dock. No Jake. From the tanning station in the center of it all Kristi lowers her aluminum reflector tray to nod her Sun-In'ed head in my direction. Her crew raises themselves to their elbows on their towels to get a better look through their mirrored lenses. Oh God. This is bad. This is bucket-of-blood-on-my-head bad. I can't— this was—I shouldn't have—

"Just about to take the boat out." Suddenly hands slide under my arms and cross my stomach from behind. Jake pulls me into him, his damp skin cool against me. "Where you guys been? You want to ski?"

"Sure." I shrug, smiling sheepishly at Laura.

Darkness at our backs, I sit against Jake's chest, feeling the vibrations move through both of us as he sings, our hands resting loosely around the bottle of beer nestled in the folds of the wool blanket. The bonfire tepee crackles, casting an amber glow over the sunburned faces ringing its edges and sending sparks up past the black tree line and into the clear night sky. I watch Benjy drum his fingers against his Coors can, eyes closed, as he pulses his head to the beat. Next to him Todd straddles a log, hunching over his bass, his hair in his eyes as he cradles the frame to play. Laura smiles contentedly as she reclines against Sam, nestled beneath his guitar. She reaches her hand over to me and I stretch mine to her, our fingers brushing before we slide them back to our respective cocoons. Kristi, Jeanine, all of them, everyone, watches from the edges of the roaring flames as Jake hums the beginning of another song and I let my eyes drift closed, confusion as distant as the specks of stars.

Jake is glowing. As he stands on the first step of the grand stairway leading to the second floor—and his bed-room—he seems to be lit from within. I look over my shoulder to see this illusion being created by the after-noon sun eking in through the stained-glass window above the Sharpe front door, the colors bouncing off the burnished wall paneling and diffusing into a refracted halo. Unaware of his incandescence, his head lists so that his hair flops into his face adorably.

"Not fair." I cross my arms, trying to hold the ground we'd sworn to when I agreed to study for finals together. "I mapped out the assignments. We have a *schedule.*" I slap the back of my right fingers into my left palm. He raises his arms in an exaggerated shrug and the tails of his white oxford lift, having already been untucked by my roving fingers the second his heavy front door clicked shut. "You're looking at me like I'm crazy."

"But you are," he says with a sweetness that suddenly gives me pride in the description. He takes a seat on the second step, reaching out to pull me closer as he slides his hands up the backs of my bare legs.

I reluctantly grab them through my skirt. "Jake, we're never going to get any homework done if I go up those stairs, and we both know it."

"You're right." He slumps. I release his hands, unwillingly extricating myself from his touch and walk back the length of the entrance hall to grab my backpack from where it fell with his in a heap by the door.

"Come on." I crook my finger for him to follow me to the kitchen. "Let's just open a book. One book—feel like we're making an effort. Somewhere on the *ground* floor."

"Come on, Katie, I hate it down here. Let's go up to my room or to the basement—I promise I'll be good."

"Okay, basement."

"Great—I'm gonna grab us some snacks." He smacks my butt as I turn away and give my hips a little wiggle before retreating to the back hall. I'm about to skip down to the basement when I spot the adjacent door ajar. Curious, I peek in, finding a formal library ringed by four walls of matching blue Moroccan bindings. As I'm reading the titles Jake sticks his head in, proffering two cans of Pringles. "Sour cream or regular?"

"Regular. What are those?" I squint at small slivers of color displayed in among the volumes.

"Hotel soaps. Every time my dad travels he brings one home for me. Apparently I really liked unwrapping them when I was little and then he just got in the habit, I guess." I follow his gaze to the shelf over the door where the slim packages are brightly wrapped in Japanese paper and stacked in a pyramid.

"He works for Sanderson, right?" I pick up an acorn paperweight from the collection of ornamental glass on the side table.

"They still give every employee one at Christmas. He has, like, twenty of them. How much paper does one person need to weigh down?" He waves the tubes of chips like landing batons. "Come on, let's get out of here."

I lift the acorn up and turn it to the light, making a rainbow. "What does he do?"

"Fiber-optic cable—some sort of regional oversight." He rests the cans down on the desktop. "Well, it used to be regional—now it's international."

"So he travels a lot?" I ask, wondering who could build this perfect sanctuary and leave it behind.

"All the time. I mean, can you blame him?"

I have no idea how to answer that question.

Thankfully his hand slides behind my neck and questions, interest in anything but this, escape me. As always, the preplanned speech breaks apart in my brain, the words softening and disappearing, only desire coming into relief as I watch him slide down, unbutton my shirt, his embrace becoming more insistent upon the discovery of the see-through cream lace camisole I found last night in an old dress of Mom's. My mouth pressed against his I run my tongue under the sharp edge of his upper teeth. "How'd you break your tooth?" I ask without moving my lips away from his.

"Hit the dashboard when I was seven."

I pull my head back—"You weren't buckled in?"

Dropping my oxford at our feet, he grabs my wrists and pins them. I bite his lip. He laughs deeply, walking me backward until I'm against a large fish tank set into the wall. I twist to get a closer look.

"No fish," he sighs, kneeling before me, resting his cheek against my thigh. "They were always dying and my mom couldn't deal with it and I got sick of dealing with it, so now it's just a water display."

"That's too bad," I say, still staring into the tank as if a lone survivor might swim out of the plaster reef at any moment. "I feel for anyone whose ambition to have pets is thwarted."

"Yeah, well, you gotta live where they are. But he's cool with it. He learned in Hong Kong that having water in your thinking space is supposed to be good for creative energy—" He's interrupted by something over the burbling water—a high-pitched tremor, an animal cry, coming from the front of the house. I look down at Jake, but he's gone completely inert, his face slack.

"Jake?" I whisper.

The waves of sound Doppler their way to us, rising in pitch as they seek their target. Phrases emerge, *make me sick, fucking sonofabitch father.* I touch his shoulder and he flinches to standing. *"Where the fuck are you?! Are you downstairs?!"* She flies in, sweaty, the blood vessels constricting her face a bright red. *"How many times have I told*

*you not to leave your fucking backpack in the front hall for me
to trip over, you worthless . . . worthless—"*

"I'm sorry, Mom," his voice small. "What happened
to your match?"

Eyes locking with me she pulls herself up short and,
panting, her tone drops an octave. "It's started to rain."
With a shaking hand she smoothes her ponytail. "Barbara dropped me off." She takes a step in the door in her
pleated tennis dress, her sneakers pristine bone white
against the dark Persian carpet. "Is your guest staying
for dinner?"

"I'd love to, um, stay for dinner, thank you," Crazy
Lady. "Sorry. I'm Katie." I wave across the six-foot distance between my body and the top that should be covering it. "It's really nice to meet you." And, these would
be my nipples. Nipples, Crazy Lady.

"We're eating at seven. Hope salmon's all right. I'm
sure it is," she answers for me, her breath still coming in
ragged spurts. "I'm going to make some martinis and
change out of my dress. Jake, will you keep an ear out
for the door? The Humbolts should be over soon—let
them in?"

"Sure."

With a tight smile in my direction, she leaves.

I scramble for my blouse, buttoning it all the way to
my throat. "Oh my God, are you okay?"

"Come on." He walks toward the basement and I
follow down the stairs, unsure what to say. "Hey, shut
the door?" he asks casually. At the bottom of the stairs he
flicks on the light, the stereo, the amps, and commences

tuning his guitar, the sound filling the space with a warm human rumble. Helping with the pretense that this didn't just happen, I pull out my history textbook and open it, but I only stare at the pattern of ink on the page as if it were Cyrillic.

"Hey, pass me the phone," he says after a few minutes, and I lean behind me to grab him the head of the plastic mallard duck.

Benjy looks at his watch. "My Calc final's tomorrow, dude. We shouldn't even be here."

Thankful someone else has broached it, I stand to zip my backpack. "Jake, I've really gotta study."

"Guys!" Jake pleads. Sam shoots us a look behind his back, where a V of sweat marks his T-shirt.

"Okay." Benjy raises his drumsticks in defeat as I sit back down. "One more time—but that's it. I gotta pass Calc."

"Sam?"

"What if I try it like this?" He riffs on the tune of Jake's they've been trying out for the last half hour, upping the tempo and infusing it with some minor chords.

"Yeah, I like it," Jake says, listening with a displaced intensity. "Good, great, yes."

"Jake?" Todd actually raises his hand to near face-level before he realizes he looks like a tool.

"Todd, you gonna punk out on me, too?"

"Nah. Well, I mean, at some point." He turns pink as he hedges. "What should I do?"

"What?" Jake asks, distracted by Sam's new melody.

"Should I be doing anything differently?" Todd repeats in the unctuous tone that sets my teeth on edge.

"No, you're good. Just keep doing what you're doing."

Purpose restored, Todd smiles down at his bass before planting his tongue between his lips in his pose of concentration.

"Okay, great, guys. Let's take it from the top. We have our Lady of Inspiration here today, so let's really wow her." Because I can't leave, because after seeing her like that, seeing him like that—I could never. I give a supportive wave from behind my Physics book. And they play, his friends' fingers and feet all jamming in unison to keep that bubble of sound in place around Jake.

15

December 23, 2005

Pulling Dad's thickest Fair Isle sweater over my head I round the corner to the kitchen. Mom is at the sink, head bent, arm furiously moving back and forth as the faucet runs, a trickle of steam rising from the water. Braced, I beeline to the coffee maker. "Hey," I call to her.

She turns, pushing up her sweater sleeve with her cheek, a hunk of steel wool foaming blue in her yellow glove. "So."

"Mom, first let me just say I'm sorry about last night." I take a speckled tin cup from the drain board. "I did not invite him here. That was definitely not part of my plan—"

"I've booked you a ticket on the plane leaving an hour after ours out of Burlington this afternoon. We're going through Atlanta and you're going through O'Hare, but it was the best I could do, and we're lucky to have that."

"What? No." I snap the glass carafe out of its holster. "I thought you were leaving tomorrow morning."

"We were. But I was able to buy a set of tickets for today."

"I see." Not wanting to clip the wrong wire I nod to myself as I focus on pouring the coffee and walk to the table, my eyes landing on the *Croton Sentinel* tented atop the lone place setting left for me. Resisting the bait I wordlessly lift Jake's headline and drop it on the chair next to me, inwardly scoffing at the picture of the Main Street welcome banner snapping in the wind.

"Read it." She clatters the scoured manicotti pan onto the counter.

"Mom," I sigh.

"Read it."

I tuck my knees up into her nightgown, shifting on the hard wood seat as I scan the article, which differs only from the usual pabulum in its mention of his scout badges. "Yup." I start to fold it.

"Keep reading." Standing where the counter corners, she grips the perpendicular ledges with her gloved hands.

"Why don't you just tell me what—" My eyes land on my name. Lifting the page closer, a sweat breaks out beneath the lace bib of my borrowed Lans as I read that Jake's new single, far from being changed to "Tallulah," has dropped this morning. "Shit," I murmur through a rapidly drying mouth.

"Let me make you some eggs. And then you can pack."

"I don't have anything to pack," I say dumbly, buying myself a second to think.

Whipping off her gloves she opens the fridge, withdrawing the cardboard carton and porcelain cow butter dish. "Whatever you have to do then. We're leaving at noon."

"I don't—I'm not ready to—" I push my fingertips along my scalp as she cracks an egg into an earthenware bowl, her hands furiously whisking the yolks into a froth. "I'm not leaving today."

"Let me be explicitly clear. I do not want him on that lawn, on my porch, or in my house."

"Okay, neither do I."

"I don't believe you." She bangs the whisk against the side of the bowl, the yellow viscous mixture dripping off the metal springs. "You know you're just giving him more material." My palms slide down my face. "He's a narcissist, Kate." She pours the mixture atop the spitting butter. "He's a taker. There is no getting through to someone who would subject us to this."

"Okay, *this* is not happening to you." Eye sockets constricting, I dare her to go there. *"You* are on the sidelines for this."

"There *are* no sidelines with Jake Sharpe!" My cell peals Beth's ringtone from my purse, the electronic squeal of UVA's "Good Old Song" vibrating through the leather on the stool by the side door. She flings the spatula at the uncooked mess curdling in the pan and balls her apron, hurling it onto the counter as she stalks out.

Through the twist of pain behind my brow bone, I fumble for the phone and my eye drops, craving the distant sanity of my friends in Charleston.

"Holy shit!" Beth screams, "Where are you?"

"I'll hold the phone out the window so you can hear the cows lowing."

"I'll hold the phone to the dashboard so you can hear your serenade."

"Motherfucker." I tip my head back, the saline hitting my retinas.

"Yeah, I almost ran off the road. *When* did he write this—and are you gonna marry him?"

"What? God, no." Blinking through the saline, the flung apron comes into focus. "Eleventh grade, when I wasn't even talking to him, which should tell you something, and God, no."

"And he comes out with it now? Have you seen him?"

I hold the strawberry-leaf-patterned cotton against me, smoothing the wrinkles before rehanging it by the stove. "Yes."

"And?"

"Believe me, I'd like to report otherwise." I pull the flung spatula out and clasp the insulated handle, tremoring the blue pan over the flame. "But I get around him and it's like we've only been apart a few hours."

"That's just the chemistry—hold on. Toasted biscuit with butter and a black coffee, please."

"Fuck chemistry." At the mention of biscuits I reach over to slide up the wood door on the bread bin and rip out a slice. Glancing back at the drying yellow curds with revulsion I spin the black knob off. "Where are you?"

"Drive-through. On the way to my dad's."

"Is Robert with you?" I ask through a mouthful of buttery challah.

"He had to work, so he's driving up tomorrow with the dog. Besides, he likes having separate cars so he knows he can make a midnight getaway if necessary." A blitz of static fills the line.

"What? Beth?"

Her voice comes back into range, "—soooo two days ago, but how was your date?"

Tearing another slice from the loaf, I try to conjure my real life. "Actually pretty great—he picked a cool little restaurant. He was smart, much better-read than I'd have guessed—very funny. *And,* I gotta say, great kisser."

"Mmmm."

"He did the hands-on-face thing." I flush.

"I love hands-on-face." She sighs.

"And there was some hands-in-hair," I say, fully there.

"Hands-in-hair." She sighs again. "Good times."

"But I am the Queen of the Great First Date. He's probably either going to reconnect with the girl-next-door or die in a hideous freak Christmas turkey carving accident."

"Or come back from the holiday dying to see you again," she says with her usual optimism.

I pull a jar of plum jam from the cupboard. "That'll be my New Year's wish."

"Mine, too. How you holding up?"

I rub my eyes. "Yesterday was the longest day of my life, no kidding, bar none." I dump the pan full of congealed eggs straight in the sink and crisscross squirt it with Joy, sizzling on contact.

"I'm so proud of you, K. You're *taking it on.*"

"Or something." I look around the half-dismantled kitchen, the bare shelves where all the cookbooks once were. "On top of everything I've somehow kicked off week-with-parents two days early."

"Fun."

"All the judgment, half the calories." I fetch my coffee from the table. "We have our whole thing down in Florida. Mom and I market. Dad and I grill the fish. It's great. Or when they visit me in Charleston. But here . . . we . . ."

"Reenact your highlight reel?"

"Exactly." I take a lukewarm swig. "Speaking of which, we're mid-screening, so . . ."

"Keep me posted?"

"Of course." I wipe my mouth with the back of my hand, my eyes landing on that stupid fucking banner.

"Just don't go postal. He's *so* not worth a CNN mug shot."

"He's not worth a CNN mug."

"Really? Ceramic? Two handles? No?"

I laugh. "I love you. Safe driving."

"You, too, man. You, too."

I flip the phone shut and down the rest of my coffee. Dropping the cup in the sink with a clang I see she left our e-tickets on the counter. I swipe up the paper, taking the steps two at a time to the landing where the attic stairs have been lowered into the hall. I grip the railing extension, hoisting the end of the nightgown to climb up, calling, "Listen, Mom, if you guys want to go early that's fine, but I'm going to change my ticket—"

"Did she get another set?" Dad rises from where he's kneeling under the eaves at the far side of the attic. My eyes adjusting to the dim light I step through the maze of opened cartons to where he stands, stretching his back. "I told her not to do that."

"Sorry, I thought you were Mom," I cough in the dust he's unsettled with what looks to be a frenzy of unpacking everything boxed away. "What's going on up here?"

"She went out. What in the bloody hell did you say to her?" He wipes his blackened hands off on his gardening trousers. "She was in a state."

"Nothing."

"I hate it when she gets like that," he says, erasing the smudges from his glasses with the hem of his sweater.

I nod, "So what's with all this?"

"Just wanted to see what was up here and sort it out." I look down to his feet, surrounded by his emerald-bound rare set of Thoreau. The ones he took with him.

"These never made it back on the shelves?" I ask, quietly.

"No. When I came back, we just . . ." His head swivels, his gaze arcing over the knee-high piles. "Put everything up here." My heart pounds at this acknowledgment, but he quickly moves us along, pointing me through the gutted garment racks to a cluster of boxes. "Here, lend a hand."

I step over, unfurling the cardboard flaps of the top one to reveal a tight cube of squashed animals. "Oh, this can all go."

"Even Mr. Lephant?" Standing over my shoulder he reaches past me to greet the folded fur, extending its crushed trunk. His elbow as fulcrum he swings it into my face, touching its nose to mine. I pull away, coughing again. "You couldn't say *elephant*." He gazes at its accordion face. "Some kid will love him."

"I think these're too dusty for Goodwill, Dad, not with the kind of asthma kids have now."

"Oh, right, of course." He shoves it back in the box and presses the flaps shut.

I look past him, from the colorful jumble of my childhood bits and bobs to the boxes of belongings he had to assemble for what was almost a second life for all of us. "It can go."

"The lot of it? Yes, right, right."

"Dad?" I touch his arm and he startles, facing me in the slatted sunshine slanting over the chairs stacked by the window, his eyes wet. My ribs knit together. "Dad," I say again.

"Katie, I'm fine, it's just the dust. Run down and fetch me a tissue?"

I nod and weave around the stacks to the lit hole in the floor.

"Katie?"

"Yes?" I turn back.

"Keep this." He lifts his old university blazer from the last box of his things, the thread holding the pocket crest in place unraveling. "You could dry clean it, fix the patch, get a whole 'nother life out of it."

"Sure. Just put it aside for me?" I ask gently, hoping he'll forget, knowing I couldn't bring myself to jettison it en route and I don't want it in my home.

He holds it out to me. "Carry it downstairs with you then."

"Be right back." I push myself across the creaking boards to take it, before hastily retreating down the ladder.

A Sierra Club travel mug of hot chocolate in each hand I carefully push backward through the storm door. Clomping down the drift-covered deck steps, I steady my hands as wisps of steam emanate from the small plastic openings. The late afternoon sun ricochets off the Langdons' satellite dish to the ice cloaking the snow-filled backyard.

"Keith, watch your brother's eye!" Laura, snowman foreman, monitors construction from her perch on the dry corner of the picnic table. "Thank you."

She takes a mug as I hop up beside her, my ear still cocked to the street. "Hear anything?"

"Like . . ." she prompts.

"Sound of a car, bike on the snow. A rabbit with a note tied to its neck." For a minute we both slant our heads like sibling retrievers. "Enraged woman driving a Honda."

"Katie!" We startle and I jerk my head up to where Dad peers from the tilted attic window.

"Yeah?" I shield my eyes with my mittened hand.

"What about your toboggan? It has your name on it."

"Well, as of today that's officially a collectible!" I turn to Laura. "Want a Katie toboggan that weighs a hundred pounds?"

"Well, there are two of them to drag it up the hill," she considers. "So, sure."

"Lor'll take it, Dad!" I shout over my shoulder. He nods, letting the dormer slap shut.

"Shouldn't we be helping him?" she whispers over the top of her mug.

"No—and he can't hear you. I offered for a while after noon came and went."

"And her cell's still off?"

"Yup. So he's in the zone." I take a swig. "But better packing than making birdhouses."

"Oh, I liked the birdhouses," she says nostalgically. "As therapeutic distractions go, they were pretty cute— I still have mine. The squirrels love it."

"Really? 'Cause we made a campfire with ours when the Prozac finally kicked in." I drop my head.

"Oh, Katie, it's going to be okay." She rubs the top of my back where my shoulder blades pinch together. "He's bound to have ups and downs as he comes off— what was it?"

"Zoloft."

"Isn't he? *Keith, his eye!*" she calls sharply, startling us, before shaking her head. "Last Christmas I was right there with 'em, rolling in the snow and making angels, but this year . . ." She rubs her down-clad belly. "Don't get me wrong, I'm excited to have this baby, but I honestly don't know what I'm going to do in a month. Sam's mom'll help, but . . . this was so not planned."

"It wasn't?"

"No—watch the eyes!" She extends her arm, the milk sloshes, dampening the edge of her black down sleeve.

I pat her wrist, helping to absorb the spill with Mom's mitten. "Why didn't you tell me?"

"Because I couldn't admit to being a thirty-year-old with a shaky handle on birth control." She shrugs, looking all of twelve, despite her bump.

I pivot toward her embarrassed expression. *"Hey, hey,"* I say gently, tapping my thigh against hers until she lifts her eyes to mine. "My mom had me while she was still in grad school. She took me in a bassinet to all her finals. Talk about so not planned. Yet, *somehow* it all worked out," I say, willing the summation to apply to now, too.

"But you still have a fear of enclosed spaces."

"True. And exams."

Smiling, she pulls a string cheese stick out of her pocket and peels it. "Thanks. I appreciate the pep talk," she says, taking a bite.

"Anytime. I will pep-talk you through delivery and beyond. I will be pep-talking you down the aisle at their graduations."

"Shhh." She holds up a finger and we tense as a car comes closer . . . passes . . . and drives away. Toward sane people. "Did he say anything?" she asks, shoving the empty wrapper back in her pocket and bringing the green mug to her chapped lips.

"Anything . . ."

"Time related. Did he say anything pertaining to the sun or our orbit of it?" She blows into the steam before taking a tentative sip.

"He just said he'd come find me—" Another car passes. "Do I need to reapply my lip gloss?"

"Do I need to beat you?" My cell rings and we both freeze. I pull it out of my pocket and we slump upon seeing the Charleston area code.

"Hello?" I answer.

"Kate?" my boss's assistant's voice crackles down the line. "I'm sorry to bother you."

"Hi—no, no bother at all. What's up?" As she fills me in I mouth, "Sorry," to Laura who waves a gesture of no-problem. I hop off the picnic table, looking for a clearer signal, getting alternate earfuls of pressing update and static until I'm hovered over the garbage cans. "You can tell Lucas everything about Argentina is in the red binder on my filing cabinet and that I cc'd the Gates Foundation and the U.N."

"And the U.N.," she echoes as she types. "Okay, got it."

"Thank you so much, Hannah." The cell slips in my mitten.

"What?"

"Thank you so much," I repeat, tightening my grip. "I hope you're getting out of there soon."

"A few more hours."

"Well, Merry Christmas."

"You, too. And I hope your mother makes a speedy recovery."

I cringe. "I'll send her your wishes. See you on the third!" I slap the phone shut and hop back onto the table, where Laura greets me with a funny expression.

"What?" I ask, slipping it back in my pocket.

"You cc'd the U.N., Kate." She readjusts her hat, pulling the blue wool over her earlobes. "Jake's a tool."

"Yes, I know. I know." I take a deep whiff of the steeped cinnamon. "The irony being that the more of a tool I think he is, the more insulting-slash-enraging the whole thing becomes. I just want two days ago back. I was *great* two days ago. I had a maybe-sort-of promotion and was starting to see someone who could be a maybe-sort-of boyfriend—"

"The civil engineer?"

"Surprisingly great first date." I flash to the sensation of inquisitive lips on mine.

"Excellent." She cracks the lid of her mug for a moment to let the steam escape.

"Mostly I was living in two thousand five and liking it. And now suddenly I'm Loony McLoonington."

"Because *that's what he does*. He turns sane people into raving turbines of implacable rage." She balls her free fist. "And now my children will grow up and, despite our best efforts, in a town this size, inevitably find out about what Jake stole from their father and then *they* will be the next generation of implacable rage. It just . . ."

"Unless we can get him to right this." We hunch over our mugs and watch Keith and Mick scavenge the snow for twigs around the woodpile to decorate their friend. Or poke into each other's ocular cavities.

"Micky?" Laura calls with forced casualness. He turns from across the lawn, dropping his little head back to see her from under his hood. "Is Keith made of snow?"

Mick turns his hooded vision to his brother. "What?"

"Does he have hands and feet?"

Keith shifts his red hood to check his mittens. "I have hands and feet!"

"Does he melt when he goes inside by the fireplace?"

"He doesn't melt!" Mick erupts into giggles.

"Then he's not a snowman," Laura delivers her summation.

"I'm not a snowman!"

"Which means he doesn't need new ears and eyes."

The two look at her, glossy-nosed and mystified. She slows down her explanation. "Those sticks and rocks go *on the snowman and only on the snowman.*" They return to their foraging around the tarped pile.

"This baby's covered." I smile and pat her belly.

"You're too kind."

"But am I a snowman?"

She chuckles.

"Lor?"

"Yes?"

"Is this okay?" I grip and regrip my mug, unable to meet her gaze.

"What?"

"Can I be doing this?" I shift my feet on the ice-patched bench. "At our age? Is Jeanine right? Shouldn't I have moved on to some alternate state of Zen?"

"Honey, let alone the far-from-minor fact that he set your family tragedy in four-eight time." She cocks her head at me, her blond ponytail swishing over her shoulder. "He came on your tits, wrote a song about it, and won a Grammy. I say you have carte blanche."

"Thanks." I rest my head on her quilted shoulder as we return our attention to the street.

❦

"Sweet potato?" Dad asks across the dinner table. "I was thinking three, but chopped for thirty." When really we're two, each awaiting the sound of a car in the driveway, neither of whom are eating. I stare at the copious Brussels sprouts, neatly stacked, their eight-inch round world perfectly ordered.

"Thanks." I take a spoonful of the rosemary-flecked roasted wedges and add them to my untouched plate as the sound finally comes, followed by the geriatric grind of the garage door lifting, drowning out the classical station. Dad's eyes are trained on the side entrance.

"Hi, everyone." She comes in, stomping her puffy boots intently on the mat and lowering her purse and coat to the wood stepstool. "Okay. So, I've come to some clarity. Kate, no matter what has transpired with this boy, you need closure. I understand that. And you should get it. And we should support you in getting it. And then this will all be over." Wiping her hair off her forehead with the back of her wrist, she walks to us in her worn argyle socks, looking from him to me, her face expectant. Mouth puckered, he taps his fork against the chicken breast grown cold.

"Thanks," I manage to recover from my surprise. "That's great to hear." I stand to fill her wineglass. "Dad made his chicken, if you haven't eaten yet."

"Thank you." She takes a sip, putting the business of her revelation behind her. Dad does not ask where she went to find it as she takes her place and serves herself. "Simon, this looks delicious." Napkin in hand, he pushes his chair back from the table. "Simon?" But, back to us at the cupboards, he doesn't answer. "Simon?" she repeats.

"I've lost my appetite." Napkin still absentmindedly balled in his fist, he pivots against the counter with a box of Wheat Thins. "But, Kate, you should eat something."

"If I was in Charleston I'd be scooping frosting out of the tub by the fistful right now and you'd never know," I say lightly, trying to levitate him.

"If you were in Charleston, we'd be leaving for the trip we paid for. Twice," he mutters into the box.

I stiffen. "You are. Dad, I'll have this thing with Jake wrapped up by the time you're supposed to leave tomorrow morning." Or I won't. And I'll have to spend the rest of my life praying I outlive him so I can pee on his grave.

"Right." Mom nods as she cuts into her chicken. "And we will get on with our Christmas and on with our lives. Kate will be fine—"

"But, she's *not* fine, Claire!" Dad slaps the yellow box

to the counter, crackers scattering. "She's sitting here waiting for Jake Sharpe to call like she's thirteen years old!"

"Dad," I say slowly, trying to pull him back. "I am fine. I mean, obviously, I don't want to be sitting here waiting for Jake Sharpe. I don't want to think about Jake Sharpe, thinking about me, sitting here, waiting for him. And I *especially* don't want *you* watching *me* sitting *here* thinking about Jake Sharpe thinking about me, sitting here, waiting for him." I look to Mom. "I do just want this to be over. O-ver. So let's just please finish our dinner and I will come up with some new plan of action, maybe something involving a snowmobile and some sparklers—"

"How could you just walk out of here and not even *call* us, Claire?" His face instantly furnaces. "And then just waltz in ten hours later and condone the *filth* that little shit has put out there about our daughter? About *you?*" My breath stops to hear him speak of Jake's songs. Mom flushes in turn, her eyes dropping down. "You may be ready to give him a grand-marshal parade, both of you, but he disgusts me. He cannot, *should not* be trusted." His tremoring body is echoed by the rumbling approach of the three thousand, seven hundred and forty-second car. I twist away from their stricken faces as the headlights suddenly flood the kitchen, the black rectangle above the sink turning bright white in the mirror over Dad's empty chair.

The rusted horn lets out an asthmatic bleat, sending me bolting for the side door, bracing myself in the spikingly cold air. *"This* is your version of tomorrow!" I shout at the old Corvette, its headlights stinging my eyes. "You self-aggrandizing, narcissistic fuck!"

The passenger window squeaks down. "Hey, Hollis."

"Sam?" I stop. "Hey!" I run to him as he hops out, lifting me in a big guy embrace that penetrates the no-man's-land that's been keeping this all at a tenable distance. Before I can give way I pull back, drying my eyes. "I saw the boys—God, they're amazing. They're looking more and more like you." Sniffling, I ruffle my hand through his thick blond mop. "God, it's good to see you."

"You okay?" Concerned, he tucks his head down to catch my eye, freckles dotting his wind-burned cheeks.

I lean into his ear. "He's in there, isn't he?"

"You're going to love this." Sam claps his cupped palms, the leather making a hollow *thwack*. "He wants us all to go to the lake."

"The lake." I wrap my arms around myself against the chill. "Is he kidding?"

"He can hear you." Jake lifts himself up and sits on the ledge of his open window. The dead beaver hat is gone, along with the stylist's take on lumberjack, replaced by a thin black Henley. "I thought we'd go skating, the five of us."

"Are you kidding?" I repeat. "You show back up here after thirteen years and you want to take me to the lake?"

"He wants to go skating," Sam kicks his boot heel into the plow drift lining the driveway. "With the band."

"What's wrong with skating? I never get to do it anymore. I thought it'd be fun."

"Fun," I echo as Sam puts a warming arm around me and rubs my shivering shoulders.

"Come on, guys, we love it out there! We had some of our best times at that cabin."

"*Best* times?" I thrust myself out of Sam's embrace. "*Really,* Jake?"

"Sam's down—right, Sam?"

I look up into Sam's face, and he shifts his gaze to the driveway across the street.

"Look, I get it, you're all pissed. Keith and Mick wrote *Jake sucks!* in the snow with twigs—"

"Yeah, that was Laura."

"Fine, I suck. But I'm here. And I've been doing a lot of thinking and I just . . . we should all . . ." He exhales, looking from Sam's face to mine. "It's your call." He slips back in the window and rolls it up.

"She let you get in there with him?" I ask in disbelief as exhaust chugs out of the muffler, dissipating over the pavement.

"If playing twelfth grade is what it takes to get him to sign over our share of the royalties I'll give myself a mullet and sing 'Free Bird.' "

"Okay," I sigh. "Got it."

I head inside to grab my peacoat.

Jake pulls up across from Todd's house, where a Christmas party has filled the street with salt-crusted cars. "Fetch him?"

"Me?" Sam balks. "We're not exactly on the best terms."

"I can't ring his doorbell if he's having a party. It'll cause a fucking riot," Jake retorts wearily, "And then we won't get to spend any time together." Travesty.

"Fine." Sam climbs out and approaches the twinkling house through the mechanized lawn ornaments. He presses the bell, and after a few moments Todd answers, the foyer chandelier revealing his dramatically thinned hair.

"Wow," I whisper. Sam gestures to us. Todd steps out and squints, his face lighting up when he spots the Corvette.

"I thought you'd be flattered," Jake mumbles from the front seat.

"Excuse me?" I rev with alert.

"I thought you'd be flattered."

"You thought I'd be *flattered?*" I lean forward as Todd closes his front door and Sam ambles back down the walk. "Think the peasants on the plains of Mongolia were flattered?"

"What?" He turns to me.

"When they were raped and pillaged by Attila the Hun—think they were *flattered?*"

Sam opens the door, flips the passenger seat forward, and squeezes in next to me. "He said to pull around the corner."

"At your service." We cruise the bend just as Todd comes flying out the side door, hunched, bent-kneed, barn coat flapping, inviting an unfortunate mallard-comparison. He dives into the waiting passenger seat, a pair of skates clutched in his arms.

"Drive. *Drive!*"

Jake belly laughs as he shifts gears and lurches us out into the street. "My God, man, is this the fucking escape from Alcatraz?" He reaches over to pat Todd's pate.

"Katie, hey!" Jake's hand on his gleaming head, Todd leans around the seat, the springs squeaking.

"Hey." I smile awkwardly, not wanting to betray my allegiance to Sam. "You okay?"

"Michelle doesn't know I'm gone."

"I can't believe you bagged Michelle Walker." Jake chuckles, returning his hand to the wheel as we roll across the river.

"Bagged her. Married her. Had two kids with her." His voice flushes with pride. Sam and I exchange silent glances at the shared vision of Michelle's prom triumph, a decade and a hundred pounds ago. Todd turns back to us. "Katie, you look great."

"Thanks. You, too, Todd."

His bare crown tinges crimson. "Michelle has me on Atkins."

Sam turns to me. "We were doing South Beach until Laura got pregnant. You do not want to see a pregnant woman on a low-carb diet."

"My nutritionist makes these seaweed shakes," Jake pipes in as we take a hard left and I careen into Sam. "They're supposed to be prenatal—"

"Fitting," I interrupt and Sam grins.

"They taste like foot," he continues. "But they're supernutritious. Hey! I could have her send Laura a few bottles."

"Thanks, but I'm guessing the only thing scarier than my pregnant wife on a low-carb diet is my pregnant wife trying to suck down seaweed." Or, seven-figure royalty check outstanding, unwrapping a gift basket from Jake Sharpe's nutritionist.

Todd twists in his seat again. "We saw your parents at the kids' pageant, they said you're doing something with the environment?"

"Yeah." I nod. "I'm a sustainable development consultant."

"A what?" Todd asks.

"Basically the way manufacturing operates globally pulls more resources from the planet than it puts back," I explain. "I work with a firm that shows them how to be eco-friendly—self-sustaining."

"And they just comply?" Todd asks skeptically.

"Tax deductions."

Sam snorts, "Of course."

"Fighting the corporate choke-hold on our planet will be the great war of this century," Jake states, the phrase sounding teleprompted. And at the same time eerily like a pamphlet I handed him in tenth grade.

"You said that at the VMAs," Todd exclaims. "Last year when you got that environmental award for promoting . . . what were you promoting?"

"Recycling in high schools."

Todd takes off his coat to remove the reindeer sweater. "That's awesome, Jake." And the vehicle's biggest sycophant is . . . "So, hey, can you autograph something for me to put up at the dealership?"

"He probably has to get his *federales* to clear it first," Sam grumbles, staring out as our headlights illuminate a passing cluster of teenagers, cameras and cell phones primed as they erroneously hike in the opposite direction toward the Sharpe house.

"No, man, of course." Jake glances at Sam in the rearview.

"Great. And something for my nine-year-old, too. She'd love that. I tell her about the band, but I don't think she believes me." He pats his belly with that same self-deprecating expression he always used with Jake.

"What, she doesn't recognize the skinny kid in the photos?" Sam asks.

Todd ignores him. "I display the old bass in my sales office, though. Keep her tuned up and everything."

"We're coming up on the turn to Benjy's folks, right?" Jake seeks confirmation.

Todd straightens. "Yeah, but—"

"Let's just go without him," Sam adds.

Ignoring them, he makes the turn. We pull up in front of the run-down ranch house. "Man, it feels good to drive."

"He's still here?" I peer across the dark yard. Devoid of holiday decoration, the only sign of life inside is a low lamp lit behind the front curtain.

"That's what I heard," Jake affirms.

Sam looks to me. "He Googles," I quip.

"And my mom still lives in this town," Jake huffs, challenging his outsider status.

"If by *live* you mean rack up DUIs," Sam whispers to me.

"Ben's dad's shop went under when the Home Depot opened," Todd adds loudly, drowning out Sam's vicious, albeit true, aside.

Jake honks the horn, its echo fading into silence broken only by the chugging engine. We watch the still house for a response. Finally, someone inside pulls the fabric in the front window back an inch . . . then releases it. The lamp goes out.

"Pass me my jacket?" Jake reaches his arm back.

Sam unearths a brown suede ski parka from between us and hands it up. Apparently no longer concerned with inciting a riot, Jake turns off the ignition and gets out of the car.

Todd pats the dashboard. "I can't believe this thing still runs."

"Jake Sharpe's first car?" Sam scoffs. "His mom probably keeps it swaddled in a diaper in a heated garage. Been to the compound yet?"

"Just for a moment," I admit. "It seemed the same. You know, plus the floodlights."

We watch as Jake skips up the front steps to the listing porch.

"Nah," Todd says as he strokes the maroon Naugahyde. "After Jake's dad split—what was that—like, 'ninety-three?"

"Right after graduation," Sam answers.

"Right, well, like a few years later she started buying

up all the surrounding houses—left the shells, but gutted each one and made it something crazy—stables, a screening room—an indoor pool. Apparently in the summer she shuttles around on a golf cart, going from one building to the next."

"Fucking insane." Sam shakes his head, the thought sliding in a well-worn groove.

"It's so sad."

"What?" Sam turns to me.

"She never wanted to live here—Susan. Jake's dad dragged her from Boston for work and then traveled nine months of the year, leaving her totally alone. And then after all that he gets out and she's somehow . . . stuck. I don't know. It's sad."

"We were in that house as much as you were, Katie. That woman's a bitch."

"Oh, I'm not saying she isn't a bitch. I'm just saying it's sad."

We watch as Jake stops knocking and leans his finger into the bell.

"Well, this isn't awkward at all." I pull my fists up into my sleeves.

Sam hands me his gloves and I slide my hands into them gratefully. "He's here in person instead of sending another letter from his lawyers—it's a start."

"You still at that?" Todd asks, pulling his sweater back on.

"Yes," Sam replies, "We're still *at that*. No thanks to you, you big fucking pussy."

Todd whips around, "I have the number-one chain of dealerships in the state. In the state. So, no, I am not suing the town hero."

"Only because you make more money telling everyone you're still his best friend. I guess this little outing should pay for your retirement."

"You will never win, Sam," Todd's measured salesman tone returns. "His lawyers have lawyers. Let it go, already."

"That money belongs to my kids," Sam snaps.

"Benjy!" Jake shouts from the porch, his breath visible. "Get your sorry ass out here! We're going to the lake!"

The front door flies open and Ben, clad only in boxers and socks, bursts out, paper plate of pizza in one hand, beer can in the other. The old drumming arm winds up—

"What the fuck?!" Jake leaps back, utter disbelief on his sauce-splattered face. Ben seems to consider Jake's question . . . then pelts him with his Bud.

"Shit," Sam and I say in appreciative unison as the can bounces onto the porch, brown liquid pooling in the snow.

"Dude!" Spluttering, Jake backs down the steps, brushing off foam-sprayed gobs of pepperoni and cheese from his torso as Ben reaches in a frenzy for the mail by his feet. "Dude! Benjy, come on!" But Ben, his body taut with rage, follows down the steps, throwing anything he can get his hands on—the welcome mat, a watering can, string-tied recycling.

"Should we lock the doors?" Sam asks gleefully.

Jake leaps into the car just as a bag of garbage slams against the rear window. We peel out, a porch chair smashing on the asphalt behind us.

Breathless, Jake pulls over at the first stop sign. "Jesus Christ." He wipes at the suede. "Anyone have a napkin?" Todd offers up tissues. "Thanks." He pulls a piece of lettuce from Jake's hair. "I mean, what the fuck is his—"

"Do *not* finish that question," I interrupt him.

He winces, but says nothing as he restarts the car.

Seemingly as frustrated as its backseat passengers, the Corvette starts to register protest when Jake makes the turnoff for the lake, drowning out Todd's patter with an ominous grinding. A mile later it shudders to a grateful stop under the skeleton of the towering oaks, a deep silence enveloping us as Jake cuts the engine. I do not want to be here, do not want to get out. Todd squeaks open his door, making a show of stretching his stiff legs. Sam climbs out behind him, but I can't seem to move.

"Cold as balls," I hear Sam mutter. Jake grabs his jacket off the driver's seat before flipping it forward. He extends a hand to me, his forearm bare, his hair ruffled by the wind whipping through the open doors, suddenly looking all of the seventeen I feel. Have been plunged back into. "Come on, Brainy, I'll help you."

I clear my throat, sliding myself away from him and through the passenger door. "I forgot cars came without heat," I muster bravado, stomping feeling into my feet.

"Or windows that roll all the way up," Sam adds.

"Wusses," Jake tosses off, grinning affectionately. "It's good to rough it."

Sam's ribs spread as Jake breaks away, pushing through the knee-deep snow with a six-pack wedged under his arm to unlock the cabin door. "Hey! Grab some wood. Let's get her roaring," he calls from the door as he lights the porch lantern.

"On it!" Todd yells, and Sam follows him to the vestiges of the pile under the eaves.

I lean back against the warm hood, staring at the little house under whose roof, now weighted with snow, I once sought refuge.

Sam manages to coax a smoky fire from the frozen logs before joining Todd on two low beach chairs under a dust-packed wool blanket and producing a bottle of Jim Beam. I creak open my own rusted chair and lower myself, only to be greeted by an icy breeze rising through the crudely joisted floorboards. I extend my hand for the brown bottle as Jake flops down on the hearth's ledge, his skates beside him. "Oh, man." He hops up again, reaching over me. I twist my head to see him tapping the uncooperative power button on the cobwebbed boom box. Finally it lights and he presses PLAY on the tape deck. There's a crackle and then—

"I'm hot, sticky sweet, from my head—"

"To my feet, yeah!" he shouts as three heads immediately dip and rise.

"Pour some sugggggggggggrgghgphm." The tape grinds to

203

a distorted halt, the vocals dipping into a satanic register. Then there's a pop.

I take the bottle from Todd's hand and gulp down a burning shot.

"So, after the plaster dust clears I realize I've blown it." Buzzed, Sam gestures a wide circle with his beer can. "Literally. There's a three-foot hole in the wall where the window's supposed to be."

"I can't believe she never told me." I huddle under the scratchy wool pulled taut to my chin.

"For the first three months of their lives the twins slept under giant garbage bags taped to the wall—"

"Thank God they were born in July." I laugh.

"I know. Can you imagine? Every morning we'd have had to dig 'em out like a car."

"When I got my promotion I decided to splurge and put in a bathtub." Rolling my eyes at the memory, I extend my hand from under the blanket for the bottle as the fire snaps, "So I leave the plumbers doing their thing and head to work. When I come home my toilet is sitting in the middle of the living room." Sam and Todd start laughing, the creases around their eyes deepening. "When I asked the guys what the story was they told me it didn't 'fit' anymore, but that was okay—I could use my 'other' bathroom until they could get a smaller one. I was like, okay, that closet door, there, that does not go to Narnia. This is the whole apartment. There is no other bathroom."

"Oh shit," Sam snorts, "What did you do?"

"For a month I pretty much lived in my office. And I cut my liquid intake waaay down."

"When I had my place in L.A. redone"— At the first sound of his voice in a good hour, I loll my head on the metal bar to look over at Jake. —"the designer put in this koi pond that flows right into my studio 'cause it's supposed to be good for my creative energy." After discussions of skyrocketing car insurance rates, the looming financial burden of aging parents, and DIY, he finally relates. "So, the day it's done, they fill the pond and drop in the fish and it looks great and we have people over and everyone loves it and we all go out to dinner. Right?" We nod. Yes, dinner. We do that. "Anyway, I get home around four in the morning and, I don't know, there was a leak or something, some drainage problem, but the water was almost completely gone and the koi are just flapping and gasping." He flails his torso, mimicking koi in their death throes. "So now I'm shitty drunk and running around trying to find bowls, but I don't know where they keep the bowls, so I'm racing back and forth in, like, total circles just trying to find a bathroom on the ground floor. See if maybe there's one with a tub. But I can't find one. And at this point I'm losing it. I'm trying to get my assistant on the phone. I'm convinced I can hear the fish suffocating. So then I pass this wall of, I don't know— these huge antique Asian-looking container things and I start running them over to my office and trying to get the fish in them. By the end I must have had fifty of them on the floor, just filled with the most fucking grateful fish you've ever seen in your life."

The fire sputters; we sit in the near darkness. The draft renews its strength, filtering in between the planks in the walls and floors, winter restaking its preeminence.

"Early Japanese bronze hand warmers," Todd volunteers.

"What?" Jake asks, extending his legs and brushing off his jeans.

"You put the fish in your nineteenth-century bronze hand warmers," Todd explains, peeling off the Jim Beam label. "You have the largest private collection in the U.S."

"I do?"

"Architectural Digest." He rolls the gummy paper into a tight scroll between his palms.

Gap-mouthed, Sam stares at Todd, incredulous.

"Michelle subscribes." Todd shrugs.

"Eden must've bought 'em." Jake recovers. "She's always buying shit and not telling me. You know."

"Yeah, I hate it when I send Laura to Wal-Mart to pick up a few things and she comes home with a trunkful of Japanese hand warmers." Sam tosses his beer on the last anemic flames and we listen to the sizzle. Stymied, Jake stares into the gray smoke. Todd taps the rolled label into the neck of the emptied bottle.

"Okay, time for a skate!" Jake abruptly swipes the last beer from the floor and throws open the wood door, racing down the steps and across the snow. As we slowly make our way to standing we watch through the doorway as he kicks across the powder to where the lawn slopes, scampering sideways down the bank to the edge of the ice and sitting on the old dock to strap on his skates. He pushes out onto the frozen surface, his legs propelling him away from us. Without breaking stride, he pops open his can, an arc of spray glowing blue in the moonlight. He whoops with joy, his arms wide, spinning, his face turned to the dark sky.

"It's beautiful!" he exhorts.

Todd heeds the siren song, shuffling outside to the car to grab his skates from the front seat before scrambling down the bank. Sam turns his attention back to a mess of equipment in the corner, walking over to lift a deflated inner tube halfheartedly from the floor. I pull the small chain at the base of the nearby buoy lamp, its pool of light enumerating the cracked canoe oars and abandoned swimsuits. He picks up one of the umpteen compressed bottles of Coppertone and shakes it.

"Here," I say, pointing to the corner where Jake has left the lid up on the splintering wooden trunk. Brushing aside the cobwebs I hand off a pair of men's skates.

"Fuck, why not? I bought the ticket, might as well take the whole ride." He resigns himself, tossing the plastic bottle into the canoe. "You good?" he asks from the door.

"Fantastic. You?" We look at each other, two distant relatives at a funeral who can't find the words.

"See you down there?" he finally asks, knocking the doorframe. I nod as he gives a small smile and heads out.

I turn back to digging, lifting skates and snow boots

and waders. Then, at the bottom, I see, not just a smaller pair, but the ones with KATIE written on the side in faded red Sharpie.

In the few minutes it takes me to get laced up, the guys are already crisscrossing each other, cans in hand, athletic activity and alcohol lubricating their overriding masculine desire to just have a good time, to just have it all be okay, to just have it back to when all any of us needed was the proximity of each other.

I step gingerly out, my ankles wobbling before I can find my stride. Then I start taking even glides on the silvery ice, remembering, remembering, remembering how to do this. It darkens and I look up to see a thick cloud cover the moon. I falter—just as hands close in on my hips.

16

TWELFTH GRADE

"Sam, you're supposed to put it on your lap." Laura, carrying the soup tureen into the dining room, provides what one would imagine to be a self-explanatory direction for the napkins she and I painstakingly shaped into Mom's good wineglasses.

Sam shrugs and pulls it off his head, laying the linen over his lap with an extra flourish. Jake laughs, whipping his out of the glass and snapping Sam's nose before draping it over his cords.

"Boys." Laura sets the dish on the table and, smoothing her peasant skirt beneath her, sits.

"I'm starving." Jake looks over the spread she and I have spent the day camped out in my kitchen preparing.

"Music!" I push back my chair and glide to the stereo in the living room. Flipping through Dad's records, I find the Miles Davis and shake it deftly out. The slow bass fills the house—this weekend—*my* house.

"Nice." Jake bobs his head as I return to the table, dimming the chandelier on my way, feeling every bit the fabulous hostess.

"If you're sixty." Sam takes a roll from the basket.

"I'm going to toast." Laura raises her wineglass brimming with Zima. We lift ours to her. "To our lovely host. To her parents' weekend in England. To senior year. To getting through this college bullshit and—"

"Getting out." Jake clinks his goblet against ours.

"Getting laid." Sam's glass reaches out for our retreating rims.

"Sam," Laura groans to remind him that only one couple at this table has cleared the starting gate. My stomach contorts as I avoid Jake's eyes.

"Soup's good." Jake swirls the creamy broth with his spoon.

I lift my own to my mouth—"Ugh, it's not."

"It's not?" Laura dips into her bowl.

"Way salty!" I reach for my Zima and chug it down to no avail.

Laura's lips curl. "Four tablespoons?"

"Four *dashes.*" I push my bowl away.

"Crap." Laura swigs from her glass.

"Four dashes of crap?" Sam delivers straight. "What's the recipe, I wanna give it to my mom." Jake cracks up.

"The chicken's almost ready," I say, not hungry anyway, the looming chaperone-free night zapping my appetite.

"And crap free," Laura adds. I join in their laughter as I enviously study her, for whom the hours ahead are already a known.

• • •

I drop the last plate into the dishwasher, using the counter to steady myself as I lift the door closed. I dance in front of it for a moment, the warmth of my buzz making the music my own. Eyes closed I hear Laura and Sam laughing from the backyard and I can't imagine better than—more than, this.

"What are you smiling at?" At the sound of his voice my eyes drift open in the dim light of the stove hood to see Jake grinning by the side door. "I was going to ask if you wanted to smoke with us, but you seem pretty . . ."

"Perfect." I sway over to him, opening his jacket and pulling it around me. He nods down, his eyes dropping to a sexy slit.

"You are."

It's all I need to curl my fingers into his and, like I've seen in every movie, lead him into the front hall and up the stairs. Walk him to my room, not letting the three generations of family pictures break into the scene. Push open the door and stop in front of the bed with my back to him. The height of myself. Warm from head to toe. Spotlit in the triangle of yellow spilling in from the hall lamp. Jake is behind. His hands at the hem of my dress, gripping it, lifting it up over the length of me. I raise my arms and it is perfect as he slides it up, the last of the cotton grazing my nails. I hear a moan escape as he registers that I stand before him in only the white thigh-highs Laura and I painstakingly picked out at Victoria's Secret yesterday.

Part of me splits off and runs downstairs to tell her that they are perfect, I am perfect, that this is going perfectly. The other part is turned around by Jake who is all warmth and motion and gripping. Then we're on the quilt, seizing skin till we feel the shape of the bones beneath. Pulling at his belt and zipper and cotton to find, to get to—he sits back, jacket still on, eyes wide as he fumbles with a square package, a string of sweat over his lip.

And then we are closer than it is possible.

And then—"Hi," I say as we blink at each other. He squeezes his arms around me, wrapping me in his jacket for a second time. I feel him open his mouth against my hair. Car headlights arc across the ceiling as someone passes.

"What?" I pull my head back to focus on his face, his beautiful face, his expression earnest, about to divulge—what? "What?" I repeat.

And I'm hit with a wall of vomit.

I stand in the shower and stare at the curtain, now more sober than it is possible. This is the scene they never show—the newly de-virginized Julia Roberts rinsing puke out of her thigh highs. And what is the perfect thing to do now? What are the chances I can sneak in and wake Laura? What are the chances Laura, herself, is covered in puke? That this is the part of the sex nobody talks about? I'll just stay in here till I think of something to say. Like, how about getting up from my fucking sheets so I can wash off the contents of your stomach before I have to sleep in them?

I reach my hand out for a washcloth and scream when it meets Jake's jacket. I pull the curtain and peek out.

"Sorry! Sorry." Still fully dressed, he steps back uncertainly.

"Have you been standing there this whole time?"

He stares at the ceiling like he wishes it would zap him into vapor. "I was going to go, but I don't know if that's . . . Then I thought I should stay. Then I came in here to tell you . . . I don't know what."

"Okay!" I nod helpfully, water dripping down my face.

"This . . ."

"You want to disappear?" I ask, licking the drips as both hands are occupied gripping the curtain in a frame around my head.

"Yeah, yes I do." He nods at the ceiling.

"Look, it's not the end of the world."

"Not the end of the world? We made love and then I yakked all over you."

"Made love?" I repeat.

"Yeah," he sighs, shrinking in his jacket. "And I yakked."

"So what? So, you yakked." I shrug.

"So, you've been in there for like an hour."

"I didn't know what to do next," I say honestly.

"Me neither." His face contorts. "Shit, I can still smell it."

"It's on your shirt." I point the curtain out at his congealing flannel.

"You want me to leave and never bug you again?" He drops his head.

"You mean kill yourself?"

"Or that."

"No, Jake Sharpe, I don't want you to kill yourself." A smile breaks on his tense face. "You might as well come in here and rinse off while I figure out the right way to handle this."

"Shit, you're trying to figure out how to handle me?" He picks off his clothes and drops them into a heap in the corner.

"For years." I step back under the spray.

"Any ideas?" He opens the curtain and steps inside, pulling it closed before standing like a sad little bronze medalist, shoulders hunched.

"Still in here, aren't I?" I wave for him to move under the water and we switch sides. "Soap?"

"This is weird," he says, taking the bar.

"You're weird," I say, leaning back against the cool tile.

"Shut up." He laughs.

"Or what," I giggle, relaxing. "You'll puke on me?"

❦

"What's up with the birdhouses?" Jake asks, pointing to the row of brightly painted seed-filled chalets lining the porch.

"Dad's gotten into making them since the research center shut down. They give him what my mother calls a productive outlet. Here, hold this," I say to Jake, handing him the bundled mail as I fumble with my keys on the porch. "See if my Dartmouth application's in there."

He flips through the catalogs, extracting an envelope. "Nope, but here's UVA." I push the front door open into the almost equally cold front hall and we stomp the snow off our boots. The warble of Judge Wapner greets us from the back of the house as I swivel the thermostat up to sixty-five. "I bet my basement's really warm right now. I bet it's toasty."

"Shut up." I laugh. "One afternoon here isn't going to kill us." We unlace our boots, kicking them onto the mat by the door. Jake goes to hang our coats on the pegs, giving in to his routine compulsion to hold my sixth-grade Venetian mask up to his face.

"The Phaaaaaaaantom of the Opera is here," he belts. He bites my neck and I squeal. Swatting him, I deposit the rejected mail, UVA envelope included, on the hall table. "Admit it, you've missed the mask."

Jake circles his arms around me in response, pulling me into a kiss.

Reluctantly I break away, keeping hold of his hand. "Let's just say a quick hi and then we can go upstairs and study." I raise my eyebrows suggestively, letting the tip of my tongue protrude from beneath my top teeth.

He makes a low growl as he follows me through the swinging door to the empty kitchen. "Dad?" I call out. The large stainless pasta pot teeters on the stove, its bottom blackening above the flame. Switching off the burner, I grab a dishtowel to lift the lid, a blast of steam revealing that the water has boiled out. The open package of lasagna noodles lays strewn on the butcher block alongside a gummy red ring of paste where the top has been taken off the can. I reach for the sponge to wipe up the smattering of green spice flakes from the open bottles. "Dad!" I call again.

Jake remains by the doorway, hand holding his fist. "The den?"

Darting past him I follow the sound of the television to where Dad's splayed in the armchair, as if he hasn't moved a muscle since I left for school.

"Dad?"

He rolls his head to gaze at me, his eyes red-rimmed.

My stomach twists in on itself. "Dad, the water boiled down."

"What?" he asks dully.

"The water," I repeat, trying to figure out what it is that isn't registering for him, my words or my presence.

"Oh." He looks baffled for a moment before dragging the worn afghan from the arm of the chair and laying it over his corduroys. He reaches for the remote and turns up the volume, but misses the table's edge as he goes to return it, the device clattering to the floor. The plastic panel breaks off the back, sending the batteries rolling along the wood to my loafers.

"Bugger," he sighs.

I swipe up the Energizers and broken remote and step in front of the television. "Dad, Mom's going to be home in, like, ten minutes."

His eyes drift closed.

"Okay, so Jake and I are just gonna, yeah." I leave him

with the blasting TV and return to the kitchen, greeted by the smell of scorched steel.

"Is he okay?" Jake still hovers in the doorway.

"I don't know. No." I go to the window over the sink and push up the pane. "I just don't get it. How someone can go from being fine, from being a fine person, to . . . Listen, maybe you should just go home, tonight's not really—"

"I can help." He darts to the window by the broom closet and lifts it an inch, a cross-breeze sweeping past me. "It's not like I'm missing dinner with the Cosbys."

"Right," I say, not wanting my father to be the reason he eats alone. "Okay." I open the fridge and toss him a tomato. He catches it like a fly ball as I pull out an armful of salad fixings.

"What do you want me to do?"

I glance at the stove clock before sliding him the plastic cutting board and a paring knife. "Chop like you mean it."

I'm dumping the spaghetti into the colander when the garage door purrs open. I drop the pot back onto the stove and jog over to stick my head around the den doorway. "Dad." Immobile beneath the afghan, he gives no indication of having heard her car or me. I step to the television and hit the power button. "Dad! *She's home.*"

"Hello!" Mom trills. "Something smells delicious." I swing back around the doorjamb to where, hand gripping her knit hat, she pauses in a teapot silhouette to take in Jake standing over the stove in her apron. "Hi, Jake. Where's Simon?"

"Here," Dad answers, stepping heavily in behind me in his leather slippers.

Unzipping her coat I watch her eyes go from his patchy stubble to the rumpled shirt he was wearing yesterday to the jam splotches on his trousers. Without ceremony, he crosses to the table and folds into his chair.

"It's almost ready, Mrs. Hollis," Jake says with an enthusiasm that makes me want to marry him, sliding the spatula around the rim of the blue cast-iron pan.

"So how was the Amherst meeting?" she asks, pulling a bottle of wine from the rack along with the opener.

"Well," I begin as she walks to the table and places the bottle heavily in front of Dad with a dull thud, extending the opener to him. "The school sounds great, but—" He doesn't move. I look to Jake.

"But by the time the recruiter finished describing it," he steps in. "It sounded like all twelve students come over to her house every night to have dinner and watch *Jeopardy*."

"It's small." Carrying the wooden salad bowl to the table, I pull out a carrot sliver and pass it to her. She pops the orange disk in her mouth, giving me a small smile of gratitude for the gesture as she busies herself with the bottle of Chianti.

"Great!" Jake proclaims, "Done." He starts ladling the sauce onto the noodles and I ferry them to the table.

Mom swipes a finger into her bowl as she sits. "Mmm. Jake, your mother taught you well."

"Actually, my mom's not big into that stuff." He shrugs, untying her apron to sit. "But our cleaning lady—Jackie—this is one of her standards." He slides into his seat and we tuck in, reaching for salad and bread and cheese. Dad's hands remain slack in his lap as he stares into the middle distance, prompting me to draw out my AP Bio test into a five-minute anecdote, acting out every stumping question, and Jake, following my example, reenacts Sam blowing a fuse trying to set up for last week's Sweet Sixteen at the country club.

"What did you do today, Simon?" Mom breaks in.

"I laid some more glue traps in the attic," he says, gaze still unfocused, wiping his clean mouth with his napkin. "And then after lunch it occurred to me it'd been years since I'd seen *The Man Who Would Be King,* so I rented it."

"Oh, I'd love to watch that again." Mom gives a thin smile, taking a sip of her wine. "Katie, if you finish your homework, you and Jake should watch it with us. It's a classic."

"Sure, if we get our homework done."

"I watched it this afternoon."

"Oh," Mom says, sucking in her cheeks.

"So," I rush. "The regional debate championships are right after Christmas break and I have the permission slip—"

"Did you hear back from anyone today?" she asks over me, regripping the delicate rim of her wineglass with her fingertips.

Scraping his chair, he stands and shuffles away from the table.

"Simon?"

"No." Rifling the cupboard, he extracts the canister of oat crackers.

"What about the man who told you to call him this week?"

"It's only Wednesday." Slouching back into his seat, he pulls out a round biscuit, methodically breaking it in halves and then quarters. "He said *middle* of the week. I don't want to seem desperate."

"I heard today there's an opening at the library with Disalvo's departure," Mom keeps on, trying, but failing, for breeziness, "Wouldn't that be a good fit for you?"

He crumbles one of the quarters back into oats. "I am an educational researcher. *Maybe* I could go back to teaching. I am *not* a librarian."

"So," I jump in. "The debate competition runs for two days over a weekend and the best people in the northeast will be there. I'm really nervous." I scan my brain for an amusing, yet long-winded, debate practice story that will buy us some time to finish eating and get away from this table. "I told you how Denise and I were practicing with, oh, this is funny, you guys are gonna laugh, we were—"

"How much is it?" Mom asks, her eyes still on Dad.

"What? I don't know. For the room and gas and the entrance fee and meals, I think, altogether, a hundred?"

"I'll have to let you know after break." Miserable, Mom stabs at her salad. "We'll have to see if we can afford it."

"But," I stammer, "if we make it to nationals I won't be eligible. It's my last year."

"I can give you the money," Jake says quietly, as if somehow meaning for only me to hear.

"See, Simon?" Mom's face curdles further. "See what happens?"

"Jake's just joking," I scramble. "Oh my God, Jake, it's okay. Guys, it's fine. I don't have to go. Let's just talk about it later, okay?" I plead.

We sit in awkward silence as Dad presses his fingers to the oat flakes wedged into the weave of his placemat, transferring them to his napkin one by one. Jake glances at the clock. "Hey, Mr. Hollis, the Bruins game starts in five minutes. Wanna watch?"

"I'd like that," he says, unexpectedly perking up.

"Great, I'll bring you dessert," I encourage as Jake half rises and Dad takes the tartan tin to the den. "Enjoy the game! *Thank you,*" I mouth as Jake follows with his glass of milk.

When I look back two thin streams of tears are slipping down her face.

"Mom?"

"He's got to get it together." She takes a deep breath, drying her cheeks with her napkin. "With your tuition next year . . . I just don't know, Katie, I don't know *how.*" She rests her forehead on her fisted napkin. I scoot my chair over and touch her shoulder. She leans into my hand, her soft hair slipping across my wrist.

"I'll go back to Ms. Hotchkiss and tell her scholarships are the first priority."

She blows her nose. "I want you to be able to go wherever you want to go."

I find a smile. "I want to be a blonde—we can't all have what we want, right?"

She laughs for a moment before her own smile evaporates. Two whoops of joy shoot out of the den as the puck goes into play.

※

So groggy I could easily slip into a coma if I could only put my head down on the particleboard desk, I stumble out of sucky AP History. The tedium of that man droning on about the Corn Laws is so intense I don't see how I'd get any less out of it if they just put headphones on my prone body. As I twist my locker combination I calculate—a forty-minute study hall gives me thirty to do a week's worth of journal entries, three to finish Spanish, and a full seven minutes to crank out the lab report. Fantastic!

"Fine. Don't say hi to me."

I spin to see Laura's departing backpack.

"Hey!" I jog to catch up, but she makes no effort to wait. "I'm dying of exhaustion."

"I'll throw a pity party for you." She speeds up, her half-cowboy boots scuffing the linoleum.

"Hey, what's wrong?" I grab her shoulder.

"Nothing." She jerks it away, her backpack slinging forward.

"Nothing?"

"Hate to bore you."

"I'm standing here asking you." We're pushed together by kids squeezing by on both sides.

She pulls a hair off her sweater, avoiding my eyes. "I'm gonna be late for gym."

"Since when do you care about being late for gym?"

"Like you'd have noticed."

"What's wrong?"

She pushes out her lips. "Nothing. Not that you'd care, but I just had my meeting with Ms. Hotchkiss."

"And . . ."

"Oh, it was great! Yeah, she thinks I should be *realistic* about my expectations." Water spills over the rim of her navy lashes and she blinks. The bell rings and a football thug lurches between us to dive into class. "Shit." She throws her hands up. We're alone in the hall.

"Come on." I take her arm. She breaks into fluid sobs. *"Come."* I tug and she follows; we race through the empty halls, our backpacks' contents shaking heavily from side to side. We dart through the corridor linking the two buildings to the first secluded spot on school property: the stairs to the balcony of the middle school pool. At the landing I drop to the cement and push backward into the alcove, pulling her down next to me. We sit and catch our breath for a few moments before she breaks out into fresh tears, dropping her head onto my shoulder.

I squeeze her hand. "It's okay."

"No, Katie, it's not. You're, like, practically married to Jake and you two are all like fucking soul mates now and will probably go to some perfect Ivy League somewhere and all Sam can talk about is how that stupid band tape they've been sending out to everyone is going to get them discovered or some shit. Meanwhile I need to be *realistic* because my boards were, quote, *mediocre* and my activity list is, quote, *frankly* mediocre. Hi!" She attempts cheerful through her tears, "Laura Heller, your frankly mediocre candidate!" She swipes her free hand under her streaming nose.

"Laura, you're not mediocre! You're going to get in everywhere! You interview so well! And your grades are really solid—"

"Translation: mediocre."

"Compared to who? Dana Dunkman? Come on, don't let Hotchkiss get to you like this. She makes everyone feel like shit. That's her title, Shit Adviser. She and my mother are on some shared mission to ship me down to Duke or UVA, some stupid southern—"

"You met with her already?" She withdraws her hand from mine.

"Tuesday. Tuned the entire thing out. I just remember the South part 'cause it was the height of her crazy."

She stares past me at the semicircle of dust-caked ficuses. "Why don't I know you did that?"

"What do you mean? It's no big secret."

"I bet Jake knows. I bet he knew right after the meeting."

I have to think about it. "I guess . . ."

"What's happening to us?"

"Nothing."

"Fuck you." She reaches for her bag, and so tired by all of it, I'm suddenly sputtering in the chlorine-soaked air.

"*Laura!* I have a million fucking things to do, that's

what's happening! In addition to the full-time job of keeping my parents from being total assholes to each other, I'm doing a zillion hours of homework, and debate, and these interviews, and getting these applications and trying to keep up with all of it, but really just going through the motions because I finally got Jake, but all of a sudden everything's telling me I'm just supposed to go off to college and have this great life and forget all about it—"

"But this is it, Katie," she interrupts me, her voice heavy.

"I know."

"I mean, this time next year we'll all be—"

"I know that," I cut her off.

"You and me, too."

"It's different."

She twists the claddagh ring Sam gave her for her birthday. "It's not."

"We're best friends! It's not like we're going to date other people, marry other people. Nothing's going to change the fact that you've been my best friend since that ass-freezing Indian hop." Her lips break into a small smile. "Hell, I'll strip down right now and do a commemorative lap if you need proof."

"Please, no."

"Then stop, okay?" She nods against my shoulder. "Wherever it all ends up, you and me are a team deal." I reach in my bag and hand her a napkin.

Laura laughs and blows her nose. "I guess I am losing it if I'm thinking Jake Sharpe's getting into an Ivy. Like he wouldn't be a pig in shit playing in the back of a bar for the rest of his life."

"So would Sam." I'm surprised by the defensiveness that flares.

"We should become pool sharks," she says, her humor returning.

"That would definitely keep the family together."

"The kids could bartend." She snorts.

"I'm in." I fumble around my bag and find another napkin. She dries her face while I rest my head back against the tiles, wishing I could just know already.

🜋

"Dad," I whisper from where I crouch by their bedside. *"Dad!"*

"Yeah." He grunts awake. "Katie. What now?"

"When did you become a citizen? What year?" I try to keep the flashlight steady with my chin so I can write as neatly as possible on the application.

"Jesus." His breathing starts to deepen.

"Dad! Come on. When did you become not-British?"

"Sixty-eight." Mom's voice cuts into the darkness from the far side of the bed. "How is it that you are officially doing this at the zero hour?"

"Great, you're up—you've got a what in ed?"

"I *have* an M.S." she corrects my grammar.

Pen poised. "What?"

"M.S.! M.S. in ed, Kathryn! When does this have to be postmarked?"

"Uh," I write *M.S.* "Tonight. But this is it. I was just

heading to the copy store and saw this bunch of questions on the back page of the Swarthmore application. Right, so Dad speaks how many languages?"

Silence. I take the flashlight from under my chin and direct the beam into Mom's glaring face, her arms crossed tightly over the jacquard bedspread, each of their rigid bodies at polarized edges of the mattress.

"Mom? Dad?!" I nudge him with my knee. "Dad!"

"Huh? What?"

"How many languages do you speak?"

"Three, for God's sake."

"Great. Thank you. Great. Great!" I flip through the paper-clipped pages. ". . . And we're not agnostic." I check the box. ". . . And Mom never fought in the army." Check again.

"I'm going to if you miss this deadline."

I flip the pages over and slide the application in my backpack, dropping the flashlight on top because there's no time to put it down. "Cool! Great! Thanks. So, sweet dreams. Back as soon as I get these in the mail." I race out.

"And copied!"

"Mom, I know!"

"I'm not impressed!" she yells as I jog down the stairs.

"Good thing you're not Swarthmore!" I call back as I slam the front door behind me.

Screeching into the parking lot I drive full speed up to the clump of cars in front of the Mail Boxes Etc. 10:57.

Totally doable. Three copies of everything and done. I turn off the ignition, grab my backpack, and slam the door with my butt, all while taking in what looks to be the majority of the senior class camped in sweaty-faced clusters around the two copiers. Fuck.

I stare at the fluorescently illuminated chaos. The glass door swings open and JenniferTwo walks out, pulling her Hamilton hat on.

"Really bad?" I ask as she approaches.

"Ridiculous." She nods wearily. "And the second machine just broke. So . . . lucky I got here at nine."

"You've been here since nine?"

"Yeah. Got here right after Jake." She slides her keys out and jangles them.

"Jake's in there?"

"Over there." She nods toward his Corvette, parked away from the others, headlights still on. "Later." She unlocks her Honda and drops into the driver's seat, Tone Loc blasting as she backs up. Stepping out of her way, I see Jake sitting on the pavement in front of his car.

I walk over, buttoning my coat. "Jake?" Getting closer I see papers spread out over his hood, motionless in the still night. He taps at the pavement with his fingers, legs crossed, Burton hat pulled low. "Jake." I crouch down, but he doesn't look up. "What are you doing out here?"

His beautiful face is vacant as he nods to some drumbeat only he can hear. "Nothing."

"You been sitting here since nine?"

He continues to nod steadily, his expression blank. Standing back up, I look down at the Common Application forms, recognizing Susan's handwriting every-where.

"Your mom filled out all of this?" I pick one up. "So then you just have to stick it in the mail, right?" He doesn't respond. "Where's the essay?" I shuffle the papers, but there are no copies attached. "Jake, I thought you've been working on this all month?" Now I am my mother. I pull back my sleeve to check my watch. "Jake, come on, talk to me. I have to do my own shit, too, you know."

"Couldn't do it." His words come out in foggy puffs.

I crouch to hear him. "What?"

"I couldn't do it." He lifts his eyes to mine. "I don't want this. I couldn't do it."

"I have to get my stuff copied," I plead for this not to be happening.

"Go," he says.

"But, Jake—"

"Go."

I rip open my bag's zipper, the bundles of applications sitting inside. I glance back at the line. Fuck. I grab the stack from the hood, pull out my pad, and turn to a fresh page, simultaneously throwing open the passenger door. "Get in."

"Katie."

"Jake Sharpe, you are five hundred words away from getting this shit done like everyone else. We have fifty-eight minutes at ten words a minute, so you talk, I'll write, but I swear to God I'll run you over myself if you don't get into the car right now so my fucking fingers don't freeze! Move!" I bop him on the head with the notebook and he pushes up to standing and slides in, lifting himself over the gearshift to the driver's seat. I tuck in beside him and slam the door against the first flakes of a fresh snow. "Okay! Here we go." I sort through the applications, scanning for the essay question. "What person or experience has been the most influential to you and why?"

He clicks off the lights and stares at the steering wheel.

"Jake, come on." I hand off the questions and tap the notebook with my Bic. "What person or experience?" He opens his mouth . . . and closes it. "Okay, skiing. How about skiing? Or lizards? That trip to Arizona? Or the band? The band works. Do the band—"

"You," he interjects quietly.

"What?"

"You." He swivels in the bucket seat. "Are the single most influential person, or experience, in my life."

Astonished, I lean to kiss the ridge of his knuckles resting on the gearshift. "Thank you," I breathe, before forcing myself to return to the responsibility of our reality. "But, Jake, you can't do that—they don't want to hear about me."

"Well, that's what I have to say." He takes the pen from my hand and starts scrawling directly on the application. I sit beside him, unable to get out of the car, take my place on the copier line, move this whole process toward its completion. "*Central* America, right?" he checks, glancing over at me uncertainly.

"Yes." I smile.

"She taught me you have to stand up, all the way up, on a desk, for what you believe in . . ." he scribbles furiously. "Katie?" He looks up.

"Yes."

He leans over, his lips meeting mine. "Thanks."

※

Denise Dunkman pulls her Nissan into our driveway and I reach for my seat belt. "Great!" I say, unhooking myself.

"I just don't know how this happened," she says for the three hundredth time since we arrived this morning at the empty parking lot of Smithton High, off by a full week for the Regional Debate Competition.

"Seriously, it's okay, Denise," I say again. "I repeat: I'm happy not to sleep at that creepy motel tonight."

"But I wrote it in my calendar, I double-checked the materials," she continues to re-review her erroneous plan. The last three hours on the highway apparently not having turned up any satisfying answers for her.

"I believe you."

"I just don't know how this happened."

"This will be like our practice run, okay?" I give her a quick hug and grab the door handle, eager to exit this Beckett-esque loop. She continues to shake her head as I step onto the snowy pavement, the silence of our street a welcome break from her Edie Brickell tape—a tape I was quite fond of at seven o'clock this morning. I tug my overnight bag from behind the seat and heave it onto my shoulder, feeling the stiffness of the six-hour round-trip when I stand to slam the door.

"I wrote it in my calendar! I double-checked the materials!" she shouts from inside the airtight vehicle, and I smile and nod. Waving good-bye as I cross in front of her receding headlights, I see she's still shaking her head, as she will be on Monday and, I'd bet, when we make the drive again next weekend. Note to self: bring tapes. Or a mallet.

Trudging up to the porch I see a car parked in front of the garage. Ugh, company. Completely drained from the buildup of competition adrenaline that fueled the first half of the day, I'm way too tired to be cordial.

I turn the handle and lean into the door, but it doesn't give. Dad's visiting Uncle Daschle in Dorset. Did Mom go out with a friend and lock the door? Shit. I move backward down the steps, hoping I brought my key, looking up to confirm that the lights are on upstairs. They are. I ring the bell just as the door pulls in and Mom steps onto the threshold, her hair tousled. "Katie." She blinks at me, the collar of her dress tucked under.

"Hey." I drop my duffel to the porch and arch my back. "The regionals weren't until next weekend." But she doesn't step aside. And her feet are bare, not even slippers on.

"Um . . ." I look over her shoulder to see someone coming down the stairs. A man I don't know. I go numb. I am not supposed to be here—not supposed to see this—know this. "Katie," she says again, stricken, but still not moving.

"I just wanted to take the car," I say, suddenly needing an excuse to come into my own house. They both stare at me, her in the doorway, him halfway down the steps, a tie hanging limply in his hands. I ignore it, trying to make him a plumber, an exterminator, someone with a reason to be upstairs that is not—is not—

"This is—" She goes to make the introduction, but I push past her, diving to the side as she reaches to touch me.

"I'm taking your keys." I swipe them off the side table, cool metal filling my palm.

"Katie," she says with false calm. "This is Steve Kirchner. He teaches at the middle school and just came by—"

"I'm taking the keys," I say again, because it's all that comes to mind that does not grant approval or even acknowledgment. I scramble away through the kitchen toward the garage, where the door whirs to life as I start the engine and hurl the car into reverse. But I can't. I can't go because his car is in the middle of the driveway. I shift into neutral, leaving the engine running to open the side door and call shakily into the house, "Can you move your car, please?" I fumble to unhook the plastic lid of the garbage can before vomiting up my rest-stop lunch.

"Sure. Yes. Definitely." He steps quickly past, his cologne filling my nostrils as I wipe my mouth on the sleeve of Dad's university blazer, and in moments his car has backed up, muffler pumping gray fumes beneath the streetlamp as he hovers. Hovers and does not go.

I rev her car backward until it is in front of his and shift gears to leave. It is only then that she comes down the porch stairs calling my name, the border of abandoned birdhouses at her bare feet. I don't look back to see what his car does next.

My hand knocks against the Sharpes' front door. I watch the steady motion of it back and forth, like those windup things they put over babies' cribs to keep them distracted. *Knock, knock, knock.* And then Jake is there and I fall into him, against him, my knees giving way as I try to get out what has just happened—that everything in my life that was the before him will now be the before *this,* and I am in the early minutes of the rest of it, the After. My first memory of the After will be this very moment beneath the yellow glow of Susan Sharpe's glass lanterns.

"Sshshhh, Katie," he murmurs softly. Bending to keep hold of me as I crumble, he pulls my body up and into him as tightly as he can. I push my face into his sweatshirt, try to meld myself all the way into his bones, my mouth open, sound barely coming out as I gasp. "It's okay. It's okay, Katie."

I lift my chin and look up, try to burrow into his worried eyes. "My mom," I try. "My mom . . ." He rocks me into him on the cold brick, as I gasp and sob and try to form a sentence that will name this.

• • •

I wake on Jake's chest, both of us wrapped together in all the blankets he was able to find in his cabin. My sore eyes focus over the scratchy wool, into the glowing embers of the fire, before I'm blinded by the image of Mom immobile in our front door. Hot tears begin again, sliding down my cheek and onto Jake's bare skin, slipping around his ribs. He inhales deeply, tightening his hold on me. "Hey there," he murmurs. "Awake again, huh?"

"Hi," I say, running my tongue along the wetness lining my mouth as he strokes my hair. I lift my head to look at him, his own eyes red-rimmed in the firelight. I reach up and touch the salt tracks on his cheekbone. "You okay?" I ask.

"Yeah," he says, shaking off my hand. "Just sad. It's sad." He runs his hands over me.

"I don't get how we got here." I blink up at the ceiling, an image of her kissing Dad at his birthday last August seizing my chest. "My whole life she's always been fucking on about fortitude and loyalty, and it's all bullshit, everything she stands for is bullshit. My dad falls apart for a few months and she just fucking cuts."

"Shhh," he says gently, though his eyes are welling and I realize I'm officiating at the funeral of his escape family, but I can't stop.

"How can I trust anything now?" The tears come faster. "How can I trust *anything* they say or do? Why did this have to happen, Jake?"

"I don't know." He rubs my back through the blanket. "Why is my mom like she is? Why does my dad travel all the fucking time? I don't know."

"I don't know either." I roll onto my side facing him in the crook of his arm and he rests his hand on my hip, pulling me closer to kiss my forehead.

"Because they suck?" he offers.

"Yeah." I manage a laugh before biting my lip. "What did you do when your mom ran into that tree? Where did you put it?"

"I don't know. She just . . . I just sat on the floor by her bed all night and felt like shit and then, I don't know . . . it doesn't stay this bad. Just at first."

"Really?" I ask, needing him to know, deciding he does.

"Really." He looks at me and the broken in him resonates with the broken in me. "Right now you're just on the floor at the end of her bed, that's all, Brainy. Sun's still gonna rise."

"But I hurt so much." I slide my hands around myself. "Everywhere, it hurts." He gently lifts my fingers and lowers his head. I feel his warm lips on my side, over my ribs. He moves his mouth up my skin, along my neck, and to my lips.

"It doesn't have to. I don't want it to," he says, his face just above mine. He kisses my cheekbone, the bridge of my nose, circling his soothing warmth around my eyes. I close them as I weave my fingers into his hair.

I awake to the sound of a car engine turning off, the cabin filled with the blue light of early dawn. Nausea envelops me as I unhook Jake's arm to stand and step over him to peer out the window where Dad's car is parked at the top of the road. The headlights go out. I shakily pull on my wrinkled black dress pants and push my feet into my loafers, shrugging Dad's blazer over my skin, the smoky scent of last night's fire puffing up from the fabric as I unlatch the door.

Upon seeing me, she gets out of the car and I pull the cabin door closed, silently replacing the latch. Still only in her dress, her arms wrapped around herself, she is surprisingly small beneath the towering oaks. I descend the steps, my loafers crunching the white down. I cannot—do not want to see this her. The her of the After.

Her breath fills the space between us in a visible cloud. "Katie." She is hoarse, her face swollen, raw, and I will the cold to fill me up, allow no room for feeling. "Laura told me about the cabin. I couldn't stand the idea of you out, driving around with this . . ." She breaks into tears I can't let in. "He won't talk to me, Katie, he won't let me help. I don't know how to make him better. I don't know how to make him employed. I don't. I've applied to jobs in Burlington, Boston even, wherever, whatever he wants, but he won't *do* anything. These last few months I've been trying, you have no idea how hard I've been trying." I gird my whole body not to throw myself into her embrace, let her make this better, the familiarity of her, the most familiar I know. "And then to have someone want to make me laugh, it just . . ."

Our eyes meet. "You have to tell him."

She reaches out, but I step from her. Her gaze flickers, swiveling me to where Jake leans in the doorway cloaked in a blanket, face tight with concern. "I'm not going back until you do," I say, retreating to the cabin, my shoes retracing their tracks.

"Katie," her voice is thick with tears. *"Katie."*

I push myself up the steps, buckling into Jake's arms.

17

December 23, 2005

Abruptly the lid of clouds is lifted and the pendant moon once again illuminates our converging and diverging paths on the ice. His touch slips away.

I slice to a halt, a spray of flakes arcing, the famous lyrics of her arrival that morning, which I am forever keeping at bay, flooding me. *And shielded in his blazer, razored against your skin, you walk down the steps, but you won't let her in, the one who made you, and broke you——*

"Dude, we're going up!" Sam shouts as he picks up his skates and starts hiking back up the white bank.

"Should probably head back!" Todd adds as he finishes lacing his boots on the log bench and follows. I rest my hands on my thighs, steadying myself as Jake throws a thumbs-up to the hill, atop which the house I hid in for days erodes against Jake's immortalization of the event.

"Ready?" He slices past me toward the dock. I take off in a hard fast loop, pushing into the wind as I cut along the perimeter of the overhanging tree limbs, with every slicing stride reassigning my rage from the excruciating imagery of that album to its creator.

We pull up at Todd's house behind the few remaining cars. Someone has left a knit hat on the electric snowman. "Katie, it was great to see you." Todd reaches back to pat my knee.

"You, too," I say.

"Sam," Todd acknowledges.

"Todd." Sam nods wearily.

"And I'll have my guy send you those autographs," Jake reassures as Todd grabs him in a bear hug, his hands slapping against Jake's suede.

"Thanks, man." The dashboard lights illuminate Todd's beaming profile as he opens the car door, collapsing the passenger seat forward for Sam to boomerang around. "Merry Christmas, guys."

Jake parallels with the curbside snowbank at Sam's house. It's dark save the kitchen window throwing a low light onto the garage, the sheer plastic walls of the partially completed addition above billowing in the breeze. He shuts the engine off again.

"Cool." Sam swings the door open. "I'll just run inside and get the papers."

"Sam," Jake catches his wrist. "Man, you know I can't. I wish I could. But the label owns the songs—"

"Fuck you," Sam spits, pulling his arm away, before letting out a long breath. "Or fuck me, right, Jake? Fuck me for thinking that playing Reunion would get you to pony up."

"I wasn't playing."

"You said you'd been doing some thinking."

"I have—*for years!* I've missed you guys! I feel like shit for losing touch. I can't believe the boys are three already—they do look just like you. It's awesome, you and Laura—just awesome."

"That's . . . that's what you have to say to me?" Sam stares at him, his jaw clenching.

Jake's eyes drop to his lap. "I miss you, man."

Sam pivots to me and I mirror his disbelief. "Well, Jake, I'm sorry," he says slowly, nodding as he speaks. "That must have been hard for you." Another deep breath, a smile of incredulity. "But I was right here. I own one of those telephone things. I even fly. So . . . yeah." He swings his legs out onto his driveway. "It must be something, Jake. To be where you are."

"Where's that exactly?" he asks quietly to Sam's back.

"Wherever it is you made a decision to keep us from being there with you." Sam slams the door behind him so hard the window rattles. As he stalks up the driveway Jake suddenly revs off, sending me flailing back against the bucket seat, an empty beer can lurching to the floor with a hollow pip. I brace myself against the ceiling as we race past a stop sign.

"*Jake!*" I scream.

He screeches to a halt at the side of the street. "Get up front."

"It's safer back here, thanks."

"Dammit!" He slams the steering wheel. "It's not that simple. You know it's not that simple, right?"

I suck in my cheeks, my eyebrows lifting.

He spins around, craning to the side of his headrest. "Crediting them at this point is just *not* possible. The label's lawyers have said no fucking way."

"Please," I cut him off, my fury spiking. "How you can sit there and feel you don't owe—"

"What?! What do I owe everyone?!" He throws his hands up. "It was *my* vocals that got that scout out here— to watch some stupid garage band."

"That stupid garage band helped you write some pretty fucking amazing music," I sacrifice admission of my opinion to make my point.

"None of you have any idea what it's like out there. They never would have made it—they would have fucked up their whole lives."

I hold his gaze. "Well, how incredibly selfless of you to save them from fame, fortune, and their very own koi ponds."

He closes his eyes for a second, shutting me out. "He didn't want them," he says evenly.

"Who?"

"The scout. It was me, solo. Or nothing. I didn't know how to tell them, so I just . . ."

"Took off. With *their* guitar riffs and drum solos."

"Fuck!" He twists back around. "Should I tell them now? So, sorry guys, but you actually weren't wanted. Isn't it better to let them have this dream? Let *me* be the one who thwarted it? And what's your fucking deal anyway? You weren't in the band. I didn't take anything of—"

"*Except my life!*"

"What?" He blinks into the rearview, genuinely confused.

"My life! My *life!*" I hurl the beer can at his head.

He ducks. "I didn't take your life!" He slaps his hand to his heart. "Those are *my* memories!"

"Of *me!*" I kick the back of his seat. "*My* mother! *My* body! *My* bedroom! The freckle on *my* neck!"

He twists himself back to me, a stunned expression on his face. "I wanted you to hear the songs and know that I never stop thinking about you."

"*That's* what I'm supposed to think?"

"Don't you?"

"Oh yeah. Right after I realize all my fellow shoppers at the Piggly Wiggly are being treated to a lyrical blow-by-blow of my oral sex capabilities I usually abandon my cart, blaze screaming from the store without my purse, and the whole time all that's running through my mind is, *aw, he never stopped thinking about me.*"

"They don't play *that* song at the Piggly Wiggly," he duhs me.

"No," I smile, ultra-chipper. "But they do play it in a lot of bars." I look at him with insouciance, cocking my head. "Do you enjoy coming along on all my dates? Is that it, Jake?"

He turns away.

"When I start a song"—he sighs—"no matter where

it begins I just end up seeing . . . you. It brings you, I don't know, closer."

"I'm not dead, Jake!" I scream at the back of his head. "I haven't been in hiding—you could have come found me at any point!"

"I've been on a tour bus for the last ten years!" he shouts to the roof before spinning back to me. "There's no nurseries to renovate, no neighborhood parties, no Christmas pageants." He searches my face with the same expression that he had on his mother's stairs that first afternoon. "It's not a life. You didn't miss anything."

My chest feels manacled. "Except your face in the morning." My eyes prickle. "Except the prom. Except you looking me in the fucking eye and telling me you're leaving."

We stare at each other.

Suddenly he turns away, his hand twisting the key. "The prom I can do."

18

TWELFTH GRADE

En route to Georgetown I reach into the McDonald's bag lodged between my coat and the gearshift to feel around for any remaining french fries, folding them into my mouth and pretending they're hot. Pretending I'm driving over to Jake's. Pretending it's Laura asleep next to me. I turn up the volume the tiniest notch on "Jake's Tape for Katie" as the car rears onto the roaring grate meant to wake dozing truckers.

"Stop fiddling." Mom opens one eye. *"Please."*

"Fine. But I can't hear anything."

"Just put on NPR," she murmurs, her eyes drifting closed.

"There *is* no NPR. We're in the middle of nowhere and it's the middle of the night," I mutter back, glaring at the black hills barely visible against the sky.

"NPR is everywhere. You just have to find it." She pops her seat upright and rolls the volume, the Pogues blasting us. *"I love your breasts, I love your thighs, yeah, yeah—"*

She shoves the eject button, sending the tape clattering to the floor. Shaking her head derisively, she begins to move the dial methodically through the fuzz.

"Mom." I feel around under my seat for the jilted cassette, my remaining link to sanity. The car swerves again onto the thunderous rail.

"Kathryn! Would you please! Focus! On your driving!"

"I can't focus on my driving when you're doing that!" The radio alternates between scratch and muffle until bursts of some guy talking break through.

"There." She sits back and crosses her hands in her lap. The static continues to punctuate his every other word.

"This is not a station."

"And then, when you have followed the directions as we have prescribed—"

"It's a call-in show, it'll be fun," she says through clenched teeth.

"Jesus will appear and you will be taken in by the righteous. And you won't have to worry about baking those pies in the kingdom of heaven."

She switches it off. We pass a road sign, our headlights arcing across its green face. "Two more hours till Littleton. You going to be all right?"

"Yeah." I rest my cheek in my free hand, my eyes aching. But anything's better than just sitting there in the passenger seat, trusting her to steer us, thoughts chasing each other from whizzing mile marker to whizzing mile marker.

"So, Mount Holyoke," she begins wearily.

"Yeah."

"It was kind of . . ."

"Freaky?" I fill in.

"Yes!" She swivels to me. "No one was smiling. Not a single person, not a student, not a teacher. Even the woman in the gift shop was grim. So strange, it's such a lovely campus."

"It was really weird," I concur, having already mentally scratched it off the list of the six schools vying for my attendance.

"God, I'm starving. Any fries left?"

"Sorry."

She feels under her seat. "I think I dropped a juice box last week on the way to work." She continues to root around. "Well, here's your tape, at least." She holds up a cassette.

"That's not mine." Mine has a lizard drawn on it by my boyfriend.

"Oh." She holds the cream plastic to the green radio light. "Oh my God, *Chorus Line.* Remember how you used to love this?" I stiffen. Although we've come a long way in three months—Dad's moving out not leaving me another option—still, I cannot reminisce with her. She pops it in and grins, singing along as she turns it up. *"I really need this job,"* she trills. "I bought this back when I was applying for my first teaching job. I used it to keep my spirits buoyed when I was finishing my degree. Burlington made me wait three months for the acceptance, you know." She readjusts her tortoiseshell combs.

"I didn't."

"It was miserable. But you used to sit in the backseat and sing your little heart out with me." She smiles in my peripheral vision. "That was great. You were great."

"Thanks."

"Really, Katie, you were." I feel her study my face, the water in her eyes glittering off the dashboard lights as she relaxes into her seat. I turn the tape up, the words coming back to me—the memory of when all I had to do was belt it out from the backseat harder to locate.

✄

"And we're walking . . . and we're walking . . ." We dutifully shuffle along in our third clump in as many days of applying juniors, accepted seniors, and potentially paying parents. The third alarmingly bubbly blonde strides brazenly backward across the third green. "And we're stopping." Heels and toes are trod as we freeze. "This is Rodin University's main building. Also known as the Harte Center, after James Harte, who was chancellor of the college from 1817 to 1842. We like to say this building is the heart of the school, or the vena cava, if you will. The main artery, get it?" The parents of the applying attempt a laugh, in case they're being secretly evaluated on how amusing they make our tour guide feel. But the rest of my, I'm now guessing, non-pre-med cohorts and I remain stony-faced.

"Okay! Let's keep moving!" Stacey keeps barreling backward and we follow like an ungainly school of fish pulled in her wake. Grimacing, Mom stops to press the back of her new tan pump down with her foot.

"We could've just watched the videos from the comfort of our own home," I remind her. "If you'd spring for a replacement VCR since Dad took the old one."

"But then you'd miss out on the chance to be her friend." Mom smiles that we're coming and nudges me onward with her shoulder.

"Are you? Ever going to buy a new one?" I keep my eyes on our guide because the VCR is not what I'm talking about.

"I suppose. Why is no one outside?" she asks chummily, once again changing the subject from the three lives she's ripped apart. "Why is no one playing on the grass? It's strange. It's a beautiful day. Where is everyone?"

"Excuse me?" a mother raises her hand, her purse, a full-size replica of a tabby cat, swinging as she keeps pace with our leader.

"Yes?" Stacey perks even further up.

"Sometimes my daughter, Jessica, forgets to take her vitamins. Is there anyone who can help her remember to do that?"

I follow Mom's gaze to assess how such a daughter, might, in fact, have gained admission to this school. But, other than wearing Buster Browns, Jessica shows no sign of being in need of a personal vitamin assistant.

"That's a great question! There are R.A.s in every freshman dorm, and I'm sure Jessica and her R.A. can work something out."

Mom widens her eyes at me and we stare at the mother and her feline accessory. She does realize Jessica will be leaving home, right? That Jessica could, say, choose to blow the entire lacrosse team and her lack of B_{12} will be the least of this lady's worries? Mom slackens her expression as the tabby cat turns in our direction.

"And here is the Pilgrim Building, where the bulk of freshman classes are held."

"Woooow," Mom whispers in awe, *"Ugly."*

"This building was a gift from the class of 'seventy-three," Stacey announces.

"And no one kept the receipt." Mom tries again, eliciting laughter only from the father-daughter team behind us. Stacey beams at the feedback.

"Yes! So, all freshmen are required to check in here at weekly meetings to share feel-ings and feel-outs. And here is our freshman dining hall!"

We peer in the yellow-tinted windows on what looks like a circa 1970s production of *Oliver.* The faux-wood mustard-yellow mirror-shard decor says "Brady den," but the collective facial expression on the picking masses says "Inedible."

"We have over twenty different kinds of cereals and toaster strudel available three meals a day!"

Jessica's mother shudders.

I watch a student, a look of dismay on his face, raise his spoon high over his bowl and let the contents splash back down in beige clumps. I try to picture myself on the long line with my tray, eating below the sign for VAGINA AWARENESS or standing on the equally long line to heat my toaster strudel, and my throat tightens. Not a single Laura. I scan the greasy faces. Or Jake. No one close.

"Great! I'll take you back to the Admissions Building where some of you are scheduled for the three o'clock group interview. Congratulations to those of you already accepted. Remember, I'm Stacey and my door's always open!"

We plod in silence along the vast green, the spring wind whipping through my coat. I look at the faces of the kids readying for their three o'clock, one kid's eye visibly twitching with nerves. In passing classrooms students sit staring at teachers obscured from my view, googly-eyed with witless intensity as they take dictation. To what end? More papers, more grades, more teachers, some stupid job, and then what? If Jake and I can even make it through all this together, then we just—what? Have some kids so we can start them on the whole stupid path all over again? Rip their hearts out filing for a trial separation along the way? It all just seems so, so—

"Your door won't always be open, will it? That doesn't sound safe."

"Mom."

She pushes into the gift shop, the buckle of her raincoat tapping the glass. "Katie, we need to have a discussion about how you're going to protect yourself when you—"

"Mooooooom!" Several beats of inflection convey that I cannot even begin to discuss my safety at a school

I cannot even begin to imagine myself at, when I can't even begin to imagine myself anywhere else, including what *was* my own home, and I might be having a breakdown right here by the wall of purple Frisbees, coffee mugs, key chains, and visors, so please, please justbackoff.

"Okay," she channels my frequency. She picks up a little mongoloid-looking bear and squeezes it in my face. I stifle the impulse to hurl it across the crowded shop.

"I need, like, five minutes."

"To call Jake," she strains for impartiality.

"No. To just . . . take a walk or something."

"Kathryn, you have to be able to assess your own needs without constantly factoring in Jake's." She squeezes my forearm. "I'm grateful he's been there over these hard few months, but I'm worried you're getting too dependent on him and losing yourself in the process."

"Oh my god! I'm just taking a walk!"

She studies my face. "Honestly?"

Fuck. You. "Yes." I step back from her gaze. "I'm saying I *need* to be *by myself.* Not in a group of freaked-out kids and parents, not in a car with you."

"Fine." She hardens.

"Fine." We walk out of the shop into the lobby of the Admissions Building, where we wordlessly part ways. She continues on to the parking lot and I'm left standing in the pavilion. Alone. I take a deep breath and let it out, not sure what to do next. Not wanting to go back out onto the prairie-size green. Not wanting to hang out in here. I walk obediently past the pay phones, continuing to assess my needs, and on to the bathroom as I check my watch. He'll be practicing now anyway.

Coming out of the stall, I see Jessica in a new college sweatshirt bent over the sink counter, holding her hair out of her face with her left hand. Catching my eye in the mirror she straightens, holding a small straw in her right.

"You still have the tag." I point to the nape of her neck, where the Champion logo dangles.

"Thanks." She smiles, her Scottie dog earrings glinting in the reflection. "This place seems awesome," she says as she runs her finger over her compact and then across her gums, catching the last particles of powder.

❦

Stepping out of the UVA bookstore I squint in the strong sun, wishing I'd brought Jake's Ray-Bans, but how could I have known it'd be spring here, real spring—full-bloom, sweet-air summer's-around-the-corner spring, not the lame depressing April-shower spring of home? At the bottom of the steps I pause, undecided where to take myself next—a library, a cafeteria, another charming brick building—and suddenly the cloud of lung-stifling ache that has been lodged there since February surfaces. Here, under the hazy sun, surrounded by Technicolor grass and the fragrant blooms of stately gardens. It all reaches me through a web of tissue in my chest straining under the weight. Like I have just been beaten. Only it isn't "just." Without the noise of Mom trying to chatter over it or the warm drug of Jake to distract it, I am freshly, acutely inside the pain of what has transpired, what has been lost—the comfort of who we were together.

I emerge from the walkway to the stretch of green leading up to the Rotunda. It is, like everything else here, heartbreakingly beautiful. And dotted before it, in some *Alice in Wonderland* twist, are rocking chairs. I slip off my flats and collapse into the closest one, letting the ground cool my feet.

"Hey, do you know if the Treehouse's open today?"

I squint up at an approaching guy, blond hair flopping as he jogs over. "Sorry, I'm just visiting."

"You don't go here?"

"Undecided." I gesture down at the bookstore bag.

"Well, you seemed right at home." He grins. I am unused to being grinned at by anyone but Jake. The guys at school know not to bother.

"Is that a good thing?"

"Could be." He playfully taps my exposed shin with his flip-flop.

"Yo, Jay! Stop picking up the ladies and let's go!" Jay looks over my head and I peer through the slats of the chair at a group of guys waving him back to the walkway.

"Sorry, Undecided, that's my ride. Good luck—I mean, I guess, good luck to us."

"Thanks!" I watch him jog off and realize I'm smiling. And flirting. And, for one second, forgetting.

∷

". . . *Further compounding the devastation,*" the British voice intones from the Motel 6 TV, "*is the inability of the baby elephant to leave his mother's body once the hunters have removed her tusks. He will stay by her side, crying, until eventually he, too, dies from dehydration and starvation.*"

She lowers her glasses to shoot me an inquiring look from where she sits on her own double bed, reviewing her staff's lesson plans for next year and drinking Fresca. I hate her. Hate her look. Hate her glasses. Hate her lesson plans. I even hate her Fresca.

"Yes, Mom, if hunters shoot you for your precious silver drop-ball earrings I will stay by your side, keening, until I, too, die of dehydration and starvation."

"Good." She returns her attention to the pile of binders in her lap, neither of us discussing the day or my undecided-ness. Or the fact that I hate her. Hate her.

"*The ivory is then smuggled across the border . . .*" My eyes swing from the screen to my backpack hanging from the chair, its small side pocket filled with hoarded quarters.

"We're switching over to *90210* at nine, right?"

She makes a red swoop on the page with her ballpoint. "I want to see how this ends."

"The world runs out of elephants and all we have to remember them by are a few Babar cartoons and *Horton Hatches the Egg.*"

She pauses her sanguine marking. "That was a wonderful book. That's when we got you Mr. Lephant." She smiles. "You couldn't pronounce elephant."

A group of men encircle the felled animal with hacksaws. "Mom, seriously, this is stressing me out."

"Perspective. It's meant to give you perspective."

"So that when I end up snorting blow with Jessica in matching dog sweaters I'll think, hey, this sucks, but at least no one's trying to kill me for my eyeteeth?"

"Exactly." She scribbles a note on the last page and sets it down, not looking at me. "Does that mean you're still undecided?" It means I need to call my fucking boyfriend! "I hear Swarthmore has a high rate of cannibalism, actually. Not surprising, given the aroma emanating from that dining hall." She takes another swig of Fresca.

"Isn't your soda warm?" I ask, hopping off the faded floral coverlet.

"Kind of." She swishes the can in a little circle before sliding it onto the table.

"I'll get ice."

"Oh no you won't." She points her pen to freeze me, the backpack already slung over my shoulder. "This is the land of and-we-never-saw-her-again."

"Are you kidding?"

"We are probably the only guests of this establishment"—she circles her Bic in the air—"who don't have a teenager gagged in the trunk of our car."

I pick the plastic ice bucket off the table by the window and unchain the door. "I'm going to college next year."

"And here I thought this was a pleasure cruise."

"I mean I'll be doing this on my own," my voice tightens in annoyance as I gesture to the world beyond the closed curtains.

"On your own? Or with the *ice* you're getting?" Her fingers bob in cruel quotation marks.

"On my own." I grip the door. "And you have *forfeited* your right to worry—prod—pretty much have any kind of opinion at all. So, just stop, okay? Stop pretending like you're still my mom, because it makes me sick." I finally release the phrase that's been ricocheting through my head since her car pulled up at Jake's. "You make me sick."

My backpack thumping against my side, I race along the long concrete walkway and down the steps to the lobby. "Pleaseohpleaseohpleaseohplease," I intone with every rushed step. I pull open the glass door to the cramped room, relieved to see the pay phone unoccupied.

"Help you?" The manager sticks his head out from the office, where I can hear a rerun of *Three's Company* starting.

"Just using the pay phone."

"Oh. 'Kay. Just don't take too long. That there's communal," he grunts, retreating.

I set my backpack down on the shiny plaid loveseat and retrieve a fistful of quarters. Holding the receiver, slick with trucker hair cream and sweat, to my ear, I dial carefully, punching the numbers with force enough to make him be home.

The phone rings and rings. "Pleaseohpleaseohplease-ohplease." And rings. I wait eight, sixteen, twenty-four rings. Finally the line cuts.

"Shit."

The head pops out again.

"Sorry!" Girl Scout cookie?

"Hmph," he grunts.

I drop the quarters in again and redial. On the second ring it answers.

"Hello?" Susan's voice snakes through the line.

"Hi! It's Katie. Is Jake home?"

"Jake, are you home?" she asks snidely. "He's right here," she says without enthusiasm.

"Hey." One low syllable and the tense hours and tours and Public Broadcasting and Wendy's and moldy showers all swirl away. "Hold on, I'm gonna go pick up in my room, okay?"

"Sure," I reply uncertainly, pulling out my last clump of change. I drum my fingers on the scratched plywood wall, pumping in another twenty-five cents each time the line starts to beep.

"Still there?" his voice finally fills the connection, low and husky.

"Yes," I say, turning into the phone as if it could put its arm around me.

"How's it going?"

"Seventy-two hours in a car with my mom—what's not to love?"

"But you're almost done, right?" he asks encouragingly.

"Yeah, we'll be back late Sunday night."

"That'll be me, throwing Brainy at your window."

I smile, the corners of my mouth suddenly trembling as I try to imagine going months without seeing him, our life together lived only on greasy pay phones.

"I'm glad you called," he says.

Swallowing, I try to relax my mouth. "I couldn't get through before."

"Oh, was that you? Yeah, we were fighting."

"What about?"

"Same old shit. Well," he pauses, "not exactly. I got into UVM."

"Jake!" I try to exclaim, but my throat constricts around the air as I push it out. "That's great! You guys'll all be together."

"Yeah, Sam's already trying to see if we can room and Laura's figuring out sharing a car," he laughs, but his voice sounds no more enthused than mine.

"That's so . . . great. Congratulations." The last word comes out strangled as the tears break.

"Hey, hey, don't be sad."

"But I'm leaving all of you," I choke out. "You'll all be together, building these great college memories and I'm going to be . . . Jake, UVA was so much more beautiful than any of the other places even though it's, like, a sixteen-hour trip home. People seem nice and relaxed, but not too relaxed, and they smile, but not like zealots. It doesn't feel like they're going to be snorting vitamins with Westies—"

"What?"

"Nothing." I reach into my backpack for a wad of napkins. "No, that's great," I repeat, "It's really great. I'm so happy for you."

"I love you, Katie."

Now it's my turn to, "What?" as I blow my nose.

"I love you. And no amount of distance is ever going to change that. Do you hear me?"

"Yes," I affirm.

"No. Listen. I—love—you." His voice slows, as if trying to carve these words into me. "And *no* amount of distance is ever going to change that. Remember that? Promise."

"So does that mean—so what should I do?"

The line starts to bleat, having swiftly digested my last quarters. The manager sticks his head out again, his gaze suspicious, resentful.

"Katie? Katie?" cries down the line. "Promise?"

"Jake?!"

❦

My arms tightly crossed, I slouch in the passenger seat and struggle to keep my eyes closed. My mouth dry from a night of crying, it's easier to pretend to be asleep than admit consciousness and risk another round of screaming. The car thuds rhythmically over the highway joists and I lift a lid to peek out at as we go over a bridge. The sun glints off the water below. Screw it. I "blink" awake. Mom grips the wheel, her face taut and pale.

"I'm not trying to make you perfect," she says quietly, her voice hoarse. I stare out the window at the dandelions spotting the wayside beneath a sign informing me that this mile is being maintained by Bette Midler. "I'm not aiming for perfect and I never have. Neither has your father."

I clench my jaw at her invocation. "I know that, Mom."

"I took a week off from work to do this—"

"Because Dad's library job just started."

"*Because* I want you to see what your options are— how big the world is. You think I've forfeited my right to advise you, Katie, but you *need* to see—" She waves her hand. "How big your life can be."

"I know. And I don't want to rent an apartment over a convenience store in Burlington and be a waitress."

"I only said that because if you're so sure that your life is about Jake Sharpe, then we'd rather see you take a semester off and *really* see what it's like to have Jake be your first priority."

"*We'd?*" I bite the inside of my cheeks. "Okay, well, I'm *not* so sure." I throw my arms open. "About anything—any of this! How could I be? I know you've done it before, I know, but you're not me, you're you." I take a deep rattling breath, feeling the loss of her. "And you didn't have a Jake."

"Not at seventeen, I didn't."

"So you don't know, either. About anything." I root around for napkins and, giving up, swipe my sweater across my face. "It just sucks that the one thing I do know right now, and I do mean *one thing,* is that I love him and he loves me, and that's a really good thing. And to choose to leave that behind like it's a box of my old toys just 'cause I'm supposed to follow in this path that *arbitrarily* comes in September feels so . . . *reckless. Reckless,* Mom. You guys always said it's people that matter and here I am making this decision and you're questioning my priorities and I . . . I . . ." My chest shakes with sobs. I feel her warm hand on my head, which only makes me cry harder. "Fuck, Mom, why didn't you just let me apply to UVM?"

Hearing nothing, I look up to see tears streaming down her face as she pulls to the side of the highway. Hunched over the wheel, she pushes the leather into her forehead and scrunches her eyes.

"Mom?" She turns her face away from me, her shoulders shaking. Cars race by honking loudly. "Mom, maybe we should put on the hazards?"

She whips her head up and throws the switch as she pulls her hand across her nose. "No fucking napkins?"

I feel around fruitlessly again. "No fucking napkins."

"Okay, Kathryn. Here's the truth. I don't know what I'm supposed to do here. Neither does Dad. And I miss him. And I fucked up. But I'm still your parent. There you go." Tears roll down her cheeks and she focuses her eyes in the distance.

"Okay," I say, thinking I'd finally feel better with this

admission, but instead feel only more nauseated at the seemingly bottomless revelations of their fallibility.

"We wanted to throw you a big graduation party in the backyard and send you off to an amazing adventure somewhere wonderful and new that you could make all your own and instead, every single discussion we have about what's next for you is a ringing chorus of JakeJake-Jake. He can't be the core criteria for your life planning, Kathryn. I know he's been a wonderful friend to you through this . . . this time, but you can't plan your life with a man as the primary building block."

I feel the ache of another hit. "You say that like I'm ruined."

"You're not. You're not ruined." She leaves off the *yet.* "You're great."

"This again." She smiles, licking under her nose. "I'm making this decision for myself, Mom, not you or Jake or Ms. Hotchkiss."

"That's all I'm asking."

"Really?" I inquire sarcastically. "'Cause it feels like when we get home you're going to sleep in my room and follow me everywhere."

"I am!" she says, flicking the hazard lights off and scanning over her shoulder for a spot to pull back on. "Everyone should. You're such a charmer, especially since you ate those sour cream and onion potato chips for breakfast."

"You showed a lot of restraint there."

"I'm 'letting you go,' remember? God, we need napkins." She sniffles.

"And snacks." I crack my window, letting the racing air dry my face.

"And a prom dress!" She flourishingly flicks the turn signal as she nods at a billboard for a mall. "Think they have a family therapist at the Jessica McClintock Factory Outlet?" She pulls us onto the exit ramp.

19

December 23, 2005

Jake pulls us into the Croton Falls Country Club, driving the length of the empty parking lot and around to the back where the last trickle of kitchen staff emerge, hunching against the wind as they stride to their allotted parking spaces at the far end.

"Here, this way," Jake says, hopping out of the front seat and coming around to my door. He pops it open, holding out his hand.

Immobile, arms crossed, I stare at the weather-beaten changing cabanas. "Jake, it's closed."

"Just come on." He smiles entreatingly. "Please?"

I glance at my watch. "Can't we just sit in a heated diner and have a discussion like normal people do in the middle of the night?"

"Not unless you want it broadcast in thirty-two countries."

"Why here?" I point at the dark brick building.

"We're gonna have ourselves a prom. If you would please get out of the fucking car."

Rolling my eyes, I nonetheless extract myself from

the vehicle and fall into step with him across the recently plowed concrete. As the last two men round out of sight he points to where the service door is still propped with a brick. "See? It's practically an invitation."

I look at him, trying to suppress a smile.

"Come on." I nod and, ducking, follow him as he snakes through the kitchen and into a darkened back hallway smelling of salmon steaks and tartar sauce. "This way."

"How do you know?" I whisper.

"We played here, like, a thousand times."

"Right," I remember, as we hustle along the corridor in the dark. "Your 'Feelings' had 'em on their feet every time."

"*That* is an underrated song."

"Really?"

"No." He pushes against the swinging door to the dining room and we stand at its edge. The starkness of the round folding tables, bare without their starched linens, is softened by the moon reflecting off the snow-blanketed golf course, filling the space with a milky light.

Even though I haven't grown a centimeter since senior year the room feels, if slightly ethereal, predictably smaller and infinitely less glamorous—the walls ringed with fake holly wreaths, the stage offering a small tin-seled tree. Jake walks backward away from me across the parquet dance floor, his arms outstretched. "So? What was it like?"

"What was it like?" I echo.

He stands in the middle of the floor. "Yeah. Describe it for me."

"Well . . ." I look around, the room filling in my mind's eye with beaded satin and rented tuxes, the ec-static couples, the stag tables, swept-up hair and let-down girls, open disappointment and hidden flasks. "This is all through a thick veil of tears, mind you."

He nods, his acknowledgment buying him a guided tour.

"Okay, the theme was Shoot for the Stars, so there were star-shaped Mylar balloons all over the ceiling." I gesture up to the fireproof tiling. "Which sounds heinous, but I thought it looked like the 'Modern Love' video and kind of liked it." He raises his eyebrows. "It was *controversial*. Anyway, everything was silver and twinkly. Michelle and her crew had put in a lot of effort and . . . it was a prom." I shrug. "The drink tables were set up here, I think . . . and here."

Jake is watching my arcing arms, looking at each place I point as if it were all reappearing. He beams at me.

"Sam, Todd, Benjy—they were playing. Sam sang."

"And I'm up there, too. In this version."

He hops effortlessly onto the stage and stands by the unplugged microphone. "What were you wearing?"

"A pink satin Jessica McClintock bubble dress." I ges-ture to mimic the pouf.

"Hot."

"Donna Martin wore one just like it."

He smiles and starts to sing, *"Is it getting better, or do you feel the same?"* his voice filling the room with "One," which he'd always dedicated to me. Prophetic. "Then we'd finish our set and the DJ'd take over and we'd all get to come dance with our girlfriends." He steps off the stage. "May I?"

"I—" I protest, but, continuing to hum the song, he slides his fingers into mine, lifting my hands to the back of his neck where they rest against his warm skin. His hands grasp my hips and we start slow dancing. And I am overcome by how good this feels as we sway to the suggestion of music that vibrated out into the universe over a decade ago. I breathe in deeply, smelling his skin beneath the cologne he endorses, that familiar scent I always likened to fresh sweet corn.

He whispers in my ear. "Prom . . . check. What else you need?"

The realization strikes me. I summon the strength to suspend this fantasy in order to get what I have come for. I pull back to look him in the eye. "I need you to break up with me."

He casts his gaze to the floor.

"I need to hear it."

"Okaaay." Raising his lashes, he searches my face. "Um, I guess I would have told you—"

"No." I shake my head. "Not 'would have.' "

He nods, getting what I'm asking. "Katie?"

"Yes?"

"There's something I've been needing to tell you, try-ing to . . . figure out how to tell you. You know how that scout came and saw us play and . . . well, he wants me to

come out to L.A. He thinks he can get me a record deal."
He rubs his chin, slipping into seventeen.

"Wow, that's amazing," I say, feeling an unexpected
flicker of authentic enthusiasm.

"So, I've thought about having you come with me,
and I've been playing it through and playing it through,
but . . ."

"But?" I peer at him, desperate for this impossible
question to finally be answered.

"You have college and I have no idea what it's going
to be like out there and . . . and . . . everything in your
life is so fragile right now." He slides his hand through
my hair to cradle my head, his expression agonized. "If
this doesn't work out, I couldn't live with myself if I drag
you down with me. Anyway, I know I'm going to miss
you so fucking much it's going to be hard to breathe. I
know I'm going to wake up every day . . . *every* day and
wonder if I made a huge mistake . . . but I've gotta go.
I just have to, Katie."

"I know," I say, finally able to give the benediction de-
nied expression.

"You do?"

"I do. Everything, everything you've achieved, Jake,
I wanted for you."

"I'm sorry."

"You are?" I lunge once more. "For what?"

"For ever leaving you." He leans in and our lips meet
and we sink into each other, our hands sliding under
wool, finding skin. He tastes the same. Tastes exactly the
same.

"You taste the same," I murmur into his hair as he kisses my neck. Knees bending we melt onto the scuffed parquet, hands finding familiar tracks. Then he undoes his buckle, pulling a condom out of his pocket.

"No, no. Oh, God, no, stop." I sit up. "We can't do this." I pull down my shirt.

"Yes. Yes, we can." He reaches for my belt.

"Well, obviously, yes, we're physically capable. But you have a fiancée. Here. Now. In 2005. And three friends who you do owe, yes, Jake, *owe* royalties and credit. You have *got* to make good on that."

"But we've wasted—"

I shoot him a look.

"I've wasted too much time." He slides his hands back around my hips.

"Jake." I unlock his grip. "This is . . . I don't know what this is. A time warp. Remnant hormones." I stand, collecting myself as I refasten my bra.

"Come on, we've already done the deed before, so it doesn't really count."

"That's the most specious argument I've ever heard."

He leans back on his elbows. "My point is, our confessional lists won't get any longer. Come here."

I stare down at him. He pulls himself up to standing, stepping close, our faces almost touching again. "Jesus, Katie, are you telling me you don't feel this?"

I blink and steady myself, trying to reconnect with every minute of my twenties spent ranting in a parking lot outside some event that had just been sabotaged for me by its own soundtrack, swearing that if I ever got the chance . . . Pulling the words from half-remembered speeches that once pounded through my head on long morning runs, "I'm telling you that you don't deserve it. Yes, this was prom and you fucked it up. Yes, we have chemistry. *Huge* chemistry. Multiplatinum chemistry. Yes, you've been missing out all these years. But you left, Jake. You left. And I built a whole life that has nothing to do with you. Which, and let me be abundantly clear, is not available to you as creative material. Nor those of its auxiliary players, no matter how poetic their actions may strike you. So, while I appreciate the apology, I'd appreciate it even more if you took me home so I can finally get on with it."

20

UVA

Walking out from the air-conditioned chill into the afternoon sunshine, I drop my backpack at my feet to pull off my cardigan on the steps of Cabell Hall.

"See you Tuesday!"

I look up from tucking the pointelle cotton into my bag. "Yeah!" I smile back to Cute Lacrosse Shirt Guy. "Enjoy the movie."

"Right." He slaps his palm against his forehead. "See you at the library, then." He walks backward, waving, before turning around and merging into the buoyant traffic of sun-kissed faces.

I lift my pack onto my bare shoulder and grin up into the cumulus-cloud-dotted sky. I fucking love Charlottesville, Virginia. Fucking love that it's given me a To-Do list that doesn't include Go to Crap Summer Job and Sob into Ben & Jerry's Apron. Love that it's filled with people who don't know a goddamn thing about said previous sobbing. Love that everywhere I go, every hour of the day, there is, at minimum, one jogger chugging past in pursuit of health and clarity, flying the flag, forward focused. I just stick-mein-the-sweatshirt, put-me-in-the-postcard, bumper-sticker-my-notebooks, L–O–V–E, love it.

I slip my sunglasses on and bounce down the brick steps into the J. Crew flow. Checking out hot guy with soccer ball. Checking out hot guy with other hot guys. Smiling at hot guy walking past. And somewhere in all this relentless navy and orange possibility awaits flip-flop-wearing Jay. Who I shall find and fall in love with, if I have to date every hot guy here to do it.

❧

"I *hate* her," my roommate Beth spins around to announce, her eyes wide with surprise at her own vitriol as we inch along in the miserably hungover Sunday morning O'Hill cafeteria line.

"Who?" I look around for the enemy.

"Her," Beth mouths, jerking her head at the Patagonia-clad blonde in front of us.

"Why?"

"I don't know," she whispers with alarm, her face twisted in confusion. "I've never met her. But her perfume, her voice . . . I feel like I could whop her over the head with this tray." Her petite hands grip the peach plastic.

I look past Beth to her heedless torturer, giggling with friends as she picks through damp Tater Tots, unaware of the potential untimely end posed by the sleep-deprived, dehydrated, five-foot redheaded first-year behind her.

"When did you stop the pill?" I ask, reaching for a fistful of steaming wet silver.

"Um . . . like three weeks ago, right after I broke up with Mike, why?"

"PMS," I pronounce. "Real PMS. The natural high."

"Really?" Beth's horrified.

"Welcome back!" I clang my fork to hers.

"I thought maybe it was the rain." She shakes her head and grabs a limp waffle, biting into it. "Or someone wearing that much Calyx assaulted me in my formative years and I'd repressed it."

"Rain isn't helping," I sigh, looking out the steamed windows. Gross guy in muddy sweatpants passes. Grosser guy chugs milk with his grosser friends, spitting it up all over himself while they laugh gross laughs. Grossest guy walks past, burping hello to the entire line. All in all a sea of pasty, oily, bloodshot, beer-reeking gross.

Six months at UVA and no Jay. No hot guys. It's like the cold froze their cuteness and now it's chipped off to reveal their bloated inner selves.

"I fucking hate Charlottesville, Virginia."

"Where!" Beth's eyes light up.

"What?"

"Oh," she deflates. "I thought you saw it on a T-shirt. One in each color, please."

I stick a mug under the coffee spout and watch the soapy water rise, indulging for only a moment in the imagined feeling of Jake's flannel shirt against my collarbone.

"This is so not how I pictured this," Beth says over the plastic cup of beer almost as large as her face.

"You were expecting crystal?" I ask as I watch Laura chatting with a bunch of the Phi Mu girls, seeing her break into her first genuinely relaxed smile since she got off the bus this afternoon.

"When your friend was describing how fun it would be I purposely tried to picture it as not-cliché, but how is it possible that there is *literally* a guy over there in a toga chugging from a funnel?"

"Let's just take a moment to celebrate the 'over-there' part," I point out as Beth leans in to clink plastic, foamy amber liquid spilling down my wrist and soaking the sleeve of my borrowed bodysuit. I watch Laura circle the keg with the Phi Mus and expertly take the dripping tap in her mouth. As her legs are lifted in the air Beth and I instead opt to keep slurping out of our relatively sanitary cups, eagerly awaiting, with the rest of the crowded room, the draft's alleged goggle effect, which will hopefully scrub about a decade's worth of nasty off these walls.

"Listen!" I put my hand on Beth's leopard-print forearm as I make out the opening bars of George Michael's "Freedom '90." Her eyes widen. She grabs my arm in turn and we quickly plow our way into the other bodies thrashing on the sawdust-covered floor between the Ping-Pong table and couch. Suddenly Laura is caroming the lyrics in my face, taking my hand. We throw our arms up and sing along, because no matter the Jake-size hole in my heart, I do have this. I could do whatever with whomever. I close my eyes and shake my hips, smiling as I look back out to see the cadre of girls around me, the circle momentarily completed by Laura, all blissfully doing the same.

Unable to fall asleep as the habitual 4 A.M. eddy in my rib cage builds in strength, I study the stucco ceiling. Laura chokingly inhales. "Laura," I whisper. More snuffles. "Laura," I try again, peering down at her sprawled across the stretch of carpet between Beth's and my beds, her right arm still akimbo around the plastic wastepaper basket. I sit up and reach my foot out to nudge her prone figure. "Laura!"

Her eyes squint open before focusing on me. "Huh?"

"Hey."

"Hey." Her lids flutter closed and her breathing slows, resuming its sharp increase in sonorousness. I pull my knees up under my T-shirt and stare out at the sliver of world visible between the shade and sill. The pain in my chest spreading through my limbs, making me cold, I lift the comforter around my shoulders. "Where is he?"

"Huh." She tucks her left hand under the pillow.

"Where *is* he? Where *is* he, Laura?" I curve over the edge of the bed. "Where did he go?"

"No," she says, her voice low and scratchy from

yelling lyrics, smoking, and puking. "Go—to sleep." She rolls away from me.

"I can't."

She mutters, feeling around her for the second pillow, pulling it over her head. "Sam that fucking postcard—"

"What?!" I drop to the carpet, the comforter slipping off as I grab the pillow from her. *What postcard?*

"Didn't tell you 'cause it's—"

"What? It's what?"

She lifts onto her elbows, taking a deep breath, her gaze regaining clarity. "Big nothing. 'Hey, what's up? Hope school's good. Miss you, man.' Big. Nothing," she finishes, disgusted.

"From?"

"L.A., but led nowhere." She collapses back. "Not that Sam didn't dust it for prints."

"Does he still have it? Can I see it?"

"Oh my God! I did not sit on a bus for thirteen hours to talk about Jake Sharpe when I could be doing that in my own bed!" Suddenly she jerks to her knees over the plastic wastebasket, dry heaving, and I reach out to curtain the hair off her face. As the wave passes she rests her damp forehead against her arm on the plastic rim. "Eight months later—eight *years* later, he's still a total fuck." Her voice amplifies inside the wastebasket. "That's the news from Vermont, so can we please just go to sleep?" Nodding I pass her a glass of water as she wipes her mouth. *Hey, what's up—hope school's good—miss you, man.* Doesn't miss me.

"I think I'm gonna head back," I say to Beth as we pass the brick path to Delta Zeta.

"I don't know," she prevaricates. "Two years of this and I'm getting kind of drawn to it." Rows of acapella–singing Laura Ashley-clad sisters conduct wooing choruses to the first-year girls walking Chancellor Street. "I'm not saying it isn't a touch Stepford."

"A touch." I nod. "Although the prospect of all that free ice cream is pretty enticing. But, hey, go for it. They're playing *Jaws* on the big screen and Lindsay's making a 'Candygram' sign."

We exchange a quick hug and I cut behind the trilling houses onto Rugby Road, where the fraternities seem to be staging a wildly subtler recruitment: Dave Matthews drifts over lawns dotted with couches lounging near lazily smoking barbecues. The sun shifts further, dipping behind the rooflines of the once-grand homes as I continue along the sidewalk.

A Frisbee clatters to rest at my feet.

"Hey, pink skirt girl!" I look up the lawn and point to myself. A tall blonde grins. "Toss it back?" I swipe up the orange disk and skillfully fling it back, restraining myself from blowing my knuckles and rubbing them on my camisole. "Not bad." He wipes the gleam of sweat off his chest with the T-shirt hanging from the belt of his cargo shorts. I shrug and continue walking, *praying to God—* "Hey!" *Yes?*

I turn to see him watching me, tapping the Frisbee against the heel of his hand. "Yeah?"

"Hot dog?" he calls, flicking it back into play. "I mean, we're barbecuing. You want a hot dog?"

"Sure." I shrug.

"Cool." He jogs backward up the grass and waves for me to follow, leading me to a tiny grill with a not very tiny guy sweating over it. "Load her up, Cord," he directs. While draining his beer can Cord grabs one of the hot dogs squeezed across a tower of white coals and drops it into a bun. He squirts it with toppings and extends it to me.

"Thanks, Cord." I take the paper plate and Cord nods, wiping his brow with the back of his chubby hand. I take a bite, wincing.

"Oh, dude! It's hot. Hold on." He bolts to a dented trash can at the base of the front steps and whips out a beer while I huff around the steaming meat to cool my tongue. He snaps the top and I take a soothing sip through the foaming opening, profoundly relieved at not having to resort to spitting it out.

"Thanks."

"You got it, pink skirt."

"Katie." I wipe my mouth with the back of my hand.

"Drew." He crosses his muscled arms over his lovely chest while, beside us, smoke continues to billow from Cord's makeshift hibachi.

"This is great." I attempt another chew.

He grins. "Liar."

"No, really!" Cord tosses a hot dog up and tries to catch it behind his back with the bun. I eye the growing pile of blackened misfires at his feet.

"Couldn't figure out another way to get you up here," Drew says, sending the heat from my mouth into my cheeks. "Had to think on my feet."

I glance down at his Tevas. And they are nice feet. "Well, hot dogs are always a sure thing."

"Yeah, Rush is all about seduction. We start with the roasted meat product and move on to the Jell-O shot."

"An art form." This is banter. We are bantering. I swig my beer, smiling at the couple sprawled on the couch beside us singing along with Dave.

"So, Katie?" He swivels his torso abruptly to the left to dodge the incoming Frisbee. "You a first-year?"

Sipping my beer, I shake my head.

"Second?" he asks, pulling the T-shirt from his waist again and holding it behind his neck like a towel.

"Guilty." I take another sip. "You?"

"As charged." We smile at each other. Where the fuck you been, Drew?! "Streaked yet?" he asks.

Oh. "Can't say as I have."

"A couple of the guys here are making their run tonight." He boldly takes my upper arms to step me out of the path of the hot dog fumes as the smoke shifts. "We should check it out."

"Are you—"

"No! No." A flush spreads up from his jawline. He is nervous. I am making this boy nervous. "So, want to meet at the Corner around ten, pick a spot for some drinks, then head over?"

"Yeah, I could do that." He takes the can from me, our fingers brushing. He holds out his other hand for my napkin.

"Full service," I say appreciatively as I pass it off.

He smiles again. "So, ten, at the Corner?"

"Yup."

"I'll be waiting, Katie."

But he isn't. I am. Again. Always. Eternally. Tombstone imprint: Katie Hollis, She Waited. I inhale the last of a bummed cigarette and stub it out on the brick wall. Fuck this. Fuck him, never again, not for all the tan lanky in the world. I'll just grab an ice cream with fudge and meet up with the girls. I kick off my borrowed beaded sandals and turn toward the bar.

"Pink skirt! Yo, Katie, wait up!" I spin around to see him doubled over, gripping his knees. He looks up and attempts a grin as he pants. "I ran all the way over. The shower backed up and I wanted to rinse off and change and my room was a mess." My pulse ramps from the implication, from the trickle of moisture moving down his jawbone into the neck of his Polo where the fold marks are still evident.

"Okay," I say, not moving.

He stands and runs his hand across his forehead. "Shit. You're pissed."

"I just don't do waiting really well."

"Try cleaning a drain shared by five guys." He grins hopefully. I allow myself a smile, willing away my misplaced ire. "So are your shoes, like, an accessory or something?" He nods at where I clutch the sandals under each crossed arm.

My turn to blush. "No they're a—I was just going to—"

"Carry them like a clutch or something?"

"You're pretty versed in women's fashion for a frat boy."

"Two older sisters." He shrugs, dropping onto his khakied knees as he reaches for the sandals. I hand them down and he places them on the pavement in front of my toes.

"They've trained you well," I murmur, slipping my feet back in.

Leaning against a fluted column on the edge of the lawn a few hours later I am tingling with the warm buzz of many gin and tonics and first-rate, spark-laden banter. Drew cheers on the dark profiles of the guys racing drunkenly in the shadow of the Rotunda. He whoops, the vibrations moving along my side—his hand placed carelessly on my thigh like we've been dating for years. Memories swirl and I push them aside by focusing on the outline of a rocking chair near the center of the rolling grass. Studying how the moon glints off its finish, I feel myself grinning. I made it.

"Oh, shit!" Drew jumps up. Two runners careen to

Cord's sprawled figure, members flapping as they right him. Cord stands stunned for a moment before sending his arms into the air in a rock-on pose. Drew doubles over in hysterics. "That's gotta hurt."

Standing, I watch him as the laughter of the guys fades down the lawn with their retreating posteriors. "Let's go." His eyes widen for a beat before he slides his hand into mine. He swipes up my sandals and we walk the cricketed gardens as the red lights of arriving campus security bounce off the old brick wall. He weaves me through the grounds toward 14th Street, floating, gliding on anticipation—a narcotic I haven't felt in so long there's a muscle pain surrounding its release. I stand just behind him while he fishes out his keys, feeling his warmth through his shirt.

He switches on the desk lamp in his room. "Room-mate's out."

I look around the tidied space, laundry peeking out from beneath the bed, my eyes landing on a picture taped over the desk—four blond kids jumping into a swimming pool. Two girls, two boys, one of them—"Is that Jay?"

"You know Jay?" he asks, surprised as he pulls two beers from his mini-fridge.

"How do you know Jay?"

"He's my brother. Wait, you're not from Newton?"

"Vermont." I turn my back to the desk. He walks to me, leaving the bottles behind, and puts both his hands lightly atop mine where they brace me against the wood, then leans in for a sweet, gorgeous kiss.

"You're so fucking beautiful," he murmurs before kissing me again. My palms fly to his cheeks, pressing his head against mine, pressing Jake's imprint into oblivion. His fingers slide up my bare arms and then pull me forward toward the bed. We tumble down, laughing. Drew reaches out to his nightstand, his lips still on mine.

"Wait." I touch his arm. "I don't think we should—"

"No, I was just going to—" He flips on his stereo.

"Right." I blush. He smiles, his eyes drifting closed as we continue to roll into each other. I am losing myself in the ecstasy of being here, of finding how much I want this and didn't think I ever could. The knowledge that I am not ruined. That I am wanted as much as I want. That Drew hums sweetly along with the music as he slides my jeans off. I lean back and close my eyes— the melody seeping into my senses. The melody of desire and . . . and . . . hurt and—

I bolt up, kicking him off me.

"What the fuck?" he asks, kneeling up, my jeans in his hand.

"Shhh!" I fumble for the volume, rolling it all the way up.

"You okay?"

"What is this?" I gasp, my mouth dry.

"We were hooking up."

"No! This song! Where did you get this?"

"It's the radio. Campus station. Uh, some new release they started playing a few days ago. You're really freaking me out here."

I grab my clothes up, pulling them around me as I try to stand.

"I have to . . . I have to . . ."

"Okay." He backs against the wall.

"I just have to—"

"I'm losing, my eyes on the towering golden gods over our heads. I put my hand to your skin and you tell me come inside I come inside—"

I force sound, numbly gripping my clothes as my eyes blink for the door. "—go."

21

December 24, 2005

Laura's singing on the stairs pulls me from restless sleep. I crack my eyes, squinting against the sunshine as my door flies open. *"He is a loooo—ser 'cause you are the cham—pion!"* she belts out, jogging in fists aloft, an eight-months-pregnant Rocky. Her down coat open over her pink maternity hoodie, she swings her right arm in a wild arc of air guitar. "Whew!" She looks up from her Wembley Stadium finale and pushes her hair back out of her face as I sit up. "Tell me *everything.*"

"Laura, it was . . ." I inhale, looking at her expectant expression, finding myself unable to put an adjective to it. "There he was. And there I was." I hold my palms up facing each other, fingers splayed to mime the moment. "And . . ."

"You left him at the height of it all regretting his entire existence!"

I flip my pillow around and hold it against my stomach. "He thought I was going to do him right there on Harriman's parquet."

"He took you to the golf club?!" Her pert nose wrinkles.

"Prom," I explain, the sensation of his mouth on mine suddenly vivid. I reflexively drop my face into the pillowcase, reflushing at the memory, an estrogen tremor going up the back of my neck.

"Right, continue," she insists. As I pull my head up, she gingerly lowers herself to the bed, the next pending round of motherhood sitting low on her hips. And, right, this is not eleventh grade. This is not the night-after-of-nights-to-come. This is over. "He said he was sorry," I offer. "Twice." I hold up two fingers. "And he looked sorry. He sounded sorry. Mostly what I got was sorry. And then I got out of the car because he just sat there as his sexy, smoldering—"

"Sorry!"

"Yes." I catch myself. "Sorry self, with his thumb up his ass. And . . . I got out of the car." I fall back, now fully awake and fully unsure. "I got out of the car," I repeat. Because it's true. I blink up at Keanu. "Wait—this was all after we dropped Sam off. How did you?" I jolt back up as Laura, beaming, produces a folded piece of paper from her pocket.

"*Evicted?*" Laura reads. She flips it around, revealing a Web site printout.

"*You* read E!Online?"

She sniffs. "I started when I was breast-feeding. It relaxes me and increases milk production."

I hold up my palm. "You had me at 'breast-feeding.' "

"Listen, this was the home page. *'Are Jake Sharpe and Eden split? Only hours before they were scheduled to start performing their live MTV Christmas special, Eden and her entourage have reportedly decamped—'* "

"Decamped?" I echo.

" *'Decamped,'* " she repeats with emphasis, " *'From the Sharpe mansion where she was supposed to be spending the holidays cozying up to the family—'* "

"That family doesn't do cozy," I contradict.

She shoots me a silencing look and resumes, " *'A source close to the couple said that Jake returned home around two A.M. last night and then,'* quote, *'fighting and hysteria were heard coming from the third floor.'* "

"Fighting and hysteria?" My stomach drops.

She slows, tapping the paper for emphasis, " *'Whether a lover's quarrel or a full-scale split, this most likely means Eden's diamond may be returned under the tree and MTV may be acting pretty Grinch-like themselves when it comes to promoting Jake's new album.'* " She cuddles the paper to her chest like a valentine. "It's so much more than we could have even hoped for, dreamed of, prayed up! So much better than regret!"

"But why would he—when did he?" I stammer, stunned. "They've been together for like—"

"Two years," she fills in, resting her swollen fingers on my knees. "Which is, like, *twenty* in musician years."

I push the pillow off my lap. "But why would he—"

"Because you seriously messed him up! Now he's reportedly broken off the first major relationship he's had in forever and she's probably his perfect match and now he'll wallow in lonely misery, never write another thing, go bankrupt Michael Jackson–style until he's brought up on charges of lewd indecency in a public bathroom and—"

"*Kathryn!* Could you come downstairs *right now?*"We both look to the door.

"Kathryn?" Laura echoes. "Your mom still scares the crap out of me."

"What time is it?" I swing my feet to the floor.

"Eight thirty."

"I'm not late yet." I take the printout from her, scanning through it. "I guess I really won," I murmur.

"Won? Are you kidding? You can take every last one of *these* down." She flutters her fingers toward the array of gold debate trophies above the headboard. "And stick *this*"—she flicks the paper between my hands—"up in their place."

"Kathryn! NOW."

"Coming!" I slip my E!Online diploma into the pocket of Mom's nightgown. Laura descends the stairs with me at her heels, slowing as we take in what awaits us.

Mom and Dad stand at the open front door by their packed suitcases, gazing in alarm out to the porch where a late-forties-ish, well-heeled blonde looks—between the cell phone headset she's muttering into and the massive Atlas-size ledger she's reading from—as if she's coordinating the launch of a space shuttle from our lawn. Her head whips up at our approach. "Fuck me," she barks into her headset as Laura and I take the final stair. "She's pregnant. Tad, I need the medical team—I need tests. Pronto."

Mom turns to me, her tight expression telegraphing that we are on a sixty-second countdown to Principal Hollis. I quickly join her in the doorframe. "I'm sorry, but who *are* you?"

"Jocelyn Weir." Dad passes me the red business card with distaste.

"I work for Jake." Clasping the ledger to her chest, she tugs her fingers up into the sleeves of her silk Chanel duster.

"And based on your manners, I'm assuming you're a relation as well?" Mom states more than asks.

"You have *no* idea what kind of *shitstorm's* been dropped in my lap this morning—what?! No! No! STOP! Not the panty photos, the sex tape, Christ!"

Mom tightens her grip on the doorknob. Dad tightens his grip on Mom. Jocelyn Weir tightens her grip on the wire dangling from her ear and holds it to her mouth. "Tad, you tell Eden's people not to even go there or we'll have that tape running in Times Square by noon." She turns her focus to Laura. "Katie, I need a glass of water, filtered, no ice—lemon if you have it, but only if it's organic."

"I'm Kate Hollis." I step onto the porch, pulling my hands into my sleeves.

Jocelyn's face momentarily relaxes with relief. "Oh, God, fantastic! Kill the medical team, Tad." She pushes a buttery chunk of hair out of her eye line. "Okay, so, Katie, here's the deal. You're the girl in the songs, yadda-

yadda-yadda. I can get, *maybe,* a day of press out of that, max—what? Whatever, Tad! I'm not talking about fucking France—I'm talking domestic! Jesus." She shakes her head, looking at me for professional commiseration, which I do not give. "Eden is *the* story, she gives me *years* of material: *InStyle* wedding, MTV series, adopted babies from Third World countries, joint albums, a Christmas special. Get it?"

"No."

Laura impatiently pushes through my parents, joining us on the porch. "Is he just sick? Is he literally green with nausea? Paint a picture for us."

Jocelyn adjusts her headset.

"Is he?" I ask. "Green?"

"Katie."

"It's Kate."

She fixes her gaze on me. "Okay, Kate, here's your part," she pauses for dramatic affect. "There is no you and Jake."

I am dumbfounded. "*This* is what he sent you to tell me? *I* rejected *him,*" I retort as I step back, beyond bristling. "Last night, that's how it went down." I turn to my parents. Laura nods emphatically. "*I* got out of the car."

Mom beams proudly.

"Well done, bun." Dad palms my shoulder.

"That's fantastic!" Jocelyn smiles to the full extent her dermatologist will allow. "So, I repeat, Kate, there is no you and Jake."

My face sets in disgust. "He really sent you here to

EMMA McLAUGHLIN AND NICOLA KRAUS

reject me, so as to unreject himself, so he can have the final rejection?"

"No relationship of any kind," Jocelyn barrels on.

"None," I confirm. "This is pathetic. When you talk to him, tell him I think he's pathetic."

Clasping the leather-bound tome with one arm, Jocelyn swipes her free hand definitively. "No—future—to speak of."

And suddenly it registers that this is a negotiation. "Okay, Jocelyn, let's get to the point. I'll sign your nondisclosure, or whatever, but only *after* he pays my friends their royalties."

Laura jabs a fist. "Right."

Jocelyn's mouth twists, her voice steely. "There is nothing for you to sign, and that other discussion is not on the table."

I turn to Laura as she shakes her head in disbelief. "So if this isn't about a nondisclosure, what *do* you want? A framed photo of me keening in wounded heart-break?"

Jocelyn pulls a folded sheet of lined paper from her pocket. "I personally needed to get clear on a few things, because Jake can be shortsighted and my job is to keep him focused on the big picture. You have helped me with that, and I am grateful. Now, the reason I am here is that he entrusted me with giving you this, which you are to take a look at and then give back to me so I don't find it on eBay five minutes from now. Understood?" Her manicured fingers extend toward me.

I grab the paper. "You were right, Mom, it's probably

a song. Another goddamn song. Where I get out of the car, but with toilet paper stuck to my shoe." As everyone watches I tear into the folds, braced for Jake himself to rise up out of the creases and take it all back, his apology, his desire—

"What if I never left? Meet me in the daylight. J."

Laura rips the paper from my fingers and reads it before it's passed from Mom to Dad. "Thank you." Jocelyn plucks it from his hand and sets a lighter to it, dropping the flaming tail in his coffee. "Fantastic. We're through. So, I was never here. This never happened. That's a wrap." Jocelyn charges down the steps as a white van with AMERICAN EAGLE AIRLINES emblazoned on the side pulls in with my restored luggage.

"Perfect timing." Mom starts to move from the open door toward the staircase as Dad sets his fouled coffee on the railing and picks up the bags by his boots. "Kate, we're leaving in *half* an hour," he says as he carries them past the hole I dug in the zinnia bed.

"There's toast for you on the counter, and if you could strip your sheets that would be great," Mom calls back over her shoulder. "Merry Christmas, Laura!"

"Merry Christmas, Mrs. Hollis," Laura shouts up the stairs. "Have a great trip!"

"Wait," I whisper, my head reverberating with his question as a man gets out of the van with my bag and a clipboard. But nobody stops. Dad signs the release, dumping my wheelie in their trunk. "Wait," I say. "Wait!"

Jocelyn stops at her car door without turning around.

"I think I need to see him," I call out.

"No," Laura gasps. Dad slams the trunk. The van peels away. Mom tears back down the stairs.

I hold my tensed palm up as she approaches. "I've got the counterargument covered, thank you."

"We just talked." Jocelyn stalks back up the drive, Dad on her heels. "You understood your role."

"You're not coming?" he balks.

Mom steps onto the porch. "You agreed, we're leaving for the airport."

Jocelyn tugs out her earpiece. "Listen to the mother."

I drop my head back, unable to look at their confused, hurt faces. "Listen, everyone, I appreciate how involved in this you all are, but I can't just . . ."

"You can *just,"* Laura cries. "That's the whole point! Of course *now* he wants to see you! Of course *now* it's all about you! But you got out of the car, Katie! *You got out of the car!"*

"Good, that's good," Jocelyn strides toward me. "I like that. Yes, this is not your vehicle. Get the fuck away from the car!" Her gold bangles make a discordant clang as she motions to Laura. "Good, what else you got?"

"I did get out of the car, I did." I look from Mom, Dad, and Laura's alarm to Jocelyn's ire. "I—I—don't know. Sometimes, not often, maybe once a year, I'll have been on a bad date, or something, or something that seemed like it was going to be a thing turned out to be a nonthing and I'm driving home and it's late." I try to take a deep breath against my tightening chest. "I'll turn on the radio and look for him." My gaze lands on the porch banister and I leave it there. "And I'll let myself pretend, for just a minute, that he's singing to me. Just to me. And I wonder if I'll *ever* feel like that again." My stomach twists as I watch the color drain from Laura's pregnancy-flushed face.

"*How* can you be so gullible?" Dad's voice is hushed.

"You're standing here romanticizing this lunatic like some naive adolescent." Mom's head shakes in disbelief. "Have you learned *nothing*? I don't know, Simon, I don't know what we're supposed to do. She's clearly incapable of thinking rationally and with any shred of self-preservation when it comes to this boy."

"He's not a boy," I manage. "And I'm *not* seventeen."

"Really Kathryn?" Mom steps past him into my face. "Because you sound like some lovesick, simpering child, and a stupid one at that."

I lean away from her contorted features. "You just hate Jake because he had the gall to write a song calling you a bad mother and a bad wife."

"Katie, don't," Dad snaps.

"No, Simon, it's fine. Fine, Kathryn, hate me. Hate your father. Feed that edge of disdain you always shroud yourself in around us." Her voice stretches in desperation, "But *don't* fall for this, not when you've made it this far—a note passed to you by a *publicist*, like he's in grade school—"

"Oh, yes, so far!" I back from her, tripping down the steps. "I'm standing on the porch in your nightgown! But now I'm finally being given the chance to get out of here, *fully* out of here. Why can't you give me that?"

"Because here's what this looks like, Katie. You get in

295

that car." She extends her arm down the driveway, leaving it there as she continues, her eyes burrowing into me. "Go to him, sleep with him, share every intimate detail of your years of sanity and then, out of nowhere, he's done again and dumps you off some concert tour. You're left flat on your ass with nothing. On the tarmac in Beijing or Moscow. Only now he's got a whole new host of material, so when you show up on our doorstep—" Her lips shake. "And we have to institutionalize our only child, we can still look forward to hearing about the lurid details of her sex life on the speakers of every mall in America!"

I cross my arms, shielding myself against her toxic prediction. "That's what it looks like, huh, my life? *I'm* institutionalized?"

She drops her arm, hunching into herself. "If you go to him."

"If I go to him I am taking a chance to talk to him. Talk to him, Mom, work through the pain and confusion and hurts. We'll discuss it, we'll heal it. We'll move forward through this, not *over* it, which is what you do. So that when you get to Florida and find Dad crying on the floral couch on week whatever of no medication, because he claims he doesn't need any—" I turn to him, looking recalcitrantly impotent in our raging midst. "And you do, Dad. I'm sorry, but you do. Even though she doesn't have the guts to admit it. So, *instead,* she'll solve it by going off and fucking someone, someone you know—maybe the pool guy, or a neighbor. But wait, I forgot, it doesn't matter—it's all good! We don't even need to discuss it. So go ahead, Dad, wallow in depression. Mom, fuck someone, do it right in the condo—Dad can move out, move back in six months later, what does it matter? We'll still sit around Christmas mornings like nothing ever happened. It's all fine. We're all fine. I'm glad Jake wrote that song. I'm grateful Jake wrote that song. Even if you never forgive me for it. Who are *either* of you to talk about learning from the past?" I glare up at her standing on the porch steps, the miserable porch steps. "You know what? It's perfect that you didn't bother to tell me about the house sale. Because as far as I'm concerned you can burn the motherfucking thing to the ground." I turn to Jocelyn. "Take me to him."

22

LAURA'S WEDDING

I grip the spray of flowers at their ribboned base and lick the tear that has slid down my cheek as it hits my lip. *Must not let makeup smear. Must be hottest have ever been.* I look past the seven French twists that separate me from Laura and over to Sam, whose face is flush with emotion as he repeats after the priest. They kiss, the organ swelling into the recessional and Laura turns to the applauding congregation, her eyes sparkling as I well up with joy for them—the surrealism of their grown-up-ness surpassing the surrealism of what will happen next. Deep breath, shoulders back, boobs lifting and . . . turn.

My eyes go directly to the empty seat next to Benjy.

Benjy meets my gaze and shakes his head flatly from side to side, lips puckered. I glance over to see Sam register the same and then to Laura, her expression faltering as their eyes meet. She takes Sam's hand and they beam again, beginning to recess down the cheering aisle.

The wire stays of my dress hold me upright as I trail behind Laura's sorority sisters and step down into the dusky light outside the church. Everyone veers to gather in front of the photographer, while I go directly to the curb, looking from one end of the street to the other—no limo, no entourage, no paparazzi.

"Bridesmaids gather round the bride!" The photographer waves his free hand to me and I go stand where instructed as these strange girls fuss at her veil, laboriously laying the white netting out behind her.

"He didn't come," I murmur, unable to access restraint. Her smile hardens and hurt flickers in her heavily made-up eyes.

"Everyone look at me! Big smiles!"

As the next song starts on the backyard dance floor Dad says something in Mom's ear. Nodding in agreement, she smiles and touches his lapel with her manicured fingers, part of the Day of Grooming I suggested to gird her for spending an evening with a hundred people who have probably deduced she's the selfish floozy currently residing at the top of the *Billboard* chart. They make their way over to their table, where I've been holed up with my third slice of cake and seventh cocktail, knees up between two chairs I swiveled together into a hard-backed chaise. "I think these gave me a blister," she says, slipping her heel out of the crimson pump to check.

"Right." Dad pats the pockets of his seersucker blazer, "I'm going to say our good-byes. Pick you up in front?" he asks. We nod as he goes in search of the Hellers.

"But you were right, Katie," she says, tipsily twirling her foot at the ankle, "Red shoes do give one a boost."

"I didn't say it, Sigourney Weaver did." I run my finger over the gold-rimmed plate, swiping up the last trails of frosting. "I read she always wears red shoes when she has something to do that makes her nervous."

"Well." She drains the remainder of her flute. "Turns out I was in a state over nothing. Walk me to the car?" She picks the last cookie from the plate.

"Claire?" a fuller-figured blonde in a sea-foam evening dress shuffles into our path, a matching clutch held to her side with her upper arm. "Marjorie. Laura's aunt—Jane's sister," she introduces herself, pumping Mom's hand, petals from her wrist corsage fluttering to the grass. "From the Minnesota Hellers."

"So nice to meet you," Mom says as I stare at Laura's teenage cousin from Dubuque dismembering a centerpiece. "Laura made an absolutely beautiful bride. It has been such a privilege to watch that girl grow up."

She continues to clasp Mom's hand, her avid expression not registering anything Mom just said. "I told myself, if I ever got the chance to meet you, I hope you don't mind . . . It's just that Jane's told me all about your horrible situation and I just wanted to say how aghast I've been, how *awful* I think the whole thing is."

Mom's eyes widen. Better accustomed to these pinpricks in my privacy, I cut her off. "Thank you. So kind. We were just heading out."

"That boy should just be taken out and shot. I can't

imagine what you've been through this last year. Every time I hear that song I think, *If you only knew,* if you only *knew* what a horrible *horrible* person that boy is you wouldn't be calling in for it." Out of steam she just nods at Mom, her speech of support trickling away.

"Thank you," Mom says, withdrawing her clasped hand, dying through her glazed smile. They nod at each other, Marjorie looking expectant.

"Well . . ." I search my cocktail-soaked brain for a more pointed extraction.

"I apologize," Mom fills in, "but my husband's waiting with the car."

"It is so great that you made it through all that—he must be a very understanding man."

Mom's smile finally collapses, as does my stomach. "He is." Mom swipes her purse from the table.

"Nice to meet you!" she calls after us, and I wave.

I go to slide my arm through Mom's, but she slips a step to the side. In the glow from the tea lights lining our path to the front of the house I see her face set in a grim line.

"Mom?" I ask as she glances up and down the car-filled street, unable to look at me. "Mom."

She swivels around, her hand hitting my cheek in a swift stinging slap. I stagger back.

Dad pulls up and she folds into the car beside him. I stand motionless. Stunned. "Have fun!" he calls, pulling them out into the dark street.

"Fun," I manage at their retreating taillights as I slowly extend my lower jaw. So done, so over it, all of it,

I slip out of my strappy sandals and unceremoniously drop them into a curbside trash can before wandering back to the house. Taking in the dense June night, letting the sweet air cool my pulsing cheek, I weave along the neighbor's hedge so as to keep soft lawn beneath my feet. Crickets chirp, infusing the humid air around me. My head thick with champagne, I feel my dress, designed to make him regret his entire existence, taut at my every curve, and want him more. Here in the lush heat of Vermont summer. Here on the hood of that parked car—

"Hollis."

A hand grabs me as I trip over big black shoes. I readjust my focus to the lawn, where Benjy sticks his cigarette in his lips and squints up, steadying me with his other hand.

"Woo," I murmur, sliding down next to him at the base of the elm.

"Smoke?" He reaches into his blazer abandoned on the grass. I nod, taking the burning cigarette from his lips and inhaling deeply. He grins.

"Thanks," I exhale, feeling the earth's dampness sinking into the sateen. "Happy wedding." I return his cigarette.

"Yeah." He props his wrists on his knees and, for a moment, looks enough like the memory of Jake that I find myself leaning in, eyes drifting closed. Our lips meet, the taste of tobacco traveling between us as we move apart.

Nothing.

He stares at the sidewalk in front of us. "I should go find my date. Jen'll be looking for me."

I nod, pushing off this humiliation into the cattle car of humiliation that is this weekend. "I'm . . ." I search through words. "I thought tonight I'd finally get—"

"Yeah." Benjy rocks to a stand, lifting up his blazer and flipping it over his shoulder. "Thought I'd get a ticket out of my dad's shop—pay for school. Should've known he'd chicken out. Fucking wuss. Always was." He looks toward the house glowing over the hedge. "Walk back with me. You don't want to pass out here."

"I don't know," I mutter. "It'd top the whole experience off quite nicely."

He lifts me up and I sink into his side as we walk around to the backyard, crossing a pair of waiters balancing trays of emptied glasses. Arm around my waist, he stops us by the poles of the tent to watch as the flower girl, white Mary Janes abandoned, spins like a dervish on the burnished parquet.

"Nice lipstick." Jen comes into view. My fingers go to my mouth. "Not you, bitch."

I pull away from Benjy, refocusing on the smear of MAC's Film Noir across his lips.

"Katie." We spin to see Laura standing in the doorway. Jen pushes past her, running inside and up the darkened staircase. Benjy's shoulders slump as he follows. "Were you hooking up with him?" Laura's face twists in disgusted disbelief.

I stumble, trying to regain my footing now that I have to ballast myself. "We just kissed, it was nothing."

"I can't believe you—" She is cut off by an amp crackling with loud guitar. We both turn to where a bunch of the groomsmen lounge around a table as Sam strokes his old Fender, Jake's chords breaking through the lingering conversations. Laura's eyes harden as she looks from them to me, her face flushed. "I don't get it."

"What?"

"How you could *still* . . . after *everything*—" She stops herself, straightening her pearl combs.

"Want him?"

"Yes!" she exclaims as if just getting through to a recalcitrant child.

"I'm sure you don't," I sneer, the disappointment of the last forty-eight hours spiking in my chest.

"You're sure I don't?!" she shouts, lunging forward. "I have listened to every last *word, hope, dream* and *fantasy* of Jake Sharpe."

"You don't!" Rage breaks open at her and her chilly posse of engaged Phi Mu sisters. *"What* have you *ever* had to want?! You've had the utter devotion of your soul mate since *eleventh grade!* He just *married* you! I'm the one in the bridesmaid's dress."

"The bridesmaid's dress I had to force four busty friends of mine into so that you could look unforgettable for the return of the rockstar who's *not coming.* You hear that, Sam?" she yells across the tented lawn, *"Not coming!"* The guests quiet. "I can't wait to tell our children about the wedding theme Mommy and Daddy chose, 'Jake's Not Coming'! And we'll have to tell them something, won't we, while we're using the money for their college tuition still paying off this event because the royalties sure-as-fuck won't." Her hands go to her temples and she scrunches her eyes.

"Laura." I murmur.

"What's it going to take, Katie?"

"I'm not proud of this," I say, shrinking.

"But you'd still give yourself to him, if you could. If he'd showed up tonight. With or *without* the papers for everyone to sign and the checks for everyone to cash. You would have—tonight—forgiven everything to be back in-the-presence-of. And so would you." She shakes her thin arm out at Sam as he stands, the Mc-Clellan's blush drained from his face. "This was my day. Just one. And that's what you have to say to me after all these years, my best friend who never comes home— he's not coming? You break my heart. Both of you." I step toward her as she crumples into her dress, but Sam pushes past me, wrapping her in his arms and, against her protests, guiding her gently into the house.

23

December 24, 2005

Avoiding the rowdy throngs of paparazzi barricading the Sharpe gates, the rental car—"A Dodge Daytona!" Jocelyn shouts into her cell from the front seat, "I know! How Andy Griffith is that?"—pulls in half a mile down, curving past skeletons of barns from a different era eroding in snow-covered fields. My suitcase open beside me on the backseat, I zip the cashmere hoodie over my bra and extract my hairbrush, trying to slow my lungs, my heart, my brain, trying to ignore her stream of invectives—"Vermont! Fucking Vermont!"—and use these last few minutes to debate if this is a massive mistake. Decisively tossing Mom's balled-up nightgown out the open window I press the button to raise the pane before crisply snapping the hem of my jeans over my kitten-heeled boots.

The car slows to a stop along the dirt road.

"Here?" Jocelyn asks the driver. He hands her yet another sheet of lined paper with Jake's scrawled instructions and hops out to open my door.

"Oh, okay, thank you," I say to him, now actually

obligated to leave the heated vehicle. The supple leather sinks into the deep snow as I stand. "Are you *sure* this is right?"

"Hey! Up here!" Jake's voice calls and I pivot around, blinking up to where he sits, smoking a cigarette, his legs dangling over the edge of a decaying tree house. Out here in the middle of a field, in the middle of winter. He waves. "Good morning."

The Dodge suddenly revs its engine, the back wheels unearthing a spray of snow as it pulls away, leaving us in chirp-filled stillness. Shielding my eyes from the crisp sun, I look to where his suspended boots swing like Kermit feet. "Of course you're up a tree."

"The view's really something!" he shouts down. "Promise!"

"Okay . . ." I clomp through the powder and begin to ascend the rough-hewn planks of wood nailed through the bark. His hand reaches to pull me assuredly to the platform.

"Lost your coat?" he asks, unsnapping his jacket.

I slip it on, feeling how his body has warmed it through. "No time to get it in the Exodus." I swivel myself around and let my legs remain hanging off the side beside his. And the view is gorgeous, acres of branches forming a black lattice against the ivory and the Sharpe house sitting upon its cake platter in the distance.

"Smoke?"

"Not since college. I'd think with your voice . . ."

He looks down at the stub of his butt. "Recording

industry keeps the tobacco industry alive. Backstage at the Grammys, everyone's got a honey bear in one hand and a pack of Marlboros in the other. But I try to confine it to late-night or when I'm . . . a little nervous. Otherwise my team gets on my case."

"You have a team?" I ask, straightening my arms against the wood floor.

"Well, you know, my throat guy, my trainer, my publicist—"

"Yes, we've bonded. What, you couldn't get an *actual* deposed dictator?"

He laughs. "I know, she's fierce, right? I need that though. I thrive on it. I believe you planted those seeds pretty deep." He stubs out the cigarette in an ashy semicircle and flicks the filter to the ground. "Come on, let's go inside, I think it's a little warmer in there."

"Is it really a sauna?"

"What?" He whips his legs around and crawls into the small room, which is empty, save for the blanket and thermos.

"Todd said your mom had hollowed out all the structures on your property and built stuff inside—you know, basketball courts and the like."

He laughs as I crawl in beside him. "Well, there's an indoor pool behind the garage, but that's it. Good idea, though. Here." He unfolds the blanket and drapes the heavy wool over my legs.

"Thanks. Why haven't I been up here?"

"I don't know, I kind of outgrew this place by the time we got together. You're the first girl up."

I rub my tingling palms together. "Tell the next one to bring earmuffs."

"I don't want there to be a next one." He puts his hand on my thigh.

"Jake." I take it off.

"I shouldn't have posed the question?" he asks.

"No. Yes. We should've talked first."

"We did talk."

"I mean about making huge changes. About hurting other people. I'm touched, I am. But our lives are so far apart—"

"You're touched?"

"Yes, but—"

"Look, I did what I did because I want to." He takes my chilled hands in his and holds my gaze. "I owe that much to both of us. To just put it out there, clean and simple."

"But, here's the problem, Jake." I slip from his grip to gesticulate. "And I should mention, problem, like, one hundred three out of about forty-two thousand. I don't know you. I mean, yes, it's clear we still have, you know, heat. But I don't know who you are now."

"Well, for starters: this is my tree house." He swings his right arm in introduction. "Tree House, this is Katie."

"It's Kate, now. I'm thirty."

"Sorry, tree house—Kate—drop the *i* on her guest towels."

"See?" I shiver. "I don't even know about your tree house, and this was around before me."

He unscrews the thermos lid. "Okay, let's see. After

Return of the Jedi came out I was driving my dad nuts about wanting my very own Ewok village—hot toddy?"

I nod, plunging my hands into his jacket pockets.

"I just kept bugging him and bugging him." He pours me a shot. "When he put me off I started twisting screw-drivers into trees with that kid with the Coke-bottle glasses—"

"The one with the lazy eye?"

He nods. "We were best buds back then. So, like, three trees die, my mother goes nuts."

"I bet she did," I laugh, raising the little metal cup.

"Cheers." He clinks it gently with the thermos. "So my dad got some guy at the factory to build this place. And it was pretty cool, even if it wasn't inside the tree." He knocks back a swig.

I down the cupful, liquid coating my throat, burning its way between my ribs as I ready myself. "Jake," I look down at the cap, circling my thumb around its rim. "That you wrote about me, about us, I understand. I get that our relationship was yours, too. But to write about my mom . . ." I look over at him.

"That was about you seeking refuge in me, the closest I ever felt to you, that we ever got."

"But to come back to her infidelity album after album, I honestly don't know if I can ever—"

"That's not your family." He taps the bottom of the thermos against the edge of the platform, his mouth twisting. "That's my dad."

"What?"

"He had this other woman set up in Denver. They have two kids now and he stopped traveling, so yeah."

"Oh, God, Jake, I had no—"

"Me neither." He clams his left hand shut and starts methodically pressing each joint in, cracking the knuckles. "Mom found out my first year in L.A. when she contested the settlement her lawyer unearthed this woman."

"Jake, I'm so sorry."

"Yeah, it's pretty sick. The divorce took years and the details that came out." He grimaces as he switches to his right hand. "Like he used to collect things from his trips—"

"Those soaps, I remember."

"Yeah, turns out he had guys from work bring them back from *their* exotic trips—he was in Denver the whole time. We don't talk. So"—he forces a laugh—"that's that."

That's that. Calculating the hours, the years, the decade of wasted ire, I pass him the cap back and watch as he refills it for himself. Chagrin burgeoning into relief, I study his face up close in the sparkles of reflected daylight, the shadow of stubble that wasn't there before, the little spray of creases from his eyes, the cluster of pale freckles the camera doesn't read. "Wait a minute—didn't Kristi Lehman get a hickey up here? She did!"

"God, that's right! I totally blanked on that."

"So, I'm not the first girl up here!" I slap his knee.

"You're the first woman, Ms. Thirty. Jesus, what do you think Kristi Lehman's doing right now?"

"Rubbing her neck wistfully and praying you'll write a song about it." I take another sip, the liquid going down easier. "Actually, Sam saw her. She's running the mini-mart in Fayville. You so wish you were here with her right now."

"Not a chance. It was awkward as hell and I got a massive splinter trying to get her bra off." He leans back, letting his torso rest on the gnarled floor. I prop myself on my arm and look down at him, his hair falling away from his chiseled face, the angle so intimate, a view of him that's still somehow privileged.

"Come here." He pulls me down, his arm wrapping around me, my head coming to rest under his chin. I lie there with him, our breath falling into sync, feeling like a strewn toy suddenly remembered and returned to the privileged crook. The masking Gucci smell from the night before is gone, letting the sweet scent of his skin disorient me, making me want to turn my face up and kiss. I take a deep breath, letting the icy air ensnare me in my purpose. I sit up.

"Jake what went down between us, well, we're figuring that out. But it's untenable that you never gave those guys any credit. Untenable."

He pulls the blanket over his head. "I know."

"Don't joke." I pull the blanket down, its weight flattening his hair. "This is a deal-breaker."

He sighs. "I told you, it's totally complicated."

I push myself away from him. "And this isn't?"

He lifts the blanket over my head, covering us both as

he pulls me down next to him. "No work talk, I'm begging. We're hanging out. What did you call it?"

"Getting to know you."

"Yes, that."

Flailing the blanket off, I pull back and stare at his sheepish expression, determined. "If you don't do right by my friends, there is no 'you' I want to know. Are we clear?"

He sits up, the flirtatious boy energy suddenly dissipated. He looks me in the eye. "Clear."

"Really? You'll tell Jocelyn and your lawyers? You'll sign the papers?"

"Yes." An unfettered lightness floods through me as he takes my face in his hands. "I need you—Kate," he emphasizes my adult name. "I think I keep writing about you just to keep your voice in my head."

"I'm your Jiminy Cricket?"

He laughs. "*You* are the best thing that ever happened to me."

"Can your lawyers draw up something to that effect, as well?" I laugh with him, finally able to let myself feel the elation of being right where I am.

He kisses me gently. "I can't be apart from you again."

"You just got one ring back," I deflect, though his words outstrip my most outlandish fantasy.

"No, listen, I have a week in New York before my Asia tour launches. Spend it with me."

"Jake, I don't know if we're ready to . . ." I hedge.

He runs a finger along my jawbone. "I promised I'd

have Christmas Eve with my mom. Are you up for some Sharpe Family Holiday Festivities?"

"Where we douse her in sherry and set her alight?"

He laughs. "She'll be good, I promise. And we have a beautiful tree." He leans in and kisses me. It is delicious and insistent. "We'll fly to New York tomorrow morning first thing. We'll have an amazing week together and get to know each other for real. And then we'll see, *you'll* see that you and I are—that we've been waiting thirteen years for our lives to start—" He's interrupted by the sharp crack of a tree branch breaking. We turn, following the sound to the scratched plastic window as brightness, infinitely whiter than the sunlight filtering in a moment ago, explodes around us.

✿

"They're taking pictures of the carolers." Susan lets the taupe silk curtain drop back. "What kind of inhumane outfit makes its photographers work Christmas Eve?"

I set my champagne flute down on the coffee table, wishing it were whiskey. "Actually, I think they all work freelance, so they're sort of out there by choice."

"It's always tempting to open the door and just let them take their pictures so they can go home," Jake says from atop the ladder where he's straightening the angel. The last chorus of "O Tannenbaum" grows quiet as they move on to a house not under siege. "But it doesn't work like that."

"There, dear, that's much better," Susan nods approvingly from the brocade settee and Jake beams, reaching in to space the garlands and lights. "It was making me seasick. Smoked salmon?" She nudges the sterling tray of pristine triangles toward me.

"No, thank you," I say, my stomach not having caught up to a festive holiday meal from running through fields with a charge of telephoto lenses at my heels. "They did a great job of putting everything back together," I offer to mollify declining her canapés, looking around the room, the silence I remember about this house once again stiflingly thick. "Speaking of carols, could we put some on?" I ask.

"Oh." Her lined face sinks. "This is my first Christmas here in ages. I wasn't even sure we still had ornaments. I usually meet Jake and my brother's family in Vail. Let me check." Knuckles against the brocade she pushes herself up and makes her way, reasonably steadily, to the bookshelves where a row of CDs sits among picture frames and a few velum-bound volumes on Nelson. She unfolds her glasses from the gold chain around her neck and peruses the labels. "The Vienna Boys Choir," she announces after a few moments of browsing. "That'll sound festive." She puts the disk into the machine and strains of "Exultate Jublilate" fill the room. Not exactly chestnuts roasting, but better than the deafening nothing.

"Ma'am?" A woman in a crisp gray uniform pushes open the swinging door. "The roast'll be ready in a few minutes if you want to make your way to the table. The bisque is served."

"Thank you, Mary."

"Who wants their gifts?" Jake asks, hopping off the ladder.

"Jake, the bisque is served." Susan smoothes her nubby tweed skirt.

"I know, but I can't wait. You go to the table. I'll be right down." He bounds up the stairs, leaving us to each other.

"You have such a beautiful home," I say, joining her at the threshold of the French doors that lead to the dining room.

She looks around, her eyes landing on the MTV-gouged wood paneling, her lips pursing, rose lipstick feathering into the deep smoker's creases. "You have no idea what it took to get all of this installed properly up here. I had a whole team from Boston round the clock."

"Well, it's always been beautiful," I say, taking a seat opposite her place at the grand table. We sit in silence beneath the crystal chandelier throwing stripes across the brown jacquard wallpaper. "In high school. I always remember how well-appointed everything was." She allows a thin smile.

We both lift our heads at the clomp of Jake's feet taking the stairs two at a time. He tears in and, tossing a small robin's egg blue box to me, rounds the table to his mother, handing her a large glossy brown package with J. MENDEL printed on top. He pulls in the chair closest to her as she empties her flute and reaches for the decanter of red.

"Well?" He looks from her to me. "Open them!" He hops his chair one inch closer to his mother's side.

Taken aback, I look down at the ring-size box. "Jake? How did you?"

"Had one of my people there at ten A.M. when they opened and in a car on the way here by ten fifteen." He beams. In the absence of any motion from Susan I untie the red ribbon and lift the lid. Inside is a small velvet box in the same blue. I look at him questioningly. He smiles back, but he's not leaping to his knee, so I exhale and crack the lid. Inside is a square-cut sapphire the size of a Scrabble tile framed by two diamond baguettes.

"Jake," I say, floored. "Oh my God."

Susan drains her glass.

"Do you like it?" he asks.

"It's gorgeous." I tilt the box so the sapphire can catch the light. "But I can't accept it."

"It's just a promise ring. For your right hand. I figure I've asked you to say yes to enough for one day. But I want you to have it. Think of it as a corsage, thirteen birthday presents, thirteen Christmas presents and three graduation gifts rolled into one."

"Okay," I laugh, slipping the heavy platinum on my finger, feeling the groundedness of the cool weight. "When you put it that way, where're the matching earrings?"

"Mom?" he prompts, leaning forward.

"Who wants to say grace?"

"Mom?" he repeats, elbows extended like bent wings as he grips the chair arms.

"Oh, dear, of course. Everything on your clock." One tug at the brown and white grosgrain ribbon and it falls away. Lifting the lid, she unfurls the brown and white tissue paper while Jake looks on expectantly. Breath held, we both watch her draw out a gorgeous horizontally pieced mink pullover.

"It's stunning," I say in the absence of any response from Susan. "Very Audrey Hepburn."

"Catherine Zeta-Jones was wearing one, and I asked her where she got it. You like it, Mom?"

"It's lovely, dear. Thank you." She brushes his proferred cheek with her lips. "Do you want to take your seat so we can start? There is nothing to be said for lukewarm bisque."

He gets up, returning the chair he'd slid over, and moves to his assigned place diagonally across from her. "If it doesn't fit you can exchange it the next time you come to New York."

"No, it's fine. Not sure where I'll wear it, though . . ." She dips her spoon into the pink.

"Well, when you go back to Vail," he tries valiantly. "And when you visit your friends in Boston and in Paris—it'll look great in Paris."

"I have so many clothes I never get around to wearing." She takes another spoonful. "But I'm sure I'll find a use for it. I can always donate it."

His face slackening, he reaches for a hunk of bread hiding beneath the damask in the sterling lattice bowl.

"I love this ring, Jake," I rush in. "It's absolutely gorgeous."

"You do?" He smiles. "I picked it out. I didn't go in person, but I selected it online."

"It's beautiful."

Jake's phone rings and he pulls it from his pocket to glance at the number. "Jesus," he mutters. "I've gotta take this. Tokyo is not having Christmas." He pushes back from the table and stands up. "Yeah. Hit me," he says as he walks with the call out to the living room. I stare past his retreating torso to the tree, whose bare base only now strikes me.

"This soup is delicious," I say.

"Mary's recipe." She reflexively touches her velvet headband. "I shall pass on your compliments."

"Did you get Jake anything?" I ask.

"What?" she asks in turn.

"For Christmas? Did you get him anything?"

"Oh," she tuts, fingering her glasses chain. "For the man who has everything? What could he want for?"

I picture my spoon hitting her forehead, leaving a creamy pink circle above her stunned expression.

Jake sticks his head in, still on the call, and presses his hand over the mouthpiece. "Actually, Mom, looks like we have to fly back tonight," he whispers. Relieved, I nod supportively. He retreats back into the living room.

Holding my gaze, she clinks her crystal glass with her fork.

The door swings open. "Yes, ma'am?"

"You can clear, Mary."

"Thank you, ma'am."

As Mary circles the table there is a pause that even the Vienna Boys Choir and Jake's low murmur of assent from the other room cannot fill. Susan stares, her gaze starting to cross as she bores into me. Finally, her eyes descending to her gilt charger, she speaks, "I have a beautiful home. You have a beautiful ring."

I lean back so Mary can take my bowl. "Sorry?"

"Jake's father was in Saskatchewan when I was in labor. Not quite Asia. But still, not with me."

"I don't see—"

"Ask yourself, where is he on my birthday? Where is he on my child's birthday?" She takes another sip. "Then admire your beautiful ring."

✼

Jake leans across me and presses PH on the brushed steel panel. He squeezes my hand as the industrial-style elevator slowly glides up the concrete chute, the locked doors to each passing apartment visible through the burnished slats. "God, it's so late. Thanks for doing this," he says the thousandth time since we got in the car for the airport. "Do you hate me? I just couldn't take . . ." he trails off.

"Jake, it's *fine*," I repeat. "The thought of spending the night under the same roof as your mother was not thrilling me, either. It's all good. Really, truly, I mean it."

"Good." He smiles, seemingly finally able to take in my stream of enticed reassurances as we slow our ascent, strips of light sweeping over us from the first open door. The gate slides aside.

"This is us." He beams welcome, guiding me into a vast loft ringed by spectacular twinkling views of Tribeca and the New Jersey shoreline beyond. "Pretty great, huh?"

"Wow. Yes." I let my fingers slip from his to walk to the windows and rest my forehead against the frosted glass. I look down to the winsome cobbled street, its margins covered with days-old mounds of snow that look from here like cappuccino froth dotted with a liberal sprinkling of cocoa powder. I turn my gaze up to the avenue and recognize the awning of the restaurant that guy took me to last fall during our romantic-oh-wow-we're-really-not-right-for-eachother weekend. If I'd had any idea, as I endured his pontification about the advantages of tax cuts for the top one percent, that all this was possible only a few feet, a few floors away, I'd have scaled the building.

I feel Jake behind me, his hands sliding under my hoodie, fanning across my back. "It's after midnight," he whispers. "Merry Christmas."

"Merry Christmas." I twist my head to the side, our mouths connecting as his fingers slip around to my breasts.

"I want you to like it here."

"I do," I say, replying to his touch. He takes my hand again and leads me past the lustrous David Smith sculptures hazily reflecting the collage of Eames and early American furniture, down a hallway that seems to run the length of the block.

"Here." He smiles as he opens the last door into a lacquered rust red room, and we both look to the bed, piled invitingly with plush gray flannel and black silk. He picks a remote off the bedside table and points it at a panel in the wall and then at the curtains, which commence jerking open and closed, drowning out the sound of a CD starting to whir.

"No music," I preempt.

"Sure?" he asks, remote poised.

"Not even 'Michael Row Your Boat Ashore.' "

As he zaps the device again, silencing the panel, I walk around the room, peering at the personal effects on the bookshelves and mantel—a small soapstone polar bear, a mosaic dish, a souvenir shot glass from Perth.

"Come on," he begs the renegade curtains.

I bend to get a closer look at the bottom shelf of the closest bookcase, where a few framed photographs sit in the shadows—his father feeding a radiant Susan wedding cake in sepia tone, Jake in a cowboy hat, his cheeks puffed out as he blows out a melting 3 candle on a cake bigger than him, a lithe Jake cannonballing off the dock, and then, tucked behind all of them—a small heart-shaped frame that I remember picking out with Laura. And there I am in his basement, cracking up at something with Sam right when Jake snapped the picture.

"Thank you," he says, and I look up to see the fabric finally sliding closed with a contented sigh.

I cross to him, take his face, and kiss him deeply, last reservations gone.

24

TWELFTH GRADE

"Yes, I picked them up—they look *awesome*—but the guy said if it starts to rain we have to take them off *immediately* or our feet will turn periwinkle and bubblegum," I say, scratching *shoes* off my list.

"If it starts to rain," Laura declares, "I will kill myself. So having periwinkle feet will only add a jazzy touch at the open casket."

I twist the spiraling cord. "Light a candle, do a dance, offer to give up sex."

"On it. Love you, 'bye."

Holding the phone by its head I replace the mallard in its cradle. Twisting around on the green couch I look over to Jake tuning his guitar in the rays of afternoon sunshine streaming through their basement dormer window. "Okay, so Laura says Sam dropped off the deposits for the tuxes so you just need to pick them up by three tomorrow—he'll meet you there. That'll give you guys time to get to Harriman's and set your equipment up before going home to get ready."

"Cool," he says, not looking up.

"You'll remember? Because Laura and I have our hair and nails starting at two so we won't be home to call and remind you."

"No, got it," he says, his eyes on the strings as he strums, searching for the perfect pitch, but not finding it.

"And Laura decided we do want to go to the preparty at Michelle's, so you guys're gonna pick us up at seven. We'll both be at Laura's, because my mom wanted my dad to come over for the pre-prom pictures and it just started to turn into this whole big drama and I couldn't deal, and she was crying, so I've decided, rather than having the most depressing preprom photos ever, I'd just skip out of the whole thing and stand between the Hellers."

"Great."

"Jake?"

"No, great." He finally stops tuning and lifts his head, his expression anguished.

"What?" my voice drops with concern. He stares, his face emptying as he studies me. "Jake? Is everything okay, is your mom okay?" Suddenly the intensity of his gaze stops my breath. "Jake, what?" But he just continues to concentrate on me for a long moment like he's seeing really far and I don't know what's coming.

He clears his throat, not taking his eyes off me as he lowers the guitar to the floor. "Come here." He pats the top of the washing machine. "Hop up."

"Okay . . ." I slide my backpack to the floor, standing and crossing to him. Apprehensive, I spring onto the cool white metal with a hollow thud. He twists toward me and I move my knees apart so he can stand between them. Again that anguished look, but only for a moment before he reaches past and I turn my head to try to see, but only hear the clicking and feel the washer turn on, sending a vibration through my hips.

He pulls back, pressing his mouth onto mine and we kiss, deeply, our tongues sliding against each other, consuming. He pulls away, running his lips over my neck—sternum—breasts—hands sliding up my thighs. The room drops into shadow—the sun moving out of their yard—his chin on my stomach—staring up at me—sliding my underwear down—I fall back on my elbows—his chestnut hair disappearing beneath my skirt—his tongue—and never—never—never have I—my head drops back—he tilts my pelvis—pressing me into the churning metal—fingers slipping in me as his mouth his mouth his mouth and I . . . and I . . . and I want . . . I want . . . I want . . . I want life always . . . to . . . always . . . to always . . . be . . . this.

25

December 26–December 31, 2005

I flip one of the black European square pillows from the floor against the headboard and prop myself up bent-kneed while Jake scans through his DVD library, retying his pajama pants. "Ready for the next one?" He queues up *Godfather III* on the flat-screen over the mantle.

Tucking the front tails of his flannel shirt between my bare legs I ask, "Shouldn't we actually leave this room at some point today? Or at least this bed?" I look out at the flakes of snow drifting in the coral radiance of the setting sun.

"Do you have a need not being satisfied?" He lunges onto the mattress, the down duvet puffing around the impact as he bites my thigh. "What do you want?" He leans across me to pull open the mini-fridge under his night table.

"Any more Fresh Samantha?" I crawl onto his back and kiss the sweet saltiness of his neck while gazing down at the dwindling supply of blue-topped Fiji.

"Nope. No worries, I'll do a kitchen run." He swivels his head to kiss me, his fingers running under the shirt, mine moving over his body in turn as we start to miss yet another substantial chunk of Coppola's opus. His cell shudders on the lacquer tabletop for the tenth time this hour.

"Don't you need to answer that?" I ask, bracing my hands on his chest.

He pulls himself off and slides to the floor where he stands, smiling down at me, his hands resting on my feet.

"What," I ask, self-conscious.

"Nothing. You just look so right here, all bed-headed and bed-worn, beautiful." The phone continues to rumble its way across the table. He pats my feet. "Fuck 'em." He crosses to the door. "I haven't had a day off in three months. They can sweat it for a few." At the threshold he turns, cocking his head. "Aren't you having fun?"

"I am." I wrap my arms around the huge pillow, watching the dusk bask the walls in a lustrous sheen. "I just don't want to get you fired."

"Ah, but I'm the one who fires." He taps the bookcase framing the doorway with his knuckles. "And does kitchen runs, sit tight."

"Something crunchy!" I call after him as I get up from the tousled silks to pick some lighter holiday viewing from the cabinet. I skip over the foreign films, the Japanime and the large selection of documentaries, looking for anything comedic or maybe holiday-themed. Dispelling the image of my parents probably at this moment nestled in front of *Kind Hearts and Coronets,* I land on Jake's name and pull the case from the shelf.

"Your concert footage," I read from the back as he returns, bags of popcorn in his arms, bottles and glasses clamped between his fingers.

"Oh God, yeah." He tips forward to set down the smoothies and spill the foil bags onto the bedside. "That shouldn't be there. I try to keep all the work stuff contained in my office. It's bad feng shui."

"I want to see your office."

He gives me a skeptical look as he twists off the cap and pours the lumpy banana-scented concoction into the vintage Happy Meal glasses. "Okay, why?"

"Just 'cause."

He passes me a full glass and we clink before he chugs his down, slapping it onto the table like it was an empty beer stein, licking the thin yellow film from his upper lip. "Then I will give you the tour." He gestures to the doorway with a concierge half-bow. "After you. Take a left."

I set my glass down and follow the long hallway, my bare feet curling away from the cold poured cement.

"Third door on your right."

I twist the knob and enter into what I'd mistakenly imagined Susan Sharpe would've turned her own house into, a shrine to Jake. Part wood-paneled office, part pillow-strewn creative nest, every surface blazens with his image and accomplishments. I cross to the teeming wall opposite the desk where his six multiplatinum albums hang above framed cover art, tour posters, and photographs with everyone from Leonard Cohen to Jay-Z. Over the curved art deco desk is the Gus Van Sant film he had the cameo in and did the soundtrack for.

"Ah, yes, that." I shake my head at the poster.

"Yeah? What about it?"

"That was *supposed* to have been a raging fiasco. For *months* I looked forward to raging fiasco. But, of course, not so much."

"I told you—there's nothing interesting in here." He takes my hand and tries to pull me out, leaving me hopping on one foot across the Tibetan rug.

"No, wait." I right myself as I wriggle from his grasp. On one of the teak bookcases is a row of DVDs. "Let's watch one of these," I say, sliding out the first one, a collector's compilation of all his music videos.

"No, God, no," he laughs. "And watch how awful my hair was? And those mid-'nineties outfits? I am wearing leather pants in one of them. Leather pants! God, no."

"Come on," I plead. "It'll be fun." I sidle up to him in all my half-nakedness. "I've been studiously avoiding all this stuff for years. You can immerse me in your oeuvre."

"I'll show you what I want to immerse in you." He lifts me up and tosses me onto the desk. I squeal as he slides on top, pushing more memorabilia to the floor to shimmy me across the ebonized wood. He slips inside and I ballast the soles of my feet along the scalloped edge, meeting him. Suddenly he stops and peers into my face. "Not because you didn't like it, right?"

"What?" I ask, breathless.

"You didn't avoid all my stuff because you don't think it's any good?" His face is suddenly awash in the wound I was braced to see at Christmas Eve dinner that never surfaced.

I push myself up on my elbows, with him still inside. "Jake, no, of course, I love your music."

"You don't have to say that," he bites as if I've just lied. "It may not be your taste. Neil Strauss said my last album was reductive and atonal."

"Who?" I ask, now so far from an orgasm.

"The *Times*."

"Oh." I inhale sharply, trying to catch up. "But it was a huge hit. So, who cares about him?"

Somehow he is still hard. "We're not talking about Neil Strauss," he sneers. "We're talking about you and if you like what I do."

"Oh, God," I struggle to erase the exasperation from my voice. "I love your music. What do you want me to say? I listen to it every day? No. I don't. You left."

Suddenly his demeanor abruptly relaxes. His hips start to move again. "But I'm here now."

⁂

I slowly blink awake, starting to renestle my naked frame against Jake's, when I become aware that something woke me, aware of movement in the dark room. "Jake?" Suddenly there's a loud crack. I whip up, clutching the covers to my chest. But the man in the jumpsuit prying the Damien Hirst off the wall opposite takes no notice.

"What the fuck?!" Jake leaps out of bed. *"Joss!"*

She appears in the doorway, silhouette backlit by the sunshine streaming down the hall. As she strides into the room and my eyes adjust I realize, that, while Joss-like in every way, down to the clanking Chanel bangles, she is,

in fact, not Joss. Her diaphanous blouse billowing behind her, the woman looks down at Jake over her own
leather-bound binder. "Well Eden's certainly not missing
out on much, is she?"

Unfazed, Jake plants his muscled legs. "What are you
doing here?"

Jocelyn flaps through the door, looking harried.
"Gwen, *what* is the fucking rush?" She strides up to her
doppelgänger. "Is Eden having an antique emergency?
She can't live without her Chippendale tchotchkes for
one week?"

"She is not leaving her invaluable collection in the
hands of this maple syrup hick and his outlet mall strum-
pet." Gwen glances over at me, gripping the cashmere
throw around my bare torso with my elbows. "Wow,
you *have* seen the softer side of Sears."

"Everyone out!" Jocelyn shouts, her taut body emanating an enormous sound. *"Now!"* She walks Gwen and
her orange-suited henchmen to the door, shooting a
withering glance back at Jake's nudity. "When I call, you
fucking answer. Put your pants on. This is not a performance day."

Looking duly slapped, he pulls his jeans up and
reaches for a kimono hanging on the back of the closet.
"I'll take care of this. Here." He tosses the embroidered
silk toward the bed as he follows them out, forgetting to
shut the door behind him.

"Oh." I sit for a moment contemplating my next
move as the men in jumpsuits carry packing crates back
and forth a few feet away. I lean forward, keeping the

throw at my breasts and reach to the far corner of the mattress, grasping the tip of the belt loop with my fingernails, and drag it to me. I swing around to face the curtains and slip into the oversize robe in one quick motion.

"Is she fucking *kidding*?" I am beaconed by Jake's distress down the hallway, past a parade of life-size black-and-white Meisel nudes of Eden making its way to the front of the apartment—as if the jumpsuited men were marching in protest of naked thin people.

"Jake?" I ask, lifting the long rectangular sleeves to block the rising sun reflecting off the Hudson, lighting a living room transformed into a chaotic obstacle course of crates and straw. The walls are bare, the couch is gone. A mover stomps past carrying a metal pole.

"Is that a—"

"Eden's." Jocelyn nods. "Want it?"

"Uh, no . . . thanks."

She bellows from her diaphragm again. "GWEN, DON'T FORGET YOUR SKANK'S SKANK ROD!" She turns to Jake, who is looking increasingly panicked as his home is dismantled into bubble-wrap rolls the size of hay bales. "Jake," her voice lowers, "I will take care of this." She bends her knees, swiveling her face up into his sight line. "I will take care of everything." One of her freckled hands squeezes his arm. "I will have them out of here in a few hours and I'll get Richard McGeehan on the phone and he will have this place re-designed to perfection by the time you get back from Asia. I promise."

At those two words Jake relaxes. "I'm sorry I went AWOL—it won't happen again." He bends down to rub the top of his head against her shoulder. "And make sure none of my midcentury modern *accidentally* wanders into their crates. You're an angel."

"Well, you're a little devil." She smirks, patting his hair.

All forgiven, Jake lightens. "Breakfast?" He turns and offers me his hand as Joss shouts, "HELLO?" into her headset and I trail his naked back, eager to get away from their *Manchurian Candidate* rapport—and the hordes of strangers who have infested our cloister.

But I follow him instead into a kitchen clearly designed to cater parties. Big parties. Two Viking ranges, two Sub-Zeros, three sinks—all stainless steel, all gleaming, and all populated. A man in a chef uniform is pulling a tray of steaming croissants out of the oven to the salivating coos of two women filling their coffee cups from a massive urn. At the sink a uniformed woman scours the last few days' dishes as she carries on about the snow with a man in a tracksuit reading the paper over poached fish in a sort of postmodern breakfast nook. And it dawns that, in fact, the cloister is theirs.

"Hey, everyone, this is Kate." I wave to a chorus of heys.

"Have a good break?" Jake greets the chef in passing. "Dude, are we out of kimchi?" he asks into the fridge before the man can answer.

"Third shelf," he replies, as I back myself toward the large neoprene-upholstered banquette, feeling my distinct lack of panties.

"Whoa." I spin into the face of a faux-hawked man in black jeans tight as Capezio leggings.

"Sorry."

He reaches down to brush off the pristine white tip of his black Converse, even though I am barefoot. "Hey, Jake. Niiice move, man. You dominated Christmas. You had better ratings than Santa."

"Thanks, dude!" Jake grins, swilling from a glass bottle. "Kate, liquified kimchi?"

I wave a no-thanks as Jocelyn does a glissade through the door, headset framing her like swan feathers. "That was Jann, calling from his holiday in the Maldives. *Rolling Stone* wants the cover—"

"Excellent."

"With Katie."

"Kate," he reminds her.

"Annie Leibovitz's gonna shoot it—she's thinking something Byzantine to comment on contemporary iconography in American culture—maybe trick you out like Justinian and Theodora."

"Okay, I need to step in here," I start as Jake reaches for the pastry platter, "I don't think, for me, professionally—"

"NO STARCHES!" shouts the man in the tracksuit.

Jake drops the criminal cruller while the chef slides some aromatic fish/seaweed concoction on the table next to the waiting rainbow fan of today's periodicals. Jake squeezes the back of my neck before swinging around to his seat.

"Excuse me," a woman nudges my arm to get to the *Post*.

"Sorry." I pull the robe tighter. "So, as I was saying—"

But before I can finish registering my misgivings Jake unflaps one of the napkins and blows his nose into it. I watch as he then opens the cloth like a hymnal. "Joss?"

"Yes, honey."

"Can you get Elizabeth on the phone? Tell her there's still a slight green cast—wait, is this green?" To my horror, Faux-hawk leans over the extended napkin and nods. "And my sweat's had this, like, tinny smell." She writes this all down as he speaks. In fact the entire kitchen is rapt. "Tell her I'm out of formula."

"Is Elizabeth your doctor?" I ask, suddenly stricken that he has a horrible wasting disease kept under wraps.

"My herbalist. She's amazing. With all the flying I do, I have to keep my immune system strong. She's in L.A. but you should do a phone session."

"Okay!" Jocelyn leans against the counter and crosses her arms. "So, since I'm guessing you haven't listened to your voice mail while you've been playing *Blue Lagoon,* MTV's ripping me a new one over pulling the duet with Eden. They're threatening to cut all promos for the album, so I told 'em at midnight, when the ball drops, you'll sing 'Katie' with the genuine article right by your side—they can run it on 'Best Of's' into the next millennium. Fantastic, huh?" She claps her hands.

"Gluten-free French toast?" the chef asks me in a low voice.

"Actually," I turn, overwhelmed and not a little grossed out, "I'm going to get dressed."

"Sit tight for five, okay?" Jocelyn puts a bagel in my hand. "So, today's rundown: work out, meet with the execs from Japan, who did a circle jerk around your signed contract last night, by the way. Then rehearsal."

Jake gives a thumbs-up as he shovels in his macrobiotic breakfast. "Great," I say. "I'll go to the Met."

"No." Jocelyn snaps her ledger shut and turns her attention to me, fighting the reflex to cross my kimonoed arms in front of my face like Lynda Carter. "So far, all the American public has seen of you is postcoital shock, a shot of you with a blanket over your head climbing down a tree, and one *very* heinous yearbook photo—"

"It was not postcoital. There was no coital." I put the bagel down on the table. "And everyone had Julia Roberts eyebrows."

"Uh-huh. So, today, we set the tone. We let America see who Katie is."

"Kate," Jake reminds her again, his face hidden behind *Spin*.

"Thanks, but, Jake, are you listening?" I tap the glossy cover. "Because I don't really—"

Just then a flushed blonde in her mid-forties strides in shaking out the pelts of a gray shearling, whose suede is the matte complement to the polished stainless steel. She brings her fingertips to her pursed lips and splays them with a kiss. "Thanks for the Maserati, darling. My husband's already absconded with it."

Jake drops the magazine. "Glad he liked it." He leans coquettishly across his place setting and lifts his stubble-glazed face up to her. "Never leave me again?" he pleads. "Those MTV people had me in a Wookie hat, Kirsten." He smiles, winking at me. "I looked like *such* an asshole."

"Oh, baby, you have to learn to say no." She twirls off her coat and tosses it on the counter, revealing a very expensive looking charcoal cashmere sweater and matching velvet jeans.

"I didn't want to get them angry at me." He pops open another bottle of kimchi the chef deposits between us and raises the *Times*.

"Kirsten manages Jake's brand," Jocelyn informs me as Kirsten grabs a croissant and rips the tip off. "She's here to give you yours."

"Howdyado?"

My mouth opens as I try to formulate a response, but I am now, like, twelve responses behind. I maneuver the corners momentarily to turn up in acknowledgment of Kirsten's greeting. "I don't need a brand."

Jocelyn slaps her ledger closed. "Then you need to go back to cow country and get a new boyfriend."

"Joss . . ." Jake sends out a warning flare from behind the wall of newsprint.

Kirsten shoots Jocelyn a look. "Katie."

"Kate," I correct, staring imploringly at the Business Section. "Jake?"

"Kate," she continues. "People are a little overinvested right now, with the upcoming album, the Christmas breakup—"

"The fact that newlyweds have been stomping on each other's toes to your story for almost a decade."

Kirsten shoots Joss another silencing look and I'm sensing some sort of good-cop bad-cop as Kirsten leans in to lull me with dulcet tones. "Today is a wonderful opportunity to get off on the right foot with the American people."

I pull my robe closer. "Except the American people already know way more than, frankly, is appropriate. Whatever foot we got off on was ten years ago. They have six albums about me. That's all I'm gonna give."

The man in the tracksuit folds the last section and stands, suctioning seaweed from his molars. "Ready?"

Jake leaps from the banquette, abandoning his fish to come around and kiss me. "Have fun," he whispers in my ear. "We'll catch up in a few hours." He starts to pad out.

"Jake, can you at least stay until we've finished this conversation?"

"I really can't, but don't worry, that's the whole point. You don't have to worry. You don't even have to think about it. Everyone here is going to take amazing care of you." He gives me a quick kiss.

"I don't need to be taken care of!" I call after him as he waves from the door. But Jocelyn and Kirsten are staring me up and down. "I don't need to be taken care of."

"What's the reconstruction?" Jocelyn punders. "She's certainly not Eden."

"No, she's not. So, that's what I'm working with—playing up the contrast. How youthful you are. You radiate . . . youth. So, starting right now no cigarettes, no Red Bull, no diet pills, and whatever you do, I *beg* you, when you exit a car *knees together.* So first we're gonna get you in some fabulous Stella McCartney gear and send you around the reservoir a few times, let the paparazzi chase you. You're a runner, am I right? No matter—your adrenaline'll kick in. Then we'll all spend the day shopping organic, eating vegan, visiting a rock-climbing wall, and getting a colonic. By the end of the day every magazine will have gorgeous shots of this youthful, healthy girl."

"Um, no. No, no, no and absolutely, positively, over-my-dead-body no."

Jocelyn slaps her binder on the marble counter. "Okay, look, Yokel Ono, update: the box set drops in less than two weeks. Jake reuniting with his long-lost love buys me exactly one news cycle. One. So, we need you to fucking maximize." She pauses. "We could knock you up?"

"No."

"See, now you're just being an asshole."

"Now I'm just being a woman in a bathrobe in a strange kitchen being told she has to square dance with the American people while her boyfriend has his snot analyzed."

"But Jake's not just a boyfriend, is he?" Jocelyn cants her head. "You love him. You want the best for him. And you have decided to come on board his life."

I hold her gaze, letting that sink in. "Okay. I will give

you one day. One." I turn to Kirsten. "No cigarettes, no Red Bull. But no colonics, no running, and no, and I mean no, baby. Certainly not *this* news cycle."

Jocelyn consults her schedule. "Fine. Tonight you're having dinner with Chris and Gwynnie."

"Paltrow?"

"There'll be paparazzi outside the restaurant—so, remember, healthy!"

※

At midnight I finally hit SEND on the mea culpa e-mail to my boss its taken me four days in New York to get up the nerve to write. A butter-colored bar appears at the bottom of the screen, *"Wireless network unavailable."* Annoyed, I get up from Jake's bed with my glowing laptop and circle the dark room, trying to reconnect with the evasive signal. "Come on, come on," I mutter, eager for him to get my impassioned argument for why he should continue to employ a tabloid-strumpet.

I open the door and start haltingly walking the unlit hall, waiting for any sign of connectivity, praying my battery doesn't die. Then a door halfway down opens, shedding a trapezoid of light on the black cement. "Hello?" I call.

"Hey," one of the office staffers says as I walk in. She's flipping the collar of her coat out and shutting down the computers.

"Hi, I didn't realize anyone was still here."

"Oh, yeah," she says, sliding a stack of file folders into her white patent leather tote, the canary yellow wood bangles on her wrist clacking. "We're in the home stretch." As her Mac screen pops to black she reaches behind her to pull a poster-size 5 off the wall, revealing a 4 beneath it.

"Oh, the number of days until the Asia tour launches," I say, getting it.

"No." She pulls her ponytail out and sticks the rubber band between her teeth. "Well, yes. But it's *our*—" She swirls her arm at the elbow to indicate the office. "Countdown to getting our lives back." She pulls the holder out and refastens her hair. "I mean, it's totally exhilarating, but when he's in town it is just nonstop. That man has the work ethic of the Pilgrims."

"He does?" I ask. "I assumed this pace was being dictated by the label."

"Oh no." She clicks off the desk lamps. "When he's not in the studio, he's touring. While he's on the bus he's reading scripts, while he's filming he's reviewing contracts, while he's promoting he's researching every global problem you can name. And he takes insane care of himself, just insane." She shakes her head, like a parent at the school play. "The man cannot stop. So . . ." She blows her bangs up. "For three months matching his pace is the touring team's problem, and we can catch up on laundry and sleep. But we do miss him."

"Yeah, I guess that's just what being someone in his position looks like," I say, trying to reconcile this new image and wondering if he'd had unlimited funds at s eventeen to fill that house with an entourage, this isn't exactly what Susan's replacements would've looked like.

"Oh, no." She heaves her tote up on her shoulder. "No. We've all come from other offices and no one experienced anything like it. Except Sadie, who did two years with Madonna. I don't think he's taken a vacation since I got here."

"Really." The vision I'd been nurturing of Jake and me walking our children, sand buckets in hand to the shore, ebbs away.

"Yeah. Can I help you with that?" she asks, indicating the laptop as she backs me out the door, looping her floor-grazing scarf around her neck.

"Oh, just trying to send some e-mails for work, you know, explaining the tree house debacle, but I lost the connection."

"Oh yeah, here." She pulls a file folder from her tote and hands it over. "Your clippings."

I flip it open in the crease of my laptop and finger through the calculatedly apple-cheeked pictures of me, all under varying captions of *Jake's Katie—why we love America's new girl-next-door.* "Wow," I say as she watches me watch myself touring New York, Kirsten and Jocelyn half out of frame. "You guys just decide 'healthy' and then they . . . and these. Wow." Stunned, I hand it back to her.

"You okay?" she asks, slipping it in her purse.

"Sure, yeah, I mean, it's wholesome and that's the important thing. I think my career can survive this," I say, praying I'm right, praying I haven't just flushed my master's degree.

"And try the sauna. It's never worked, but, for some reason, the signal's really strong in there."

"Okay . . ."

"Fourth door down on your left. Off the massage room."

"Great. Thank you." With a wave she heads toward the elevator, and I burrow deeper into the apartment to see if a dormant sauna can open my Bluetooth, if not my pores.

❦

Well past hungry as it is well past the after-hours supper Jake was supposed to pick me up for, I recross my legs on the extra-long ottoman where I'm slouched in the now mostly empty living room. I tried sitting on the floor, but the poured cement sent a damp chill into my lumbar. In the dim light provided by the skyline below, I stare at the shadowy bare spaces left by Eden's departure and try to picture my Pottery Barn chair or garage-sale desk filling them in. But the result is so laughable I return to the previous hour's game of imagining kids hanging out in here after school, sprawling on the cement, a Heller-esque tray of goodies between them, small fingers leaving Cheetos imprints on the pony-skin chaise. And where am I? What will I be doing?

"Waiting," I mutter, stretching to grasp the Pellegrino left for me by the chef as he departed for the night. I pull the slice of lime off the rim and squeeze it, making a satisfying hiss as the juice sprays into the water, the density getting trapped by the bubbles. I take a sip, pressing smy lips together as the elevator starts to move, the cables visible through the open door across the room. *Clack clack, whir.* I breathe, my own motor in sync. It shudders to a stop, the bars parting. Coat open, he stretches up, his fingertips catching the doorframe as he leans forward. "God, it's amazing to have you there—"

"Waiting."

"For me." He lunges across the room, covering the twenty feet between us in a pace. "You were all I could think about," he says into my neck.

I twist out from under him to place my glass on the floor. "So, was this like a hot thing for you and Eden?"

"What?"

I slide my hips over so I can face him. "Like, you'd spend the day, or month or year with your people, and she'd be with her people, and you'd be thinking about each other. Was that, like, foreplay?"

"What's your problem?"

"My problem is that I've spent the last three days, no, not with my boyfriend—"

"I'm more than your boyfriend—"

I hold my palm up to silence him. "I've spent the last three days being baby-sat by Satan's minions while being chased, and I do mean *chased,* by paparazzi. *I* got a smile of sympathy from Nicole Kidman as we both tried to leave the Mercer Hotel—only they followed *me.*"

He takes off his coat and lays it beside him. "You went to the Mercer? Did Joss get you their blood orange mojito—it's awesome."

"Oh my God, Jake!"

He stands up. "I can't talk to you when you're like this," he says with a defensiveness that only spurs me.

"Like what? Annoyed?"

"It's not my fault," his voice rises. "You keep talking to me like any of this is my fault. Stop blaming me."

I stand, straining to temper my anger. "I am not blaming you. I just—" I'm brought up short by his suddenly stricken expression, some seed of panic rising in him I'm compelled to quell. "I just missed you. I'm here to be with you."

At my words he pulls me into him, enveloping me, his voice once again deep and calm. "I know. Today sucked. It sucked. Everything ran over. I was miserable." He kneads his fingers through my hair the way I adore, the way no one else has ever been able to, although it seems so obvious and what is wrong with boys? I slide my arms around him, my hands slipping under his T-shirt. "Tomorrow we'll spend the day together. We have three more days till New Year's and they'll be fantastic. I promise. I'll make it better. Just hang in through New Year's." He pulls his hand away, his ring caught in my hair.

I reach up to help him untangle me, but we are two hands too many for the project. "Just take it off," I say, my eyes watering from the tight pain.

"What?" He tugs.

"Ouch! Stop! Just take it off and I'll do it."

He fidgets for a moment before the ring drops, the metal pulling my head to the side. I catch the platinum skull, flipping my hair forward to see the strands barbed in its ruby eyes.

"I'm starved." Jake drops back onto his elbows on the ottoman, idling back on its tufted expanse. "You?"

"Yes." I unhook my hair and smooth it over my shoulders. "No. Actually, I was starved three hours ago. Now I'm just tired." I slouch to the floor next to his boots, looking down at the knobby silver cranium, sliding my thumb in and out of it.

"So, I'm your boyfriend, huh?" He nudges my thigh with the rim of his sole.

"I guess." I toss the ring to him and he heists up to catch it, sliding it back on.

"Someone's pouting."

"I'm not pouting." I scowl, pulling my legs up. "I'm just kind of . . ."

"What?"

"What are we doing here, Jake? How does this work?"

"It . . . is working." He looks at me blankly.

"No, I mean, this is your life. I have a life of my own. How do we combine them? I've been thinking we could get a house down in Charleston, something beautiful on the water and you could set up a studio down there, I guess . . . make it a home base so I can continue with my—"

He arches an eyebrow. "I already have three houses."

"Okay. So, maybe we can pick one of them. I mean, I guess I could telecommute. I don't know. I still don't know how this is all going to shake out at work."

He reaches down to take my promise-ring-laden

hand. "I've spent enough time apart from you. I want you on tour with me. I want to see your face in the morning, like you said. Every morning."

I pull my hand back. "My children aren't growing up on an airplane, Jake."

"Children?" his voice rises.

"Don't you want them?" mine follows in tandem as I twist to face him.

"Eventually . . ." He nods down at the floor, his hand coming up to swipe at his chin.

"Like, how eventually?"

He shrugs.

"Jake?"

"Don't know, Kate."

"Okay, but this is the stuff we have to figure out." I feel like crying.

He shakes his head, letting out a little laugh. "I'll tell you what."

"What?"

"I'd like to make them, I know that much." He reaches down to take my forearms and pulls me up onto him on the smooth leather as he reaches for my zipper. "So much thinking, Hollis," he murmurs as he bites ever so gently into my neck. "Always so much thinking. Let me." His mouth roves to mine. "Let me show you how to stop."

༄

"NOBODY MOVE! WE BLEW A FUSE!"

I sit up in bed.

"CALL THE SUPER!" Joss brays as my cell peals from the bedside table. People are shouting responses to her and running back and forth outside the door as I reach for the phone.

Seeing my boss's number I take a deep breath and answer. "Lucas, thanks for getting back to me."

"Kate, hi. Happy New Year."

"Thirteen more hours," I say, slipping my feet to the floor. A charge of footsteps thunders past in the hall.

"So, Kate, had a good holiday?" he asks, his tone nervous—so much better than the outrage I've braced myself for. "I was glad to hear your mother's okay."

"Lucas, please do not fire me. *I promise,* this whole thing will blow over in one news cycle and I can retreat from the spotlight with Trudie Styler and Ali Hewson and no one needs to know—"

"Kate—"

"Lucas, I know this is awkward, but I assure you I have no plans to be publicly or, more importantly, professionally associated with Jake. My work is my work and his work—"

"But you can call on him, right?"

"I'm sorry?"

"He'll come with you to Argentina, tour the factories with you and some photgraphers, this could be very good for us."

I reach for my jeans. "Uh, I hadn't even considered—"

"Well, consider. Consider the attention Jake could bring to sustainable development. The impact he'll have if you channel his fans' attention. Can you set up a call with him?"

"Well, he's about to go on tour . . ."

"Just a quick five minutes to get things in motion, Kate."

"I'll see what I can do, but—"

"Fantastic. This is fantastic. Call me back."

"Okay." I click the phone off. So the good news is I still have a job. The bad news is that job is now about getting a good photo-op with my boyfriend. Nauseated, I reach for yet another new TSE turtleneck from the pile Kirsten left for me.

Halfway to the living room I hear Joss shout, "OKAY! GOT IT! TRY IT NOW!" and *Poltergeist* light blasts down the dark hall.

"HAS ANYONE SEEN THE DIOR?"

I step tentatively into the room teeming with dancers contorting and stretching against every surface while they wait for one of the numerous mirrored stations, manned by makeup artists wielding brushes and hair stylists wielding dryers, to free up. "KATE, YOU'RE IN FIVE!" an impossibly slender black man in stiletto heels shouts to me from across the chaos.

"Jake?" I cup my hands to my mouth and call directly out.

"Champagne?" Faux-hawk crosses to offer me a black-stemmed flute, a glitter 2006 tiara squashing his crest.

"No, thanks. Where's Jake?"

"Suit yourself, but tonight'll be all work, so you may want to have your New Year's now," he says, knocking back his own glass.

"Kate!"

"Jake!"

"Yeah, babe, over here," he beckons from the other side of a rolling mirror.

I step over its sandbagged base to see Jake sitting in a director's chair getting facial acupuncture from a petite young woman while he and a man in a baseball cap watch the tape of rehearsal on a small monitor stuck in among the jars of pancake. And Jake is naked. Balls-out. Naked. "Uh, Jake . . ."

"Yeah, babe, can you grab me a rice cake—they're on the buffet table."

"And a robe?" I ask as a cadre of dancers walk past to get their costumes pinned.

"What? No, it's Naked Day!" He throws his arms up, the needles shaking. "And could you put a little dollop of almond butter on it? Thanks."

I turn away, my eyes watering from the whatthe-fuck that is careering around my skull. I spot Joss by the buffet flipping through the ledger. "Joss." I grab her arm. *"Whatthefuck?"*

She peels my fingers off her silver-flecked Chanel jacket. "Is there a problem?"

"Why is Jake naked?"

"It's Naked Day," she says with none of his enthusiasm.

"There are at least twenty young women in this

room who are eighteen at best. At best. Get him to put a robe on."

"Okay, tweedle, I can't *get him* to do anything. And he is performing live for millions of people tonight. As are you. So let Miss Thomas get you started." She trills her fingers at the man in stilettos.

Jake is suddenly at my elbow, needles still jiggling. "Jake, put some fucking clothes on."

"Kate, I have to get up there tonight and bare my soul. I'm sorry if it offends you, but its just what I need to do to tap into the vulnerability they expect." He reaches over me for a rice cake and takes a grinning bite as he orbits back to the chaos.

"*How* is this not a massive liability issue?"

She smacks the book shut. "You have no idea how good I am," she states. "Before Jake I had a client who cooked his wife's afterbirth on a hot plate in the hospital room and ate it in front of at least eight witnesses. And no one ever knew. I am that good." I can't close my mouth. She shrugs, clearly unenthused, but tempered by a pay-check. "He needs to commune before he performs—"

"Which, when he's on tour . . ." It sinks in.

"Is every day. But don't worry, all the surfaces in the bus are slip-covered."

"Great. Great," I exclaim with manic sarcasm. "No, that's a comfort."

"MISS KATE!"

I wave at Miss Thomas as he taps his palm with a golden canister of Elnett and nod that I'll be right over. "We're not due at MTV for twelve hours," I appeal to

Joss. "I'm not spending all day trussed up like a Vegas showgirl."

Eyes back on her plan of attack she pronounces, "They want you in extensions, and that takes hours. Get over there."

"Right-o." Before she looks back up, I dodge into the hallway reeling from the bedlam and the fact that the love of my life needs to be—needs to be—naked in the middle of it. I push against the nearest door, finding myself in a pitch-dark space, running my hand along the wall for the overhead. I wince as the heel of my palm is scratched by something. Trying again more carefully I brush the plate lightly with my fingertips, finding the small switch. I toggle it, illuminating the room, and see that the vertical dimmer has lost its cover, the razor sharp half-inch of metal sticking out unbuffetted. I turn around to find I'm in an emptied dressing room that immediately recalls those teenage girls' bedrooms where the parents have invested way too much money or emotion to update it, so heavy metal posters are taped up over preexisting murals of unicorns and fairies.

Here the decorative motif is dolphins: holding up the vanity table, sparkling in tiny gemstones at the juncture of the floor tiles, frolicking in the ceiling frescoes, arcing across the turquoise silk of the curtains. And somewhere in the back of my brain it clicks that Jake's girlfriend prior to Eden had one hit titled "Angel of the Sea." Layered over the polished travertine is Eden's handiwork—photos from magazines of the Southwest taped up haphazardly over the walls and mirrors, a cow skull atop the jewelry case, and poetry on every wall—written in ink, in lipstick, in eyeliner—lyrics I recognize that made it into her songs and meters of verse so raw, so personal, I cannot imagine anyone sharing them from a stage.

Unsure if reading walls is the same thing as reading a diary I nonetheless take in every word, riveted. She writes about the road, about wrestling with addiction, about her mother, and about a son whom she wants to protect always. Did she have a baby? Back in Arizona? I read on, piecing it together through the metaphors, his heart is a radiant bird, his smile a crooked line she cannot cross, his voice a fall of ash, a flight of dandelion, a ring of smoke. And, oh. It's Jake.

A chill runs up my legs from the stone and I take a seat at the vanity, pulling my feet up. And there, taped to the mirror, is a fertility chart, her basal temperature written in the corner of each day—97.6, 97.6, 97.6. It spikes to 98.6 and then the three following days are circled with big exclamation points. And over that in eyeliner she wrote *Jake can go fuck himself. And Madrid.* I'm guessing he didn't make it back for her ovulation.

There's a firm knock at the door. "Kate?" a male voice asks.

"It's open!" I call, suddenly eager for company even if that company wants to give me extensions.

Faux-hawk pushes it in, his tiara askew. "For you." He proffers a FedEx box.

"Me?"

"I was told." He sashays over and places it on the table

in front of me before giving the walls a once-over with his kohled eyes. "God, she's brilliant."

"Not crazy?"

"Nah." He positions one hand on his slender hip. "She's an artist, the real deal. But that's one artist too many in a marriage, if you ask me." He looks in the mirror over my head and refluffs his crest.

"How about two artists too many?" I ask.

Tipsy, he shrugs, not doing the math. "Oh, and don't take too long. Miss Thomas is running around the place gripping your hair like he scalped someone."

"Thanks," I say as he shuts the door, the noise of Jake's circus suctioned out behind him, leaving me in the sealed silence of Eden's refuge. My stomach squeezes as I recognize the scratchy slant of Dad's handwriting on the address label. Right, that. Them. I carry the cardboard over to the clenched drapes and drag the swaths of silk open, the bright December sun washing through the floor-to-ceiling window, muting the collage around me with its whiteness.

I take a seat on the floor, positioning her room at my back. Willing the redbricked vista before me to keep my perspective buoyant, I slide my fingers ambivalently along the Overnight Express tape. Grabbing a forgotten cowboy boot from beneath the dresser, I sliver the seam with its brass-tipped toe. The flaps rise as they're released. I drop the tan crocodile to lift out balled tissue paper, my hand encircling Mom's old microcassette recorder taped to a card with 1 written on it. I take the black plastic brick between my hands, fingering the little yellow Post-it with an arrow to the PLAY button where she has written simply, "Please." I let out a long breath. Don't want to. Don't want to please. Want to leave them on that porch and have the whole history evanesce. Want to be done.

I hit PLAY.

"Is it on?" Dad's voice ekes into the room. I press my thumb into the volume wheel, moving it up until it's at its peak.

"I think. Try testing," Mom says as if next to me. I slide my thumb down.

"Testing," Dad says. "I feel like I should sing something."

"Moonlight in Vermont," Mom warbles. My cheeks lift in an uncertain smile.

"Seriously."

Mom clears her throat. "Yes." She takes a breath. "Kate, hi."

"Hullo," Dad chimes in.

"So, it's Christmas. And we've opened our presents and your dad's barbecued the shrimp. And we've missed you. We've spent the day, well . . ."

"Fought like hell."

"Yes, we've fought and talked and really had ourselves quite a row. And here's where we're at . . . we're really just terribly—"

"Sorry," Dad says, the word sounding utterly foreign not couched in a joke.

"Sorry that I had an affair," Mom pushes on as heat rises up to my forehead. "And that you had to stumble upon it, be alone with it."

"Sorry I lost my marbles and made everyone feel so rotten," Dad says with such clarity that I stop the tape with my trembling hands, rewind it a slippery beat and press PLAY again.

"Lost my marbles and made everyone feel so rotten. And I'm saying it here where you can listen as many times as you need to."

I press the pads of my fingers to my mouth as Mom takes an audible breath. "And after Dad moved back in we never talked about it with you because we were trying to get you back to a happy family as fast as we could. We didn't want to burden you, drag it out. But that clearly didn't, well it didn't—"

"Bloody dreadful tactic, apparently. So Kate, here it is. We're going to tell you everything now, all of it. From the day the research center closed to the day I moved back in. We're going to tell you everything you could ever want to know about those months and you can listen to as much or as little as you want."

"We've got ourselves a full pitcher of piña coladas," Mom says, and I smile deeply as I picture her shoulders rise. "And I even treated us to pigs in a blanket from Publix in your honor."

"Even got the little umbrellas," Dad adds. "One other thing, before we start, I want you to know I went off my medication under supervision. I don't like to discuss it with you, Katie, because it's not my proudest quality as a parent . . ." His voice has gotten so quiet I have to press the box to my ear. "The blubbering's only supposed to last a few weeks."

"You did well up over the kids' bell choir this morning."

"Claire, he said I'd be normal. Not an android," Dad scoffs. "Those little angel robes with the bells bigger than their tiny heads, I'm not immune."

"All right, then." I hear Mom smile. And that she is nervous. "Let's get to it."

"Yes. So, let's see, to the best of my recollection I just woke up one morning, feeling like I hadn't slept, feeling heavy tired—"

I click STOP, absorbing the magnitude of their gesture, realizing, now that they've been cleanly offered I don't need to hear the details. What I've needed is to know they've been voiced, dealt with, laid to rest. Closing my eyes, letting the brilliant sun burn through my lids to turn my focus a warm pink, I lift the recorder to my heart.

Blinking, I reach into the box and feel a wrapped bundle. I withdraw it, taped to a card with 2 written on it. I wriggle off the recycled ribbon, unfurling the gold tissue from Neiman Marcus in which I wrapped her slippers last year, and pull out a seashell she's slid inside the folds. I place it next to me before crinkling the paper back on familiar worn wool. I lift the blazer up in front of me, realizing almost every inch of fabric has been safety-pinned with our old pictures—the metal carefully pricked through fading photos of Croton Middle and

Croton High, the winter choir concert, family birthdays, debate championships, the seventh-grade play, every stop of my adolescence, and there at the heart, where Dad's university crest used to be, a picture of 34 Maple Lane with the three of us out front taken the day we moved in.

My cheeks wetting, I pull it on, looking down at everything I've done in all its carefully pinned-on glory, everything they wanted for me, even when clinically depressed and cheating. I catch sight of the Princess phone on the chaise and pull it over, lifting the receiver as I punch in the number.

"Hello?"

"Dad?"

"Kate?"

"Happy New Year's." I swipe a hand across my damp face.

"Isn't that tomorrow?" he asks playfully, but I can hear the relief in his voice.

"I figured since I missed Christmas—"

"The Battle of Sarasota?"

"That bad, huh?" I smile.

"We were due—we hadn't had a good dust-up in years. And your mother makes her jam tarts when she's feeling contrite."

"What do you do?"

"A soft-shoe." I hear the twinkle in his voice.

"Yeah, me, I like to run off with a rockstar."

"How's that going? Gotten a tattoo yet."

"Dad?"

"Yes?"

"Thank you." I fit the smooth shell in my palm and pull the jacket around me. "For the blazer and the tape and everything—"

"If Jake as son-in-law is part of your package deal, I will learn to love him again."

"Really?"

"He was a good kid. Hold on, I've got Mom bouncing up and down for the phone. Happy New Year, bun. I love you."

"Kathryn?" she asks furtively.

"I *love* it."

"You didn't burn it?"

"No." I smile.

"But you can if you want to, it's your choice. Number three."

"Of course I'm not burning it," I say as I tip the box toward me to see the round tube of fireplace matches roll along its emptied bottom. "I'm sorry I lost it back there."

"Oh, I don't know, it was kind of nice having a teenager in the house again."

"Referring to me?" She laughs and I squint against the graffiti pullulating from the surfaces surrounding me. "Tell me what you guys're up to."

"Well . . . I'm working on a puzzle."

"Of course."

"And your father is about to grill up some swordfish and vegetables for lunch—"

"I miss you," it fervently escapes me, the acknowledgment of this lost feeling, the revelation of its long absence overwhelming. Silence. "Mom?"

"I'm here."

"I don't know if this is . . . I don't know how I should be . . . how to make this real."

"You shouldn't be *making it* anything. That's the whole point of trying this on, isn't it?"

"Is that what I'm doing?"

"Yes, trying this on, seeing how it is."

"How did you know with Dad?" I wrap the blazer closer around me. "How did you know to hang in?"

"How do I phrase this?" She pauses for a moment. "Because he hung in for me, Katie—the real me, not the concept of, not the abstract. And we share, not only the last thirty-five years, we share you. He's my partner—in all his grumpy, silly, smart, smart glory."

I smile at her summation of him, of them. "Mom, I found out all the songs after 'Lake Story' were about his father."

The line is silent. "Well, I'm sorry to hear that, for his sake."

"That's gracious of you."

"I know." She laughs before sighing, "Wow." I sense it sinking in for her. "Oh, your father's having trouble with the grill—"

"Yes, go."

"Love you."

"I love you, too."

The door wedges and Jake's voice belts, *"Kaaaa-tie,"* through the opening, startling me.

"Yes?" I stand, blanching as he strolls in, full makeup, full-frontal flapping flesh framed by the scrawled door he closes behind him. He reaches his arms out, fingers waving for me. "Is that Croton?"

"My parents sent it as a peace offering. It's my—" He takes my face in his hands, staring comfortingly into my eyes. "Hi," I say softly. He buries his airbrushed face in my neck. "Jake." I push back from him. "Stop."

"Can't," he groans, perspiration beading above the makeup. "Only have five before I have to go through the lineup again." He tugs at my turtleneck, knocking me off balance, forcing me to grab back for the chaise as I land on it. "Sorry. You get undressed. I'll turn around."

"Jake?" someone yells from behind the door before I can respond.

"Yeah?" He jogs to it, bare feet slapping the stone.

"Call from Tokyo."

He spins to me, feet squeaking. "Got another break in thirty. Get changed and we'll meet, oh—" His face falls. "But not in here, okay? Bad vibe. In the bedroom. In *that.* Love you." He tugs open the door and disappears, singing, *"I'm gonna fuck you, Kaaa-tie!"*

I sit up, touching the smear of foundation on the fawn-colored cashmere, my eyes landing on the picture Mom pinned beneath the right sleeve. There, nestled in with every other milestone—sits the unmistakable cake-platter of Jake's childhood home.

As the limousine inches into Times Square I peer out at the elated throngs, screaming the New Year in. Beside me Jake sits with his eyes closed, doing his visualizations, wriggling uncomfortably against the confines of his suit while nursing a Marlboro. My cell vibrates and, seeing Lucas's number, I press IGNORE, letting him add yet another voice mail to his cache of "brainstorming."

"Who's stalking you? Should I be jealous?"

"My boss. It's about you, actually." I shift to alleviate the chafing of the tape securing my cleavage. "He has this cockamamie idea about making you the face of global sustainable development."

Jake's eyes open.

"Don't worry, I told him you were going on tour. You don't have to get involved at all. I'm sure I can mollify him with some sort of anonymous donation, I mean, if you wanted to, no pressure."

"Anonymous?" he asks.

"Totally. Not a problem—"

"Oh, okay, I see." He sits up, blowing a strong stream of smoke out his nostrils. "So your boss likes me enough to want to make me the face of this cause, but you . . . you, what? Think I'm not serious enough? Think I'd embarrass you?"

"Jake, *no,* that's not it at all," I say, taken aback. "I just didn't want to tell you what to do with your money."

"No, I get it. I get it." The limo inches into alignment with the red carpet where Joss waits with our security detail. "Ready?"

Before I can say no the door swings open. "JAKE! JAKE! JAKE! OVER HERE, JAKE!" We make our way down the red carpet, through blinding flashbulbs and the defeaning hysteria of the crowd. My hand clasped, I stop when he stops, angling my chin down as Kirsten instructed. *"JAAAAAAAAAAAKE!!!"* Behind the phalanx of press, the crowd of girls screams themselves hoarse. He smiles, waves, says, "Hedi Slimane for Dior Homme" over and over, signs autographs.

We squeeze through the revolving doors of 1515 Broadway. "Jake. Jake. Jake." A corps of MTV staff wearing headsets descends, tobacco-stained fingers grabbing his arms and pulling him from me. I don't even make it into the elevator.

The studio floor is packed, every corridor crammed with revelers and handlers and reveling handling. Holding up the pass around my neck, I snake through the throngs, choking on the mushroom cloud of perfume and nicotine billowing from their clothes. I find the dressing rooms. "Jake?" I call out. A multiplatinum rapper struts down the hall with his entourage, sweeping me up in their cannabis wake. Disengaging myself before I'm pulled onstage I fold into a miraculously empty nook and peer out through the black felt flaps. The rapper takes the mike from a scrawny man old enough to be grandfather to the prepubescent audience screaming their appreciation of his serenade.

God, they're so young.

Registering the trilling of my phone as speakers break out the driving beat, I lift my clutch to my ear. I fumble to crack the crystal minaudiere and let out a cry of de-light when I see the glowing Vermont area code beside my lipstick. "Laura!" I exclaim. "Hi!"

"Happy New Year!" she calls down the line. I hear the boys echo her in the background.

"How are you?" I press my finger to my other ear and huddle into the wall.

"I am e–la–ted. I'm on a crack high, you brilliant, brilliant girl. I'm sitting here with my hysterically happy husband and my brand new Chloé bag. You know what it goes with?"

"No?"

"My pajamas. My big swollen tummy. I might take it in the bath with me later. I've never loved anything so much in my whole life."

"That's fantastic!" I cheer, her unadulterated joy infectious.

"Oh my god, Kate, we left the kids with my parents and had a romantic weekend in Boston. It was phenomenal—we went for long walks, went to the Isabelle Stewart Gardner Museum, had fantastic meals—we got a couples massage!" She lowers her voice. "And had lots of sex. The big kind."

"Are we ready to roll?" I hear Jake's voice coming from behind the flat on my left and try to make my way around the maze.

"Shit, I better go."

"Yeah, go get ready for your *debut*. We're watching! We love you!"

"Love you!" Again the boys echo.

"Love you, too!" I click off. "Jake," I say as I spot him sipping water from a clear plastic cup.

"Shh," a man admonishes me and I take in the boom he's holding. I obediently freeze as Jake sets down the cup in the bright lights and his interviewer, a guest VJ for the festivities, some recent one-hit-wonder, nods he's ready to go.

"We're here with Jake Sharpe. Hey, Jake, I'm such a huge fan!"

"Thanks, man." Jake smiles. The guy with the unwarranted arrogance of the newly famous waits for Jake to return the compliment. "Right, so you'll be rocking us into the New Year in a few short minutes."

"Looking forward to it." Jake nods at the camera.

"Yeah, we just kicked it," he offers Jake another chance.

"Cool."

"Right. So this has been quite a season of revelations for you. The muse of your hit songs has been revealed to be your high school sweetheart, uh, Katie Hollis, who'll be onstage with you a little later." He looks to the camera. "So, stay tuned for that. And on your greatest hits CD, songs from your first album will no longer be credited solely to you . . . but to, let's see . . . Samuel Richardson, Todd Rawley, and Benjamin Conchlin." I feel us share this moment and grin from the sidelines, picturing them all glued to the TV. "So, why now, Jake?" he departs from the teleprompter. "With a new album to promote, why choose this moment to reveal that you didn't actually write the music that first made you famous."

Jake blinks at the ignored screen for a quick second as he regroups, "Right, okay."

"Tell us more about who wrote it."

"It was a collaboration." He shifts in his seat. "With some great guys—my best friends." He looks over and we share a smile as I think it might be possible—not best friends, but amends made, gaps bridged—it's a start. And I'm proud of him.

"Then where are these other musicians? They 'collaborated' on pretty groundbreaking stuff, some argue your best work." He smirks.

"Yeah, well," Jake runs his hands over his thighs, "collaboration is an art form, definitely. I'm still pretty fanatical about the talent I surround myself with—hunting for the people who bring out the best in me, like Mirwais, who produced my last album. You know, you want the best backup, the best support, so your talent can fly. What those guys gave me in terms of emotional support while I wrote those songs—" My skin grows hot and I can feel Laura's face fall as he thumps his fist twice against his breastplate. "—I will never forget it. Never."

"*Asshole.*"

Everyone's eyes fly to me, Jake's locking with my disgusted expression and I turn before the camera can, pushing against the throngs to find the exit, elbowing my way against the crush trying to make it to the Times Square windows before the ball drops. Reaching the elevator bank, I pound the button, spinning around for the stairwell.

"So what, you're just gonna leave?" He rounds the corner on my heels, tugging at his mike. "You're just gonna walk out?"

"Yes."

I spot the red sign and try to step around him to the door, but he catches me by both elbows. "I told you this was going to be complicated. I have millions of fans who want me to have written those songs. I have a responsibility—I have an *obligation*."

"You have a *big ego*."

"Fuck, Kate!" He drops my arms. "That kid was being a dick! You were standing right there, you saw what a dick he was being. They have their money. It'll be printed in the liner notes. *What's* your problem?"

"You. You are my problem." I stop myself. "Were my problem. You were the fucking millstone of my twenties."

"Yeah, and you were mine and it's fucking amazing that we found each other and here we are doing this."

"Doing this. Is that what the last week has been?"

"Yes! We're doing it. And I love it! I love that we have this crazy insatiable passion and I see you in my apartment, in my life, and we make this crazy love and we bump up against each other and you put me in check with all these fireworks. We have this insane roller coaster—I love this."

"*This* is being seventeen." I step aside as a cluster of kids run past blowing cardboard horns. "Or younger.

God, they're all so young. They're babies. We were just babies, Jake."

"I'm not a baby."

I stare at him, epically, cosmically clear. "Jake, I don't want this. And, just so you know, it's not your schedule, or your team, even Joss. I could acclimate to all of it—eventually. It's you, Jake—who you are. Who you grew up to be. Or more precisely, didn't." I step closer, continuing in range of his pheromones, no longer potent. "I'm so thankful we did this, because now I can admit to myself that some part of me will *always* be a little in love with you, the seventeen-year-old you. Who you *were*. And that's okay. It doesn't mean I'm stuck, or stilted. It just means that for the first time I'll hear 'Losing,' and instead of changing the station, or marching out of the supermarket, I'll appreciate it. I'll listen, and smile, because it's a beautiful song." I search his eyes. "A beautiful song that lasts exactly three minutes and forty-eight seconds."

His face twists. "You're scared shitless. You know that we're soul mates and you're terrified—"

"No, actually, Jake, I'm embarrassed. I was about to dismiss the last thirteen years of my life for the shot of adrenaline you give me for three minutes and forty-eight seconds. Three minutes and forty-eight seconds! At seventeen that was a lifetime. At thirty . . . it's just a song."

"Jake!" Jocelyn flaps down the emptied hall. "What the fuck? Those were *not* your sound bites. And, Kate, thanks to your outburst I'll be spending the weekend fellating every major network. Now, move—you guys're on!"

He gives me one last agonized look as I reach for the door, pushing into the stairwell— "Take care, Jake"— leaving him to go where he's told.

Downstairs I press against the revolving glass, the suctioning swish propelling me out onto the cleared red carpet just as the ball starts to drop. I raise my hands overhead, my eyes catching on the sapphire ring. I go to slip it off, but stop. Thirteen birthday presents, thirteen Christmas presents, three graduation gifts . . . all totaling one fully earned royalty check. Filling my lungs with the brisk air I look up at the six-story screen across Broadway, the live studio feed lighting the crowd below; Jake sings his heart out to the hysterical adulation of his juvenile fans. If his world has just ended, you would never know it.

Making my New Year's wish I smile deeply, blinking up as the liberated confetti falls from the sky and, finally inured to the cold, I walk away.

26

LAURA'S WEDDING

"Katie?"

At the sound of Laura's voice I lift my cheek from the bathroom floor. Holding my robe closed, I pull myself up to sitting with the edge of the tub and look through my hair to see her crouching in the doorway. "I'm so sorry." I drop my cheeks into my hands.

She reaches to hold my arm, her brand-new wedding band ballasting the sparkle of her engagement ring. "We all had way too much to drink. The look on Sam's face at the church, your face, it was too awful. Have you been in here all night?" She takes my chin, gently lifting my gaze. I nod.

"Yes. But it's not . . ." I shake my head, my heart starting to pound again. "I just . . . can't . . . catch my breath. My chest is so . . . tight . . . I feel like someone's . . . standing on it."

Her face contorts with concern. "I'm getting your mom."

"No." I wave my hand weakly. "Please."

"Okay . . . well, let's get out of the bathroom, at

least." She helps me up and we shuffle back into my bedroom, settling down in unison on the quilt. "Let's breathe together, okay?"

I nod. She inhales dramatically, pressing my hand to follow. I do, in and out. In and out. "This is going to be forever—"

"Breathe," she reprimands sternly. We do. A few more before I squeeze her hand and let go.

"I don't know how to end this. Every time I try there's another song—" I wring my hands together tightly. "This is the rest of my life."

"Hey." She grips my shoulders.

"What?" My words blur with tears.

"We have to have more control than this. Don't we?"

I shake my head, collapsing forward.

"Hey!" She lifts my face to her. "You listen to me, Elizabeth Kathryn . . ." I stare up at her.

For the first time I see that she is in a skirt suit. "God, you're on your way to the airport. Please, you have to go. I can't bear to ruin your honeymoon, too."

She holds her hand up to silence me. "*You* did not ruin anything." Her eyes land on the clothes draped over my desk chair and she hops up off the bed. "You brought these for the weekend, didn't you?"

I nod.

"You brought them to finish this, right?"

I nod again, wiping my nose.

She lifts the butterfly dresses and lingerie with both arms and drops it all on the bed. "So you're ready."

"I can't if he's not—"

"Here." She swipes the collapsed duffel bag off the floor and tosses it onto the quilt, followed by the heels.

I grip the clothes to me. "I don't . . ."

She slides the top dress from my grasp and gingerly folds it into the bag. "You already packed it. To get on with your life, right?" She cocks her head, "Right?"

"Yes."

She slides the next dress from my hands. "Yes. So, you will repack this bag and put it away and someday, somehow, he will come home."

"But what if—"

"He will have to. He will come home and I will be here and I will call you." She puts her hand over both of mine, still clutching the platform heels. "I promise you, Katie, I swear it on us, I will call you."

ACKNOWLEDGMENTS

We deeply thank Suzanne Gluck, Alicia Gordon, Sara Bottfeld, Eugenie Furniss, Suzanne O'Neill, Judith Curr, Ken Weinrib, Eric Brown, Addie Szabo, Larry Heilweil, and everyone at Burton Goldstein & Co. for their continued support, encouragement and guidance. We could not ask for a better team.

Emma wishes to thank her family for the giggles they abundantly share to accompany her on the ride, Shannon and Sara for the same, Christine Ranck, whose invaluable work makes the past feel inspirational, Sarah M., Minnie M. and Ashley E. for being the best Lauras a girl could have hoped for, and D.B.H. for being perfect.

Nicki wishes to thank her family for their unflagging enthusiasm, Mary Herzog for her wisdom, insight and care, Stephanie Urdang for her wonderful energy, Kevin Jennings, a brilliant man, for always getting me revved up when I've gotten bogged down, Kristi Molinaro, my inspiration, for always making it fun, Patricia Moreno, guru of joy, and Dr. Szulc, the master.